Florida WEDDINGS

Romance Blossoms in Three Novels Set in the Sunshine State

LYNN A. COLEMAN ‖ KRISTY DYKES ‖ KATHLEEN E. KOVACH

BARBOUR
PUBLISHING

Published by Barbour Publishing, Inc., P.O. Box 719, Uhrichsville, Ohio 44683, www.barbourbooks.com

Our mission is to publish and distribute inspirational products offering exceptional value and biblical encouragement to the masses.

 Member of the
Evangelical Christian
Publishers Association

Printed in the United States of America.

Cords of Love

by Lynn A. Coleman

Dedication

To my granddaughter, Leanna Marie, who was going through the "why" stage when I was writing this story. I love you and pray God's continued blessing on you. Leanna, you are growing up so quickly and left the "why" stage many years ago. Now you are a fine young lady, and you make your grandma real proud. My prayer is you continue to grow in the Lord and develop into the woman God has blessed you to become. All my love, Grandma

Chapter 1

The bell above the door jingled. Renee looked up. "Aaron, how'd the appointment go?"

"Not good. They went with the competition." Aaron Chapin, her boss, rubbed the back of his neck.

"What?" Renee stood up. That was impossible. They'd worked hard on that proposal. "What happened?"

Renee sent a quick glance to John, an art major at a local college who did part-time work for Sunny Flo Designs. He bit his lower lip and looked back at his drafting table.

Aaron's gaze locked with hers, his dark brown eyes appearing almost black. "They said we weren't original," he answered, his words tight.

"They're crazy. No one, absolutely no one, has anything on the Web marginally like that. I checked." Renee tapped the top of her desk with her recently manicured fingernails.

"Apparently, that's not the case. The competition gave them something very similar at a fraction of the price." In a couple of brisk strides, Aaron sequestered himself in the back room of the store, where he kept a couple chairs, coffee table, refrigerator, coffee machine, and a love seat. He often used the room to go over proposals with customers.

A desire to comfort him washed over her. The poor man had seen more than his share of suffering. His wife had died in an auto accident two years before. Her heart went out to him, a single parent raising a four-year-old son, Adam, who happened to be the cutest little guy she'd ever seen.

She squeezed her eyes closed and covered them with her thumb and forefinger. *Why'd he have to be so vulnerable, Lord?* she silently prayed. *What if I become attracted to him?*

She'd keep her distance. Renee sat down at her desk, glanced at the computer monitor, then retyped the advertising slogan she'd been working on all morning.

"Psst," John whispered. "I'm bailing before Aaron asks me to put in overtime tonight. Midterms are staring me in the face. I haven't even cracked the book open from my civics class."

"No problem. I'll stay if he has a mind to work."

John reached for his blue backpack, swung it over his shoulder, and hustled out the door. "Tell Aaron I'll be in after class tomorrow."

Renee waved him off and turned back to her computer screen. The I-beam blinked at her, beckoning some new words of inspiration. She snuck a peek back toward the open door to the back room. No sound. Nothing. Should she check on him? *No,* she reminded herself. *I've already decided not to pry.*

She tapped the keys of the keyboard. "Office relationships never work out," she mumbled.

⚭

Aaron stirred his coffee. How on earth could he have lost this account? They'd come up with a unique angle and twist to the Web design. Something not yet on the Web. He dropped the wooden coffee stirrer into the trash.

The phone rang.

"Sunny Flo Designs, Renee speaking. May I help you?"

Renee Austin had been a gold mine. The woman knew Web design and graphic layout, and she added the creative edge he felt he'd been losing. But how long could he afford to keep her on if he kept losing accounts like this one? *Stop it,* he reprimanded himself. *It's only one account; it's not the world. There will be more accounts, Sunny Flo is—*

"Aaron, Adam's on line one," Renee called out.

He picked up the receiver and sat down on the soft white leather love seat Hannah had picked out the set; it worked well with the laid-back yet professional atmosphere. "Hey, buddy, what's up?"

"Dad, Grandma said I had to call you about supper."

"Oh." Which meant Adam had been giving his grandmother a hard time about what he wanted to eat. "Tell Grandma I'll be picking you up for supper."

"Really?" The joy in his son's voice tugged at his heart.

"Really. My appointment canceled."

"Yipee!" Adam screamed as Aaron pulled the phone from his ear.

"I'll see you in a little while, sport."

"Okay. Bye, Dad."

"Bye, son." He clicked the portable phone off.

Of all the days to have an account fall through. Perhaps it had been his fault. He never should have scheduled such an important client the day before. . . .

Yes, he'd lost the account, pure and simple. His mind hadn't been on his work. "God, why?" He rubbed his face as tears threatened his eyes. *Not at work.*

He picked up a tissue and blew his nose, then stormed into the bathroom and splashed his face with cold water and patted it dry. He heard the phone ring again. Aaron listened, thankful Renee hadn't called him. He sat down for a moment with the light off. His mind drifted back to the accident. Shaking, he recalled the vision of Hannah's mangled car, the blood—so much blood. "Oh God, please take these memories away. I. . . When won't I have to deal with them anymore?"

Who was he kidding? He knew those images would be with him the rest of his life. He'd been told not to go see the vehicle. He'd been told to get a close family friend to go, but he hadn't listened. He'd always been stubborn. Aaron didn't know if he'd gotten that from his prideful Yankee father or the hot-tempered blood of his Cuban mother. Often he figured it came from both of them, making him an immovable object on far too many occasions. And because of that streak, he'd been left with nightmarish images. Currently those images tore at his soul, tore at the fabric of his beliefs. No man should see how his wife suffered before her death, especially following the impact of a tractor-trailer careening into a small SUV.

His eyes fully adjusted to the darkness of the small rest room as the meager light revealed the mirror and sink, the toilet paper roll that needed to be replaced soon, and the framed picture of his first layout ad. He'd been fresh out of college and on top of the world then. Hannah had saved it, and when he'd branched out to start his own business, she'd had it framed and then presented it to him the day Sunny Flo Designs opened.

"Enough." He stood and washed his face with cold water once again. *It's been two years. Get used to it,* he resolved. Stepping back into the conference area, he picked up the phone and called his mother. "Hi, Mom. Did Adam tell you?"

"*Sí,* when will you be arriving?"

Aaron turned his wrist and glanced at the metal hands that displayed the time. "I figure in an hour."

"All right, son. I'll have him ready. Unless you'd like to stay for dinner?"

He'd love to. His cooking skills were vastly inferior. But he didn't want to leave himself vulnerable with his family. "Thanks, but no. I think I'll take him to his favorite restaurant."

"The cheese place?"

"Uh-huh."

His mother groaned. He couldn't blame her. The place was for children, and they ran wild from one game to another. The food was for kids, too—pizza, hot dogs, hamburgers—and the noise of the place sent more than one parent home with a headache. Grandparents seemed particularly susceptible.

After a quick good-bye, he went to his desk.

"Aaron, John has a layout on his drafting table you'll want to look at." Renee walked over toward John's work area.

Why'd he have to hire a woman, a blond-haired, blue-eyed temptation? He should have known better and overlooked her superior work compared to the other applicants.

"Thank you. How's the work on this year's tennis championship coming?"

Renee stepped back to her desk. "Take a look. I've just about worked out the kinks with the Java script. The tennis ball isn't too busy, and I like the speed at which it comes across on my screen. But we need to check it out on the older computer and see how it performs."

Renee thought Aaron wise to keep an old computer with a dial-up modem off-line to check out the Web pages they were creating. They'd upload them in a secured location on the company's Web site and view them on-line. They'd circumvented quite a few problems that way. Not everyone had the latest and greatest software on their personal computers.

She glanced over to Aaron. His face seemed puffy, his back stiffer than usual. The tension he'd been carrying for the past week seemed to be growing.

It's none of your business; just keep your mind to yourself. You don't need to be messing with this man's troubles. Didn't you have enough problems before? The sting of Brent's horrible actions came back into focus. How could he have done such a thing?

"Renee, look at scores.htm."

Renee clicked on the button. What was he seeing? "I'm there."

"Scroll down halfway."

"I'm there." She scanned the document. "What's that?" she yelped. *Where'd that purple line come from?*

Aaron chuckled. "That was my question to you."

Renee looked over the code. Sure enough, it was in there, but how? She hadn't put it in, had she? What was she working in purple for? "That's really strange. I don't recall doing this."

"Probably a copy and paste without realizing it."

Renee quickly fixed the glitch.

The phone rang. Aaron picked it up. "Sunny Flo Designs."

"Hi, Mom." He paused, then added, "Sure, you can drop him off."

He leaned forward in his chair. "What? Is she all right?"

Renee watched him clench his fist, then swivel the back of his chair to her. Right, it was none of her business. Then why did she care so much?

Aaron's mumbled words ended with the click of the handset in its cradle.

"I'll be right back." He stormed out the door and marched across the parking lot to the small café.

Renee shrugged her shoulders and looked back at the screen. Aaron Chapin didn't need her messing up on any further accounts.

"Hey, Renee, how's it going?" John walked back through the doors.

"Fine. I thought you were studying for midterms."

John came over and looked past her to her computer screen. "I forgot my textbook. Where's the boss?"

"Next door; he's on edge." She highlighted the foreign coding and hit the DELETE key.

"Well, it is that time of year." John's thin frame, wild curls, and baggy jeans reminded her of her own college days.

"What time of year?"

John straddled his stool like a cowboy on a horse and thumbed through the piles on his desk for the book. "Anniversary of his wife's death. It was sometime this month. I wager by the way he's been acting, it's this week or next."

And to have lost the account, too—no wonder he retreated into seclusion. "Guess we better just mind ourselves and keep busy."

"Nope, I'm outta here." John jumped up and slipped out the front door as fast as he'd entered.

"Does he go off the deep end, Lord?" Renee looked for her purse. Perhaps she should call it a day, too. She opened her desk drawer to retrieve her wallet.

"Where'd John go?" Aaron asked as he came back in.

"Uh, he said he'd be back tomorrow."

"Great." Aaron's temper was beginning to show.

"Aaron," she whispered.

He turned toward her and came up beside her. His finely bronzed skin, dark eyes, and dark hair seemed imposing. She'd hate to anger the man.

"Are you all right?" she asked tentatively.

"I'm fine." The edge on his words could have cut steel.

Instantly a look of regret crossed his face. "Sorry. Look, I know you're a Christian and, well, I'd like you to pray for someone. She's just been beaten by her husband and has landed in the hospital."

"Oh my. I'll definitely pray. What's her name, if you don't mind me asking?"

"Marie." His hands shook. "She's my sister."

Her sympathy for this man took control. She eased out of her chair and walked around her desk. "I'm sorry, Aaron. I'll pray."

He nodded and started to retreat toward the back room.

Renee hesitated. Should she follow? Should she show compassion? Did he want it? She wouldn't be much of a Christian if she didn't reach out to him. Cautiously, she entered the back room.

He sat on the chair angled to the right of the love seat.

She sat down in front of him on the coffee table. "Aaron, John said your wife died around this time of year."

He raised his head and narrowed his gaze upon hers. "Yes," he croaked out.

"I'm sorry. Can I do anything for you?" She cupped his hand with her own.

His gaze changed. He reached out and touched her hair. She didn't move—she couldn't move.

"It's so silky," he whispered.

Odd, he'd been married; he knew what a woman's hair felt like. Then she remembered that his wife was Spanish. Perhaps she had more of the South American Indian's style of hair.

He slowly rubbed the ends of her hair with his thumb and forefinger. "Hannah's was soft, but in a different way," he mumbled. "I miss her, Renee. I really, really miss her. Why did God allow her to die?"

What could she say? She didn't know? She'd never understood her own losses. Her parents had died when she was only eight. She'd been sent to live with her aunt, who gave her a roof over her head but was too caught up with her male friends to take much notice of her niece.

His thumb touched her cheek.

Renee closed her eyes and swallowed hard.

He pulled her toward him, then his soft lips blazed against her own. She pulled back and reached up to slap his face but caught the shock in his eyes.

"I'm sorry. I don't know what came over me. It'll never happen again." Aaron jumped up and rushed out of the room.

"Daddy!" Adam called as the front door banged behind him.

Chapter 2

Hey, buddy." Aaron scooped up his son and held him close. What had come over him? He didn't want to know. He didn't want to explore it. He didn't even want to think about it.

Noticing his mother waving from her car at the curb, Aaron returned the gesture as she drove off. And what about Marie? What could he do for her? Manuel needed to go to prison for his actions. He was a drunk and abusive. As much as Aaron wanted to go to his sister's side, he had an errand to do.

The café sent over two brown bags full of the meals he'd ordered. "Miss Austin," Aaron called, "I'm leaving now. Would you lock up?"

"Sure," she squeaked out from the back room. She hadn't come out. He couldn't blame her. He wouldn't be surprised to find her resignation on his desk in the morning.

Aaron didn't want to face her; he couldn't. He put Adam down and gave him one of the bags to carry. "Here ya go, son. We'll bring these down to your cousins."

He'd ordered enough food for his sister's four kids, Adam, and himself. He'd take them to a park to eat. He had no idea what condition the house was in or if Manuel would be there. In one warped part of Aaron's brain, he hoped he could show Manuel what it was like to be beaten to a pulp. Not that the man would feel it in a drunken stupor.

"Daddy, is *Tia* Marie okay?"

Sweat beaded between Aaron's shoulders as they crossed the parking lot to his van. Aaron secured Adam in the booster seat. "She'll be all right, son. She's been hurt."

"I know. Uncle Manuel beat her."

"Who told you?"

The boy looked down at his sneaker-covered toes. "No one. I heard Grandma telling you in Spanish."

"You understood those words?"

Adam nodded his head.

Aaron grinned and mussed the boy's hair. "You're too smart."

"Momma spoke in Spanish, and Grandma speaks in Spanish all the time. Grandpa does a little."

Aaron hadn't been teaching Adam Spanish, hadn't thought about it one way or the other. He knew Adam knew some phrases, but apparently he'd picked up far more.

"Is your dog red and your nose green?" Aaron asked him in Spanish.

He wiggled and giggled. "Daddy, we don't have a dog."

Aaron slipped behind the steering wheel. "No, we don't. Can you answer me in Spanish?"

"No. I understand it, but I don't say the words so good."

"We'll work on it together, okay?"

"Sí." Adam grinned.

The entire trip to his sister's place in Homestead, south of Miami, they practiced Spanish. Adam had a natural ear for the language. He'd grown up with it. They practiced silly sentences that worked on rolling the *R*s, which became more and more difficult as silliness worked into the conversation.

On their arrival, they found Aaron's nephews and nieces at the neighbors and no sign of Manuel. Reluctantly, the children piled into the van. He took them to a park and made a picnic out of the meal he'd brought with them.

Aaron tapped out his father's cell phone number. "Hey, Dad, how is she?"

"She's going to be all right. He broke her arm this time."

Aaron kicked a hunk of coral. "He needs to be arrested," he mumbled into the phone and prayed the kids didn't hear him.

"Yes, but your sister is too afraid of him once he's released."

"It's not right." Aaron knew his father felt the same way, but until Marie was ready to remove herself from the situation, their hands were tied. In the past they'd tried to file police reports, only to have Marie lie and say she fell down or walked into something. She would never admit the truth to the police officers or doctors. She always covered up for Manuel.

And he thought he was stubborn! Marie won that award hands down.

"No, it isn't." His father's voice brought Aaron's mind back to the current situation. "But until she's ready, we can only try to encourage her to seek shelter away from Manuel."

"Sí. I'll be leaving with the kids shortly. They've eaten dinner and will need a good bath." Aaron could hear his father chuckling. He knew his father wouldn't be in charge of baths. "I could have them spend the night at my house tonight so they could swim in the pool."

"Chicken," his father teased.

"Hey, the outdoor shower is a lot easier to clean up." Aaron ended the conversation with his father. "All right, gang, let's pack up our mess, get some clothes from your home, and go to my house. It's a pool party tonight."

"Yeah!" they all screamed and scurried to pick up the debris around their picnic table. With the kids loaded in the van, he drove back to their house. Aaron clenched the wheel tighter as he pulled in the driveway behind Manuel's truck. The day couldn't get any worse. First he lost the contract, then he'd heard about Marie's beating. Then he'd done the most foolish thing of all and kissed Renee.

Renee, of all people. Lord, protect me from myself, he silently prayed. *And protect me from what I want to do to Manuel.*

∞

Renee cleaned up the office, set the alarm, and left. Would this be her last day working for Sunny Flo Designs? She couldn't work for another man to whom she found herself attracted. *Do I have some sort of weird psycho-thing going, Lord, that I can only fall in love with my bosses? Sounds pretty sick.* Office romances never worked out. She'd heard it ever since entering the business world. But she'd fallen for Brent hook, line, and sinker.

Now she was attracted to Aaron; and while he didn't look or act anything like Brent, he still fit the role of her boss. Of course, she hadn't done anything to bring about that kiss. And she was about to smack him silly for having done such a thing. Why, oh why, had she tried to comfort him? *Ultimately, it's my fault. I should have left the man alone.*

Renee continued to mentally thrash herself throughout the supermarket, down the streets of North Miami, and to her seventh-floor apartment. Once inside, she removed her business suit and relaxed in an old pair of cutoff jeans and a T-shirt. *Hard to believe it's October.* The eighty-degree temperatures seemed more in keeping with early summer than fall.

She flipped open a can of diet cola and went out to her deck. She was several blocks from the ocean with a good view of Biscayne Bay, if she leaned slightly over the edge of the rail. Which she did all too often. Fortunately, it was an easy jog to the beach and the lower campus of Florida International University. The school's property abutted the bay, and it made for a delightful place to run. Tonight she needed to run.

She placed her apartment key in her front pocket and set out at a mild pace. At the edge of the bay, she sat at the water's edge and watched for manatee. She'd never seen the gentle mammal but heard they started migrating north around this time.

"Lord, what happened today?" She paused, waiting for an answer. When nothing came, she continued. "Father, I can't fall in love with my boss. Once was bad enough. I can't put myself through that again."

I know it was Brent's fault, and he should be the one suffering, yet he's fine. He's happily married. His business is intact. There isn't anything the man lost from our broken engagement. She'd even been foolish enough to toss his engagement ring back at him. Of course, it had felt right at the time. But she'd die seeing the same ring on his wife's finger.

That's when she'd left. She'd left the job. She'd left the city. She'd left her past behind. And now, it just didn't seem fair to be here in a strange new city with a growing attraction to Aaron Chapin.

She wanted to smack him for being so forward, but the sweet feel of his lips flooded her with passion and desire. Admittedly, she hadn't felt that kind of connection with Brent—ever. Which had made it easy not to give in to his constant demands to have sex before marriage. No, Brent wasn't the best choice for a husband; she saw that now. But it didn't stop the hurt he'd caused her when he'd married another woman without first breaking off their engagement.

Brent Cinelli was a first-class cad with a capital *C.*

She gazed off toward the horizon, where the sky turned the color of orange rose. Renee pushed herself up and ran a couple hard laps on the service road before heading home. She'd have to start looking for another job. She couldn't work for Aaron Chapin any longer.

She entered the apartment to the sound of her answering machine taking a message. "I'm sorry I missed you. I really miss you, Renee. We need you to come back."

Her body stiffened. *Brent? Why would he call me now? How'd he find me?*

That wouldn't be too difficult, she realized. All he'd have to do was contact accounting. They had her change of address.

"Please, Renee, pick up the phone. I want to talk with you."

Her hands trembled as she reached for the phone. "I just came in, Brent. What's up?"

"Oh, baby, I've missed you," he cooed.

Renee let out a nervous cackle. "Yeah, right. How's your wife, Brent?"

He cleared his throat. "She's fine. I'm just saying the company really misses you. I miss your inspiration. You've put a tremendous hole in our team by leaving, Renee."

"You've got no one to blame but yourself, Brent. Just how long were you going to hide the fact that you'd married someone while you were still engaged to me?"

"I told you I was planning on letting you know," Brent defended in his nasal tone.

"Of course you were." She bit back her anger. "Get to the point, Brent. You can't charm me any longer." And for the first time she knew the man's spell had no control over her. He meant nothing to her now, other than a sorry man who needed the Lord in his life.

"All right, here's the deal. I need you back here. I'll give you ten grand more than you were making when you left. You'll have full artistic license and at least two assistants doing layout, secretarial, anything you need."

"That's a nice offer. But I have a job. Sorry."

"I'll send you an offer in writing so you can reconsider."

"Brent, the answer will still be no. I'm not interested in your offer. I could never work for you. I don't trust you."

"Ouch! What did I do that was so wrong? Come on, Renee, answer me that. You and I both know our marriage wouldn't have worked. It was for the best."

"You're right, our marriage wouldn't have worked. But I'm a human being with real feelings and didn't deserve to be treated in such a slimy fashion." She stopped herself before she said something she'd have to repent of.

"Well, no matter what you think of me personally, Renee, I always respected your work, and it's your work I want back. Not our relationship. I'll send the offer." He cut the line before she could tell him no.

∞

Aaron worked the kinks out of his back and poured himself another cup of coffee. Memories of Hannah had haunted him all night. Milk swirled in his coffee like the confused images spun in his mind. *Two years, and you're still not over it,* he chastised himself.

He looked at the calendar hanging in the small kitchen. October 4 seemed to stand out above the other dates. "Lord, I still miss her. Has it really been two years?" He placed the quickly drained mug on the Spanish-tiled counter and headed back to the master bathroom for a shower. The pulsing water pounded him, his muscles relaxing in its heat. "Get a grip, old boy. Adam will be awake soon."

Thoughts of his responsibility to raise their son rejuvenated him. His stance surer, he scrubbed his body clean. Wrapping a towel around his waist, he entered his bedroom. There on his bed lay Adam, his black curls resting in stark contrast against the white pillowcase that encircled his head. Aaron smiled at the angelic image. So much like Hannah, yet Adam had some of his own features as well. He slipped on his pants and lay down on the bed beside his son.

"Morning, Adam."

Adam's dark brown eyes blinked, his dimples accenting his smile. "Daddy, I was pretending to be asleep."

"You were, huh?"

"I was going to surprise you."

"Oh, well, I'll pretend to be asleep, and you can surprise me now."

Adam stood up on the bed and towered over his father. "Daddy, that won't work," he said, hands on his hips, confident he knew all the answers in life.

Aaron laughed. "Well in that case, I guess there's only one thing to do." He reached up and grabbed his son, tickling his waist. Howls of laughter filled the room. All the darkness of the previous night faded. Life was here. Adam was the blessing of Hannah's and his life together, merged for all eternity in one little four-year-old boy.

After the tickling match to end all tickling matches ended, he told Adam to go get dressed for the day. And following a gentle tap to his backside, the boy ran down the hall to his room.

"Thank You, Lord, for Adam. Thank You that I still have a piece of Hannah alive and with me."

Dressed, Aaron went into the kitchen and made their breakfast.

"Daddy, is today the day Mommy died?" Adam climbed onto the stool at the counter.

"Yes, Adam, it is."

"Are you going to her grave today?"

"I was planning on it, why?"

"I want to go."

Aaron had never taken Adam to Hannah's grave—the boy had been only two when she died. "I guess you can come."

"Grandma says she's not there, but. . ."

He needs reassurance she's gone, Aaron thought. "Sure, son. I bring flowers, white roses, your mommy's favorites. And then I usually say a little prayer to God."

"What do you pray about?" Adam took a fisted hold of his fork and scooped up some eggs.

Aaron straddled the stool, placing his plate in front of him. "Well, I usually thank God for the time Mommy and I had together and for you. . .and I ask for strength."

"Daddy, why did Mommy have to die?"

"Because bad things sometimes happen to good people, son."

"But Ricky still has his mommy."

"I know, son, and I still have mine. Your grandma is my mommy."

"I know that, Daddy."

Aaron chuckled. "Sorry, I forgot you're so grown up now."

Adam puffed up his chest.

"Grandma says Mommy was hit by a car."

A truck actually. A knot tightened in Aaron's stomach. He had always been honest with Adam, but he questioned his mother's openness about Hannah's death. "Yes, son, Mommy was."

"I miss Mommy." Adam forked some more eggs.

"I do too, son."

"Daddy, are you going to get me a new mommy?"

New mommy! Where does he get these things? Aaron wondered. "I wasn't planning on it. Why?"

"On *Barney* they were talking about how some kids have new mommies and daddies, so am I going to get a new mommy?"

Good grief, how can a purple dinosaur explain. . . He broke off his thoughts. "Son, if God sees fit to bring a new woman into my life, then maybe. But I must tell you, I'm not looking to find one."

"Okay." Adam finished his breakfast. After drinking down his orange juice, he leaped from his chair.

Aaron blinked. *What just happened here? The kid is watching too much TV,* he thought. *I need to talk with Mother.* Determined, he cleaned up the kitchen and got ready to leave for work. Adam met him in the hallway, his book bag packed with his toys for the day.

"All set?"

"Yup." Adam grinned.

How could he stay mad at that adorable face for long? Aaron mused. "Okay, let's go."

After a brief discussion with his mother revealed that Adam's questions were just natural, Aaron realized he'd been too sensitive. Loss and heartache had filled the previous night. He hadn't experienced a night like that in almost a year. He supposed it didn't help that Marie had left the hospital and returned to her own home with her children. She hadn't appreciated the family's gesture of love and support. She saw it as intrusion. He should have knocked some sense into Manuel while he had the chance last night. Of course, attacking a man in a drunken stupor would prove nothing. Not to mention, Aaron would have a hard time living with himself.

The memory of his little niece, Amanda, clinging to him, not wanting to return to her home, tore at his heart.

At the office he placed a call to the florist for three white roses to be delivered.

Renee was late. It wasn't like her. Would she return? After his inappropriate actions the day before, who'd blame her for never returning? The bell jingled over the door.

"Renee," he called out.

"Mr. Chapin, I believe we have some things to discuss."

He raised his hands. "I know, I know, I'm sorry. I promise it won't happen again. But if you feel you need to find another place of employment, I'll write you the best recommendation you ever had. You're a good employee, Ms. Austin. I don't want to lose you. But I will understand if you need to leave."

She nodded. Her honey hair crowned her head. The feel of her soft, silky locks came back to his mind. Aaron cleared his throat.

"I'll give the matter some thought," she responded. "I was made an offer last night from my former boss."

He never understood why she had left her previous place of employment. She'd only said they had a difference of opinion.

"How is your sister?" she asked.

"She'll be all right. Renee, you're a woman. Tell me why a woman would stay in an abusive relationship?"

"Fear, mostly. Personally, I'd have left the man who laid one finger on me in anger."

She bit her lower lip. Tears pooled in her eyes. Was she going to say more? *Have you been abused, Ms. Renee Austin?* he wondered.

Chapter 3

Renee kept to her space in the office. She didn't need to confront yesterday much less her past, today. As the day wore on, she became more comfortable in the environment. Aaron called her "Ms. Austin" every time he addressed her. Apparently he wasn't about to allow the kiss to destroy their working relationship. And was it really a kiss? Or was it more a man reaching out for something he'd lost?

Amazingly, Aaron seemed under less stress today. She'd looked it up—his wife had died on the fourth of October. Today was the anniversary of Hannah's death. Three white roses were delivered.

"Ms. Austin? Renee?" His voice jarred her. She blinked, seeing him standing in front of her desk.

"Sorry, I was thinking."

"Apparently." He grinned. He held an envelope in his hand. "Here's the letter of recommendation. I hope you don't feel you'll need to use it, but. . ."

"I'll stay for awhile, Aaron, before I decide. I know you were reacting to the loss of your wife."

He scraped a chair across the floor and sat down with a desk between them. "Renee, I'm not—"

The phone rang. She answered it. "Sunny Flo Designs, Renee speaking. May I help you?"

"Hi, is my daddy there?"

"Sure. Just a minute, Adam."

Aaron pushed himself from the chair he'd been sitting in and went to his desk. "Hey, buddy."

She loved how Aaron treated his son. He was a good father.

"Sure, I guess. Let me speak with Grandma." Aaron sat down. *"Madre."* His words came smoothly in Spanish. Aaron showed his Latin heritage, Renee mused, with his richly tanned skin, dark hair, and brown eyes. But his name was so contrary. He'd explained it once. His father was English, his mother Cuban. And he'd been given his grandfather's first name. The mixture of the cultures within Aaron intrigued her. Intrigued her far too much. She'd been shocked when he'd kissed her. But admittedly, another part of her had wanted that kiss, which was why she knew she'd have to find a new job. On the other hand, they were both adults; they could prevent moments like that from happening. Not to mention, he wasn't really attracted to her. She'd just been handy in a moment of weakness.

Today he seemed like a different man, back to the normal Aaron Chapin. Perhaps she could work through her own foolish attraction and continue working for him. She loved the work. She loved the quality that Aaron strived for. And she loved the integrity he insisted went into each of their products. Not like Brentwood Designs, which cut more corners and churned out more work than anyone she'd ever seen. She'd spend hours of overtime fixing and repairing shabby work. No wonder Brent wanted her back. *He's probably losing accounts without my extra work on the company's behalf.*

"Sí, Madre. I understand. Tell Adam I'll take him." He placed the handset back in its cradle and rose slowly from his desk.

"A problem?" she inquired.

"No, not really. Adam's growing up. He wants to see his mother's grave."

"Oh." Renee leaned back, crossing her arms, and hugged her shoulders.

"Renee?" he inquired.

"Sorry. I lost my parents when I was eight. The memory of watching their coffins going into the ground just flashed in my mind."

"Adam was barely two when Hannah died. I didn't take him to the funeral. I didn't have the patience for a two-year-old toddler, and I didn't want him having the memory you have."

"You're a good father, Aaron." She glanced down at the papers on her desk. "Did you find any more purple lines in the presentation?"

"No." He chuckled.

"Good. I went on-line with the old dinosaur computer, and the tennis ball coming at the customer takes a bit to load, but it doesn't run too slowly. I think it's manageable."

"I'll take a look." Aaron went over to the old computer.

Renee went back to work on the coding of yet another Web page. John should be in later in the afternoon to add the color to the logo she'd drawn.

"I agree, it works," Aaron said decisively. "It's almost at that I'm-not-going-to-wait-another-second point when the ball starts spinning at them. Put a message to click the window and move to the next page for those impatient browsers.

"I'm picking Adam up from my mother's after my appointment," he continued, "so I won't be back in today. Would you mind locking up again?"

"Of course not." She should probably protest a little, but what would be the point? She truly didn't mind.

"Thanks, I appreciate it. Have John finish what he started yesterday and whatever you need him to do for you. I'll have a list for him tomorrow."

"Gotcha." *Father, bless Aaron with a sale today,* she silently prayed.

∞

Arriving at his parents' home, Aaron stretched his arms out toward his son, who came running toward him. "Daddy!"

"Hi, buddy. How was your day?" Aaron held his son chest-high.

"Me and Grandma made play-dough."

"Really?"

Adam shook his little head up and down, then squirmed to get down. "Wanna see?"

"Sure."

The boy tore back through the front door and into his grandparents' house. *All that energy!* Aaron kissed his mother on the cheek. *"Buenos días,* Madre." His mother sat with her Bible on her lap in the living room.

"Buenos días."

"Was he good?"

"Sí, lots of questions about Hannah and death."

Aaron winced. *"Gracias."*

Adam came running in, a mound of blue dough draped over and around his fingers. "See, Daddy?"

"Wow, looks great, buddy. Are you bringing it home?"

"Grandma says to keep it here for tomorrow."

"Sounds like a plan. We'd better get going. Put the play-dough away and give Grandma and Grandpa a kiss good-bye."

Adam scurried away.

"Anything I should be aware of, Mom?"

"No. He's just old enough to ask questions now."

"I know." Aaron had hoped this day would never come. How could he explain death to a four year old? He thought back over the years when Adam had asked so few questions about his mother. Taking in a deep breath, he braced himself.

Adam placed his hand into his father's. "Daddy, are we going to Mommy's grave?"

"Yes, son."

Adam tightened his grip. Once they reached the van, Aaron hoisted the boy up into his booster seat and waved back to his mother. Seat belts in place, he turned the key in the ignition and began the journey of no return.

"Daddy?"

"Yes, son?"

"Did Mommy's boo-boos hurt?"

Aaron gulped. "Yeah, they hurt, but not for very long."

" 'Cause she went to heaven?"

"Yes, 'cause she went to heaven."

"Daddy?"

"Yes, Adam?"

Aaron's jaw clenched at the memory of the car battered and ripped open, Hannah's blood splattered on bits of broken glass and over the distorted driver's seat. Yes, Hannah did have pain, more than he wanted to tell his son. She had lived for a little more than three hours and died shortly after he arrived at the hospital. His grasp tightened on the steering wheel. His forearm muscles tensed, bracing himself for Adam's next question.

"Did you bring the flowers?"

His pent-up breath escaped with such force, his nostrils flared. "They're up here beside me, buddy."

"Daddy, why do you bring flowers?"

Easy question. I can handle easy questions. "Because your mommy liked white roses. So I bring three. One from you, one from me, and one for her."

Adam wiggled in his seat.

"Son, do you need to go to the bathroom?"

"No." He continued to squirm.

"Why are you squirming?"

"Something's hurting me."

"What?"

Adam reached his little hand under his bottom and lifted himself slightly off the seat. "I can't find it."

"Check your pocket, son."

He reached into his pocket and pulled out a small ball. "I got it." He held it proudly in the air like a prize trophy.

Aaron smiled. "A ball, huh?"

"I was hiding it in the play-dough at Grandma's."

"Oh."

Aaron parked the van in a shaded parking spot. A few cars dotted the lot. "Here we are, son."

Adam pushed the button to his seat belt and wiggled out of his restraints. As they walked toward the grave, Adam asked, "Daddy, are all these stones dead people?"

"Yes, son."

"Why do they use stones?"

"Well, 'cause a stone won't fade away like paint on a sign does."

Adam nodded. "Wow, Daddy, there's zillions of them!"

The boy looked up. "Are you going to die, Daddy?"

Aaron stroked his thumb across Adam's hand. "Someday. But I believe God will have me around for awhile."

They walked hand in hand. Aaron gained strength holding his son's warm, small hand. At Hannah's grave, he went down on one knee. "Adam, this is your mommy's grave."

"What's it say?"

"Hannah Marie Chapin, born January 5, 1974. Died October 4. . ." Aaron cleared his throat. "Beloved wife and friend." His mind ran over the entire Scripture passage the phrase was drawn from. "This is my beloved and this is my friend." A lump stuck in his throat, remembering their wedding day when he had recited that verse to her.

Adam traced his finger in the letters.

Aaron's hand trembled as he placed two of the white roses on the marble stone.

Mimicking his father's actions, Adam placed his rose. "Daddy, is Mommy happy?"

"Yes, son. She's in heaven, and it's a wonderful, happy place."

"Does she miss us?"

"I guess so. But it's different 'cause she's with God and feels things differently than we do."

"Daddy, does Jesus give Mommy a hug when she misses us?"

"I'm sure He does." Aaron reached over and gave Adam a big hug. "Hugs are good, aren't they?"

Adam nodded his head. He bent down and patted the stone. "Bye, Mommy."

Aaron's tears burned. "Bye, Hannah," he whispered. "We've got a great son."

∽

Renee looked at the clock. Half past six and she still hadn't left the office. The purple line had appeared on several of her saved files on the network. She'd painstakingly gone through every file looking for any more. She'd never heard of a glitch in software that would cause such a thing. It was peculiar, to say the least.

A bang on the door caused her to jump. She turned to see Aaron putting his keys into the lock. "Is there a problem, Ms. Austin?"

"Hey, Renee," Adam called as he came bouncing in.

"Hi, Adam. No, Aaron, well, yes, actually, but I've been working on it."

"What's the trouble?" He strolled over to her desk.

Adam went over to the old computer and clicked on one of his favorite games. "Trained him young, huh?"

Aaron's smile lit up his face. "Cheap labor. So, what's the trouble?" He leaned over, looking at her computer screen.

"It's that purple line you found yesterday. It's appearing in several pages of the uploaded files. It isn't on my desktop original, just the uploaded files."

"A virus?"

"Not likely; it's too random. There isn't a logical pattern."

"Let's contact the domain server and change our passwords. Maybe someone got in and has been playing with our files."

"But who? Why?" she asked.

"Probably some kid." Aaron reached for the phone and called the domain server. Within minutes the passwords were changed. Aaron scribbled them down on a piece of paper. "Thanks," he said and hung up the phone.

"Daddy, I'm hungry." Adam rubbed his belly.

"In a minute, son. Just let me give Renee some information."

"Okay." Adam came up to them and hugged his father's left leg.

Renee smiled. Aaron handed her the small yellow note.

"Daddy, can we go to Chucky Cheese, please?"

Renee chuckled under her breath. Adam always wanted to go to Chucky Cheese.

"What about the peanut place?"

"Peanut place?" Renee wondered where that could be. All the fast-food places she knew didn't sell peanuts.

Aaron spun around. "Road House Grill."

"Oh." She hadn't meant to speak her thoughts.

"I get a better meal if we go there." Aaron winked. "Not to mention, it's quieter. Although some nights that isn't always the case."

Renee shook her head from side to side.

"Renee, you wanna come?"

"No, I—"

"Dad, can Renee come?" Adam tugged on his father's pant leg.

"Have you eaten?" Aaron asked.

"No, but—"

"Please, Renee," Adam begged. "You put peanut shells on the floor. It's really fun."

How could she turn down the four year old? Her gaze locked with Aaron's. "Are you sure?"

He hesitated for a fraction of a second. "Absolutely."

"All right, Adam, I'll come."

"Yipee. Daddy, can I go in Renee's car?"

Aaron chuckled. "You like that car, huh?"

Adam beamed and bounced his head up and down.

Renee suppressed a giggle. Her Mustang convertible had been a necessity years ago. Now it was a classic in the truest sense of the word. She'd spent a small fortune restoring that car. "It's fine with me."

"I'll put his booster seat in your car, then."

"Sure." She reached through her bag and handed him her keys. Their fingers brushed. Her cheeks flamed. Maybe she should reconsider her position on staying on at Sunny Flo Designs.

Chapter 4

The awkwardness of the evening quickly dissipated for Aaron. Renee was a beautiful woman, inside and out. She kept an attentive ear to Adam, yet she didn't let him control the entire evening. Aaron shifted Adam in his arms. The child had fallen asleep on the way home from the restaurant. It had been a very full day, making play-dough, visiting his mother's grave, and having dinner with Renee.

He removed Adam's shoes and clothing, laid him on the bed, and covered him with the sheet and blanket. Kissing the top of Adam's head, he whispered, "I love you, buddy."

Adam mumbled something unintelligible.

He worked his way back to the living area, pulled out a bottle of water from the refrigerator, and sat down on the sofa, plopping his feet up on the coffee table. Leaning his head back, he closed his eyes. *Father, for the first time I feel I've finally let go of Hannah. It was important to bring Adam to the cemetery. Thank You for—*

The phone rang, interrupting his prayer.

"Aaron?"

"Hi, Mom, what's up?"

"Your sister. I can't get that girl to see reason."

"I can't either, *Mima*. I've tried, but she's just not ready to listen."

"I know but—"

"You needed to blow off steam."

"Sí. I called earlier. You weren't home. How are you? How did it go at the cemetery?"

Aaron sat back down on the couch. "It went very well. Something happened today, Mom. I finally released her. The burden, not really a burden exactly..." He continued to explain about his day and how it had gone.

"I'm happy for you, son. I know it was difficult. Time does wonders, but you will always miss her. It won't always ache like it has."

At times his mother seemed so wise. He'd never known her to lose someone close to her, not a spouse or a sibling or a parent, for that matter. So how she understood this...

He shook his head. It didn't matter. "Yes, that's how it is."

After they finished their conversation, he let out a slow breath and finished his time of prayer with the Lord. "And, Father, I don't know what to say about that kiss the other day. She's a beautiful woman, but am I that weak of a man?

"Forgive me, Lord. And help Renee feel safe around me. I don't want to lose her as an employee. She's helped the business in so many ways. I honestly don't know what to do or say."

Aaron clicked on the evening news. The current events rambled on, but his mind kept going back to his inappropriate actions with Renee and how much he wanted to touch her hand during dinner. He'd fought the desire to reach across the table and place his hand on hers. Why?

The blast of the station switching from news to commercials had him reaching for the remote. Lowering the volume, his hand paused. *That's my design!* Someone had stolen his design and sold it to the company he'd been bidding to. "How'd that happen?"

His phone rang again.

"Hello." He watched the screen in disbelief.

"Aaron, it's Renee. Turn on your TV." He heard the excitement in her voice.

"I'm already looking at it. How'd that happen?"

"I don't know. Aaron, I think we have a security leak. We need to get someone to come and check out the system."

"I agree. But who can we trust?"

"I don't know, but don't you have a nine o'clock tomorrow?"

"Yes, but. . .are you suggesting—"

She cut him off. "I'm suggesting that you and I work all night and rethink that proposal. There's no telling how much information has been compromised."

Aaron rubbed the back of his neck. "You're right. I'll have to call my mother to see if she can come here and watch Adam. Then I'll meet you at the office."

"I think we have to work off-line on this, Aaron. I have the entire file, specs, et cetera, on my laptop. We can work from that."

"Would you mind terribly coming here, then? It's already past ten and—"

"No problem. Give me directions."

Aaron quickly ran over the directions and clicked the phone off. He went to his home office and downloaded the working files they had on their site, then promptly disconnected the computer from its on-line service and modem. "Who's doing this, Lord?"

∽

Renee easily wove her way through the city streets. It was quarter to eleven by the time she arrived at Aaron's home. For better or worse, she had to admit the attraction to Aaron. *I'm an adult; this is business. I can control my emotions.* She hoped. She swung her laptop carrying case over her shoulder and marched up to the front door. Her finger poised to ring the doorbell, she paused, wondering if the noise might wake up little Adam. Tentatively, she reached up to knock.

The door opened. "Hi, I heard you pull up."

Aaron's handsome smile totally disarmed her. Perhaps she wasn't as adult as she'd hoped. "Hi, did you put on a pot of coffee?"

He stepped back, opening the door for her to enter. "Better, I put on Cuban coffee."

"I'll be up all night." She grinned.

"That is the idea." He chuckled. "I have a home office. It's small but workable. Or we can work at the dining-room table."

"We'll probably need both."

"True, you can work on layout while I brainstorm over new concepts."

"Sounds good."

He poured her a small cup of Cuban espresso. "Here's mud in your eye." She gulped it down and placed her espresso glass on the counter for a refill.

He knitted his eyebrows. "Are you sure?"

"Yeah, I don't feel a thing yet."

"You will." He poured her the second cup.

As she started to sip, the caffeine from the first took its effect. A sudden jolt coursed through her veins, and she felt like she could ricochet off the walls and ceiling. "Wow."

"I warned ya." He grinned. She noticed he'd only taken a couple sips from his first glass.

"What do they put in this stuff?"

"One of these little shot glasses is like four cups of coffee."

"Oh my."

He chuckled. "Come on, we've got work to do."

For the next few hours they reworked their proposal. By 4:00 a.m. they were printing it out.

"Renee, take a seat and rest for a bit," he offered.

"Thanks. You've got a nice home."

"Thank you. We bought it fairly cheap. It needed a lot of work."

"It's an interesting shape."

"The previous owners made several additions. This section we're in right now is part of the original house. Plus the rooms in the front. The pool and back bedrooms came later."

"You have a pool?"

"Yes, and a Jacuzzi. You're welcome to use it. After a long day at work, I find myself in the Jacuzzi to unwind. Then I cool off with a gentle swim of a couple of laps."

"I'd love to, but I didn't come prepared. You should tell a girl to bring her bathing suit." She winked. *Oh no, why'd I do that? I'm flirting.* She wanted to flee.

"I'll remember that. Renee, we need to talk."

She shook her head. "I. . ."

He came up beside her on the couch, then eased back a few inches. "Look, I don't know why I kissed you the other day. I'm sorry. But I don't think it was strictly as you said, that I was missing my wife. I'd been thinking a lot about her that day, no question. But you're a beautiful woman, Renee. Very beautiful. And I'm not saying that just about your physical beauty, although there is that. You're genuine and sweet. And I love the way you handle Adam. You wouldn't believe how many women have tried to use him to get to me."

What could she say? What did she want to say? "Aaron, I forgave you for the kiss. It's a dead issue."

"Is it?" He reached out, open palmed. She eased hers toward his and pulled it back. He let his hand fall to his side. "Renee, I've been out of circulation for many years, but tell me if I'm wrong here. You are attracted to me, aren't you?"

"Yes. . .no!" She jumped up. "Aaron, I can't." Tears swarmed her eyes. "I like you, but. . ."

He stood up beside her. "I won't force you, Renee. But something happened today. Something very important, and I think you should know."

She raised her head and glanced at him. "What?"

"Please sit. I want to discuss this with you. I promise I won't kiss you or try to hold your hand."

She scanned the sofa and looked back at him. Somehow she knew to trust him. She shouldn't, but she would. Renee sat down on the chair across from the sofa.

He chuckled. "Fair enough. At the cemetery today Adam and I said good-bye to Hannah. A real good-bye. For the first time since she passed away, I felt I had truly let her go. And it felt good; it felt right. I've been so afraid of forgetting Hannah, I've held on to her and her image. Can you understand what I mean?"

She nodded her head. She understood all too well. She'd been afraid to even talk about her parents after they died, fearing she'd remember something incorrectly.

"Tell me about your parents. You said they died when you were eight?"

"Yes. I don't have too many memories. They were sweet, kind, Christian parents who had forgotten to write a will. I was sent to my aunt's house. I always loved my fun aunt Ida when I was a child. But she divorced Uncle Pete when I was six, and well, she never went to church. Drinking, drugs, all sorts of male visitors passed through her apartment. I was her little slave. It wasn't as bad as I make it sound; she loved me in her own way. And she tried, but the alcohol and drugs have a way of making a person less than aware of what they're doing."

"I'm sorry." He leaned back on the sofa.

"Have you updated your will?"

"Yes. After Hannah died, it was necessary, of course. My parents will raise Adam if. . .if something should happen to me."

She rested her head back on the chair. It was close to five o'clock. They were done. She should go home and get some much needed rest. "Aaron, I need to go."

"All right, but what is it you're not telling me?" he asked.

∞

Stupid, stupid, stupid, he chided himself. *She's got a secret, and I shouldn't have pushed.* Aaron cleared the coffee cups and napkins from the dining-room table. Placing them in the sink, he stretched his back. Dusk played on the windows. He groaned. Sleep—he needed a couple hours before the nine o'clock meeting.

He sat on the edge of the bed, slipped off his loafers, and pulled off his jersey. His eyes closed, his body fell. Soft, comforting, relaxed. He yawned.

The alarm blared in his ear. His hand patted the end table. One unfocused eye peered at the red digital lights. "Six." He hit the snooze button.

Fifteen minutes later he fumbled for the snooze button and didn't bother to check the time.

He waited for the next alarm. He didn't want to get up but knew he had to. He listened for a moment longer. *It should be ringing now.* Aaron turned his head and peered over his pillow. The lights were out on the clock.

He bolted out of bed and scrabbled to his bureau for his watch. "Argh," he groaned. Ten minutes to nine, and all was not well.

"Adam?" he called, running down the hall to his son's back bedroom.

"Hi, Dad." Adam sat cross-legged in front of the laptop, playing a computer game.

"Do you know what time it is?"

"No, the TV isn't working either."

Of course not, the power's dead. Which is really odd since there wasn't a storm last night. Must have been a traffic accident on a neighborhood pole, he reasoned. "Get dressed; it's almost nine, and I have an appointment." *Which I'm not going to make.*

He grabbed his cell phone. All the phones in the house were portable and needed electricity. "I should keep one stationary phone for occasions such as this."

He tapped in his mother's number. "Hi, Mom. I don't have time to bring Adam over. Can you go to the office and pick him up?"

"Sure, what's the matter, Aaron?"

"Power's out. I overslept. I need to call a client. I'll tell ya later."

"Adiós." His mother's voice calmed his excited nerves.

He tapped in the client's number. "Hello, this is Aaron Chapin from Sunny Flo Designs. I have an appointment with you at nine. I'm going to be a couple minutes late."

"Mr. Reynolds is a busy man, Mr. Chapin."

"I understand that, but there was a power failure at my house, and I'm running late."

"I can't promise, but I'll let him know of your delay."

"Thank you." Herbert J. Reynolds was not one to put off. Aaron would be lucky to even get in the door at this rate. "So much for last night's effort."

Dressed, packed, and in the car by nine wasn't too bad, Aaron mused.

"Daddy, why are we going so fast?"

Aaron glanced at the speedometer and eased his foot off the accelerator. "I'm sorry. I'm behind schedule."

"Daddy, you know you're not 'posed to go fast," Adam corrected.

"Yes, son." Aaron tapped the steering wheel with his thumbs. He didn't need a four year old reminding him of what he should or should not do.

"Daddy?"

"Yes, son." He also wasn't in the mood for twenty questions.

"Do you like Ms. Renee?"

"Yes." He took a sideways glance over to his son.

"I like her, too. Did you know her mommy died when she was little?"

"Yes," he said cautiously.

"Me, too." Adam crossed his feet at his ankles. "Daddy?"

"Yes, son." Aaron took in a deep breath.

"We didn't pray or eat breakfast this morning."

"No, we didn't. I'll correct that at the office, okay?"

"Okay. Daddy?"

Aaron chuckled. "Yes, son."

"I love you."

"I love you, too, buddy."

Aaron had to wait for his mother to arrive at the office. Renee hadn't shown up yet. Not that he could blame her. But he hoped it wasn't because of their discussion last night—this morning—whenever. He moaned. He'd been honest about his feelings. The fear in her eyes when he told her. . .

Aaron shook his head. Back in the car, he looked at the now green light.

A horn blared. He eased the gas and worked his way through the intersection. Three more blocks and he'd be there. He parked the car at the first available slot and pulled out the proposal. He didn't have the storyboard, but he did have the laptop. At least he could provide a visual.

Over the next ten minutes, Aaron found himself at the end of a lecture about promptness as a sign of professionalism.

"Mr. Reynolds, I apologize for wasting your time. I happen to have the best proposal you've ever received, but I won't take up your time any longer." Aaron turned to exit the room.

"Mr. Chapin, Aaron, show me what you have. Why was it you were late?"

Aaron gave a brief description of the morning and his need to take care of Adam first.

"Right, you lost your wife a couple years back."

"Yes. Mr. Reynolds, I'd be happy to show you the proposal."

"Go for it." The fifty-something man with white hair and a bulging waistline slipped into the chair behind his desk.

Chapter 5

Renee worked the stiffness out of her neck. She'd overslept. The office smelled of stale coffee. She turned on the computers and got to work changing the security passwords for every account. Someone had to be getting in, but how? She clicked through the company's Internet page and found it was vulnerable. In the original coding one could actually get the directories of all the files. So even the files they had protected were visible.

The bell above the door jingled.

"Where's Aaron?" a large-framed, potbellied Hispanic man ordered.

"I'm sorry, he's not here. Can I help you?"

His gaze scrutinized every part of her body. Renee felt like running for additional cover. "You're pretty enough, but I'm looking for Aaron."

"Can I give him a message for you?"

Renee clutched the end of the counter in front of the door and was glad for the blockage.

"Tell him to keep his hands off my kids."

"What?" The word slipped out before she had a moment to check herself.

"He'll know what I mean." He turned and, slamming the door open, left.

Renee watched his lopsided gait. He appeared drunk. She sniffed the air. The scent of stale beer wafted past her nose. Releasing the counter, she slipped down behind it. Clenching her sides, she rocked back and forth. "It's been years, Lord. Why now?"

The bell over the door rang again.

"No, God, no," she silently prayed.

"Renee?" Aaron called out. She rolled onto her hands and knees and pretended to be searching for something.

"Hi, Aaron." She forced a grin and stood up.

"We did it, Renee. We did it." He captured her in his arms and twirled her around.

Renee couldn't help but smile. "What?"

"We landed the account. Thank you, thank you so much." He placed her back down. She stepped back and looked down at her feet. She liked being in his arms. Her heart raced. Why, was it Aaron or, or. . .

"Aaron, you had a visitor. If you can call him a visitor."

"Who?"

"Don't know; he didn't leave a name. Just a message." She paused.

"And?" He placed his hands on his waist.

"He said to tell you to keep away from his kids."

"Ahh, was he in his late thirties, Hispanic, with a crooked nose?"

Renee thought back on the man's features. "Yes, do you know him?"

"Unfortunately yes. He's my brother-in-law, Manuel. Don't you worry about him. I'll make sure he doesn't come by here again. He probably had a few too many to get up the nerve to speak to me."

"He did smell of alcohol."

"Yeah, that's Manuel. I'm sorry you had to deal with him alone." Aaron headed back to his desk, placing his brown leather briefcase on top of it.

"I changed all the passwords," Renee reported, "and I found a way that someone could have gotten to our files."

"How?"

"Our index page coding wasn't set properly, and if someone typed in the right address or rather the right missing word of our address, they could pull up the entire directory."

"No way. I programmed that page myself. I know I took care of that problem."

"Well, I checked the last date that file had been updated. It was about two months ago."

"I'm certain I didn't touch it." Aaron sat in front of his computer and pulled up his daily planner. "What was the date and time?"

"August eighteenth, 10:30 p.m."

"That's a Sunday, Renee. I wasn't working here or at home. In fact, I was at my parents' all that evening."

"I don't know what to say, other than I fixed the code and changed the passwords again."

Aaron rubbed the back of his neck. "Thank you. I know it's not your fault."

"No, and I'd say someone's been messing with your work. Thankfully we've caught it in time."

Aaron pulled in a deep breath, causing his shoulders to rise. She could see his neck and shoulder muscles tauten. She took a step forward, instinctively raising her hands to massage him. *What am I doing?* She stopped in place and stared at her betraying members. *Thank You, Lord, for bringing me to my senses before I touched him.*

Aaron spun around in his chair and faced her. "Renee, are you all right?"

"Yes. . .no," she stammered. "Aaron, if you don't mind, I think I better go home and get some rest. I don't think I can be productive the rest of the day."

"No problem. You worked plenty of hours last night. Thanks again, Renee. I wouldn't have made the sale without you."

"You're welcome." She fetched her purse and practically ran out the door.

I shouldn't have picked her up, he chastised himself.

The doorbell jingled. "Hey, Aaron, how'd it go this morning?"

John ambled over to his desk and plopped his book bag at the foot of his stool.

"Went great; we got the account."

"All right, way to go, man! How'd they like the logo I came up with?"

John's logo had been put to the side when they discovered their files had been tampered with. But how much should he tell him? Was John the one getting into their system and selling to the competition? But that didn't make sense. He wouldn't need to change the codes because he knew them all. "No, I'm afraid we couldn't use it."

"Huh?" John dropped his pencil.

"Renee and I discovered someone has broken into our files. So we had to come up with a totally new campaign."

"No way, man. When'd you discover this?"

"Last night."

John whistled through his teeth. "And you redid the entire campaign in one night?"

"Yeah, with Renee's help." Aaron couldn't help but beam.

"You better treat that lady good, boss. She's a dynamo. I'd hate to see you lose her."

"Yeah, I know." Aaron stepped toward the back room. "Wanna soda? I'm buying."

"Sure, thanks." John leaned over the drafting table and went back to work. He was a blessing, but he didn't have the expertise and developed skills that would come with time and experience. John's raw energy helped keep a project alive, but Renee added to even Aaron's own creative thinking.

"Okay, Lord, I got the message. Hands off," Aaron mumbled and took out a soda and bottled water for himself.

∞

The next week passed uneventfully. Sales were made. Aaron and Renee seemed to work comfortably together, and he'd not touched her in seven days, not even a simple handshake.

"Daddy!" Adam barreled in through the office door followed by Aaron's mother.

"Hey, buddy." Aaron scooped up and hugged his son.

"Can I stay at Ricky's house tonight?"

Aaron glanced over to his mother.

"Ricky's mother invited him," she explained. Ricky was a year older and lived next door to Aaron's parents.

"A real sleepover, I don't know. Are you old enough?" Aaron teased.

"Dad–dy," Adam emphasized.

"Well? It's a big deal, you know."

"Please, Daddy, please." Adam hugged him again.

"Sure, buddy." He glanced back at his mother. "Do you need anything from my house?"

"No, Adam and I already packed his bag." She winked.

"Oh, really? Pretty sure I'd say yes, huh?" He tickled Adam on his side.

Adam laughed wildly.

Renee walked in from the back room. "Hey, Adam. Hi, Mrs. Chapin. How are you?"

"Bien." Gladys Chapin smiled.

Aaron followed Renee's movements a moment too long. His mother's eyebrows were raised when he glanced back at her. "Aaron, your father and I are waiting on your decision about us taking Adam to Orlando."

"I see, so that's why you agreed to this sleepover."

"Possibly."

He'd been hoping to put off his parents a little bit longer. Adam left for occasional visits with Hannah's parents, but each and every time, Aaron had gotten little or no sleep. The fear of losing his son was so great, he couldn't rest. Hannah's parents had been asking to take Adam for several days, not just an overnight, so that they could bring him to visit some of Hannah's relatives. Aaron knew it was right. He just found it too difficult to be alone and calm.

"All right, all right, you win. You can take him to Orlando."

"Gracias." His mother enveloped him in her arms.

"Yippee, I'm going to see Sam!"

"Sam?" Aaron, his mother, and Renee asked at the same time.

"Who's Sam?" Aaron pushed further.

"The seal."

Okay, I'm clueless, Aaron admitted to himself. And by the blank expressions on Renee's and his mother's faces, they were as confused as he.

"Grandma, can we go tomorrow?"

"It's up to your dad."

"Daddy, please?" Adam looked up to him with his big brown eyes and gave him a bright, toothy smile.

Aaron chuckled. "Sure."

"Grandma," Adam said, taking her hand, "we gotta go pack more clothes." He pulled her toward the door.

"Hey, don't I get a kiss good-bye?"

Adam dropped his grandmother's hand and came running back. "I love you, Daddy, thanks."

"I love you too, son. You mind your grandma and grandpa, all right?"

"Yes, sir." Adam wiggled free from his embrace and jumped over to Renee. "Renee, did you hear I'm going to Orlando?"

"I sure did. That's great."

"You wanna come?"

Renee's laughter licked Aaron's ears. "No, I'm afraid I have to stay and work with your dad."

"Okay. Bye, Renee." Adam jumped up and hugged her around the neck. She wrapped her arms around Adam and closed her eyes.

She loves him. Oh Father, what's going on here? Why can't we be honest about our feelings? And what are my feelings?

Renee turned and wiped the tears from her eyes. She loved Adam so much, yet she didn't have a right to feel this way, did she?

Gladys Chapin spoke softly to her son in Spanish. Aaron turned toward her, then looked back at his mother. "Sí," Renee understood. The rest of their conversation was a blur.

Gladys kissed Aaron gently on the cheek and tapped it with her hand. *Lord, I miss my mother. How's Adam going to do without his?*

Bringing her attention back to her work, she fiddled with the keys, then went over to John's drafting table.

"What's the matter?" Aaron asked.

"Not sure. Take a look at this." She pointed to the logo John had colored the previous week. "We scanned it in, and I reworked it. But. . ." She shook her head. "It's just not working."

"Let me see." Adam turned and fussed with the terminal behind John's work area. He copied the image and put it in a separate graphics program. "What if we change the color scheme here?" He highlighted the area around the circle and selected a textured color.

"All right, the beige works better, but it's a lousy color for marketing."

"True, but we are in South Florida, and the muted tones work."

"Yeah, but it needs something. That color alone will get lost in the background."

"Right. What if we target this area in the center of the logo and give it a shade of red that will blend with the beige and not overpower it? And let's move it slightly off center. There, how's that?"

Renee leaned over his shoulder, rested her hand on it, and blinked. "Aaron, you're good. You need to do more of the creative work."

"Nah, someone has to make the sales."

"True."

Aaron's gaze shifted to her hand. His scrutiny burned her fingertips. She hadn't realized she'd touched him. "Renee," his voice cracked.

Renee swallowed hard. "I'm sorry."

"I'm not offended. In fact, I rather enjoyed the sensation. Renee, we need to talk. We can't go on like this. There's something between us. I don't know what it is or why it is, but we can't just have it hanging over us. I'm afraid to move and react. I don't know what to do, but we can't keep avoiding it."

Renee closed her eyes. Her entire body started to tremble.

"What? What happened?" he whispered. Gently he pulled her into his embrace. "Shh, it's all right; I promise it will be all right. God will get us through this, Renee. Trust Him."

Tears pooled in her eyes. *Lord, I'm such a baby. What am I going to do?*

Aaron's wristwatch alarm went off. He groaned. "I've got to go, Renee. I don't want to but—"

She stepped out of his embrace. The cool air sucked the warmth from her. His embrace had been so comforting. He grabbed her hand. "Renee, speak to me, please."

She lifted her head and looked into his wonderful chocolate eyes shimmering with flecks of gold. "Later."

"Promise?"

"Yes," her voice quivered. She nibbled her lower lip. Should she tell him?

"Will you be all right? I could call and cancel the meeting."

"No, we've worked too hard on it."

"You're sure?"

"Yes, go." *Now, before I say something foolish.*

"I'll call you." He grabbed the portfolio case and headed out the door. He paused and looked back at her. "Renee, I want to be your friend."

"I'd like that. Bye."

"Bye."

He left. She watched him walk through the parking lot to the van.

"Friendship I can handle, Lord, but this attraction is killing me. Why have I fallen for another boss?" *I must be crazy. I must have some deep psychological need for an authority figure in my life.* Her Psych 101 college course came back to mind. *Maybe I'm pathological.*

Chapter 6

Aaron glanced at his watch and tapped his steering wheel. Five o'clock on I-95 on a Thursday night wasn't where he wanted to be. He pressed the autodial of his cellular phone. One ring. Two.

He slammed on his brakes.

Three.

He should have called sooner. His finger went to disconnect.

"Sunny Flo Designs, Renee speaking. May I help you?"

"Renee." He eased out his breath and watched the driver beside him vying for position.

"Hello, Aaron, how'd it go?"

"Fine. I didn't get a definite. They have another company coming in tomorrow, but it looks promising. Come to dinner with me?"

"I don't know."

"Renee, please. We need to talk."

A gentle sigh echoed in his hands-free headset.

"Adam's with his grandparents. We'll have plenty of time."

"Okay, Aaron."

"Great, I'll pick you up at your apartment."

"No," she said a wee bit too quickly.

"All right, where do you want to meet and when?" Aaron glanced in his rearview mirror. Another exit and the evening traffic would be heading in the opposite direction.

"Not Adam's favorite," she laughed.

"No Adam. No noisy kids' restaurant, trust me on that one. I know a great place for steak and seafood. It's on the bay."

"Sounds promising."

"How about I pick you up at the office? Neutral ground, how's that?"

"Aaron. . ." She paused. "That's fine. What time?"

"Seven?"

"Okay, I'll see you then." She hung up the phone before he could say another word. Two hours should be enough time for him to go home, shower, change, and be back at the office, shouldn't it? He hoped so.

The traffic opened up. Aaron pressed the gas and enjoyed the freedom of a nearly empty highway. He autodialed his parents' number.

"Hello?"

"Buenos noches, Madre."They spoke for a few moments about Adam, the big sleepover, and the weekend his parents had planned. It seemed unreal to him that in a few hours his parents could have mapped out an itinerary that took in two amusement parks and reservations made at a hotel with a pool.

He drove home, showered, shaved, and changed into a set of casual clothes. Arriving at the office early, he went over the day's work and examined the next day's schedule.

The bell jingled over the door. He glanced up from his computer screen. "Hi, Renee, I was just going over Friday's schedule."

She dropped her purse on the counter. She wore a delicate silk blouse and cream-colored skirt.

"You're lovely tonight."

A faint line of crimson crossed her cheeks. "Thank you."

Aaron stood there tongue-tied.

"Did you see the write-in for the Glickman account at three?"

Work, a safe subject. He coughed and cleared his throat. "Yes, I take it they needed to reschedule."

"Yes, but it was rather odd. Their reasons, that is. If I didn't know better, I'd say they had booked an appointment from our competition during our time slot."

Aaron rubbed the back of his neck. Perhaps discussing work wasn't the best solution. "We'll leave it in the Lord's hands, Renee. I don't want to be worrying about it tonight."

She nodded. "I updated your laptop. After last week, I think we need to keep the material close at hand."

"Good idea." He reached for his computer briefcase and left it beside the desk. "I'll leave it here tonight and take it home over the weekend."

He took a tentative step toward her. "Come, let's go before we end up talking about work all night." He braved a wink.

She giggled. "Okay."

∽

Renee found the waterfront restaurant charming. It was set at the end of one of the bridges that crossed the international waterways, better known as Biscayne Bay at this section of Miami. It was obviously built during the sixties' boom. The picture windows looked over the bay, the tables spaced with just the right amount of room between them for some privacy. And the conversation with Aaron had been quite easy up to this point.

He placed the white linen napkin on the table. "Okay, Renee, now that we've talked about everything except what we need to talk about. . ."

She gulped a swig from her water glass.

"What are you so afraid of? Have I done something to scare you?"

"No, it isn't you, Aaron. It's me. My past. . .I'm afraid. . ."

He cupped her hand with his and leaned closer. "No matter what's happened in the past, it is the past, Renee. Jesus forgives."

"I know He does. And I'm not worried about my salvation or my walk with the Lord. It's me I'm afraid of."

He pursed his lips, holding back his thoughts.

"Aaron." She pulled her hand away from his and held both of them on her lap. "I was engaged to my former employer."

His eyelids widened. He sat back in his chair and clasped his hands together, placing his elbows on the arms of his chair.

"Let me start from the beginning. I started working for Brentwood Designs while I was in college, doing much the same as John is doing for you. The firm was larger than yours, but not nearly what it became after I joined the creative team. Brent loved my work. I loved his praise. I found security in it. Eventually we started dating. I put more and more hours into the company, somehow wrapping my relationship with Brent into the need for the company to succeed. Anyway, to make a long story short, as I put more time in the company, Brent put more time in seeking solace from others. He married another gal at the firm without first breaking off our engagement. I won't tell you how I found out."

"Ouch. No wonder you're afraid of us developing a relationship."

She eased out a sigh of relief. "I promised myself I would not fall in love with another employer."

"I see. And do you keep your promises?" His words were tight.

"I try, Aaron." She reached over and touched his forearm. She needed him to understand. "It's not you. It's me. Throughout my entire life, the people I love disappear."

"Renee, that's rubbish. You're letting your experience dictate your actions. Where's your faith? If we're to develop a relationship, and I do mean if, it has to be grounded in the Lord. I trust God to lead and direct that relationship. I can't be anything more than a friend to anyone else otherwise."

"You prayed every time you went out with Hannah?" she asked.

"Yes. I'm not saying that we were perfect. We weren't. We had our problems. But I can't see entering a relationship without God being the center of it. It's too easy to get caught up in a physical relationship, a bad relationship, or anything other than a godly one, without prayer."

Renee closed her eyes. She hadn't put God at the center of her and Brent's relationship. If he hadn't married, she could have found herself giving in to his sexual demands just to keep him. She shook her head.

"What?" Aaron leaned toward her again.

"My relationship with Brent was not Christ-centered."

"Ahh." He eased back. "Renee, I have a son. I can't afford playing with his affections. I can't have him getting too attached to a woman who might not be his future mother."

She opened her eyes and stared into his. Aaron had to be one of the most honest men she'd ever met. "I would never hurt Adam."

He reached for her hand again and caressed the top of it with his thumb. "I know. I've watched you with him. I suppose that is part of what I find so appealing in you, Renee. You love Adam. It isn't phony or put on. And Adam knows it too. He responds to you. Do you know you're the first woman he's hugged outside of the family?"

"Really?" She beamed. *I feel so honored.*

"Really. Kids are pretty sensitive to phony characters. You wouldn't believe the women who've tried to buy him off in order to get to me. Oh, Adam's no saint. He takes the gifts, but then he lets me know he's not very fond of the lady."

Renee chuckled. "Phew, I almost bought him a toy the other day. But I didn't want you to think I was trying to win your affections."

Aaron roared. "You silly woman. You've already won my affections. That's why we're having this conversation. Look, Christmas is around the corner. If you'd like to purchase something for him, you could give it to him then."

"I'd like that." Renee smiled, then grew serious. "Where does this leave us?"

"Answer me one question." Aaron leaned closer.

Renee's heart skipped a beat. Her palms began to sweat. "All right." She managed to squeak the words out.

"Can you trust God to be the center of our relationship?"

"Whoa, nothing like putting a girl in a defenseless position. If I say yes, we go forward with a relationship. If I say no, then I have no faith. You don't play fair, Mr. Chapin."

"Renee, I like you. I don't have time for fair or not fair. I can only deal with straight and open honesty. So tell me, are we going to give this relationship over to God or walk our separate ways?"

"I would like to, but I'm afraid," she confessed.

Aaron took her hand into his and kissed it gently. "Then let's pray about it."

They bowed their heads, and Aaron led them in a prayer. She found herself drawn to his words, drawn to his faith. Could it really be this simple? Did God have a plan for her and Aaron?

She thought about his prayer the rest of the evening. By setting a rule for her to live by, that of not getting involved with another employer, was she limiting God?

Aaron dropped her off at the office, and she drove off in her car. He hadn't pushed for a kiss good night. And she had to admit she had been hoping for one.

"Lord, what's wrong with me? I say I don't want something, and yet I yearn for it. But I have to confess, Aaron is right about our relationship needing to be centered on You. I certainly don't trust myself. Lord, I feel so unworthy of Aaron's friendship, let alone his affections. Please help me."

∞

Aaron looked over at the office. He should probably get his laptop and go over tomorrow's presentation. Turning his wrist, he noted it was already eleven. He yawned. It could wait until morning.

He thought back on his dinner conversation with Renee. *She's hurting, Lord. Help me to be sensitive. Hannah complained more than once about how I didn't understand what she was going through. Help me not make the same mistake with Renee.*

"And, Lord," he continued out loud, "let us know ASAP if we shouldn't be developing a relationship. Give her peace, Lord."

Aaron pulled into his carport and entered the house through the side door. It felt so strange to be alone. "Lord, keep Adam safe."

He retreated to the Jacuzzi, turned on the air jets, stripped down, and left his clothes on the bench in the changing room. Slipping on his bathing suit, he settled into the small pool and let the pulsing water work its magic. What he hadn't shared with Renee tonight was that it was becoming increasingly obvious that someone was working overtime to malign Sunny Flo Designs. The reschedule with Glickman was probably similar to the encounter he'd had today. He'd thought the sale was locked in. It should have been. Today was supposed to be the final presentation. Today he learned Sunny Flo Designs was still going head to head with another offer.

Aaron rubbed the back of his neck and slipped down farther into the bubbling water. At the time he had the Jacuzzi put in, it had been an extra they really couldn't afford. Since that time, the machine had paid off wonderfully by helping him work out the stress in his body.

He angled his left shoulder blade and the base of his neck into the jet stream. He'd injured that spot years ago, and it always seemed like the first area tension started to settle in. He leaned back, closed his eyes, and drifted off to sleep. He woke with the water calming as the jets shut off from the timer.

He glanced at the pool, thought about doing some laps, and looked over to the timer. Should he stay in for another fifteen minutes?

The phone rang, ending all debate.

Who could be calling this late? Adam? The water swooshed as he climbed out and hustled over to the phone. "Hello?"

"Mr. Chapin?"

"Yes."

"Mr. Chapin, this is the North Miami Beach Police. Sir, there's been a burglary at your store."

"What? Why hasn't the alarm company called me?"

"I can't answer that, sir. I found the place ransacked on my evening patrol. I think you might want to come down here."

"I'll be right there." Aaron hung up, swiped a towel over his body, pulled on a loose T-shirt, and slipped his feet in some sandals. He heard his swimming trunks swish as he walked toward the front door.

"Ahh, phooey." Aaron stomped to his bedroom, dried off completely, and dressed appropriately. Thankfully, he'd come to his senses. Filling out long reams of paperwork in a soggy bathing suit wouldn't have been his idea of fun.

Approaching the storefront office, he couldn't believe his eyes. It looked empty. Wires hung from the ceiling. Papers and posters littered the floor. His heart sank. "What happened?"

A young officer dressed in dark blue walked over to him. "Sorry. I patrolled by here an hour before and nothing looked suspicious."

A detective approached. "Mr. Chapin, I'm Detective Diaz. Can I ask you a few questions?"

"Sure." Aaron had become familiar with the police department after his wife had died. The pending trial on the man who'd killed his wife had put him together with the police department on several occasions.

"Did you have an alarm?"

"Yes, but apparently not a good one," Aaron spat out. He needed to control his temper.

"We'll need to contact the company."

Aaron gave the detective the name of the company. The number was passed to a younger officer. Aaron was certain he'd be contacting the company. "Where's the power box for your system?"

He led them to the back room. Aaron gasped.

"Mr. Chapin?"

"They took everything. Including the safe."

"A safe?"

"I used it to keep backups secure in the event of a fire. It's a fire- and water-proof filing cabinet, not a real safe."

"Was it bolted down?"

"No. Apparently it should have been," Aaron grumbled.

"I'll need the names and addresses of your employees who had keys. It wasn't a forced entry."

"I was with Renee Austin this evening," Aaron offered. He couldn't help but continuously scan the empty rooms.

"Until the time we called you?" the detective asked.

"No, I dropped her off here around eleven."

"Do you know where she went after that?" Diaz continued to scribble notes on his small pad.

"Home, I presume. It was late." The possible meaning of the detective's question penetrated Aaron's stunned mind. "She didn't do it," he protested.

"I'm sure you're right. Does she have a key and the passwords?"

"Yes. So do John, myself, my parents, any number of people."

"I'll need all their names."

Aaron groaned.

"I also need a list of the items stolen, descriptions, serial numbers, anything that can help us identify your belongings."

Belongings? My entire office has been stolen, along with my records. "I have some information at home. I can give you a list of the types of computers, how many desks, chairs, lamps, drafting tables, furniture."

"That will be great, Mr. Chapin." The detective put his hand on Aaron's shoulder. "I'll do my best but. . ."

"I know, I know. Not much gets recovered."

"Unfortunately. It is Miami's largest crime."

Aaron looked at the scattered papers on the floor. A police photographer was taking pictures. Another officer was brushing for fingerprints. Aaron flipped open his cell and dialed Renee's home number.

"Hello," she said yawning.

"Hi, Renee. Sorry for calling so late. I need a favor."

"Aaron, what's up?"

"The office has been burglarized."

"What?" He heard the shuffle of bedcovers.

"After I dropped you off, someone broke into the place and stole everything. Absolutely everything, Renee. I don't even have a seat to sit down on."

"Aaron, tell me this is some sick joke. No, I know it's not. No one would call this late. I'll be right down."

"Thanks. Bring your laptop. Please tell me your laptop is at home, fully updated."

"Yes, I have it." *Praise God,* he had some backups.

"Great. There should be a file in there with a list of all the serial numbers of the computers, electronic equipment, and a few other things."

"Should I bring a printer, too?"

"Hang on." He covered the phone. "Detective, can I give you a CD, or do you need a hard copy?"

"Whichever. I can get it from you in the morning."

"On second thought, Renee, save yourself running out here now. The police detective said he could get the list in the morning. Call me tomorrow, and I'll tell you where to find the files."

"Are you sure? I don't mind coming down now."

"Yeah, I'm sure. Do me a favor, though. Come in tomorrow after placing some calls from your home. I believe I have two appointments, possibly three. Please reschedule for me. At the moment, there isn't even a phone here."

"No problem, Aaron."

"Thanks."

She yawned. "Is there anything left in the office?"

"There are some scattered papers on the floor. But the walls are barren. The place looks like a tomb."

"Oh, Aaron, I'm so sorry. I wish there was something I could do."

"I have it covered. I have to go, Renee. God bless, and say a prayer."

"I will. Good night."

"Night." Aaron snapped the phone shut. "She'll come in tomorrow and bring the list in."

"Great. I have a few more questions."

"Sure." Aaron pinched the bridge of his nose and inhaled deeply. "I need to sit down. Do you mind taking up some floor space with me?"

Detective Diaz quirked a grin. "Why not?"

The next hour passed quickly. The swarm of police and detectives indicated it was a slow night for crime in the area. Aaron sat with his back against the wall holding a Styrofoam cup of stale coffee one of the officers had brought in with him.

Finally it was over. "Good night, Mr. Chapin." The last of the men in blue waved as he walked out the door.

Who had a key? The possibilities were limited. The suspects even fewer. His parents were unthinkable. John had been with him for nearly four years, and nothing like this had ever happened before. That left Renee. *It can't be, Lord. How could she have pulled it off after dinner?*

The detective pointed out that professionals had come in. Even if none of the four with access had been involved in robbing him, they probably gave a copy of the key to someone else.

Aaron shook his head. "It can't be, it just can't."

Chapter 7

Renee found him sitting with his back to the wall, his knees bent and holding up his outstretched hands. One hand held a coffee cup. His head bent down. "Aaron?"

He lifted his head and gazed at her. His handsome smile slid up the right side of his cheek. She gasped. The office stood naked in the bright fluorescent lights. The only thing breaking up the room was the service counter by the door.

"You didn't need to come."

"I know, but I couldn't sleep."

"It's not a pretty sight, is it?"

"No. I can't believe someone would take everything. Computers, yes, but this is insane."

She dropped her keys on the counter and went to him. "I'm so sorry."

"Sorry? Why would you say that?"

A stern look caused her to pause. "I—I." She took a step closer. "I don't know. I suppose it's kinda dumb, huh. Isn't it what everyone says when someone's had some trouble?"

He closed his eyes and nodded. "Yeah, I'm sorry. It's been a long night."

"Apology accepted." She sat down beside him. "What are we going to do?"

"Tomorrow I'll make some calls and get some rental office furniture and equipment. There will be forms to file with the insurance company and a whole host of other things."

She looked over to the door, the various windows. "How'd they get in?"

"With a key and the security code."

"No way. How's that possible?" She placed her hand on his arm.

"You've got me. Oh, by the way, a Detective Diaz will be calling you to set up an appointment with him."

"Ah, so I'm a suspect." She winked.

"Apparently. So are my parents, John, and. . .and. . ." Aaron jumped up. "The maintenance company." He flipped open his phone and punched out some numbers.

"Detective Diaz, please. . . . Sure, give me his voice mail." She watched him pace back and forth in the empty building, his feet crunching the papers littered on the floor. Methodically, she picked them up.

"Detective Diaz, Aaron Chapin here. I just thought of another group of people who've had a key. The Flamingo Cleaning Company. I don't have their number off the top of my head, but they're listed in the phone book. They've been cleaning my office weekly for years. Call me if you have any questions."

Aaron snapped the phone shut. "What are you doing?"

"Picking up the loose papers. What's this black stuff?" She rubbed her stained fingers on her jean-covered leg.

"Fingerprint powder."

"Oh. Will they need my fingerprints?"

"Yes, if you don't mind."

"No, I don't mind. Aaron, this doesn't make sense. Why would someone steal everything?" She placed the gathered pages on the counter.

"You're right, it isn't normal. Maybe I should have given you the raise John suggested."

Does he really believe I'm responsible? "Aaron, you really don't suspect me, do you?"

"No, of course not. I don't want to believe anyone close to me could have done this. However, you are the most likely suspect, according to Detective Diaz."

Tears pooled in her eyes. He didn't believe her, not completely. What had she done to make him doubt? She scooped up her keys. "I'll see you in the morning, Mr. Chapin."

"Renee, wait." He ran up beside her and grasped her elbow. "That didn't come out right. I'm tired, exhausted even, and have been hit with a horrible situation. Forgive me."

She turned and faced him.

"Please," he whispered. "Before this we started a new friendship. I don't want to lose that."

She didn't either. The thought of them beginning a relationship with God at the center thrilled her. She'd never had that with anyone else. Oh, she had some friends who believed as she did, and they talked about spiritual matters from time to time, but she'd never had a relationship that began with Christ as the center. "I don't want to lose it either, Aaron."

"Forgiven?" His grin took her off guard.

She smiled. "Forgiven."

"Thank you. Seriously, you ought to know that's what the detective was leaning toward tonight."

"I've nothing to hide, Aaron."

"Good, then it's not a problem."

Renee bit down on the inside of her cheek. *Nothing current that I have to hide. They don't need to know about my past. It's none of their concern and totally unrelated.*

"I guess I better go home and get some sleep," Aaron said, "and you should, too. We have a full day tomorrow. Besides, you'll get to go shopping. A woman's favorite pastime."

"That's a sexist thing to say." She grinned.

"Maybe, but it's true." He winked.

"I never said I like to shop."

"Come on now, going to the store, buying tons of items and on someone else's credit card? What's not to like?" He wrapped his arm across her shoulders.

"Since you put it that way. . ." She chuckled.

Aaron roared. He clicked off the lights and locked the door.

"What about the alarm?" she asked.

"What's there to steal?"

"I see your point."

He escorted her to the blue convertible. "Thanks for coming, Renee."

His fingers played with her hair. She fought down the desire and compulsion to wrap him in her arms.

"Ah, what can I say. I like the Miami night life," she teased.

"Ah yes, the girl who comes from New York," he quipped.

"I don't know what you've heard about New York, but in its defense, I lived there for many years and never had anything stolen from me. Of course, I didn't have much to steal."

He chuckled and tapped the hood of her Mustang. "Oh yes, you did."

∞

Aaron woke with a kink in his neck. After two cups of Cuban coffee and a bagel, he began a series of phone calls. He and Renee went over what they still had records of. He couldn't stop chastising himself for having let Detective Diaz plant doubt in his mind about Renee. She worked hard all morning without stopping. By five o'clock, they had three desks, three computers, a printer, a file cabinet, phones, and even trash cans all in place.

The bell jingled over the door. Aaron looked up. "Detective Diaz, did you find them?"

He shook his head. "I'm good, but not that good. I've spoken with the cleaning company, and they're sending me a list of employees and former employees who have worked there. They do have a policy of only letting their foreman carry the keys to the customers' offices. And all of them are bonded and have been with the company for years. But we'll be checking into them as well."

The officer looked around and let out a slow whistle. "You work fast."

"Renee's a genius."

"Is she here? I haven't spoken with her yet."

"She's due back any minute. I sent her to the café for our dinners. You're welcome to wait. Oh, I did find one thing that the thieves missed."

"What's that?" The detective sat in one of the newly rented office chairs.

"My wife framed my first ad, and it's hung in the bathroom. It's worthless to anyone but me, but I'm glad to at least have that."

The thirty-something officer nodded his head in understanding. Whether he truly understood or not didn't matter. It was special not because it was Aaron's first ad, but because of Hannah.

Detective Diaz opened his notebook. "I spoke with your college student."

"John," Aaron supplied.

The officer stopped at the appropriate page. "He was up most of the night with a group of other students cramming for an exam and swears he's never lent the key to anyone. He seems like a decent kid."

"Yeah, he's been working for me for years," Aaron added.

"Your parents I haven't located. Are you on good terms with them?"

Aaron nodded. "Yes. They went to Orlando with my son. Two days' worth of sun, fun, and amusement parks."

The detective closed his book. "How old is your son?"

"Four, and he's quite a little man. He keeps me on my toes."

"My oldest is six and started school this fall. Four was a good year."

"Oh? Is there something I should be prepared for?"

"Girls."

"Girls? At six?" *How absurd.* He prayed the officer was mistaken.

"Let me put it this way. Danny came home from school engaged on his first day."

"What?"

"Seems a little girl named Sam—yes, she's a little girl, I checked on this— caught his eye, or he caught hers, no one's quite sure, and proposed marriage. Apparently Sam's mommy and daddy finally got married, consequently she's real big on engagements and marriage at the moment. My only problem came when he said he had to buy her a ring."

Aaron collapsed on his chair. "I'm not ready for this."

Detective Diaz chuckled. "Neither am I. I did, however, persuade Danny to let Sam know that before a boy and girl get engaged they have to be older and the boy has to have a job."

"I'll remember that one."

"Well, it worked, but only for a couple days. Now Danny wants to get a job."

Aaron grabbed his sides and roared.

The bell over the door jingled again.

Aaron sobered. "Renee, this is Detective Diaz. Detective, this is Renee Austin." He walked up to her and took the dinner bags from her. "He'd like to talk with you," he whispered.

Renee reached out her hand. "How can I help, Detective?"

∞

"I'm sorry you had to go through that, Renee."

"No problem." *The fact that I'm shaking like a leaf has nothing to do with anything,* she reminded herself. In all fairness to the police, the detective seemed to accept her explanations. Considering they were the truth, he should; but one never knew with police, and knowing he was looking at her as the prime suspect made her more edgy than she would have been normally.

Aaron took her hands. "Let's pray."

She nodded.

"Father, we come before You tonight asking that You give Renee peace. And that You give Detective Diaz wisdom. If it's at all possible, bring the criminals to justice swiftly. I sure would appreciate it. You know my needs regarding the missing paper files and other important information, but I trust You to help sort out this mess. In Jesus' name, Amen."

"Amen." Renee took in a deep breath. "Thank you."

"You're welcome. I'm starved. Can we eat?"

"You didn't bless the food," she teased.

He took her hands again. "And Father, we ask You to bless this food to our bodies and thank You for Your provision. Amen."

"Amen." She giggled.

"You're as bad as Adam. He doesn't let me forget either."

Renee laughed, then sobered. "Have you heard from him?"

"Yeah, my parents called shortly after you left for the café. The boy couldn't speak fast enough. He did, however, say the appropriate things and told me he missed me and loved me. A man can live on that for a long time."

She placed the mildly warm plates of food on a desk. "The café said this was your favorite, and they said no charge. They are deeply troubled about the break-in."

"I'll have to thank them later."

Aaron lifted the cover over his meal and laughed. "This is Adam's favorite."

"Oh, do you want me to go back?"

"No, no, it's fine. I order this most often because of Adam, so I guess they probably figured it was for me." He eyed her plate. "What did you get?"

"Pork, black beans, and rice. Want some?"

"No, no, my hot dogs are fine."

Renee let out another giggle. She was on the border of being giddy. Little sleep and lots of stress tended to bring this out in her. She whisked away one of his hot dogs and handed him her dinner.

"Renee, I can eat hot dogs."

"So can I. But I'm not giving up my plantains." She stuck out her tongue.

He laughed. "Woman, you're good to have around. Even a simple meal is enjoyable."

"Wait until you see me with pizza. That I don't share with anyone."

"Oh?"

The playful banter took them through their dinner. Renee looked up at the clock. "Aaron, I know I said I'd stay and work some more tonight, but I'm too exhausted."

"I'm not of a mind to work either. Can I interest you in a swim and a movie?"

"Hmm, big spender, huh?" she teased.

"Truthfully, my credit card will be humming for awhile. The insurance adjuster said it wouldn't take too long, but based on past experience, I know it will be awhile before I receive a payment."

"I was teasing. Ever since you mentioned that Jacuzzi, I've been dying to use it."

"Great, I'll meet you at my place. I'll go by the video store and rent something. What are you in the mood for—comedy, drama?"

Romance, she wanted to say, but figured there was no need to go begging for trouble. "You pick. I like everything but horror."

"You're on."

"Should I get some junk food?" she asked. Watching movies always worked up her appetite.

"Wow, a woman who doesn't care how much she's seen eating in front of a man. I'm impressed."

She slapped him on the shoulder. "Hey, I have a boss who works me hard. I have to keep up my strength."

"And potato chips does it, huh?"

"Not the chips alone. It's the salsa, dip, ice cream, brownies, and a host of other horribly good things."

"I can see I'll be doing twice as many laps in the pool tomorrow."

Aaron stood at the security pad. "What's the new code?"

"One, two, two, five, zero, two."

"Oh, right. I'm not sure I'll remember that number. Why'd you pick that?"

"Christmas."

"Christmas?"

Chapter 8

Aaron shut off the outdoor flood lamp after seeing Renee drive off. The evening had been relaxing and enjoyable. He did wonder how she could consume so much junk food and keep her figure. They were learning to be comfortable in each other's company. He went to the poolroom and picked up the discarded towels, then tested the water and put in the right chemicals. Hannah insisted that if he wanted a pool, he'd have to take care of it. She'd grown up with one in her yard and dreaded cleaning it every week. As far back as he could remember, Friday night was the designated night to take care of the pool. Saturdays were generally filled with pool parties or family time.

The pool settled for another week, he slipped into Adam's room and looked at the racing car bed. Soon he'd have to buy Adam a larger one.

The phone rang, and he rushed to the kitchen. "Hello?"

"Changed the locks, huh?"

"Who is this?"

Click. The phone went dead.

Aaron hung up and called the police station. "Detective Diaz, please."

He groaned at hearing the detective wasn't working. Briefly, he explained his situation.

"Did you star sixty-nine the call?" the officer on the other end asked.

"No, I called you. Should I hang up and do that?"

"Wouldn't hurt. If you get a number, call me back."

"All right."

He hung up the phone, and it instantly rang again. "Hello?"

"Aaron, it's me. I'm home safe and sound."

"Renee, thanks for calling." Although he wished she hadn't. The number of the former caller was lost.

"I had a wonderful time tonight. Thanks for asking me."

"I had a nice evening, too. What are you doing tomorrow?" He leaned against the counter and crossed his feet at the ankles.

"Nothing much. I'll probably go running in the morning, take care of my weekly errands, then put my feet up and read a book."

"Running, huh? I was wondering how you could put that much food away and still stay in shape." He leaned over to the refrigerator and took out a bottle of water.

"Yeah, I've run for years. I love it. Do you run?"

"Nope, I swim, remember?"

"Right. Well in New York swimming isn't always an option."

"One of the blessings of South Florida."

"One," she repeated.

"I was wondering, could I take you out for dinner and maybe persuade you to help me shop for Adam?"

"Shop for Adam?"

"Christmas. I know it's weeks away, but I hate shopping when everyone is running through the store like a madman. And your new security code got me thinking about it."

He heard the purr of her gentle chuckle. "So, will you bail me out and give me a hand?"

"I thought your credit card couldn't handle any more purchases."

"It can't. But I have some cash I set aside for Christmas."

"All right. How about lunch instead of dinner? That way we can eat at the mall and get right to the shopping."

"Lunch is fine, but I'm taking you to a special place in North Miami. It's a truly unique little place."

"What is it?"

"Nope, it's my surprise."

"Okay, tell me this much, do I need to run a couple more miles?"

"Nah, maybe one."

Renee chuckled. "Good night, Aaron. I'll see you tomorrow."

"Night, Renee."

He hung up the phone and fired off a quick prayer. "Lord, help us to keep You central in our relationship."

He headed to his bedroom. The phone rang again.

∽

Renee leaned over with her hands on her knees gasping for air. The sun, salt, and gentle surf renewed her. Running felt good, but she'd pushed herself a little too far. A week of busy work because of the break-in, and now she felt more distant from Aaron than the day less than a week ago when they'd shopped for Adam.

She kept trying to remind herself that the expansive amount of work kept them from having a moment to themselves, but had she been reading more into his friendship? Since that conversation over their first dinner together, had he decided to be simply friends and not be romantically involved? Had she allowed herself to hope too much?

Renee closed her eyes and sat down at the water's edge. "Lord, I'm losing it. I swore I wasn't going to fall in love with another boss and. . .and. . ." She leaned back on her elbows. The warm sand provided a comfortable cushion. "Why do I do this, Lord? Why am I so vulnerable?"

A gull cawed as it flapped its wings flying over her. Another dove into the water and pulled out a small fish. The gentle surf lapped the shore. Virtually alone at this hour on the beach, she decided to run at the water's edge and give herself a harder workout.

Slipping off her shoes and socks, she dove into the water, instantly chilling her heated body. A quick swim rounded out her exercise. Sunset fused the sky with brilliant colors and reminded her she needed to return home.

Lying on her counter was the unopened letter from Brentwood Designs. Brent's offer. Sunny Flo Designs was barely holding its own. Renee didn't know how much longer Aaron could keep her on. Three times this past week he'd lost major sales to another company. What bothered her most was when Aaron came back reporting that the competition had something very similar to her original designs. Who was getting into her head? Had she lost her creative edge?

Putting down the letter, she headed to the bathroom to wash up. She found the shower refreshing as the salt from her swim had already crystallized on her skin and hair.

Last weekend shopping for Adam had been wonderful. Aaron's apparent distancing really left her questioning if she'd misread his signals. After all, he hadn't kissed her or even attempted to hold her hand. Worse yet, he hadn't suggested that she spend some time with him and Adam this weekend.

The phone rang. She wrapped a towel around herself and answered. "Hello?"

"Hey, sweet thing. I left you something."

The phone went dead.

Renee clenched the receiver and scanned the room. Her heart raced. Dressing quickly, she put on her baggy jeans and oversized T-shirt. Taking the portable phone with her, she cautiously worked her way down the hall into the dining area. She sniffed the air. Nothing.

She listened.

Nothing.

She peeked around the corner.

Nothing. Everything was in its rightful place. "What's going on, Lord?"

She stepped into the living area and looked out at the patio. Still she discovered nothing.

Maybe it was a prank call.

The phone rang again.

Renee started to tremble. Should she answer it? *You can't live in fear,* she admonished herself and punched the phone button. "Hello!" She winced hearing the strain in her own voice.

"Renee?"

"Aaron?"

"What's the matter?"

"Oh, probably nothing. I just got a prank call."

"Are you all right? What did he say?" Nervous excitement filled his voice.

"I'm fine. How'd you know it was a man?"

"I guess I didn't. I just assumed. I had a caller last Friday night."

"You did? Why didn't you tell me?" *Not that he has to tell me everything. . .but it would have been nice to know.*

"Call the police. Did you star sixty-nine the call?"

"No, it just happened. I suppose this will sound dumb, but I was searching my apartment."

"What did he say?" Aaron's voice rose.

She repeated the caller's message.

"I'm on my way. Keep the doors locked until I get there."

"Aaron, I'm fine. Seriously, I'm okay."

"I'm sure you are, but I was calling to see if you wanted to join Adam and me for pizza. I know that's your favorite meal."

Renee chuckled.

"Also, we were hoping to convince you to come to the zoo with us tomorrow."

"The zoo?"

"Yeah, you know the place where we can see wild animals safely at a distance."

"Sounds like fun, and I haven't eaten dinner yet." She continued to scan her apartment looking for anything out of place.

"Good, because we already have the pizza. And I'm only a block away."

"Pretty sure of yourself."

"You betcha. Renee, I've missed you. It's been a crazy week, and we haven't had a moment to ourselves. I want to spend some time with you. Do you mind?"

Renee closed her eyes and swallowed back the tears. She'd been hungering for the same thing. Maybe this relationship could work. *God, help me to trust You here.* "No, I've missed you, too."

"I'm pulling into your parking area now. Adam and I will be right up."

"Okay." *Oh no.* "Aaron, wait, I'm not dressed." She heard the buzz of the disconnected phone. "Ugh."

She ran to her bedroom. *Presentable clothes, I need presentable clothes.*

The doorbell rang.

She looked at her baggy clothes in the mirror and groaned. *Oh well, I'll lose him for sure now.*

"Renee," she heard Adam squeal. He ran toward her as soon as the door was open.

"Hey, buddy, how was Orlando?"

"Cool. I had so much fun."

"You'll have to tell me all about it."

She looked up at Aaron, who was holding two pizza boxes in his hand and wearing a frown. She caught his gaze looking to the right of her door and followed it. "What on earth?"

Aaron let Renee occupy Adam while he stood outside the apartment and called the police. The thief had returned some of her personal items from the office in a box beside the door. Thieves never returned stolen items. Something wasn't adding up.

Aaron told the officer what he'd discovered at Renee's. Detective Diaz agreed to come over and treat the box and the surrounding area as a crime scene. Having sheltered Adam from the break-in at the office, Aaron didn't want to discuss this new development in front of him. Hopefully the pizza and the video he'd rented would do the trick. Meanwhile, he'd wait for the detective outside to keep his arrival from distracting Adam.

A short while later, the officer stepped out of the elevator. "Detective Diaz, thank you for coming." Aaron extended his hand. Fifteen minutes, not bad for a police response.

"Has Ms. Austin verified the items?"

"At a glance, yes. We didn't want to touch them in case you could lift some fingerprints."

"Wise decision. You mentioned on the phone she received a phone call first. Were you here at the time of the call?"

"No, my son and I were on our way. Detective, I've tried to keep most of this from my son. He's in the apartment with Renee. Is it possible to speak with her privately?"

"Of course. Please send her out so we can talk."

"Certainly."

Aaron went inside the apartment. "Renee," he called. He'd never been in her apartment before. Sparsely decorated but functional seemed the best way to describe it.

She came up beside him. He grinned. She'd changed from the baggy clothes. "You look good."

"Thanks." Her cheeks stained with crimson.

"You're not used to people giving you personal compliments, are you?"

She shook her head no.

He reached for her and embraced her. "Get used to it. I think you're kind of special and definitely beautiful."

He felt her relax in his arms. An urge to protect her washed over him. "Detective Diaz is outside wanting to speak with you," he whispered.

"Okay, I'll be back as soon as possible. Adam's in front of the television watching the movie you brought."

"Thanks. Call me if you need me." He squeezed her hand tighter and released her from his embrace.

Aaron followed the sounds of the television and sat down on the couch beside Adam. "Daddy, will the police fix Renee's things?"

Fix? "Sí, they'll make it all better."

"Bien."

Aaron grinned. *"Mucho* bien, Adam. You've been practicing."

"Sí," he said as if he'd been speaking Spanish all his life. Aaron chuckled and rubbed his fingers through Adam's curls.

Twenty minutes later Renee came back in and paced back and forth in the kitchen. Her clenched jaw spoke volumes. "He'd like to speak with you again," she said softly when Aaron came over to her.

"Are you all right?" He reached out and placed his hand on her shoulder.

"I will be. The man is going to drive me to drink, I swear. He's so accusing. Do you know he suspects me of planting that box on my doorstep?"

"He accused you?" Aaron's anger rose.

"Well, he didn't say the words, but that's what he was hinting at." She lowered her voice. "I'm sorry. I know it's the man's job, but really."

Aaron nodded his head. "I'll take care of it." It was time for Detective Diaz to get something straight about Renee. He caught himself before slamming the door shut on the way out.

"Why are you accusing Renee?" he asked the detective directly.

"I'm not. I have to look at all angles. And why didn't you tell me that you and she were having an affair?"

"You wait just one minute. I'm not having an affair with Renee. We are friends. Nothing more, nothing less. And this friendship has increased in the past couple weeks, but that does not mean we're having a sexual relationship. Do you think I'd be so stupid as to do such a thing in front of my four-year-old son?"

"Trust me, you don't want to know what others do. Look, I apologize for the affair comment. But you have to try and see things from my perspective for a moment. Your relationship with Ms. Austin clouds your judgment. I'm not saying that is bad or good judgment, but it clouds it, and I need to take that into consideration while I'm investigating a crime. This crime was personal. Thieves don't take everything. At least not normally. This is not your normal case."

"You're right, but do you have to be so rude to her? I know her. I know she isn't behind this."

"Look, I know you think you know her. But are you aware that she was once engaged to her former employer?"

"Yes."

"Oh. Well, did you know that engagement ended because she was too controlling and demanding?"

"That's not how I heard it. The man is a genuine sleaze. He married another woman without breaking off his engagement with Renee."

"Interesting."

"Did you ask Renee about this?"

"Yes. She wasn't as forthcoming."

"No, I imagine she wasn't. She's a rather private person. Did you tell her what Brent told you?"

"No. Look, I'm not on trial here. Renee is the one under investigation. She's still a suspect, and the fact that these items have shown up at her home says one of two things. Neither of them is very pretty."

Aaron took in a deep breath and counted to five before asking, "What are you suggesting?"

"One, that she's in on this, and with your own admission, she didn't know you were coming so she didn't have time to hide the evidence. Two, that the thief may want something more than the contents of your office."

"I don't believe this. I can't."

"Look, you can't go by your emotions here. You have to look at the facts."

"And you saw proof that she did this?" Aaron inquired.

"No, just Mr. Cinelli's word."

"And you trust that slime ball?" Aaron rubbed the back of his neck. "Look, I'm not trying to tell you your job. But Renee's been putting in tons of overtime for me. She's found areas where our company has been vulnerable. Someone's been stealing our ideas, and she's managed to help prevent some of it."

"What do you mean, someone is stealing your ideas?"

"I've lost a couple of sales lately, and one of the companies that didn't go with our design actually used our design in an advertisement recently."

The officer tapped his notebook. "Can you prove someone's been stealing your work?"

"Not now. My computers were stolen, remember?" He didn't hold back the bite in his words.

"Look, maybe your Ms. Austin is as pure as she looks, and if she is, she is vulnerable. This thief, whoever he is, knows where she lives. Does she have a security system?"

"I don't know. This is the first time I've been inside her apartment." Aaron felt a cold sweat wash over him. Renee was in danger. *Why?*

Chapter 9

Renee grabbed the porcelain sink and stared at the reddened reflection of herself. Brent had lied to the police, leading them to believe she was the primary suspect. Aaron's anger had hung just under the surface when he'd come back in and told her. She fought down her own. Adam didn't need to see her upset. *Help me calm down, Lord,* she prayed. The small bathroom worked well as a place of solace.

She sighed at her reflection. She and Aaron could talk later. For now they needed to forget the past hour and enjoy the remainder of the evening. A cool damp cloth held to her face helped to remove some of the pink, and she prayed once again to calm down.

Renee put a spring into her step and bounced out of the bathroom with a plastered smile.

"I'm really hungry, Renee. Can we eat now?" Adam pouted.

"Sounds like a good idea to me, sport. What about you, Aaron?" She winked at him.

"Better watch out, Adam. Renee loves pizza. She'll eat your piece if you're not looking," Aaron teased.

"I wouldn't take Adam's piece, but I'd take yours." She ran toward the table.

Adam ran after her, giggling. Aaron groaned as he got up and followed them in. "I bought two. Figured one for you and one for us."

Adam's large brown eyes stared up at her. "You eat a whole pizza, Renee?"

"Sometimes, but today I don't think so."

"Wow, Daddy, I never saw someone eat a whole pizza before."

The three of them laughed, the strain momentarily broken.

They enjoyed the evening together in spite of the constant undercurrent of tension in the background. Aaron had to be filled with tons of questions. What had the detective told him that he hadn't told her? Should she make an appointment to lay everything out for Detective Diaz? Having her word challenged had always been something she fought. She'd seen an aunt who lied to everyone. Her parents, what little she could remember of them, had always been honest with her. She tried to live her life after their example.

Aaron lifted Adam into his arms. The poor boy was dragging but hadn't fallen asleep. "I'll call you," he whispered.

"I'll be here."

He reached out and held her hand. "Get some rest, Renee. The zoo will wear you out."

"Oh?" At least he believed her. She smiled.

"Good night." Aaron squeezed her hand.

"Night. Good night, Adam." She leaned over and gave him a kiss on his cheek. The boy's eyes fluttered. "Take the poor boy home. Call me after he's settled."

"I will. Bye."

She waved them off and watched them until they stepped into the elevator, then closed the door. She turned to clean up the kitchen, then realized she hadn't latched the dead bolt. Correcting her mistake, she marched into the kitchen, pulled the phone down from the charger, and immediately called the police.

"Detective Diaz, please."

"One moment," the female voice responded.

"This is Detective Diaz. How may I help you?"

"This is Renee Austin. I think we need to have a talk."

"Oh? Is there something you forgot to tell me?"

"What I'd like to tell you and what I'm going to tell you are two different things. First, I won't say what I feel because I'm a Christian and the Lord wouldn't be pleased with me for saying such things. Second, there's obviously been some sort of problem with Brent Cinelli's memory if he's telling you that I've been carrying a torch for him. I've been angry at him, no question, but it's not because I'm so desperately in love with him that I can't see myself living without him. In fact," she emphasized and took another breath, "sitting on my counter is an offer from him to come back and work for him. Doesn't that sound strange if I'm supposedly chasing after him?"

"First, calm down, Ms. Austin."

"I am calm," she protested.

He coughed.

"Oh, all right, I'm steamed. But I'm being accused of something that isn't true. What can I do to correct the situation?"

"For starters, I'd like to see that letter."

"I haven't opened it." Renee held the envelope in her hand.

"Perfect, then we can open it together, and I will know for certain you didn't forge the documents inside."

She dropped it back to the counter. "You actually think I'd do that?"

"Look, I've done a check on you, Ms. Austin. The most I've come up with is a New York State driver's license. By the way, did you know you're supposed to get a driver's license from Florida within thirty days of moving here?"

"Yes, I just haven't had time. Are you going to arrest me for that?"

He chuckled. "No. But I'd like to see your Florida license by the end of next week."

Renee groaned. "Fine, I'll skip work for a day and get my license. Happy?"

"Some. Look, I know you and Mr. Chapin seem to have a more personal relationship, and this business with Mr. Cinelli makes for some interesting suppositions."

"Trust me, you haven't gone anywhere with the Psych 101 on that one that I haven't gone myself. Look, I'll fill you in with all the horrid details of my relationship with Brent if I must, but I can't prove my story over his. And I doubt there's anyone working for him at the moment who would dare say anything contrary to what he's said."

"Are you saying his employees lie for him?"

"I'm saying he calls it company loyalty."

"I see. And what about you, Ms. Austin, what do you call it?"

"I call it lying, and I wouldn't do it for him. I wouldn't answer some questions sometimes, but I'd never lie for him. He knew that and kept me from the customers he was being less than honest with."

"I see. Are you saying Brentwood, Inc., is less than honest in its business dealings?"

"No, I'm saying that from time to time Brent would encourage folks to agree with what he said. He's a salesman, and sometimes salesmen exaggerate their claims. I would stay late into the night trying to work some of the miracles he claimed the Web pages would do. At the time, I figured I was investing in Brent's and my future. We dated for two years. He told me that when we married, I'd be a joint owner."

"Is that why you agreed to marry him?"

She let out a strangled groan. "No. I thought I was in love with him. The fact is I was in love with the idea of getting married. The ugly truth, as I look back on it now, is that it didn't matter who that man was, as long as I found a good and stable husband."

"Why was that so important for you?"

"Because my parents died when I was eight, and I was forced to live with my aunt, who had more men than I can remember. It wasn't a pretty life, Detective. I'm sure in your line of work you've seen plenty of children who had alcoholic, drug-addicted prostitutes for parents."

"I'm sorry. I can come over in thirty minutes—if that isn't too late for you?" he offered.

"Thirty minutes is fine." The call waiting rung in her ear. "I've got another call. I'll see you then." She clicked the phone and answered. "Hello?"

"Hi, he was out cold before I got to the house. I almost turned around so we could talk. Renee, I'm sorry about what Detective Diaz said to you."

"It's all right. It's his job, I guess."

Aaron snickered. "It might be, but I'd like to see the man use a little more common sense." He used his toes to remove his shoes and then placed them under the bed.

"I don't know why Brent said those things," Renee said. "It doesn't make sense."

"No, I suppose it doesn't." He took in a deep breath and returned to the kitchen, pulling out a bottle of water from the refrigerator. "You know, the Jacuzzi is here if you'd like to sit and relax."

She groaned. "I'd love to, but Detective Diaz is coming over in a few minutes."

Aaron's back stiffened. "What for?"

"I invited him to. I'm going to tell him every single thing about my relationship with Brent. He'll probably be bored to tears by the time he leaves."

Aaron chuckled. "I'll pray for you."

"Thanks, you don't know how much it means to me, Aaron."

"You're welcome. Renee, can you come to my house in the morning? Then we can leave right away for the zoo. Adam loves it there and, trust me, we'll be exhausted by the end of the day."

"How about if I bring breakfast?"

"What do you have in mind?"

"Fast food, totally not nutritious." She giggled.

Aaron grinned. "Adam will love you. Personally, I like donuts with lots of fillings."

"I'll remember that."

"Renee, for what it's worth, I believe you."

"Thanks, that means a lot."

"You're welcome. I'll be praying that Detective Diaz sees the truth and moves on to the right suspects. Although I'm totally clueless. Why would they return your personal stuff to you? It doesn't make sense."

"It doesn't, and nothing they returned was that personal. I don't have much in the way of keepsakes or memorabilia."

Aaron stretched. "I better get going if I'm going to have all my work done before the zoo tomorrow."

"Don't stay up too late."

"I won't." A desire to say he loved her overwhelmed him, but reason won out. "Good night, Renee."

"Night, Aaron."

He placed the phone back in the charger, walked to his office, rolled his shoulders, and connected the computer to download. While he was on-line, he decided to check out a few Web sites he'd been bidding on to see what the competition had come up with that he'd lost to.

The first page loaded. His eyes widened. "No way!"

He typed in another page. Anger, frustration coursed through his veins. He picked up his cellular phone and dialed.

∞

"Excuse me, Detective Diaz," Renee said as she turned to answer the phone.

"Hello?"

"Renee, it's me again. I'm on-line. I've found something very disturbing."

"What's the matter, Aaron?" She glanced at the detective, his interest piqued.

"Can you go on-line right now while you're on the phone?"

She heard something in his voice—frustration, anger, she wasn't certain which. "Sure. Detective Diaz is here. Do I need to do it now?"

"Good, he'll need to see this, too. You can explain to him what he sees."

"All right. Would you like to talk with him?"

"Sure, put him on the line."

"Okay." She cupped the phone and said, "Aaron would like to speak with you. He has something he'd like us to see on the Internet. I'll boot up my computer." The detective nodded.

"Detective Diaz. What can I do for you, Mr. Chapin?" she heard him say as she went to her desk in the dining area. *What had Aaron so troubled?* she wondered.

"I'll make the contact. Let me see the evidence first." The detective walked toward her with the phone. "He'd like to speak with you again."

"Hi. You're scaring me, Aaron. What's the matter?"

"Honey, you'll see in a minute." *He called me honey.* Her heart warmed, and her nerves calmed.

"Okay, the computer's just about booted up."

"Good." His voice quieted. "Connect and go to the jaja.com site."

"All right." She paused, then gasped. "Aaron, how'd this happen?"

"I don't know, but I think someone got into our system long before we realized."

Tears pooled in Renee's eyes. Detective Diaz looked over her shoulder as she pointed out the various Web sites she and Aaron had bid on. Five sites had nearly identical copies of what they had put together. Too identical. No one could come up with the exact designs they had. No one.

Once maybe, but five times? No way.

Renee ended the phone conversation with Aaron, and the detective took a seat and patiently listened while she explained what she'd done, how the Web page coding was even the same.

"I don't know enough about computers, but I have a good pair of eyes. There's no question those are your designs."

"I can't believe they had access to our system for so long."

Renee tapped in another address. Remembering Aaron's anger, she fired off another prayer for him.

"Do you have records on your computer that prove you made these designs?"

"Yes." She opened the window to the file folder for all the projects she'd worked on for Sunny Flo Designs. She groaned.

"What's the matter?" the detective asked.

"All the files have the last date I opened them. They were reloaded onto the new computers after the break-in. All the dates are wrong."

"What about backups?" he asked.

"They were kept at the office." She nibbled her lower lip. "Wait, there may be a record of some sort in the history file from the Web browser. It shows when a file was opened. . .the name of the address and the date. Bingo. Here's your proof." Finally something was going right.

"Can you give me a printout of that? And a list of your files?"

"Sure." Renee hit the appropriate keys, and the printer hummed to life.

"While that's printing, let's open that letter you received from Mr. Cinelli."

"Sure. That's odd."

"What?" The detective leaned toward her monitor.

"The designer of the Web page isn't listed on the page. No one designs pages without having a link back to their business page. It's a form of advertising. Unless the customer pays a huge fee for not putting it on their page."

"Consequently, we don't know the name of the company that's stolen your designs?"

"You've got it."

"Okay, show me that letter."

She thought she heard hope in the detective's voice that she wasn't guilty. "Here." Renee handed it to him.

"Go ahead and open it," he encouraged.

She supposed it was a federal offense to open someone else's mail. *Who would charge him for it?* she mused. Taking in a deep breath and letting it out slowly, she slid the metal blade of the letter opener up the envelope. Inside was a cover letter followed by a two-page contract.

"Here, as I said, is Brent's latest offer to me. Please note, I'm not chasing him; he's chasing me down. Not personally, just professionally." The detective scanned the various pages. "As I said on the phone, I did a lot of extra work for him, fixed a lot of problems he was even unaware of at the time. Now I imagine he's realizing just how much I did to keep that office running smoothly."

"He says here that he'd spoken with you on the phone about this."

"Yes, he called. I generally don't pick up when I know it's him but. . . You know, I think that message might still be on the tape. I didn't erase it. I don't have many calls." Renee stepped over to the counter with the answering machine, rewound the tape partway, and listened. A message from the cleaners saying her laundry was done filled the silence. "It was before this message." She pushed down the rewind key again. Counting fifteen seconds, she stopped it and listened. Brent's whining voice came on the tape. "Oh, baby, I've missed you."

Renee grinned. Not only was his message there, but their entire conversation had been taped. She'd forgotten to turn off the machine.

"Interesting," Detective Diaz said after hearing the entire conversation. "This does paint a different story than what he claims. Can you tell me what's in your sealed juvenile record?"

Blood pounded in her ears. He'd found it. She paled. "It's sealed for a reason, Detective," she replied, her voice tight. He didn't need to know; no one needed to know. Why would he even ask?

Chapter 10

A sigh of pleasure escaped Aaron's lips as he leaned back into the jet stream of the Jacuzzi. He hadn't planned on a seven o'clock wake-up call from the police. *It seems Detective Diaz doesn't sleep. When the man gets ahold of something, he goes at it like a shark on a feeding frenzy.* Monday morning Diaz would meet them at an agreed-upon spot. Maybe the accounts were lost, but Aaron might still see some justice come from this.

Resting his head on the rail, he put together a plan to make the company's computer system completely separate from outside lines. He wouldn't be taking any risks during the next few months. He couldn't afford it.

"Hi, Daddy!" Adam stood in his pajama shorts and overstuffed truck slippers.

"Good morning, son."

"Are we going to the zoo?" He placed his hands on his hips.

Aaron fought down a chuckle. "Yup, I'm just relaxing before you wear me out today."

"Dad-dy, we're just going to the zoo," he protested.

Oh, to be four when your biggest problem was going to the zoo. "Wanna come in?" Aaron tapped the water for emphasis.

"Will we still go to the zoo?"

"Of course. And the zoo isn't open yet, so we have plenty of time."

"Okay." Adam ran to the changing room.

Aaron chuckled as he heard the thumping of the boy struggling to remove his slippers.

"Dad?" Adam called.

"Yeah, son."

"When's Renee coming?"

"She should be here around nine."

"Ta-da!" Adam jumped out and posed with his superhero bathing trunks on.

"Hey, buddy, come on in." Aaron waved him over.

The doorbell rang. "I'll get it," Adam squealed as he ran out of the pool room and down the hall faster than Aaron could open his mouth to speak.

"Dad," Adam hollered. "It's Renee."

Aaron glanced at his wrist. She was early. She probably hadn't slept well either. He stood and stepped up out of the Jacuzzi.

Renee's warm smile applied a soothing balm of healing over his ragged nerves.

64

"Hi." He returned her smile.

"Hi. I brought semi-nutritious and definitely not nutritious." She held a fast-food bag with the smell of ham-and-egg sandwiches and a long box with at least a dozen donuts.

"How hungry are you?" he teased.

"Now, before you jump down my throat for my weird eating habits, there are four of the basic food groups in this bag. The box contains the necessary food group for the soul."

"The soul?" He grabbed a towel and started to dry himself off.

"I'm hungry, Daddy. I want the donuts." Adam beamed.

"After you eat the egg sandwich." He winked at Renee.

"I'll set the table while you dry off. Do you have orange juice?"

"Yup, and coffee should be just about ready."

"Great. Come on, Adam. You can help me."

"Okay." The boy followed her into the kitchen. She was good with Adam, and it gave Aaron a sense of peace to continue going forward with their relationship. No matter what Detective Diaz claimed.

Making quick work of changing, he readied himself for a day at the zoo—a pair of shorts with lots of pockets. He always needed pockets when he took Adam places. Adding a comfortable pair of sneakers for extensive walking and a light jersey top, he glanced in the mirror and ran a quick comb through his damp hair.

"What kind of jelly donuts did you buy?" he asked, entering the dining area.

"Blueberry, strawberry, cream, and spiced apple," Renee answered, giving Adam the napkins to place on the table.

"What can I do?" Aaron asked.

"Sit yourself down and eat. Adam and I have everything ready."

"Good job, buddy," Aaron praised and extended his hands for Adam and Renee to pray with him over their morning meal. "Father, thank You for giving us a great day to visit the zoo. Bless us and keep Your protective hedge over Marie and her children."

Adam added, "And God bless Grandma and Grandpa and Nana and Papa."

Aaron gave her hand a slight squeeze of reassurance. Renee cleared her throat. "Lord, thank You for bringing Adam and Aaron into my life. May I be as good of a friend to them."

Aaron concluded. "In Jesus' name, amen."

The prayer over, they all dove into their egg sandwiches.

"Renee?" Adam mumbled.

"Adam, don't speak with your mouth full."

"Sorry." He swallowed a huge amount. "Renee, have you been to the zoo?"

"In the Bronx."

"The Bronx, where's that?"

"In New York." Aaron found himself watching her every move, like the delicate way she wiped her mouth with the napkin.

"Oh, where you used to live?" Adam asked.

"That's right."

"What's your favorite animal? I like the elephants and their big floppy ears. But the lions roar real loud. Wanna hear?"

"Sure." Renee smiled.

"Roar!" Adam yelled.

"Oh my, you sound just like them. Can you sound like a monkey?"

The next few minutes passed with each of them imitating animal noises. The sandwiches done, Renee opened the box with the delightful array of sin to the waistline or backside—Aaron never was sure which. Either way, it meant more laps in the pool. Of course, he'd be doing some serious walking today. . . Aaron took two.

Renee giggled but kept her comments to herself. He supposed she had a right after the way he'd ridden her case last night about the pizza.

"I'm done. Can we go now?" Adam's smile, accented with powdered sugar and strawberries, broadened.

"I think you need to wash your face, buddy. Then you'll need to get dressed for the zoo. Wear shorts and a T-shirt, and don't forget your backpack."

"Okay." Adam's jelly-stained hands grabbed the back of the chair.

Aaron groaned.

Renee jumped up. "I'll take care of it. I brought the messy treat."

Aaron pushed his chair back and gathered the paper debris. They collided as Renee came out of the kitchen. "Oof."

"Sorry," she said, stepping back.

"How are you this morning?" he asked in a whisper.

"All right, I guess. I spent several hours looking for any other customers that we bid on. But I think you found them all."

"It's disturbing, but I don't want to discuss work today. I'd rather focus on more pleasant things, like Adam and you."

Renee's cheeks instantly blushed.

"Do you know you produce the most beautiful shade of pink?" He winked.

The blush deepened. Desire surged through him to wrap her in his arms and kiss her senseless. "Are you prepared for today with some sunblock?"

"Ah, um," she fumbled over her words. "Yes, why do you do that?"

"Do what?"

She placed her hands on her hips. "Look, I might not be the brightest when it comes to male-female relationships, but I know you were. . ."

"Come here," he cooed, pulling her to himself. Raking his fingers through her golden strands, he placed one hand behind her neck and tilted her head back. "May I?"

She blinked. He prayed it was a yes. Slowly he lowered his lips to hers. Her arms wrapped around him. He wrapped his around her. Desire and passion fused with a mind-numbing sensation, rendering him unaware of anyone, anything, other than Renee. His hands caressed her shoulders. The kiss deepened.

"Daddy, are you kissing Renee?" Adam giggled. The world, reality, came crashing back down. Aaron pulled away and stepped back.

Stunned, Renee opened her eyes. How could she and Aaron have forgotten that Adam was in the house? How could they have gotten so lost in that kiss? Renee sighed and leaned against the counter with her back to the open living area. She—no, they—should have known better.

"Yes, son, I was."

"Oh. Does this mean Renee will be my new mommy?"

Aaron glanced back and grasped her hand. "Too soon to say. Daddies and possible new mommies have to spend time together before they know if God wants them to get married."

"Good answer, son."

Renee spun around. Standing in the living room, looking right in the kitchen, were Aaron's parents. Renee prayed the floor would open up and swallow her whole. How could she have not heard Aaron's parents come in through the front door?

Aaron coughed and cleared his throat. "Hi, Mom, Dad."

His father spoke first. "I guess we stopped in at the wrong time."

Aaron placed his arm around Renee's shoulders. "We're heading out to the zoo for the day. Would you folks like to join us?" he offered.

His mother answered in Spanish. Renee couldn't speak. She couldn't look at his parents or Adam. She felt too guilty. *Why? You've been wanting to kiss him. Obviously he's been wanting to kiss you, too. It's one thing being caught by Adam, but by his parents. . .* She felt the heat on her cheeks increase enough that a cool compress sounded desirable. Of course, with the amount of heat she was feeling, steam would probably rise from the cloth.

"Speak in English, Mom. Renee doesn't understand."

"Sí. Yes. Sorry. I was apologizing for walking in," Gladys Chapin explained to Renee.

Embarrassment flooded her cheeks. Renee realized she wasn't being condemned. And it wasn't her place to say whether or not it was a problem. Obviously they had a key and were used to just walking in. Which would be perfectly natural with Gladys taking care of Adam.

"Mother, relax, no harm done."

Adam went to his grandmother and hugged her.

"Excuse me." Renee stepped from Aaron's embrace and left to finish clearing the table. She needed to do something, anything. How could she have allowed herself to get carried away like that? Or Aaron, for that matter?

He came up behind her. "Renee," he whispered.

She jumped and turned to face him.

"I won't apologize for kissing you, but I am sorry that we didn't pick a more appropriate time. Next time, I'll be more careful."

"Aaron, I'm so embarrassed."

"Shh." He pulled her back into his embrace. "Don't fret about it. My parents were well aware of my growing affections toward you."

"But. . ."

"Shh." He placed his finger to her lips. "It was an awkward moment, but we'll survive. Come on, the zoo awaits."

Renee picked up the box of donuts and handed it to him. The rest of the items she removed.

"Are you folks going to join us?" Aaron asked upon re-entering the kitchen.

"No, son. One of the reasons we came over was Marie."

Aaron stiffened. "Is she all right?"

"Yes, Manuel's disappeared again. I figure he came into some money somehow and is drinking it away." Charles sighed. "Your mother and I thought it would be good to visit Marie and the children."

"I'll pray for you and your visit." Aaron placed the box of donuts on the counter.

"Thank you." Charles turned toward Renee. "It was nice to see you, Renee. Perhaps you can get this guy to invite you over to the family meal tomorrow after church."

Renee cleared her throat. "Food?" She wiggled her eyebrows. The room erupted in laughter.

"Grandma, Renee can eat a whole pizza," Adam boasted.

"She can? My, my." Gladys giggled. "Where does she keep it? She's too skinny."

It was true, she was skinny, always had been, despite eating like a horse. It had made so many of her roommates in college jealous of her eating habits.

Aaron lifted his hands in surrender. "You invited that one on yourself, girl."

"I run," she defended.

∽

Aaron put the dollar in the machine that would make a plastic model of three monkeys. He remembered having his own set of zoo creatures when he was a child. He chuckled. They hadn't improved on the machine. It still worked the same, smelled the same. Memories washed over him to a time when he and Marie were both small and didn't have a care in the world.

"Penny for your thoughts," Renee whispered.

Aaron turned. "Where's Adam?"

"On the slide. It's great that they put these play areas in for the children."

"Yeah, gives the parents a chance to catch their wind. Why can't we bundle that energy? We'd make a fortune."

Renee chuckled.

The large spatula pushed the newly formed plastic monkeys down to the bin waiting below.

She scrunched her nose. "It's a noisy thing."

"Did you put sunblock on your nose?"

"Yes, why?" She placed her delicate fingers on the top ridge of her nose.

"It's turning pink."

"Oh no." She ran to her backpack and ruffled through for the sunblock.

"I burn easily," she mumbled.

"I figured." Aaron sat on the bench and watched Adam for a moment. "Here, let me reapply it to your shoulders and back."

She handed him the bottle, then lifted her ponytail.

He pressed his finger against her pink skin and saw the white imprint. "You might already be burnt."

"Ugh," she groaned. "I probably should have worn a blouse with short sleeves and a high neckline."

"You look just fine, but you probably would have been better prepared for the sun. I've heard people with fair skin really have to be careful. You ought to wear a hat, too."

"Yeah, right and look like a tourist. I don't think so," she quipped.

"Oh, so sun poisoning is a better alternative?"

"I'm not that badly burnt, am I?"

"I don't think so, but like I said, I'm not used to such fair skin."

"Where's the nearest rest room? I'd better go check."

Aaron pointed it out on the map. "Adam and I will wait right here for you."

"Okay." She bolted off. He'd never seen her run. Her form was excellent. *Had she competed in college?* he wondered.

"Daddy," Adam squealed as he slid down the slide.

"Hey, buddy, having fun?"

"A blast."

Aaron's cell phone rang. "Hello."

"Mr. Chapin, this is Detective Diaz."

Aaron rolled his eyes and leaned his head back. "Yes, Detective?" Why'd he ever given the man his cell phone number?

"Your store's been vandalized."

"What?"

"It doesn't appear that anything is missing, but someone threw a huge hunk of coral through the front door. I'm afraid I need you to come to your office to verify that nothing was stolen."

"I'm in South Miami at the Metro Zoo. It'll take me an hour to get there."

"No problem. I'll have an officer stand guard until you come."

"Thanks."

"Adam," Aaron called. "We've got to go, son."

"But why, Daddy? We haven't seen the zebras yet."

"Next time, sport. Someone threw a rock through the office door. I have to take care of it."

"Why would someone throw a rock, Daddy? Didn't their mommy and daddy tell them not to throw rocks?"

"I guess they weren't listening to their parents."

"They need to get a spanking and be sent to their rooms, huh, Daddy?"

Aaron scooped up his son and held him close to his chest. *Lord, help me protect Adam from the truth. And what is the truth, Lord? Why am I being targeted? No other storefronts have been recent victims. At least not that I'm aware of.*

Aaron straddled Renee's backpack over his left shoulder and left the play area to walk in the direction she'd been going. "Look for Renee, buddy."

"Okay."

"Ugh," he grunted, wincing from Adam using his hair as an anchor. "Son, would you mind leaving my hair on my head?"

"Sorry, Daddy.

"I see her," Adam shouted, bouncing up and down. Which was worse—ribs kicked or hair pulled—Aaron wasn't sure. He bent down and let the offending feet hurry off to their target.

Renee opened her arms wide and cradled the boy as he slammed into her with full force. Aaron grinned.

Her eyes locked with his. Aaron nodded. Obviously Adam had shared the news.

"Can I drop you off with Adam at my place while I deal with the police?"

"Sure. I'll make supper. Leave me Adam's car seat, and we'll go grocery shopping if I can't find what I need."

"And she cooks," he chuckled.

Chapter 11

"You better believe it, buster," Renee snapped. "I had to in order to survive."

"Huh?"

Oh dear, I've said too much. . .think, quick! "Remember I told you my aunt wasn't much of a parent figure?"

Aaron nodded.

"Well, she didn't cook. And you know how much I like food."

"Junk food," he corrected. Pulling out his keys, he handed her the backpack. "Hop in, sport."

Aaron opened the door for Renee. *A gentleman.* She melted into the front seat.

"Buckle up, Adam."

Renee heard the click of the buckle latching. "Did you have fun, Adam?"

"Yeah. I liked the giraffes. They have really long necks."

Renee thought back on how far they had to spread their front legs in order to bend down far enough for them to eat the grass.

Aaron slipped behind the wheel.

"What about how slow that tortoise moved?" Aaron asked as he turned the key in the ignition.

"The gorilla scared me."

"Me, too," Renee agreed. "I thought he was going to come through the viewing window."

"He picked his nose, Daddy. It was gross."

"Eww," Aaron and Renee said in unison.

They spoke for awhile about the various sights and sounds of the zoo. In spite of the wonderful day, her mind kept jumping to the office. Who had broken the door? Was it another robbery attempt?

Aaron reached over and took her hand. "I'm sorry about this."

"Phooey, you didn't break the door." She glanced back. Adam was nodding off to sleep. "Do you think it's the same person as before?"

"I don't know. I guess I just assumed it was, but more than likely it was kids with nothing better to do."

"True. The last time it was at night, and they were professional. This time, well, we don't know yet, but it seems like it's possible the two are unrelated."

"Quite." Aaron glanced over at her. "So, what are you fixing for dinner?"

"You'll just have to be pleasantly surprised."

"Hmm, well you know how I like my steak," he rambled. "I had a wonderful time today, Renee. Thanks for coming."

"I wouldn't have missed it."

He lifted her hand and kissed it. "I'd like to take you out on a real date, just the two of us. What do you think?"

Was she ready to go to the next level in the relationship?

"Renee?"

"I'm sorry, I guess I'm still afraid."

"I thought we settled that last week."

"We discussed it. Sometimes deciding something isn't the same as acting on it."

"Okay, I'll give you that. Let's pray about it; does that sound reasonable to you?"

"Aaron, you're unlike anyone I've ever known. I love that you want to pray about everything, but I'm also taken aback by it. Do you pray before you decide on all matters?"

Aaron let out a guttural sigh. "No, I'm not perfect. I'd love to say I always act in a spiritual manner and put the Lord first in everything, but I fail miserably at times. I do want the Lord to be central in our relationship. I don't want to have Adam's expectations high when it's possible nothing more will develop other than a mutual friendship."

"Has he been asking for a new mother for awhile?"

Aaron released her hand and placed both hands back on the steering wheel. He leaned back in his bucket seat and nodded his head. "For a few weeks now. Honestly, when he first approached me about the idea, I couldn't see past the loss of Hannah. Now, well now, I think it's possible. But I want to be cautious. There's no question about the attraction between us, and I truly enjoy our conversation but. . ."

"But are we good for one another?"

He glanced over at her and smiled, then broke the connection and concentrated on the highway. "I don't have time to waste on dating anyone who comes my way. I'm just not interested in frittering away my time on such relationships. I do believe the Lord is bringing us together, but the questions remain."

Accepting the possibility that this attraction to Aaron could come from the Lord had kept her tossing and turning more than one night. "Aaron, I don't want to repeat my past mistakes. Brent used me. I know that now. But I used him. I wanted a husband. I felt I needed one to be complete. I've been working on trying to be complete in who I am with the Lord and understanding that I don't need a man for that."

"You're right. You don't need a man to be complete."

"I also have a past that's been colored by my environment. I'm concerned that I didn't have a good role model, at least one I can remember, on how to have

72

a good relationship with the opposite sex. I thought I'd been a good partner with Brent, but apparently I was fooling myself. There's so much you don't know about me and—"

He covered her hand with his again. "Shh, that's why I want to spend time with you. Let's take this to the next level and see."

"I'm just afraid."

"Honey, I know you're afraid, and I'll try not to hurt you. But if we put God as the center, He'll make it clear whether we should go forward or if we should simply shake hands and be friends."

Did she trust God? Could she trust God with her heart? "All right, I'll try to step out in faith and trust that the Lord knows what He's doing. Because truthfully, I promised myself I would never fall in love with another boss."

"I can remedy that."

"How?"

"You're fired." He wiggled his eyebrows and flashed a white toothy grin.

"You can't be serious," she protested.

"Of course not. But if that's what it takes, I'm attracted enough to you that I'm willing to risk losing the best employee I've ever had in order to date her and explore the possibilities of another partnership."

"You're that confident?"

"Renee, I'm not looking for a business partner. There are tons of people who could do your job. Probably not as exceptionally as you can, but there are others out there. What's developing between us is worth far more than any business. I'd risk it all, if I was certain you were the one."

"But you don't know me."

He paused at that.

What is he thinking?

"Look, I know you have things in your past. I have things or events in my past you don't know about either. You don't know how I fell in love with Hannah, how she meant so much to me that she was a part of the very air I breathed."

"Could you love someone like that again?" she asked.

"Honestly, I don't know. I suppose it would be a different love because we are different people. But I swear to you, I would never enter a relationship in which I didn't feel God making us into a threefold cord."

"Threefold cord?"

"Ecclesiastes 4:12. Solomon writes that a threefold cord is not easily broken. One cord made of three parts."

"Ah." *How can I argue against scripture?* She'd never met a man with his head so straight about the Word, life, love. It was a wee bit scary. "Are you like some sort of superhuman, spiritually topnotch kind of icon?"

Aaron laughed. "Once you get to know me better, you'll start finding my faults. But it's nice to know I don't have any at the moment." He winked.

"Hmm," she mumbled and looked ahead to the oncoming traffic. They'd be at his house in a couple minutes. "Aaron, why don't you take my car to the office, and we can let Adam rest for a moment or two longer in yours."

"You don't mind?"

"Nope. I like my car, but I'm not overly attached to it."

"Woman, you scare me. That's a classic in prime condition."

"I bought it secondhand, possibly thirdhand, when I was a kid. I gradually had the work done on it. It was a real bomb when I first got it. Which is why I could afford it. Brent paid me well—that's one good thing I can say on Brent's behalf. As you can see by my apartment, I keep a simple life. Computers and gadgets are my biggest weakness. I don't know if you saw my system."

"I noticed. Okay, I'll take your car, and I'll be back as soon as possible." He pulled into the parking space next to her car and turned off the engine.

She handed him the keys.

"I'll call you when I know what's up. Take my cell phone." He unclipped his phone from his belt and handed it to her.

A pregnant pause passed. Did he not want to leave as much as she didn't want him to leave? They were just beginning to open up to each other. Could she be patient and allow the Lord to work here? "Be careful."

"I will."

He leaned closer. Was he going to kiss her again? Did she want him to? *Ha, no question.* Her skin tingled in anticipation. He cupped her chin in his palm.

She reached out and traced his lips.

He rested his forehead on hers and slipped his hand behind her neck. "Father," he whispered. "Help us stay focused on You and not our own desires."

The tension broken, he kissed her gently on the lips. "I'll be back as soon as possible."

Before she opened her eyes, he was getting out of the car and into hers, murmuring, "Lord, give me strength."

Stunned and uncertain if she was pleased with his prayer, she leaned back in the bucket seat and looked toward the white wisps of clouds spun like cotton candy. *Who is this man, Lord? I've respected him in the way he's conducted his business. But he'd never seemed overly Christian. Am I less of a Christian? Have I messed up that part of my life, too?* She had remembered the verse he quoted once he said where it came from, but. . .

I feel like a beginner next to him. Lord, something's wrong here. You can't possibly think that I have anything to offer him to make him complete.

Then it hit her. Aaron was complete without her. Just as she was complete without him. The cord was something God created when He united two people. It wasn't something lacking in her or in Aaron, or Brent, for that matter. *Why have I believed for so long that a man would complete me?*

Because your aunt did and tried on every man she could find.

Renee nibbled her lower lip. *Lord, help me trust You, not myself.*

"Renee, why are you crying?" Adam asked.

∽

Arriving at the office, Aaron found a minor mess. Nothing missing, nothing disturbed. Even Detective Diaz had left word at the scene that he felt the two events were unrelated. Aaron called a glass company that said they could have someone there in an hour. He dialed his home phone number. No answer.

He dialed his cell. Adam answered. "Hi, Dad."

"How's it going, buddy?"

"Good. We're shopping."

"Oh, what's Renee buying?"

Adam giggled. "She said I couldn't say. It's a secret."

"Oh. Can I talk to Renee?"

"Okay. Renee," Adam yelled. Aaron pulled the phone from his ear.

"Tried to get it out of him, huh?" she teased.

"Can't blame a man for trying. I'm stuck here for two hours, I think. The glass man said he'd send someone here in an hour."

"No problem. Adam and I are having a good time. And he's telling me all your secrets."

"Oh, and what secrets are those?"

"Something about how I shouldn't open up any of your closets because I might not be able to get the doors shut."

Aaron groaned. "Hey, I never said I was a good housekeeper. Mom comes by every few months and takes care of some of my cleaning."

"You don't pay that woman enough."

"I know. I don't know what I'd do without her. I'll let you get back to your shopping. I should be home around five. I'll call if it's going to take longer."

"Bye, Aaron."

"Bye." He hung up the phone. "What could she possibly be making?"

∽

Over the next few weeks Aaron discovered that Renee definitely could cook. From Italian to stir-fry, he hadn't sampled anything that didn't please his palate. They'd also gone out a time or two alone and several times with Adam. Work had kept them busy, but with fewer and fewer sales. Even his attempts to approach new customers had failed. Someone else consistently beat him to them. How could one area of his life be going so well and another area be failing so miserably? It was almost like someone was reading his mind.

The initial contact with the police seemed pointless. Even Detective Diaz had uncovered nothing. All that equipment and not one item showing up in a pawnshop.

Aaron came into his office and found John working at his new drafting table. "Hey, John. Where's Renee?"

"She said to tell you she was picking up Adam and that they had a surprise for you."

"A surprise, huh?" Memories of the first surprise meal still warmed his belly.

"You two are getting pretty thick. Anything serious?" John put down his pencil.

"Too soon to tell. We're just taking it one step at a time."

"Yeah, right. One minute you're just working together, the next you're thick as thieves."

Aaron chuckled. "Maybe so."

The computer hummed to life with a few keystrokes. "John, did you use my computer to upload today?"

"Nope, haven't touched it. What's up?" John straightened on his stool.

"Nothing, I guess. Renee must have used it." *But that doesn't make sense since she has everything on her system.* Aaron scratched the day's growth on his jaw.

"What on earth?"

"What's the matter?" John came up beside him.

"My passwords aren't working."

"Did you type them in wrong?"

It was a dumb thing to say, and he knew the kid meant well, but. . . "Yes." He tried again. No response.

The phone rang.

"Sunny Flo Designs, Aaron speaking."

Click. The receiver went dead.

"Try your passwords, John."

John leaned over and typed in his code. He had access—limited, but still he had access.

"Try Renee's," John suggested.

Aaron typed in Renee's codes. He entered and had total access. But what he found on the site was a folder he'd never seen before. He clicked it open and collapsed in his chair.

"No way," John objected.

Chapter 12

"A re we really going to fry a whole turkey?" Adam asked.

"Yup." Renee loaded another gallon of peanut oil into her trunk.

"Cool."

Thanksgiving was a few days away, and together she and Adam had been planning a surprise for the holiday. A traditional family Thanksgiving lodged somewhere in the back of her mind. She remembered being six and visiting with all the relatives, everyone laughing, the house loud, and so much food. Plans with Gladys and Charles Chapin would help to make this a special Thanksgiving for Aaron and Adam.

"Okay, let's get these things to my apartment before your daddy figures out what we're doing."

"I like surprises."

She raked her fingers through his curls. "Me, too."

Adam secured himself in his booster seat, and she crossed herself with the seat belt.

"Can we put the top down?" he asked.

"Sure." Renee unbuckled her seat belt and unhooked the top's latches. She turned on the power. Adam swiveled back and forth, watching the end unfold and the roof go higher. She opened the trunk and pulled out the leather saddle that covered the collapsed top. Putting the roof down took some work, but for Adam's pleasure, why not?

Her new cell phone rang. Aaron hadn't needed to twist her arm too much to purchase one. "Adam, could you answer that for me?"

"Okay. Hello?"

Renee snapped the last snap into place.

"Hi, Daddy."

She slipped behind the steering wheel and held off starting up the car.

Adam nodded his head.

"Say yes, Adam. He can't see you shaking your head."

"Yes," he replied and smiled. "Okay." He handed her the phone. "Daddy wants to talk to you."

"Thanks, buddy." She slipped the phone up to her ear. "Hi, Aaron, what's up?"

"Renee, did you change my passwords today?"

A little testy, are we? "No, what's wrong?"

"My passwords aren't working. Yours and John's are, but mine aren't."

77

"That's weird. Are you sure you typed—"

"Yes, I tried and retried it several times. Renee, that's not all. There's a file in your secure area," he stammered. "Ah, well, it appears as. . ."

"What are you trying to say, Aaron?"

"I think you'd better come here and see for yourself. It's rather hard to explain."

Renee nibbled her lower lip. It didn't sound good, whatever it was. "Sure, I've got to run to my apartment first so some food doesn't spoil, but I'll be there shortly, okay?"

"Good, and Renee, for what it's worth, I trust you."

"Thanks." *I think.* She glanced in her rearview mirror. A man stood across the street staring at her. A chill wrapped its icy fingers around her spine. She looked again. He was gone. Her mind was playing tricks on her. *Get a grip,* she reprimanded herself.

"Change of plans, buddy. We'll drop off the turkey at my house, then head over to the office. Your dad needs me to look at something." Slowly, she backed the car out of its parking space, still looking for the stranger. Maybe she shouldn't have watched that gangster movie last night.

"Okay." Adam wiggled his feet, covered with tennis shoes.

The wind whipped Renee's hair. She grabbed a scrunchy and pulled it back at the next stoplight.

"I like the wind." Adam beamed.

"Me, too." Dreams of traveling the shoreline with no other cars on the road, the wind, the sun, the sandy beaches, filled her mind. *Get real. This is Miami.* Skyscrapers and tourist-filled streets—she wouldn't be putting the pedal to the metal here. *Ah, but one can dream,* she mused. A gentle smile erased the tension she'd been feeling since Aaron's call.

A few minutes later she was in the basement garage of her apartment building. "Okay, buddy, let's get this turkey in the refrigerator." Renee sorted through the various bags, taking out the food items that needed refrigeration. The rest could stay in the trunk.

"What can I carry?"

A grin swept over her face. "Here ya go."

"Renee?"

"Yes, Adam?" They walked toward the elevator.

"Do you like my daddy?"

Uh-oh, where was this going? She gave a tentative, "Yes."

Adam nodded his head. She pushed the U*p* button. He held the plastic bag with two hands. "Do you want to be a mommy?"

Swoosh. The elevator doors opened. "Uh, yes, someday," she stammered.

They stepped inside. She pushed the button to her floor.

"Grandma says mommies and daddies have to marry before they have children."

Renee nodded her head. She looked down at him. His eyebrows were knit together, his lower lip puckered slightly. Something was really troubling the poor boy. The doors opened. "Come on, buddy."

He followed, carrying his load.

She placed her key in the lock and turned it.

"Renee?"

"Yes, buddy?" Perhaps he was ready now to ask his question.

She opened the door. One look inside and she dropped the turkey, pushed Adam back, grabbed him, and ran.

∞

Aaron flew out of the office, stopped, and ran back in. "John, lock up for me."

"Sure."

John opened his mouth to continue but didn't have time. "Later, John." Aaron rushed through the door again.

"God, keep them safe," he prayed, jumping into his van and heading toward his parents' house. Renee had called saying she was taking Adam to his grand-parents and that Aaron needed to be there as soon as she arrived.

The fear in her voice and the short message, "I can't talk now," brought instant adrenaline to his veins. "What's going on, Lord? First I find the bogus file, now this. What's happening?"

He wormed his way through the city's back streets. Rush hour and highways were not a good combination in Miami. He'd make better time with the stop-lights of the residential sections.

The classic blue Mustang in his parents' drive gave him a smidgen of relief. He skidded up to the curb and cut the engine before coming to a complete stop. He leaped out of the car and took the front lawn in five long strides. "Adam, Renee," he hollered as he ran through the front door.

His mother's worried face nodded they were in the kitchen.

"Daddy." Adam came running into his arms. "Renee saved me from a bad man."

"What?" Adam held his son closer.

"She ran real fast. And we didn't take the elevator. She ran down the stairs so fast. We. . .we. . ."

"Slow down, sport. Where was the bad man?"

"In her apartment."

"Who is this bad man?"

"I don't know. I didn't see him. Renee just told me that's why we were running. She's still on the phone with the police."

He needed to speak with Renee, but it was essential to calm Adam. He appeared to be settling down. *But. . .* "Are you okay?"

"Yeah, I was scared at first. She held me tight. I didn't put on my seat belt right away. Renee said I could do it while we drove."

Who was in her apartment? Aaron stepped toward the kitchen and heard Renee's mumbled words from the back patio.

"Adam, will you stay with Grandma while I talk to Renee?"

"Okay." Adam hugged him hard. "I love you, Daddy."

"I love you, too." Adam slid down. Aaron watched him go to his grandmother. *Thank You, Lord. You protected him.*

He stepped onto the patio where Renee paced back and forth. She held up her hand to him, then spoke impatiently into the phone. "I'm telling you, he was there."

She walked farther away. "Then arrest me. Look." She let out an exasperated sigh. "I know what I saw. Why would I call you if I hadn't?"

She turned back toward Aaron and rolled her eyes in apparent frustration.

"Give me a break. Look, remember that sealed file you came across?"

Sealed file. What is she talking about? Aaron wondered.

"It has to have something to do with that case. No, I don't want to tell you what it's all about."

Renee stood still. "All right." He watched her close her eyes, then open them slowly. *She's shutting down her emotions.*

"Good-bye."

She closed the phone and stared blankly in front of her.

He eased forward a step.

She turned to face him. "Aaron, I can't tell you what's happened."

"No way, Renee. You owe me some kind of explanation."

"All right, my past has caught up with me. I don't know how, and I don't know why, but I need to disappear for awhile."

"You what? You've got to be kidding. You're acting like some kind of a spy or something." He calmed himself. "Renee, we mean too much to each other. Don't do this. Talk to me."

Her shoulders relaxed. Tears glistened in her eyes.

"I'd love to, but I can't. Not now; there isn't time. You'll have to trust me on this."

"Who's after you, Renee, and why?"

"I can't, Aaron. I can't put you and Adam at risk. You mean too much to me."

"This is crazy. You have to trust someone. Trust me." He pulled her into his arms and held her tight.

She circled her arms around him and shivered in his embrace. For a long moment she stayed in his arms. Finding her strength, she pushed away.

"I'll call you when I'm safe." She bolted from the patio and ran through the kitchen.

"No way," he roared and ran after her.

∽

How'd he find me, Lord? After all these years; two different states, and still he finds me. How?

Renee heard Aaron calling out to her. She had to leave. She had to protect him and Adam.

"Renee," Aaron yelled. "You can't leave like this."

She squeezed her eyes shut. Looking back would give her pause, and if she paused, her heart would win over her mind. Logically, she knew what she had to do. In the early years she had prepared for her escape if ever the need arose. But as time went by, she'd almost forgotten.

Almost.

Fumbling with the keys, she jammed the ignition key in place.

"Renee, stop! Please stop. I love you. Don't leave me like this."

Her hands shook; the tears freely fell. "Aaron, it's because I love you. I have to leave."

"Whatever it is, the Lord will see us through this."

She leaned her forehead against the steering wheel.

"Please, Renee, stop long enough to tell me."

He opened the door and placed a loving hand on her back.

"Please, trust me, Renee."

She looked up at the blurred image of the man she loved. He knelt beside her and placed his left hand on her knee.

"Talk to me. What could you possibly have done that I wouldn't forgive you?"

"It's not that; it's who he is. He doesn't forgive. He's the epitome of hatred."

"Who?"

"He must have gotten out on good behavior or something. He was supposed to be in prison for twenty years."

He rubbed her back gently and waited.

Should she tell him? If he knew, would he be in danger? *To spite me, he'd come after Adam and Aaron.* She shook her head no. "I'm sorry, Aaron, I can't put your lives in danger."

"Why can't you tell the police?"

She wiped the tears from her eyes.

"I don't know. I guess because Detective Diaz still believes I'm behind the break-in at the office. Do you know what he found in my apartment?"

Aaron shook his head no.

"The old computer. Your old computer. Can you believe that? If I was going to rob the place, do you think I'd want the old computer? It's such a dinosaur."

She shook off the train of thought. "The fact is, Diaz doesn't believe me that...he...was in the apartment. He said I was just trying to cloud the investigation. And what's this about a file of e-mails?"

"There's a hidden file on the server that came up when we logged in as you. It contains e-mails between you and another company, B&J Advertising. You were offering my database of clients for a fee."

"You can't believe I did that."

"Of course not. It's too obvious. Even if you were at fault, you wouldn't hav
kept a record that I could have stumbled upon. Personally, I think someone i
trying to set you up."

"Trying," she huffed. "I'd say Diaz is certain of it."

"Don't be too sure. He plays the devil's advocate for certain, but I think h
believes you."

"I don't know what to do, Aaron. You don't know the man like I do, and
couldn't live with myself if something were to happen to you or Adam."

"Trust God, Renee. All along our relationship has been slowly developin
with God at the center. Just because something horrible from the past has com
to haunt you, don't stop trusting the Lord."

"But—"

He held his finger to her lips.

"Honey, whoever this guy is has found out where you live. He probabl
already knows where you work and who you work for."

"True, Benny would do a thorough investigation."

"Benny who?"

Oh no. "I'm sorry, I didn't mean to say anything."

He caressed her jaw with the feather touch of his finger.

"Did he rape you?" He ached for her, his chocolate eyes so expressive.

"No, nothing like that. He lived with my aunt on a fairly regular basis for
time. He drank, and when he drank he'd beat her. I came home once when h
was beating her. And well, I tried to yell at him to stop. He didn't. He landed
solid blow to my jaw. I grabbed the closest thing handy, my baseball bat."

Aaron's eyes widened.

"I'd just come home from softball practice. Anyway, I swung and connecte
I broke his arm. He managed to get the bat from me and hit me again. By th
time the police came, the bruises were showing. Not to mention my cracked ri
He had me arrested. My aunt wouldn't back up my story. She was terrified tha
he'd be released and come and beat her again, I guess. Anyway, in a nutshel
that's what happened and why I have a sealed record. Connecticut has change
the laws recently, extending the time for sealed records to be on file. Detectiv
Diaz wouldn't have found it if the old law still applied. Benny was a small-tim
dealer and thug for hire. The cop arrested him, too, and was happy to get hir
off the streets. And since I was a minor, he received a greater sentence, and th
charges against me were dropped.

"I don't trust him," Renee continued, "and I can't have him hurt you or Adan
He's like that, Aaron. He's spiteful beyond compare. If he knows I care for any
one, he'd go after that person first, then me. Or worse yet, he'd make me watch

"Come here." Aaron directed. She leaned toward him, and he wrapped he
in his protective arms. "Father, we come before You and hand this situation wit

Benny over to You. Keep Renee safe from harm. Keep all of us safe. Show us what to do and how to handle it."

Renee cleared her throat. "And, Lord, help me with my lack of faith. Help me to trust You completely with everything in my life. And thank You for Aaron." He squeezed her hand. "In Jesus' name, amen."

"Amen."

The truth was out, and Aaron didn't think her horrible. She probably should have told him ages ago. "Oh no."

"What?" He turned the engine off.

"Where am I going to live?"

Chapter 13

Aaron slipped her keys into his pocket. "Okay, let's take this one step at a time. First, we need to go to your apartment and see if Benny's still there or if he left a message for you. Second, I also need your help in tracking those phony e-mails, how they got on our server."

"I don't know, Aaron. I think you're better off without me. Do you think Benny could be behind all the problems at the office?" Fear centered in her eyes.

"Is Benny good with computers?"

"Not that I know of. He could have learned in prison, I suppose."

"True. Come." He took her hand and encouraged her out of the driver's seat. "Let's go back in the house and talk things through."

"But your parents? Do they know?"

"About the business? Some. About the detective's suspicions regarding you, no."

"Oh." She looked down at her feet.

He lifted her chin with his index finger, willing her to look at him. "Renee, you were the victim. Why are you afraid to let people know what happened?"

"I spent nearly a year in custody. Rumors got out, and when I returned to school, no one wanted to be around me. We were living in an apartment building, and several classmates saw me carted off in handcuffs."

He held her close. *Help me reassure her, Lord.* "But, honey, that was years ago. Today people know you for who you are, not what you did. Besides, it seems to me, it was self-defense."

"Some defense. He beat me bad. The worst betrayal was from my aunt. She lied to the police. Well, she didn't exactly lie. She just refused to speak and wouldn't agree with my account of the incident. Benny supported her habit at the time. I guess she didn't want to lose that."

Benny seems like a real gem, Lord. How can she fight this monster? "Renee, we'll need to fill my mother in for Adam's sake, if nothing else. She's seen you upset. Can't you tell her why?"

"I don't want to put her in harm's way, Aaron." She pulled out of his arms. "I really should go away."

He grabbed her hand. "No, we'll fight this together. I'm not your aunt, Renee. I'll stand by you. You forget, I've dealt with a man who beats on women. I know how to stand up to these guys."

84

Aaron escorted her back to the front door. Adam would be safe here, he hoped and prayed. They went inside and, after Renee filled his mother in, she offered Renee a place to stay. Aaron had never been more proud of his mother, of her generous spirit, and he knew she would accept Renee as part of the family. The phrase "part of the family" continued to play in his mind as they drove toward Renee's apartment.

"Aaron, are you okay?" Renee's gentle touch brought him from his musings.

"I'm fine. Sorry." He noted the speed and pushed the accelerator. He glanced over. "Honey, it'll be all right. I doubt he's still around. And if he is, all the better. I'll be able to confront him."

She nodded.

His cell phone rang. He put the headset on and answered. "Hello."

"Mr. Chapin, it's Detective Diaz."

"Yes, Detective." Aaron sighed.

Renee whipped her head toward him.

"Have you heard from Renee Austin?"

"Yes, she's with me now."

"Did she tell you what we found in her apartment?"

"Yes."

"There's more."

"What?" Aaron captured her hand and squeezed it slightly.

"Those e-mails came from that computer."

Aaron glanced at the rearview mirror. "Is that really a surprise? Someone's setting her up."

"Appears that way, but you know I can't overlook the obvious."

"Yeah, yeah."

Aaron slowed down as the flow of traffic stopped for the tollbooth. "Hang on a minute." He cupped the mouthpiece. "Do you want to tell him about Benny? I think you should."

She shook her head no.

"All right."

"Is there anything else, Detective?"

"We're working on those e-mails. I've contacted the company where they came from. No one at the company goes by that name."

"I'm not surprised."

"No, I suppose that would have been too easy. Here's my problem: They were sent from that company, too. Whoever this is had to have access to this company's e-mail service and set up a dummy e-mail address. Seems to me someone is going to a tremendous amount of trouble just to try and frame Ms. Austin. But here's where it gets interesting. This frame is superficial; it would never hold up in court. Let me ask you why, Mr. Chapin? Why would someone go to all that trouble?"

"I honestly couldn't tell you."

"Also, the feds would like to speak with you about a possible sting operation."

"Great. When?"

∞

Renee tried not to listen to Aaron's conversation, but she was sitting right beside him. *Why can't I tell Detective Diaz? Am I so vain?* She worried her lower lip.

She'd never been more thankful in her life than when her aunt decided to move to New York. Her senior year in high school had brought welcomed relief. No one knew about her past, and she refused to tell anyone.

Aaron pulled up to the parking garage. She pushed her remote and the gate opened. *How did Benny get in here? Security oozes from every corner.* At least she thought it did. Now that was up for debate.

He pulled into her numbered parking spot.

It seemed an eternity ago that she'd been in here with Adam, joyfully bringing up some of the food for their Thanksgiving feast.

Aaron continued his call as they headed for the elevator.

The super, dressed in his gray work clothes, called over to her. "Evening, Ms. Austin. Did you see your father?"

"Father?"

"Yeah, I let him into your apartment earlier. He said he wanted to surprise you."

"He's not my father. My father died when I was eight." She held back the scream.

A pallor washed over the middle-aged super. "Oh dear. I'm so sorry."

"Excuse me," Aaron interrupted, clicking his cell phone shut. "You let a stranger into her apartment?"

"I'm sorry. He seemed. . ." The man stammered.

"It's all right," Renee interjected. "But in the future, no one, absolutely no one, can come to my apartment without my permission. All right?"

"Yes, Ms. Austin. It won't happen again."

"Thank you."

Aaron held her in a protective embrace. "Well that settles how he got in."

"Yeah," she mumbled. "But what about the computer? How'd that get in there? Did Benny let the guy put it in? Or was it already in there when Benny arrived? In that case, someone besides the super has access to my apartment. Either way, I'll have to stay with your parents until the locks are changed."

"You're right."

"What was all that other stuff you and the detective were talking about?"

"I can't tell you. I want to, but they asked me not to because—"

"Because I'm still a suspect."

Aaron nodded his head.

Would she ever be free of the past? Should she tell Diaz and get it over with? It's not like other people haven't been tried and convicted for crimes they didn't commit. *I was innocent, but I still had to go to counseling.* The stigma of having been beaten, arrested, and put away still tore at her heart. *Will I ever be free, Lord?*

Aaron pulled her keys out from his pocket. "Which one?" he asked.

"This one." She pointed to the silver key with a blue plastic ring around the end. She'd identified it for quick and easy recognition. Not that it mattered much if anyone could get past the super. She might very well need to look into moving.

Placing the key in the lock, Aaron opened the door. "Stay here while I check the place."

Renee nodded. Her heart started to race. Why did she let him talk her into coming back here? She could have just bought new clothes. Although she'd want to get her computer, if it was still there. Would Benny steal it?

"All clear, Renee. Come in." Aaron held the door open. Slowly, she entered.

The apartment seemed different somehow. Nothing was out of place, but the invasion hung in the air like a thick fog over the harbor in the fall.

Aaron rubbed her shoulders. "It's all right, Renee. I'm here."

"Did the police take the old computer?"

"Yes."

"Great."

"It's circumstantial, Renee. Plus Diaz has been in your apartment. He knows it wasn't here before."

She sighed. "I'm going to have to tell him, aren't I?"

"It would be helpful for him, but it isn't necessary. I understand you're wanting to keep it hidden, but. . ." He paused and turned her to face him. "I think it would be easier if you did tell him. It's not your fault, Renee. It was self-defense."

"It's not shame; it's fear. I was arrested and held for so long. If I hadn't had a Christian caseworker, I think I would have gone crazy."

He smiled.

"What?"

"I was wondering where God was during that time. You just said He was there looking out for you, in spite of your circumstances. It's reassuring to hear."

"Oh, well, I suppose you're right. I attended her church for awhile. Then we moved to New York."

"Where's your aunt now?"

"I have no idea. When I went to college, I came home and discovered she'd moved out. I never heard from her again."

"Not once?"

"Nope. She hated my going to church. I guess it reminded her of everything she gave up when she left Uncle Pete. He remarried, and that really bothered her. You know, it's strange, but why is it that the ones who do the sinning blame everyone else for their problems? Aunt Ida always blamed Uncle Pete, but she was the one who left him."

"When we're sinning, we like to pass the buck. That way we don't have to acknowledge our sin. Look at my sister Marie. She still won't leave Manuel, who, by the way, has been back for a week."

The red glow of her answering machine blinked. She hit the play button.

Aaron opened the refrigerator and took out a bottle of water. She'd started keeping them in the house ever since they'd started dating.

The first message let her know that her dry cleaning was done.

The second came from John. "Hey, Renee, if ya see the boss, tell him the McPherson account called and gave the go-ahead."

Renee smiled.

"Thank You, Lord." Aaron saluted toward the ceiling with his bottled water in hand.

They'd worked long and hard on that proposal and had kept it completely between the two of them. She turned toward Aaron. "Finally," she sighed.

"Yes, and we can prove you aren't the leak."

"Maybe. Diaz will probably say I let the sale go through to keep the attention off of myself."

Aaron shook his head. "You don't trust the police, do you?"

"No." She pushed the play button to continue her messages.

"Well, well, if it isn't my old friend. Hello, Renee, wanna come out and play?"

"Who's that?" Aaron demanded. The voice had a sinister ring to it, as if the man had been watching B horror movies.

Renee stood frozen in place. Her body trembled. Aaron slipped his arms around her and kissed the top of her honey hair. "Is it Benny?"

She nodded.

The one who beat her senseless when she was a child, Lord.

The phone rang. Aaron answered it. "Hello."

"The boyfriend, I presume?"

"Leave her alone, Benny. It's over. Go back home," Aaron demanded.

A wicked laugh pierced the phone. "She's told you who I am. Well, watch your back. I'm watching yours." The phone went dead.

Aaron slammed the phone down.

"Come on, you're getting out of here. It's not safe."

Aaron star sixty-nined the call, but it came back as an untraceable number. "We're going to the police station, and you're filling out a restraining order. This guy won't hurt you again, Renee. I promise. Renee?"

She stood in place, not moving, as if she were in a trance.

"Renee?"

Slowly she turned her head and looked at him. "I need to run."

"No, you're staying with me. You're not running anywhere."

"No, I mean I physically need to run. It reduces the stress. It's my defense mechanism."

"Oh. Can you run after we pack your bags and report this creep to the police?" He grinned.

She smiled. "Yes, but I'll need to run tonight."

"I'll run with you, unless you want to do laps with me in the pool?"

She shook her head. "Nope, I need to run. It helps."

"All right, you can run. But first, let's run into your bedroom and grab some clothes and get away from this guy. We'll order some new locks, a new phone number, and get you secure. But for now, you're staying with me."

"Aaron, stop and think for a minute. I can't stay with you. Your place isn't safe for me either. It's like you said, he's probably already found out where I work, where I run, everything about me. The best thing is for us to stick with the plan of my staying at your parents'—at least for tonight."

He hated that she was right. "All right, but first we pack, agreed?"

"Agreed."

Her cell phone rang. She went to answer it. Aaron took it from her hands. "Hello?"

"Yeah, she's right here, hold on."

He cupped the phone. "It's someone named Jean."

"Jean?"

"Yeah, she says you know her from church."

He watched her mentally calculate whether she knew the woman or not. "Oh." She grabbed the phone. "Hi, Jean." After a brief pause, she said simply, "Fine."

Fine, my foot. She's got a lunatic running around after her, and she says she's fine. He stuffed some clothing in a gym bag. He opened her underwear drawer, grabbed a fistful, and plopped it in the bag. He didn't care to look. If he didn't pull out the right stuff, she could buy more. Everyone always needs new underwear, he reasoned.

"No, you know what," he heard her say into the receiver, "I don't think I can make it to the Thanksgiving service after all."

Another brief pause. "Yeah, I know, but something's come up."

Again, the author of understatements. Not that he'd want the entire world to know his business either. But two minutes ago she was a zombie, now she was acting like she didn't have a care in the world. *She probably runs in the sun with no hat.* Down here the sun could scramble your brains. That had to be it. No one could turn their emotions on and off that quickly, could they? He certainly couldn't. In fact, he was beginning to work up to a full steam. He needed to calm down before he lost his powers of reasoning.

"Thanks, Jean, I really appreciate it. Adam's really excited. I appreciate your help on that, too." Renee looked at Aaron mischievously. "Nope, can't talk right now. He's standing beside me."

She chuckled. "Absolutely. Talk to you later."

Her duffel bag oozed with clothing that dangled from the opening. He stuffed it in and pretended he wasn't curious about Renee's Thanksgiving plans.

Chapter 14

A aron, sit down and let me explain." Renee held her hands together to keep him from seeing her shaking. "Something you said made perfect sense, but I didn't see it until I was talking with Jean."

He sat down on the edge of her bed. He held the duffel bag between his legs. "What could I possibly have said that would make you want to stay in this unsafe place?"

"It's not unsafe. Okay, tonight it is. But tomorrow I'm coming back." She came beside him and sat down. "Aaron, you said that I needed to trust the Lord. Well, I do. I can't be running from Benny the rest of my life. I'll file a restraining order, but I'm not thirteen, and I've learned some self-defense techniques over the years. I'm going to fight him, Aaron. I have to. Don't you see? It's now or never."

He rubbed the back of his neck and worked the stress out of it.

"Adam and I have gone to a lot of trouble to put together something special," she continued, "and I'm not going to take that away from him."

Aaron let out an exasperated breath. "I suppose you're right. But I don't like it. I want additional protection here."

"Like what? I've got a superintendent who now knows not to let anyone in. I've got a security system in the apartment I can put on "stay," and if someone opens the door, the alarm will go off. I can sleep with the panic button next to me, just in case. Seriously, if we look at this logically, he can only come at me via the elevator. I don't think Benny will walk up seven flights of stairs."

"Okay, but tonight you're staying with me."

"No, tonight I'll stay with your parents," she corrected.

"Then I'll stay there, too."

"Aaron," she chided, raising her voice.

"Oh, all right. I'll go home, but Adam stays with my parents."

"Agreed. Now, why don't we call Detective Diaz and see about applying for that restraining order."

Aaron shook his head.

"What?"

"You. One minute you're falling apart, the next you're the rock of Gibraltar."

"Oh. The psychologist said that shock impacts me that way. After the initial shock, I come back swinging."

"Well, keep your bat handy." He grinned.

Playfully she swatted him on the shoulder. "Thanks for being here for me, Aaron. You don't know how much that means to me."

Two hours later Renee found herself at Charles and Gladys Chapin's house. Detective Diaz was skeptical of Renee's claims until he pulled up Benny Gamaldi's file, and she was able to give him details of the dates of his arrest and the court case against him. With the taped phone message and the testimony from Aaron of Benny's phone call, they were able to put in a petition for a restraining order against the man. The judge would have to get an order to unseal her records and verify that this man was guilty of the crimes against her, since his court records only read that he'd beaten a minor.

Her running shoes and clothes on, Renee was ready for a good workout. Aaron insisted on coming with her. She didn't mind the company, but she needed to run hard. He wouldn't be able to keep pace with her. He was in good shape, but he wasn't a runner. They went to the moonlit beach where she could run for awhile and still be well within Aaron's view if he should need to rest. And she knew he'd need to rest.

To warm up, she started with her stretching. "Do you do this every day?" he asked.

"Yup." She bent down and placed her palms on the ground without bending her legs.

"Ouch, that looks painful," Aaron whined. "You sure you don't want to go to my place and take a few laps in the pool?"

"Chicken?"

"Bock, ba, ba, bock." Aaron imitated the bird with some feet scratching and head bopping along with the clucking.

"Come on, chicken, I'll run the first lap slow. Hey, what's a good chicken name? I can't call you chicken all night."

"How about Fred?"

She started a slow jog to the water's edge. The tide was low, providing lots of room for a flat footing. "Fred?"

"Yeah, it's short for Alfredo."

"Whatever happened to Frederick?"

"That, my dear, would be from my father's side, my English side."

"I see, so today you're Alfredo the Spanish chicken?"

"You have to admit, Chicken Alfredo sounds much nicer," he huffed.

Renee laughed. "Any chance we can get some this late at night?" She kept an even pace for him to follow.

"Possibly, but it's more likely we can get your favorite Italian food."

"Pizza," they said in unison.

After a fifteen-minute run south on the beach, she turned and headed north. "Okay, Fred, it's time to beat feet." She poured on the steam. Every step slammed into the sand below her as she pushed herself into a hard, brisk run. She heard him groan but didn't turn back. She went up to the wharf and turned to head south again, having made the distance in seven minutes rather than the fifteen. Aaron wasn't too far behind. She had to give him credit for sticking by her. "Come on, Fred, four more laps to go."

He smiled and watched her pass.

Lord, I don't deserve this man. He's so special. Help me be worthy of his love and affection.

The cool evening breeze swept past as her body glistened with sweat, cleansing itself from the horrors of the day. *Why, after all this time, would Benny be coming after me now, Lord? Shouldn't his temper have waned by now?*

The simple fact was that without her testimony, they wouldn't have nailed him on half the charges they had against him. She'd seen and witnessed too many of his criminal acts. It still amazed her that the police had used a thirteen year old to get to a criminal.

Her breathing deepened as she pushed herself for another lap. Aaron had jumped into the ocean for a quick swim. His lean frame sluiced through the waters as if he were native to the sea.

Her sneakers felt like lead as their weight increased with the water. *Father, remove this yoke from me. I can't bear it any longer. Thank You for helping me open up to Aaron. Why have I lived in shame for so long? I was a kid, fighting for my life.* Tears streamed down her face. *Please, remove Benny from my life completely. I don't want to be looking over my shoulder for years to come.*

Aaron swam toward shore. "Hey there, beautiful, wanna come for a swim?"

Renee removed her sneakers and dove in. "No," she said, sputtering water, "but I wouldn't mind spending some time with you."

Aaron wiggled his dark eyebrows and captured her in his arms. "So, what's this secret you have going with Adam?"

"I'll never tell." She winked, then dove farther into the waves. "Race you to the end of the pier," she challenged.

∽

Aaron worked the kinks out of his neck as he tossed and turned in bed. He and Renee had decided not to talk about Benny and his threats. She'd agreed to stay at his parents' for a couple days until the security changes were incorporated at her apartment. The fact that someone was out there watching, waiting for the right moment to strike, kept him on edge. No matter how logical it was for Renee to stay in her apartment, he couldn't rest. He needed to protect her. The nightmares of Hannah dying in the accident had changed. In the driver's seat, he found Renee, beaten and dying. How could he explain his fear to her? And did he really trust God, as he'd been asking her to do, if he worked so hard to protect her, to overprotect her? Thoughts of sleeping in his car outside her apartment made the only sense for protecting his sanity. Of course, that wasn't fair to Adam, so what could he do?

Trust the Lord.

The simple phrase required so much. The irony was that Renee saw him as a pillar of strength with his faith. Only he knew how weak he really was.

He turned to his side and punched the pillow. "Protect her, God. Please don't take her away."

Today was Thanksgiving, a day to celebrate all that God had done for them. To Aaron it had always represented the beginning of Christmas celebrations. Adam and Renee had something up their sleeves for the day. He'd tried to snoop but hadn't found a clue. She was masterful at keeping secrets.

He groaned. If he heard from one more federal agent or police officer that she was not to be trusted, he wasn't too sure he'd be able to keep from exploding. Oddly enough, Diaz had become her strongest supporter. Of course, he was the only one who spent real time with her. Everyone else looked at the paperwork.

Aaron leaned over and picked up the ringing phone. "Hello?"

"Hey, lazy, wanna open the door?"

"Renee?"

"The one and only. Adam and I have a surprise for you, so get out of bed and come into the living room."

Joy blew away his negative thoughts. The woman he loved and his son were waiting on him. "I'll be right out."

He tossed off the covers and dressed in a pair of jeans and a polo shirt. Brushing his hair, he went to the sink and then took care of his teeth. One quick glance in the mirror, and he entered the living room.

"Happy Thanksgiving, Daddy!" Adam ran up to him. Aaron scooped him up and gave him a great big hug. Yes, he had plenty to be thankful for this morning.

"Happy Thanksgiving, buddy." He glanced to the living room and found a homemade turkey on the coffee table. Renee stood at the edge of the sofa with a precious smile.

"Happy Thanksgiving, Aaron," she whispered.

He put Adam down and wrapped her in his arms. "Happy Thanksgiving, Renee." He kissed her gently on the lips.

Adam tugged on his pant leg. "Daddy, you've got to see this. You can kiss Renee later."

Aaron and Renee chuckled. "Okay, sport, show me."

"Look here, Daddy. See?" Adam bounced up and down beside the turkey centerpiece that he must have made with Renee.

"We made it." He beamed.

"It's a wonderful job, son. How'd you make it?"

"With papier-mâché, right, Renee?"

"Right."

"Open it, Daddy," Adam pleaded.

Aaron lifted the colorful head of the slightly lumpy turkey. "See?"

Aaron peered inside. "It's my letter to God. Renee said we can write God letters and read them later." Adam leaned over to him and whispered, "You're supposed to write what you're thankful for."

"Ah, thanks," Aaron winked.

"Come see this, Daddy!" Adam grasped his hand and led him toward the back patio.

"What's out here?" Aaron asked, turning back to Renee to mouth the words "thank you."

"More surprises."

Yes, he had a lot to be thankful for. *Help me keep it in perspective, Lord.*

∞

Renee finished cleaning up from the day's activities. Not only had Aaron's parents come, but Marie and her four children had also spent the day at the house. The fried turkey had been a smash, but watching Aaron and his father fish it out with the broom handle had been too precious. Thankfully, she'd caught it on videotape. All five children and the remainder of the adults stood behind the screen wall of the pool.

"Hey, wonderful, thank you for a great day." Aaron came up behind her and kissed the back of her neck.

A moan of pleasure escaped her lips. "You know what I could really use is. . ." His hands kneaded her shoulders. She groaned. "That's it."

Aaron chuckled. "You've worked hard. I can't believe all the food you prepared. It was a glorious Thanksgiving."

"I haven't had one this special since I was a kid." Changing the subject, she added, "Marie looked good."

"Yeah, Manuel took off again. She and the children are always happier when he's gone. I don't understand why she doesn't see it."

"She sees it; she's just afraid. Afraid she'll be single and alone all her life. At least that's what I figured motivated my aunt. She hated being alone." Renee put the dishtowel down on the counter and turned to face Aaron. "I should be going home."

"What's the hurry? Adam's down for the night. It's the first night you and I've had together in a long time. Or at least it seems that way. Stay for a little while."

"All right, but you can tell my boss why I'm late for work in the morning."

Aaron took her hand and led her toward the living room. "I've met your boss; he's a reasonable man."

"Ha," she huffed. "The man's a slave driver. He gives me tons of work and just leaves."

Aaron chuckled. "Must be because he trusts you."

"Hmm, I've heard rumors." They sat down on the sofa together.

"There is one other possible explanation," he whispered.

Renee closed her eyes as the fine hairs on her arms rose to attention.

"He's fallen madly in love with you and wants to keep you all to himself." He traced her lips with the tip of his finger.

He pressed his lips to hers. She wrapped her arms around him, pulling him closer. Lost in his love, lost in her own for him, could life get any better than this?

An explosion shook the house.

The room went pitch black.

Chapter 15

What was that?" Renee squeaked out the words.

"Sounds like a transformer blew. Sit here, I'll check."

The idea of staying put in a completely darkened house didn't set well with her take-charge approach to life. Renee worked her way to the kitchen and fumbled around the counter until she found the matches. She recalled seeing some candles in—which drawer? She mentally went over the contents of Aaron's kitchen cabinets. Third drawer down next to the refrigerator. Her eyes now adjusted to the darkness, she could see the long, slender white candles still wrapped in cellophane.

A nagging thought crept in from the darkness. What if Benny was behind the power outage? Gooseflesh rose on her arms.

Stop it, she reprimanded. *No use making a mountain out of an anthill. The power's gone out, plain and simple.*

Where's Aaron? Why hasn't he returned?

She struck the match. A warm glow balled in front of her around the glowing flame. She lit the candle, forgetting to take off the cellophane.

"Oh, for pity's sake," she mumbled and blew out the match. She worked the plastic down the candle and tried the process again. Successfully lighting the candle the second time, she looked for a candleholder. Not finding one, she improvised. Remembering the Cuban coffee cups looked like shot glasses, she retrieved them from the cabinet and melted some wax in the bottom and set a candle in each of the small cups. The three candles lit the area fairly well, but she wouldn't recommend reading in this light.

A thump from the backyard caused her to pause. Was Benny out there? She rushed into Adam's room and made certain the boy was all right. *Lord, why can't they find him and put him away?* She knew it would take more than the restraining order to put Benny away again, but it just didn't seem right that men like Benny could walk the streets, threaten people, and never get caught.

Renee took in a deep breath and calmed herself. No sense getting worked up over nothing, she chided.

Where is Aaron? Shouldn't he be back by now?

She left Adam sleeping soundly in his bed and headed toward the front of the house. The front door was open. Cautiously she walked toward it. Her heart raced. Her pulse drummed in her ears. She licked her dry lips and swallowed.

Pausing, she listened. Nothing. Shouldn't she hear something? Anything, a car driving by, something?

"Aaron," she called.

No answer.

She stepped closer to the door.

"Aaron," she called louder.

Father God, where is he? Please keep him safe, she pleaded.

A cold sweat rose on her skin. She was nervous, too nervous. She needed to calm down. She placed her bare arms and hands on the cool plastered walls. Reality. She took in a deep breath.

Her hand caught the end of an umbrella Aaron kept by the front door. She wrapped her fingers around it. *A weapon,* she thought. With renewed strength, she forced her steps to the open doorway.

"Aaron," she hollered.

"Over here, honey." He waved from across the street.

She leaned the umbrella against the interior door casing. He jogged back to her. "Sorry. I was bragging about the deep-fried turkey to Jerry."

You scared me half to death, she wanted to say but instead held her tongue and smiled.

"The transformer blew. Jerry said someone saw it blow with a huge fireball. But it burned itself out right away. The power will be down for a few hours. I've got a flashlight in the front hall closet." Aaron went into the darkened house.

Renee shook her head. *I can't believe I was so afraid, Lord.* The shock took hold, and her body started to shake. *Thank goodness it's still dark and Aaron can't see me like this.*

A door opened and various thuds echoed in the empty hall. "Found it," Aaron called out.

"Shh," she warned. "You'll wake Adam."

"Nah, the kid sleeps like a rock." A golden beam of light lit Aaron's chest up to his face. His handsome features calmed her frayed nerves.

"I should probably go," she whispered. "I lit some candles in the kitchen." She rubbed her arms, willing off her earlier tension. It was foolish to live in fear. She knew it, and she refused to be a victim of it. Unfortunately, knowing it in her head was one thing. Acting on it took a bit more persuasion for the body to comprehend.

Perhaps it had been seeing Marie today, knowing her situation, knowing all too well the personal anguish the woman lived through day in and day out. In Marie's eyes, she could see the fear of returning home. *Lord, give her the courage to leave Manuel for her and the children's safety.*

"You're probably right," Aaron answered.

Renee did a mental jerk. *What was he agreeing to? Oh right, my leaving.* "I had a wonderful day, Aaron. Thank you for letting me invade your family."

"Are you kidding?" He came up beside her and wrapped his arms around her.

"You made the day, silly. I can't believe you went to all this trouble. You made it special, Renee, and I appreciate it very much."

"I guess I needed a special holiday," she admitted.

"Honey, since Hannah died, holidays have been less than special. Adam needed this. I needed this. Thank you from the bottom of my heart. I could never repay you for the joy you've given me and my family today." He kissed her lightly on the forehead.

"Good night, Aaron. Thank you."

He followed her out to her car and waved good-bye. *God, help me, I don't want to leave his house. Your will, Lord, not mine,* she prayed as she drove in silence back to her own apartment. Tonight she would face the demons of years past, alone. All alone.

∞

Giving in to his insecurities, Aaron called his father and woke him up in the middle of the night. Charles Chapin was a patient man, but Aaron couldn't believe his father actually agreed to come out in response to his two a.m. phone call and for such an irrational reason.

When the older man arrived, Aaron shook his hand. "Thanks, Dad."

"No problem."

Aaron noted the pajamas, slippers, and robe his father had on. He hadn't bothered to change.

"Do you really think her life is in danger?" his father asked.

"Honestly, I don't know what to think. I can't sleep. It's the first night she's alone in her apartment since the break-in. I just know I'll rest more comfortably if I check out her apartment building. See if someone's hanging around."

"But you don't know what he looks like, son."

"Actually I do. The fellows working with me on the sting pulled up his record and showed me his mug shot."

Charles rubbed the back of his neck. "Be careful."

"Don't worry, I will. I just need to reassure myself that she's okay."

"You could call her," his father suggested. He clicked the light switch. "What's with the lights?"

"Transformer blew shortly after you left. FPL should have it up and running soon."

"Ah, well, I don't plan on staying up all night. If you're going to go check on her, scoot."

"Yes, sir." Aaron headed toward his van and turned back. "Thanks, Dad."

His father waved him off. Aaron knew the man could have lectured him about how foolish he was being, but instead he simply came over and took his place watching Adam. It was more than likely Aaron would find him asleep on the sofa when he returned.

The drive to Renee's apartment was peaceful, hardly a car on the road. The cool night air held a relaxing feel to it. He pulled over to the side of the road and waited. In the distance he could hear an occasional car driving on Biscayne Boulevard. A dim light burned in Renee's apartment. Was she still awake? Should he call? Would she be angry that he was outside her apartment building watching out for her?

No, he wouldn't call. *Father, give me peace. I need to know that You're watching over Renee, that she'll be safe. You know I've fallen in love with her. I know I shouldn't have. I should have waited until things with the business were settled. But what can I say, Lord? I want to do what's right. Are You calling us to each other? In so many ways it seems right, but we barely know each other. And yet we connect on such a deep level. Protect her, Lord. Forgive my fears and unbelief. Help me rest in Your sovereign peace.*

Aaron turned the key, put the car in gear, and drove home. There was nothing he could do. She was out of his hands and in the Lord's. That knowledge should make him feel more confident, but it didn't. Hannah's tragic accident flooded back in his memory. Days of asking God "Why?" There were no answers, at least none that satisfied. And now he knew Renee was at risk, and there was still nothing he could do. "A man should be able to do something to protect the ones he loves, Lord."

∽

The following Monday afternoon, Aaron found himself torn between doing what the investigators wanted and being honest with Renee. He didn't want to deceive her, but if the sting was going to work, he had to have her full attention. All afternoon he'd been trying to come up with a plan that wouldn't tell her what was happening but wouldn't deceive her either. The feds had set up a dummy corporation. Sunny Flo Designs had to put a proposal together for Innovative Trust, a think tank for businesses and social groups.

He had their brochures, corporate vision statement, logo, and target audience. Hopefully, Renee wouldn't ask too many questions. Entering the office, he smiled. "Hi."

"Hi, honey. How was your meeting?"

"Good. They're interested in having us put together a full multimedia package for them. But first they want to start with a Web page." He handed her the material.

She scrunched up her nose. "Who designed these?"

"They need us," he replied.

"They need an overhaul. This is really bad, Aaron. Did you go over these?"

"Yeah, did all I could to keep a straight face." That was truthful. He glanced at one of the hidden cameras and smiled. He knew they were watching.

Renee continued to work through the haphazard material. "Honey, I'm not about to tell you your business, but do these folks really know what they're doing? I mean, they are setting themselves up as consultants and, and. . ."

"I know, it looks bad, but they're not claiming to be advertising guys, just business advisors."

Renee shook her head. "Don't think I'd want their advice. No offense."

Aaron chuckled. "None taken. Besides, that's what we're here for, to take folks like this and make them shine."

"Hmm, might take a miracle." She scribbled something on the edge of one of the pages. "What about the logo? Is that set in stone?"

"Nope, they want to be completely revamped."

"Okay," she mumbled, continuing to lean over the papers. He loved watching her work. She'd nibble her lower lip ever so slightly when she got a brainstorm.

There, she's got it. He grinned. "Knock 'em dead, Renee. Get John to help you with any layouts you need."

"Uh-huh." She didn't look up.

Aaron chuckled under his breath. She'd come up with a great campaign. It was a shame nothing would come of it. Thankfully the government had agreed to pay his normal fees for such a proposal.

"How long do we have?" Renee popped her head up as he sat down behind his desk.

"Two weeks."

She nodded and continued to jot down some notes.

∞

Two weeks! They're asking a lot. On the other hand, it was more time than most gave for a proposal. But never with this much work. *Innovative Trust. Who thought up that name? Sounds more like a new bank or something.*

"Honey." Aaron's voice nipped at her senses. She paused. Had he called her? "Renee?"

She glanced over to his desk. "Yes?"

"I said, Adam's waiting for us. I think we better pack it in for the night."

"Oh, sorry. Give me a minute."

He smiled. "I knew you would dive into this one."

"There's no choice. It's a bear of a project. How long has this company existed, and who thought up the name?"

"I think they told me a year and a half."

"Do they have clients?"

"Apparently not enough. That's why they're hiring us."

"Are they? This isn't just a proposal?"

"Well, no—but I figure they'll have to hire us. Who else can do a better job on this?"

"Don't be too sure, Aaron. I'm good, but I'm not a miracle worker. That name—whoever named it that?" she mumbled, grabbing her purse and slipping on her sandals.

Sandals in December, unbelievable. Renee chuckled.

"I'm glad you find this so amusing. Do you know how much time will be involved with this project?"

He sobered and paused. He opened his mouth slightly, then closed it. "I have complete faith in you, honey."

"Nothing like adding to the pressure," she teased.

"Ah, but I've seen you under pressure. You're a wonder to watch." He wiggled his eyebrows.

And with those gorgeous chocolate eyes, he could ask me to do anything, she mused. "Kiss me before I say something logical."

"With pleasure." He captured her and gave her a quick peck on the lips.

Hmm, it must be later than I thought. Normally they'd share a warm kiss before picking up Adam, wanting to limit their physical contact in front of the boy.

He led her to the door.

Renee looked up at him as he punched the code on the security pad. "I've been thinking about Christmas and what to get Adam, but I haven't come up with anything. Any ideas?"

"He loves planes, trains, boats, blocks, all sorts of things," Aaron replied.

They stepped onto the sidewalk. Aaron turned around and locked the door.

"I know, but he has a ton of toys. Who bought him all that stuff?"

"Uh, I guess I did, why? Do you think it's too much?" He cupped her elbow and led her to her car.

"I don't know. It seems like a lot, but I can't really judge from my past." He waited while she unlocked the car door. "Are we dropping your car off or mine tonight?"

He looked up at the deep blue sky and grinned. "Mine."

She chuckled. "I'll meet you at your house after I go home and change."

"Okay." He leaned over and kissed her again. This time with a bit more passion. "Bring your bathing suit. I think we'll want to swim later."

She didn't have the heart to tell him she'd left it there Thanksgiving day. He jogged toward his car, looking both ways for oncoming traffic.

Unclasping the roof locks, she lowered the top. Adam loved the top down. Of course, Aaron enjoyed it as well. Not to mention her own particular joy in having the cool wind racing past. She'd have to take a day off and drive through the Keys soon, just for the joy of the ride.

She worked her way through the North Miami traffic and entered the secured garage below her building. Before going upstairs to her apartment, she took the time to put the cover over the collapsed roof. She waved to the super and headed up to the seventh floor in the elevator. Pressing the black button, she watched the doors close.

In her apartment, she kicked off her sandals and stretched her toes. Rolling her shoulders, she strolled into her bedroom and undressed. Seconds later she donned a comfortable pair of khaki shorts and a light cotton blouse. She pulled her hair back in a loose ponytail, did a quick check in the mirror to make certain her makeup was intact, and headed toward the door.

The answering machine's red light caught her attention. She pressed the play button.

"Renee," a voice said, sniffling. "This is Marie, Aaron's sister. I—I don't know why I called really. I guess I just wanted to say hi. We had a good time on Thanksgiving. Thanks."

"That was your last message," the machine droned.

Should she call her? Was she okay? Renee looked up Marie's phone number and punched it in. The annoying busy signal came on. She copied the number and recorded it in her cell phone. She would keep trying.

Turning her security system back on, she left her apartment and headed toward Aaron's house. Tonight they were going out at dinner to the "peanut place," as Adam liked to call it. She was grateful his all-time favorite restaurant was getting rather old.

She looped her keys around her finger and spun them around. *Father, let me know what to do for Marie,* she prayed.

Sitting behind the wheel of her car, she called Marie again. Still busy. She snapped her phone shut and hooked up the hands-free headset.

She started the engine.

The phone rang.

"Hello," she answered.

"Hello, Renee."

Her body stiffened. She clenched the wheel.

Chapter 16

"D ad?" Adam called.

"Yes, son."

"Is Renee coming with us?"

Aaron looked in the rearview mirror and caught a glimpse of his son wiggling his feet back and forth. "Yup, she's going to meet us at our house."

"Dad?" he sang again.

"Yes, son." Twenty questions. Would the child ever get beyond this stage? he wondered.

"Can Renee be my new mommy?"

Aaron's mouth went dry. To say he hadn't thought of the prospect would be lying, but they'd only been dating for a couple months. "Ah, I don't know, why?"

"'Cause I like her, and you kiss her all the time."

Hmm, he has me there, Lord. "Well, it takes more than kissing to make a woman your new mommy."

"Why?"

"Because men and women have to know it's right to get married."

"Why?"

"Because God doesn't want us marrying the wrong person."

Adam crossed his arms and knitted his eyebrows.

Aaron took a deep breath. He'd stopped that onslaught of questioning.

"How do you make her a mommy?"

Aaron loosened his tie. "First a man has to ask the woman if she would like to marry him."

"I can do that." He beamed.

Oh, dear. "No, Adam. I'd have to ask Renee."

"Why?"

Good grief. How do you explain engagement to a four year old? Father, any wisdom here sure would be appreciated. "Because you have to be a man before you can ask a woman."

"I'm a man."

"No, you're my little man. You're not all grown up yet."

"I'm getting bigger."

Aaron chuckled. "Yeah, you are, buddy, but you still need to be as big as Grandpa or me."

"I like Renee. I want her for my new mommy," he pouted.

"Tell you what, son. I like Renee, too. Why don't we pray and see if she's the one God has picked to be your new mommy?"

"Really? We can ask God?" Renewed excitement filled his dark brown eyes.

"Yeah, we can ask God." The thought wasn't an unhappy prospect. Day by day he'd been falling helplessly in love with her. If only the police would stop hinting that she was involved with the corporate espionage. Logically, he understood their line of reasoning. She had started to work for him shortly before his troubles began, she did have the expertise to set up access to his private files to be shared with others, and she had apparently called in the change of passwords. Something he hadn't asked her about. Partly because he didn't believe she did it, and he wanted her to know that he trusted her.

Detective Diaz made a point of saying he now believed Renee, but the man didn't see how Benny Gamaldi could have played a part in the break-in. He hadn't been released from prison then.

Who was it? Aaron rubbed the back of his neck.

His cell phone rang.

"Hello."

"Mr. Chapin?"

"Yes."

"This is Sergeant White from the North Miami Police Department. Are you familiar with a Renee Austin?"

"Yes, she works for me."

"Ah, well, she asked us to notify you."

"What's happened? Spit it out, man." Aaron's voice rose.

"She's been in an accident. She's at the emergency room at Aventura Hospital."

Aaron clung to the steering wheel. His stomach lurched. "Is she okay?"

"Yes, she'll be fine."

He glanced in the various mirrors and sped up. "Tell her I'm on my way."

"Sure. Mr. Chapin?"

"Yes?"

"She'll need a lawyer. A good one."

∞

"Déjà vu," Renee mumbled. Benny had come at her waving a knife. She'd reacted. Pure instinct had taken over. She'd slammed her car door into him, leaped out of the car, and jump-kicked him in the jaw with her foot. Apparently the self-defense class had paid off.

Silently, Renee prayed, hearing Benny ranting and raving with his claims that she had attacked him. She leaned her head back against the pillow of the emergency-room bed.

"It's her knife," Benny whined.

Her eyes popped open, then she closed them again and tried to remember what the knife looked like. It was possible, even highly likely. After all, he had been in her apartment. He could have stolen it then. *Has he been planning this setup all along?*

The restraining order, she thought. Perhaps that would protect her rights against his lies. Memories of the past, her previous arrest, the trial caused her stomach to tighten. "God, no, I can't go through that again," she cried into her pillow.

A sharp pain caused her to groan. "Ugh." She eased out the constrained breath. She hadn't come away from the incident unharmed. The wound to the back of her shoulder now throbbed. The small nicks and cuts to her hands burned.

"How are you?" a young doctor dressed in a white lab coat asked, holding her chart in his hand.

"Alive," she quipped.

"Sit up and let me have a look."

She sat up, and he undid the hospital gown at the base of her neck. A nurse stood silently watching.

"It's not too bad. I'm going to order a CT scan. Are you pregnant?"

"No."

"Any chance of it?"

"No." She knew it was a rational question, but her anger simmered on the surface, wanting to lash out. Thankfully, logic ruled, and she held her tongue.

"The CT scan will tell me if there's damage to the bone and the extent of the tissue damage. Let's check your range of motion."

He put her through a small battery of tests, most of which she could easily perform. Tears hovered on the edge of her lids as the pain increased. The doctor gave his orders to the nurse, who led her down the hallway for the CT scan.

On and on the tests and treatments droned. The officer at the scene now came into her area. "I've called your employer, and he told me to tell you he's on his way. Can you please go over the incident once again?"

Renee nodded her head. She knew the routine. *Lord, help me.* Renee recited her account of the "incident," as he'd termed the traumatic event.

The officer lifted his head and looked at her. "I'm sorry, but—"

"Renee, are you all right?" Aaron rushed into her cubicle with Adam on his hip.

"Renee," Adam squealed and reached out to her.

The officer stepped back and closed his notepad.

"I'll be okay," she said meekly as another man walked into her cubicle, dressed in a business suit and carrying a briefcase. She pulled the covers up to her chin.

"Renee, I've secured Mr. Stein as your attorney," Aaron announced.

She shifted her glance from the stranger to Aaron, back to the police officer, and then back to Mr. Stein. "What's going on here? Am I being arrested? And how do you know about it before I do?" She glared back at the officer.

∽

Aaron paced the waiting room while Adam sat on a seat and watched the television bolted to the ceiling. He'd never seen Renee this angry before. He couldn't blame her. He'd charged into the hospital with lawyer in tow. Thankfully she hadn't fired the guy on the spot. Why the police officer hadn't informed her and had informed him, he'd probably never know.

He found himself looking at every male coming in and out, wondering if he was Benny Gamaldi. Figuring the man to be a middle-aged Italian, he eliminated half the suspects.

"Daddy?"

"Yes, Adam?"

"I'm hungry. Can we bring Renee home now?"

"Soon, son. She should be released soon." The question was, would she still be angry with him?

Harvey Stein strolled over to him. "Aaron, Renee asked me to give you a message. She's going to be tied up for awhile and suggested you take Adam home."

"What's the deal, Harvey? She has a restraining order out on this guy."

"True, but he's claiming she attacked him first."

"No way, not Renee," Aaron protested. *If I could just get my hands on this creep,* he thought.

"Look, I think it's highly unlikely, too, but let me do my job, okay? Take the kid home. I'll make sure she gets home safe and sound."

Aaron glanced over to Adam. He sat there hugging his knees. The poor little guy was just as concerned as he was for Renee. "All right, but tell her I love her and that Adam and I will be waiting for her call."

"Sure. And Aaron, concerning the other parties who are interested in Renee Austin, let them know I'll give them a full report."

Aaron nodded his head. He'd met Harvey during the investigation being performed by the FBI. Harvey's specialty was white-collar crime. He'd earned Aaron's confidence over the past few months, having given him very helpful and useful information concerning his rights and his company's liabilities if a lawsuit should be pursued. Aaron extended his hand. "Thanks."

"You're welcome. Take the boy home and try to relax. I'll try and smooth things over with Renee."

Aaron stifled a half-hearted chuckle.

"Can we say good-bye to Renee?" Adam asked.

Aaron looked toward Harvey, who nodded. "Sure, buddy."

Adam jumped up and ran down the hall. Aaron tried to catch up. Somehow yelling in a hospital emergency room seemed inappropriate. He found Adam on Renee's bed and in her arms.

"Call me," Aaron pleaded. She glanced up at him in the doorway. He wanted to go to her, but her eyes warned him to stay back.

"I love you, Renee." Adam hugged her again.

She winced with pain.

Aaron stepped forward. She held up a hand. "Bye, buddy. I love you, too. Don't ever forget that."

Lord, please, don't take her from us. Aaron fought his anger and smiled, reaching his hand out for Adam.

Leaving Renee in someone else's care didn't set well with him. But caring for his son was his first priority. Adam didn't need to be in the hospital, and he certainly didn't need to be there if they dragged Renee off to the police station in handcuffs.

His cell phone rang. "Hello?"

"Aaron, help me."

"Marie, where are you? Are you okay? Has Manuel beat you again?" Today would not be the best day for him to confront his brother-in-law. His Christian witness would go down the drain faster than a palm tree could sway in the breeze.

"He's bad, Aaron, real bad. I've never seen him like this before."

"Where are you?"

"At the mall. He won't find me here, and the kids think we're shopping," Marie answered.

"Okay, I'll be there as soon as possible. Meet me in the food court, and I'll buy you and the children dinner."

"All right," she sniffed. "And, Aaron, thanks."

"You're welcome." He closed his cell phone. *Lord, help me. I can't be caught up in anger when I address Marie. I need to take her to a shelter, Lord. A place where she'll get real help. Please prepare her heart that this is the right thing to do.*

"Daddy?"

"Yes, Adam?"

"Is Tia Marie hurt like Renee?"

Chapter 17

Semi-dressed in street clothes, Renee tried to figure out how to keep her arm bound to her body and manage to put on her blouse. The doctor's treatment was to bind the arm to her body for a couple days to let the torn muscles begin to heal. There had been no damage done to the bones.

"Here ya go, honey." The thin, middle-aged black nurse named Jessie smiled. She'd been with Renee all evening. In her hand she held up a large T-shirt.

"Thanks." Renee returned the smile.

"Your lawyer said he'll be waiting for you."

Renee nodded. Whoever this Harvey Stein was, she owed Aaron a huge favor. The lawyer pointed out the obvious marks on her body that showed she was in a defensive posture, therefore not the aggressor. Stein had even spoken with Benny and told him if he didn't want to return to prison, he'd best leave town. Renee could have pressed charges. She wanted to, but another part of her wanted to leave the past buried. Duly warned, Benjamin Gamaldi left the hospital knowing that if he so much as passed Renee's line of vision, she would have him arrested.

The police officer informed her that he'd been the one to advise Aaron to get a lawyer because he sensed Benny would press charges against her. His word against her word would have left the officer little choice in the matter, and he would have had to arrest her.

"Thanks again, Jessie," Renee said as the nurse helped her into the T-shirt. She wouldn't be going out for a few days.

"You're welcome. You've got quite a son, looks like his daddy."

She smiled. "He's his daddy's son. We're not married."

"Sorry, my mistake. If you don't mind me saying so, they were pretty worried about you. I swear that man was going to bore a hole right through the floor tiles. He sure can pace."

Renee chuckled and winced from the pain. "Yeah, he gets that way."

He did love her, and she did love him. She shouldn't have been angry with him. It was Benny she was angry with. But he hadn't been handy; Aaron was. She definitely needed to apologize.

Renee stepped out of the area that had been her station for the past three hours. She glanced up at the clock. *Four hours,* she amended.

"Ready?" Harvey Stein asked, his suit coat opened, his tie hanging loosely.

"Yes. Thank you for taking me home."

"Not a problem. Aaron wouldn't have gone home otherwise. Besides, I need to see the area of the crime just in case Mr. Gamaldi has second thoughts and presses charges."

Would she be stuck with this man the rest of her life? *No, I can't think like that*, she resolved.

"Aaron called earlier and asked me to give you a message. He's gone to meet his sister, Marie, and probably won't be home until late."

"Is she all right?" She didn't know what Mr. Stein knew of Marie's situation, but he should be able to answer that question.

"Don't know. He didn't say."

What happened to Marie? The message she'd left earlier on the answering machine. . . Renee had forgotten all about Aaron's sister when she met up with Benny. *Benny,* she sighed. *Lord, please keep him out of my life.*

Harvey opened the passenger door to his Ford Explorer. *Aren't lawyers supposed to drive Cadillacs or Mercedes?* "Can you tell me how it is you know Aaron?"

"He's a client."

A criminal attorney? Something isn't adding up. "What does Aaron need a criminal attorney for?" *Does he have a past I'm not aware of?*

"A safeguard. He needed to know his rights with the investigation into the corporate espionage. You are aware of that investigation?"

"Yes, but. . .I didn't know he secured an attorney."

"For advice, primarily. And yes, I was aware of you and your past, which is why he asked me to come. He figured I'd be your best defense. Which, if I do say so myself, I was." He grinned.

Renee chuckled. "You were, no question. I saw visions of my arrest. Do you really think Benny's gone for good?"

Harvey Stein looked to the left, to the right, and left again as he exited the parking garage. "That I can't be sure of. I wager he'll hang around for a bit. See if there's a way he might be able to get to you without doing it personally. But after awhile he'll lose interest, and his organization won't give him too much time away. How aware are you of his previous activities before he was arrested?"

"I don't know much. I do know he was a small-time hood for some mob."

"Small-time is right, but in prison he did some favors. You are personal. I hope I convinced him you were just a kid who had paid long enough with no family, your arrest, and your captivity. However, reason doesn't always work with these guys. But the threat of arrest does. And he knows that if he so much as looks at you, I'll have him hauled off faster than he can sneeze. That's a threat he'll take seriously. He's just gotten out and regained his freedom. He won't want to lose that."

"I hope you're right. Tell me, if you can, who besides me are suspects for the espionage?"

∞

The next couple weeks were a blur. Marie was safe in a shelter. Renee was recoverng from her wounds, the proposal was intact, and soon Aaron would be addressing the man or woman who was stealing his work.

"Hello," he said, answering the ringing phone.

"Mr. Chapin, this is Detective Diaz. We've located your office equipment."

"Where? When? Do you know who stole it?"

"Hang on." Diaz chuckled. "We've located it, but we haven't caught the man who brought your belongings to the storage area. It appears as if everything is here, but we're leaving it undisturbed and hoping to catch the man who's been coming almost daily."

"How'd you find it, if you don't mind me asking?"

"The manager of the place called in a suspicious activity report. Actually, he was concerned it was a storage center for narcotics."

A genuine tip. So they do happen in real life, not just in the movies, Aaron mused.

"Hi, honey." Renee's gentle voice brought a smile to his face. He certainly loved this woman. *It's been so hard to be close with all the secrets lately.*

He cupped the phone. "Hi. Detective Diaz is on the phone. They found the office equipment."

"You're kidding. Where? Did they catch the thief?" She beamed.

"But that's not the only reason I called you." The detective's words brought Aaron's attention back to the phone.

He held up his index finger, asking Renee to give him a minute. "What else?"

"I have reason to believe we might be looking at your brother-in-law."

"Manuel?"

"Yeah, he fits the description of the man who's been coming around. Do you know why he would steal from you? And why he would hold on to it rather than sell it off?"

So, Manuel had taken to stealing from his family. How much lower could this man go before he saw the truth of his sin? How many more people would have to suffer? "I don't know," Aaron responded, then prayed the police were wrong. What would Marie say if she knew Manuel had been stealing from her own brother? Aaron kneaded the back of his neck.

Renee placed her loving hands on Aaron's shoulders and started to massage them.

He closed his eyes. He could get very used to this.

"We'll keep a lookout on the storage unit," the detective continued, "and I'll notify you as soon as our man turns up. After that I'll need you to come down and identify your belongings."

"No problem." Aaron spoke for a moment longer, then hung up. He turned and captured Renee in his arms. "Thank you. That felt wonderful. How'd your shopping go?"

"Adam and I had a good time. He's quite proud of your presents."

"Oh, should I be doing some snooping?"

"Ha, you'd never find them."

"Oh, is that a challenge?"

"Possibly." She winked.

The question was, did he dare give her the ring for Christmas? Would she accept it? Was it too soon?

"What's the matter?" She brushed his hair from his forehead.

"I have a meeting this afternoon."

"With Innovative Trust, I know. What's the matter?"

"Oh nothing." How could he explain to her what was happening?

She placed her hands upon her hips. "Aaron, when is this going to be over? Just when I think our relationship is deepening, these walls come up. I know it has to do with the investigation, and I'm trying to be patient but. . ."

He kissed her to silence her and whispered in her ear, "Come with me."

He led her to the car. "Honey, trust me, one more day, and I'll tell you everything."

She sighed. "All right, but why couldn't you tell me in the office. . . ?" Her words slowed down as realization filled her. "The place is bugged?"

He nodded.

She jumped away from the car. "How much? I mean did they see us or just hear us?"

"Both," he admitted.

"Great, those Peeping Toms watched when I kissed you. Don't they have any sense of privacy?"

"Honey." He took her by the hand. "They know I trust you. They've watched and seen you do nothing illegal. They've seen when you've come in after hours and worked on the Innovative Trust project."

Red crimson stained her cheeks.

"Honey, I know it's embarrassing, and obviously I've been told about you coming in. But they've come in after you and have looked over all your work. They know you're not the guilty party. Innovative Trust is a phony company. It's a sting I've been planning with the FBI."

"What? I—I spent all that time on, on. . ." She sat down on the curb and buried her face in her hands.

He sat beside her.

An agent approached. "She'll have to remain in my custody."

Renee raised her head. "Who are you?"

"Agent Wyman, miss. I'm sorry, but your knowledge about the operation. . . I have to stay by you."

"You heard our conversation?" Renee asked and glanced over to Aaron.

"Yes, your car is—"

"I suppose my apartment is also?"

"Only with listening devices."

"Aaron?" she questioned.

"I'm sorry. They insisted. And that's how the emergency services came to your aid so quickly when Benny attacked you."

"You mean I was never in any real danger of being arrested?"

Aaron bowed his head and shook it no. "The local police weren't aware of the situation at the time. So the threat was real from their perspective. Harvey set them straight without exposing the federal agents."

"Aaron, I love you, but I don't know what to do here. I thought you trusted me. I thought—"

"Begging your pardon, Miss Austin, but Mr. Chapin needs to make his appointment if this sting is going to work."

"Renee, believe me, I love you, and I've trusted you all the way."

For some reason his words seemed hollow, trite even. If he really trusted her, why didn't he protect her from this invasion of privacy?

"Agent Wyman, can I go in and get my purse?"

"Yes. Then I'll take you to a secure location."

"Fine." She had little choice in the matter. She loved Aaron too much to stand in the way of this investigation. Wounded pride aside, she'd do what she could to help him.

"Renee, I'm not leaving until I know you believe me," Aaron persisted. "I don't care about the sting. I care about you and me and what the Lord's been building between us. Please tell me you'll let me explain?" He caressed the top of her hand with his thumb. His dark orbs penetrated her senses.

She nodded. She couldn't speak, not and control her tongue.

"Thank you." He kissed the top of her forehead. "I'll be back as soon as possible. They'll take good care of you. I love you." He waved as he ran toward his van.

She stood there frozen for a moment, then turned and headed into the office. The phone rang. Without thinking, she picked it up. "Sunny Flo Designs, Renee speaking."

"Renee?" She could hear Brent's anger.

"Brent, what's the matter?"

"You know what's the matter. I trusted you. I thought you were a Christian. I never in a million years would have thought you would do this to me, Renee. Okay, I admit I ended our relationship badly, but did you have to steal from me?"

"What are you talking about?" Renee collapsed in her chair. "Steal what?"

"Don't give me that sweet innocent talk. I don't buy it, not anymore. How could you do this?"

"Will you stop talking in riddles and tell me what's happened?"

"You know perfectly well what happened. Why would you break in and steal my proposals? You used to be so creative. Did you steal from others when you worked for me?"

"Look, Brent. I'm not sure what you're talking about but—"

Agent Wyman picked up the phone. "Mr. Cinelli, this is Kevin Wyman. I'm an associate of Miss Austin. Could she call you back in a minute?"

"You tell that woman to stay away from me, you hear?"

"Yes, sir."

How could Brent think I would ever steal from him. Why? I was his best designer. This doesn't make sense.

Agent Wyman hung up the phone. Renee heard the electronic hum of a disconnected line. Her life seemed to be singing the same annoying hum.

"Miss Austin, we need to leave. Please come with me."

The bell over the door rang.

"Hey, Renee, what's happening?" John said as he bounced into his seat.

"Not much. I need to go with Mr. Wyman. Can you lock up when you leave?" she asked.

"Sure, where's Aaron?"

"He has a three o'clock with Innovative Trust."

"Ahh, I hope they buy it. We worked hard on that one."

"Yeah." She tried to sound hopeful, but knew she was failing miserably. "I'll see you tomorrow."

"Sure. Don't forget I go home on Saturday. I'll be back after the new year."

"No problem. If I don't see you tomorrow, have a good visit."

John knitted his eyebrows but said nothing. "See ya."

She waved and led Agent Wyman out the door. Thank the Lord he didn't have a trench coat or a field jacket that had FBI written across the back in big bold letters. Instead, he wore a pair of jeans and a light cotton jersey.

"Am I under arrest?" she asked after they crossed the parking lot.

"No, it's more like protective custody. Miss Austin, we need to contact Brent Cinelli. It sounds like he's been experiencing some of what Mr. Chapin's been going through."

The man was a regular genius. "Yeah, but I don't think he'd believe me. I hope you catch this creep. Someone's trying to make me look bad, and I want to know why. I don't have any enemies. This doesn't make sense."

"It'll work out. And we know you're not responsible. We've watched you too closely."

"Thanks, I think," she snickered.

❦

"Mr. Chapin, so glad you could come. We at Innovative Trust believe in doing business differently. Please, join me and Mr. Sutton."

Aaron kept a straight face. Sutton was a young executive type with styled hair, perfectly pressed suit, and a pin-shaped nose. Was this the man? He'd never seen him before. *Why would he attack my business, Lord? What have I ever done to him?* He playacted along and shrugged his shoulders. "Mr. Yang, I'm sorry, but I thought we had an appointment for me to show you—"

Yang cut him off. "Yes, yes, Mr. Chapin, we do, but Mr. Sutton had an appointment before yours, and I dare say the time has gotten away from me. He was just presenting his proposal. I think you'll be quite impressed with his work."

Sutton's forehead beaded with sweat. He rose to leave. "I should be going."

Agent Yang came up behind him and placed his hand on the man's shoulder. "Please stay, I think you've done a wonderful job on your proposal."

David Sutton cleared his throat. "Thank you, but I wouldn't want to impose on Mr. Chapin's time."

"Nonsense," Aaron grinned. "I'd love to see your work. I'm sure it's fine, but it can't compare with mine."

Sutton's eyes moved back and forth in rapid fire. He looked to be planning his escape.

"Very well." Sutton coughed.

"I'm sorry, are you coming down with a cold?" Agent Yang asked.

"Something's just caught in my throat." He fumbled over his words.

"Mr. Sutton is with B&J Advertising," Yang offered.

Aaron nodded and rose. "You've obviously impressed Mr. Yang. Perhaps I should let the two of you work out the details of your contract."

A narrow smile slithered up the finely chiseled face of David Sutton. "Nonsense, Mr. Chapin. I'd like you to see it."

Aaron stopped at the door. "But Mr. Yang, if you like his proposal so much, I'll spare you the time and let you settle things with Mr. Sutton."

"Better luck next time." Sutton stood tall, extended his hand to Aaron, and even sucked in his gut a bit.

Aaron put his hand to the doorknob, then paused. "You know, Mr. Yang, I think I will take you up on your offer. I'd love to see what got you so excited. Guess I'm more curious than I thought."

Sutton's shoulders slumped.

"Excellent decision, Mr. Chapin. Sit, sit." Yang pushed the keys of Sutton's laptop. Aaron glanced over to see the poor man visibly shaking. As the Power Point presentation ended, Yang hit a key to pause the demonstration. "What do you think, Mr. Chapin?"

"I think it's an excellent proposal." Aaron turned to Mr. Sutton from B&J Advertising. "I'm just curious how he stole it from my company."

"You're daft," Sutton squeaked.

"Am I? So if I go over here and click a couple keys, nothing will happen, right?"

Sutton looked over to him, to Yang, then bolted toward the door. Two agents in black field dress with bulletproof vests appeared in the doorway.

"You're under arrest, David Sutton." The agents proceeded to read him his rights.

Aaron took a deep breath and sat back down. "Just answer me one question. Why did you try to implicate Renee?"

"She got me fired from Brentwood Designs. I had a perfectly good career going, then she became Brent Cinelli's lover and, boom, I was out the door like yesterday's trash."

Aaron shook his head.

"You just wait. She's a vicious witch of a woman. And she's got you wrapped around her finger."

With any luck he'd have something wrapped around Renee's finger that had nothing to do with dishonesty and deceit but had everything to do with honesty, love, and grace.

The next few hours were spent going over details of the case with the agents in charge. They informed Aaron how Brent Cinelli's company had been compromised and that David Sutton had also left a trail there implicating Renee. Thankfully, the agents were able to counter Brent's accusations against Renee and show him the evidence against David Sutton. Brent Cinelli provided employee documents and records.

As Aaron worked his way through the city traffic back to his home, he prayed Renee would be there when he arrived. He'd asked the agents to drop her off at his house.

His cell phone rang. He slipped on the headset and pushed the button. "Hello?"

"Daddy, Daddy, I'm scared," Adam cried.

Chapter 18

What do you mean you can't find Adam?" Renee screamed.

"He disappeared," the female officer informed her.

"Disappeared! Little boys don't just disappear. Come on, we're going to find him." Renee ran out the hotel room's sliding glass door and onto the beach. He could be anywhere. She scanned the area.

"You'll have to stay here, Miss Austin," Agent Wyman protested.

She turned back to him. "Am I under arrest?"

"No."

"Then I'm leaving." She ran down to the edge of the shore. "Adam," she hollered. The female officer assigned to Adam came up beside her. "Okay, show me where you lost him."

"I didn't lose him," the officer protested.

"My foot, you didn't. It was your job to protect him, watch him, to make sure no harm came to him. I'd say you blew it."

"I bent down to tie my shoe, and the kid disappeared. He's fine; I'm sure of it." The officer's hands shook.

Renee wasn't going to argue with the woman. She didn't have time. "Adam," she called again.

She went into a full jog. He couldn't have gone too far, she hoped. "Father, keep him safe."

"Adam," she called again. Other parents stood up on the beach, drawn to the commotion. She stopped to talk with a young father playing with his son, who was building a sand castle. "Did you see a small boy, dark hair, Hispanic, come by here?"

"No," the man answered, rising from the sand. "We've been at the water's edge for about thirty minutes. If he passed, I would have seen him."

Then he must have gone the other way, she reasoned. "Thanks." She turned and ran harder back in the direction she'd come from. "Adam," she called again.

A swarm of police officers and agents huddled near the patio of the hotel room. "You could help find him," she yelled as she ran by.

After a minute of hard running down the beach, she saw him, at last, standing with another family. "Adam!" Tears filled her eyes.

"Renee!" he shouted and ran toward her.

She scooped him up and hugged him hard. "Thank You, Lord." Tears ran down her cheeks.

"I was so scared. Mr. Mike let me use his phone to call Daddy."

"Thank you." She looked over to a middle-aged man with three small girls playing around him.

"You really ought to be more careful," he kindly chastised.

"Someone else was supposed to be watching him. Thank you, I'll take him back to the hotel."

"His father's on his way here," Mr. Mike informed her.

"Granddad, can we play with our new friend?" the oldest of the three girls asked.

"Can I?" Adam wiggled in her arms.

She didn't want to let go. "Sure, buddy."

"Apparently he wandered off," she murmured, keeping her eyes focused on Adam.

"He said he was chasing a seagull."

Renee nodded. "Thanks for rescuing him."

"No trouble. As you can see, I have three granddaughters of my own. They can move quickly."

A nervous chuckle escaped her throat. "Yeah, they sure can."

"Ms. Austin," the female officer called, approaching them, "Mr. Wyman would like to speak with you."

"Later. I'm waiting here for Mr. Chapin."

The woman opened her mouth to protest, then clamped it shut.

A squeal of brakes turned Renee's head toward the parking lot. Aaron. She smiled and waved. "Adam," she called, "Daddy's here."

He jumped up and ran to his father. *I love those two so much. Could it ever work out for me to be Aaron's wife and Adam's mother?* The real question was, would he ever fully trust her?

∽

Aaron held his son tightly to his chest and shook. *Thank You, Lord. He's all right.* Renee came up beside him, and he pulled her into their embrace. He kissed them both. "Adam, why did you wander off?"

"I'm sorry, Daddy. I was chasing the seagull."

"You're forgiven, but don't do it again."

"I won't. I was scared. Mr. Mike is a nice man."

"Yes, he is." Aaron glanced over to the middle-aged man and smiled. "Let me put you down, sport." Aaron walked over to "Mr. Mike," as Adam called him, and expressed his thanks once again. How fortunate Adam had been that Mr. Mike was a teacher at a local Christian school and had come to the beach with his granddaughters. Aaron couldn't stop thanking the Lord enough for watching over his son.

Soon the small family made their way to his van. "It's over, Renee," he whispered in her ear. "We caught him."

"Who was it?"

"Do you recall a David Sutton?"

"He used to work at Brentwood Designs. He couldn't produce on our timetable."

"Apparently he's been blaming you for his job loss."

"You mean all of this is because of me?" She stopped at the edge of the parking lot.

"No, it's all because one man, David Sutton, was greedy and too lazy to work on his own. It seems to me that if he'd taken the time he spent breaking into our system and setting you up and applied it to his own job, he might not have felt the need to use you."

Renee shook her head. "But what about the break-in? The robbery?"

"That we don't know about yet. Maybe David hired someone. We should know soon. Right now, I'm exhausted. Let's go home."

Renee nodded and nibbled her lower lip. Aaron massaged her shoulder. "Later," he mouthed the words. Renee smiled.

"Daddy, are the bad men gone?"

"Yes, son, all gone."

"Daddy?"

"Yes, son."

"Can we tell Renee our secret?"

Renee looked over to him. "Nope, she has to wait until Christmas." *Seven more days to Christmas. Can I wait that long?*

"Okay." Adam shifted his gaze up to Renee. "Renee, Daddy has a surprise, just like we do."

"Hmm, should I try to find it?" She ruffled Adam's hair.

"It's wrapped and under the Christmas tree. You can't touch wrapped presents. Daddy said so. It's a rule."

Renee chuckled. "Aaron, I'll meet you at your house. My car is back at the office."

"All right. Should I stop and pick something up for dinner?"

"Hmm, want to grill some steaks?"

"Yeah, I want steak," Adam purred.

"Sounds like a wonderful idea." Aaron held his son's hand. He gave Renee a quick kiss and squeezed her hand before she ran off.

"Come on, buddy, we've got some steaks to cook."

⌒

Since David Sutton's arrest six days before, Renee's life had seemed disjointed. How was it possible to have two men from her past hate her so much that they'd come after her years later? What was it about her that brought out this kind of hatred? Old doubts from when she was a child tried to resurface. Feelings that she shouldn't be alive if her parents weren't, that she'd caused their accident in some way. At eight years old, it had been hard to realize

119

their deaths weren't her fault.

Renee jumped up and started to run. Running had been her escape for many years. It gave her a chance to pour all her energy into something other than her nightmares. Self-doubt nipped at her senses. She should end her relationship with Aaron before any other demons from her past arrived. He didn't need to suffer because of her. What other skeletons did she have in her closet? There had been no clue David Sutton had blamed her for his job loss. Benny was understandable. Sick, but understandable. David's anger had come from so far out in left field, she still found it hard to believe, except for the memory of the look he'd given her the moment he received the news he was fired. Pure rage and hatred had brewed in his eyes. Looking back now, she could see it. Then, she simply figured he was angry. Who wouldn't be after losing their job?

Ironically, Brent had called to apologize the day after David Sutton's arrest and offered her another job. Renee snickered at the thought and pumped her legs harder. Rounding the corner by the bay, she looked over the tranquil blue water. She slowed down and worked her way over to the water's edge. Stretching out her muscles, her heart rate slowed. "Father, I don't know what to do. Aaron's family has this huge feast planned for the day. I'm supposed to be there. . . ." She turned her wrist and groaned. "A half hour ago. Do I belong there? Should I be there? Am I putting their family at risk? Aaron's had so many losses, especially Hannah being taken away. I just don't want to cause any more trouble for him."

She tossed a stone into the water. "I know, I know, life is filled with heartache and pain but. . ." She picked up another stone and bounced it up and down in her palm. Actually, she noticed, it wasn't a stone but a piece of coral, rough and hard, with delicate pieces of thinner membranes inside. She examined it more closely. To think it was an animal seemed odd. An animal as hard as a rock.

"Life from a rock," she mumbled. Then verses in both the Old and New Testaments came to mind, telling the story of the Israelites being led through the desert for forty years and how a stone produced the life-giving water for the people to drink. She realized how the apostle Paul reminded the Corinthians about this story and pointed out that Jesus is our spiritual rock.

Again she examined the intricate layers of the coral. Every step of her and Aaron's relationship had been bathed in prayer. She smiled and rose to toss the coral into the water. She stopped midway and held it in her palm. This little hunk of coral would be her reminder to look to the Lord—not herself, not her past—and to keep her eyes focused on the spiritual rock, Jesus Christ.

"Renee," Aaron called as he ran toward her.

"Aaron, what are you doing here?"

"Looking for you, sweetheart. It's not like you to be late. In fact, you're always early."

She smiled. "Perhaps I've adapted to Miami time."

Aaron chuckled. "Never. Your Yankee roots go too deep." He looked at her nderly. "I've missed you."

"I've missed you, too, but we did see each other yesterday."

"Yeah, but that was hours ago. Seriously, I was afraid something had hap-
ened to you."

"I'm fine. I should have called. I haven't gotten into the habit of running
ith my cell phone."

"I'll forgive you this time." He kissed her tenderly on the lips.

She wrapped her arms around him. "Where's Adam?"

"At the house. I was also afraid you wouldn't come today, knowing how full
he house would be. Mother is quite disappointed. She was planning on having
ou help her in the kitchen."

"I'm sorry."

"Don't fret about it. Mother will get over it. I think she just wants to share
ith you the traditional Cuban Christmas Eve celebrations."

"I am looking forward to it. Although seeing that entire pig roasted. . ." She
hook away the thought.

Aaron roared. "You'll get used to it. We do it every Christmas Eve."

"Every year?"

"Uh-huh." He held her close, and they walked back toward her apartment.
Was he thinking permanently? she wondered.

Chapter 19

Aaron looked over the crowd of familiar faces. The house bulged with family. Renee had passed several family members' close inspections. His sister, Marie, sat in a corner talking with Tia Ana. Marie looked good, healthy even. She and the children would be moving in with his parents. He deepest hurt came in learning that Manuel had been hired by David Sutton to steal the office equipment. Currently Manuel sat in jail awaiting his trial. Aaron knew he'd press charges, not because Manuel stole from him, but because once Manuel was in prison, he'd be out of Marie's life for a little while. He prayed it would be enough time for her to grow secure in herself and in God.

Aaron rubbed the back of his neck.

He felt Renee's gentle touch as she started to massage his neck and shoulders. "Aaron," she whispered.

"Hmm," he moaned in silent pleasure.

"Why do you always rub the back of your neck?" Her breath tickled his senses. *Lord, I want to ask her to marry me now.* He glanced at his watch. *Seven more hours.* He sighed.

"When I was a kid, I fell and broke my neck. The doctors fused a couple vertebrae together, and as you can see, I healed nicely. However, as the day wears on or the tension increases, I feel it."

"You broke your neck? And lived?" she blurted out.

Everyone stared in their direction, then started to chuckle, going back to their own conversations.

"Yup. If you look carefully, you can see a thin line from the incision. He could feel her fingertips work through his hair. *Please, let her say yes, Lord,* he pleaded.

"I can't believe this. Why didn't you tell me before?" she asked.

He turned and took her into his arms. "Because it never came up. It happened years ago. I don't even think about it. Although having the Jacuzzi has been a blessing." Wanting to turn the conversation from himself, he asked, "So what do you think of the Cuban way of celebrating?"

"Who's celebrating? We're all working." She chuckled.

"True, but tonight comes the feast. Then at midnight we exchange the presents. And of course, by then it will be Christmas Day."

"The pig smells heavenly. I can't believe you build that pit every year."

"Takes up too much of the yard to leave it up year round."

"I'm enjoying myself. It's fascinating. I don't understand most of what people are saying, but there are enough of you who speak English."

"Actually most of us speak English but, as you've noticed, Spanish is a language that shows great expression. It's just natural to speak both." He winked.

"I'm learning."

"Good. You'll do well."

"Daddy." Adam came running up.

"Hey, buddy, what's up?"

Adam glanced at Renee, then whispered into Aaron's ear, "Did you ask her yet?"

"No," Aaron whispered back. The disappointment on the child's face was obvious. "It will be midnight soon." Adam wiggled out of his embrace and marched over to Renee. Aaron went to stop the child but remembered Renee and the boy had a secret, too. *Lord, don't let him spill the beans.*

Adam whispered into Renee's ear. Aaron tried to hear their conversation. *Lord, please,* he prayed again.

Renee giggled. Aaron eased out a pent-up breath.

"Daddy, I'm taking Renee out to see the pig."

"Okay, buddy." Adam led Renee by the hand out the patio door to the backyard. Children splashed in the pool. Others sat around in the various chairs talking with each other. Soon he'd have a full family again. If she'd accept him.

∞

The succulent smell of roast pork made Renee's stomach gurgle. She shouldn't be hungry. She'd been eating all day—Cuban pastries, croquettes, nuts, cookies. Then there was the taste-testing of everything from the black beans and rice to the plantains. "See, Renee, Grandpa and *Tio* Jorge can turn the pig by picking up here and flipping it," Adam informed her. Excitement oozed from the small boy's pores.

She had to admit the technique was quite ingenious. They used regular chain link fence to wedge the split pig, then put poles on both sides for support and easy handling. They said it would take seven hours to cook this pig, which weighed around eighty pounds. The pit was actually above ground and made of concrete blocks that they could easily take down and store for the next time.

Adam soon found one of his cousins to run with. As warm as the family had been to her, Renee still felt out of place. She helped in the kitchen by doing everything that was asked, but she wasn't much use except for chopping and assembling pieces into pots. Not to mention Aaron's kitchen was tiny—a typical Florida kitchen with cupboards on both sides and a narrow walkway between them. For a small family it was sufficient. For this mob. . . Well, it was best not to speak her thoughts. They all worked well with each other.

Renee wandered back into the living room where Aaron sat beside an older woman with a regal posture. She had bone structure similar to Aaron's father,

Charles. Aaron's grandmother, Renee recognized from pictures she'd seen earlier. Aaron's glance caught hers, and he gestured for her to come over. He stood up. "Grandmother, this is Renee. Renee, this is my grandmother, Harriet Chapin."

"How do you do, dear. It's so nice to meet you. Aaron's been telling me so much about you."

"It's nice meeting you, too."

She patted the seat next to her. "Please, sit down and visit with me."

Renee sat down, pulling her skirt past her knees.

"Excuse me, ladies, I'm being paged." Aaron squeezed Renee's hand and left.

Harriet Chapin had royal blue eyes and silver gray hair, finely placed into a bun adorned with sparkling red stones. These same stones made up her earrings and necklace.

"That's a beautiful stone," Renee said. "What is it?"

"Red jasper. My late husband, Quinton, God rest his soul, gave them to me years ago for Christmas. He purchased them on a business trip to Africa. They aren't expensive, but I love the red. I've worn them every year for Christmas." She leaned closer. "And whenever Quinton and I had a special anniversary to celebrate."

"They're beautiful."

"Thank you." Harriet leaned a little closer still and took a quick scan of the room. "Adam told me about your surprise gift for Aaron."

"Oh?" *Just how many people has Adam told?* she wondered. She couldn't blame the poor boy. He'd been carrying the secret for weeks. Of course, Charles and Gladys Chapin also knew.

Harriet whispered confidentially, "I think a family album's perfect. I haven't seen it yet, but I know my grandson will love the gift."

Renee's love and respect for this woman grew. She understood Aaron.

"After Christmas you must pay me a visit. I have some more pictures for you to put in the album. I went through our old photo albums and even contacted my sister-in-law to see if she had some photographs. We have Chapin pictures going five generations back. I know it's a gift for Aaron and one day for Adam, but the entire family is going to want a copy of it."

Renee smiled. "It's funny you should say that. I've been thinking of putting it all on the computer."

"That would be wonderful! Of course, us old folks wouldn't mind a paper copy." Harriet sat straight up in her chair. "But we'll have plenty of time to get a copy."

"The pig is done! The pig is done!" Adam cried out from the backyard.

Harriet slowly stood up. "This is part of the tradition. All gather in the backyard and watch them take the pig off the pit." Renee followed Harriet.

Aaron came up from behind, grabbed her wrist, and pressed her forefinger to his lips. She turned and followed while the others went toward the backyard.

"Renee, I only have a couple minutes. It doesn't take long for the family to come back into the house after the pig is removed from the pit."

"What's the matter, Aaron?" She rubbed the top of his hand with the ball of her thumb.

"Nothing's the matter. I just wanted to have a little private time with you."

She grinned. "I like your grandmother."

"She's a sweetheart. But seriously, Renee, I need to speak with you."

She stiffened. "All right."

"No, no, nothing bad. Oh, goodness. . ." He fumbled for the small box he'd placed in his front pocket. *I don't know why I'm so nervous.* He bent down on one knee.

She gasped, placing her hands over her mouth.

"Renee, I love you, and I prepared a wonderfully romantic speech, but for now I just need to know, would you do me the honor of becoming my wife?"

Her eyes glistened from unshed tears.

"I was going to ask you at *misa del gallo,* but I couldn't wait until midnight. And I figured you might not like to be embarrassed in front of my entire family. Please, Renee, I've never felt more certain of God's choice in my life. Will you marry me?"

"Yes!" she burst out.

He stood up and handed the small package to her. "Open it."

Her hands shook as she tore off the wrapping. She paused, holding the blue velvet case in her fingers, then carefully opened the lid. "Oh my. Aaron, it's beautiful."

"I guessed at your size. The jeweler says he can resize it if we need him to. May I?"

She held out her left hand for him. He kissed her ring finger, then carefully slid the ring onto it. Rainbows of color sparkled from the polished diamond.

"It's three bands of gold," Aaron explained. "One band for you and one band for me—both of those are the yellow bands. The third is white gold, and that represents the Holy Spirit. In Ecclesiastes 4:12 the Bible states, 'Though one may be overpowered, two can defend themselves. A cord of three strands is not quickly broken.'

"With all that we've been through over the past couple months," he continued, "I felt this scripture really applied to us. What do you think?"

Renee found her voice. "I think I love you. I can't believe this. I've wanted it, prayed for it, but I was afraid to believe it was possible."

"Renee, I love you. I want you to be my wife, my helpmate, my friend, and the mother to our children. All of them."

"I want that, too. I love you."

"Then kiss me and seal this deal," he crooned.

She leaped into his arms and kissed him soundly on the lips. "Have mercy," he moaned and recaptured her lips once again.

A round of cheers and whistles came from behind them. Slowly they pulled apart, but he held her close.

"Daaad!" Adam dragged out his name. "The pig is done. Didn't you hear me?"

"Yes, son." Renee and Aaron joined the rest of the family and roared with laughter. "Merry Christmas, Renee. Welcome to my family."

"Merry Christmas, Aaron. I'll enjoy getting to know every one of them."

LYNN A. COLEMAN

Lynn is an award-winning and bestselling author. She is the cofounder of American Christian Fiction Writers, Inc. and served as the group's first president and on the advisory board. She makes her home in Keystone Heights, Florida, where her husband of thirty-four years serves as pastor of Friendship Bible Church. Together they are blessed with three children and eight grandchildren. She loves hearing from her readers. Visit her Web page at www.lynncoleman.com to drop her a note.

The Heart of the Matter

by Kristy Dykes

Dedication

To my hero husband, Milton, who is my collaborator in the deepest sense of the word—he's believed in me, supported me, and cheered me on in my calling to inspirational writing. Thank you, Emmett and Sonja, for all the times you've entertained us at your lovely home on the water. It was the inspiration for the setting of this novel. And when you shared with me the pictures you captured of your glorious double sunset over the water—as well as your toothbrushing manatee—well, I got all tingly and knew I had to include them in the novel.

Chapter 1

I want everybody to pray that God will give me a mommy," little Brady said in a heart-tugging, grown-up way.

Luke Moore took a deep gulp as he sat in the church pew and stared at his six-year-old son—the boy who'd just made the prayer request.

Giggles and guffaws rippled across the sanctuary.

Luke felt the hair on the back of his neck rising. Was every eye on him and Brady? With a quick look around at the mostly elderly congregation, he noted nearly everyone was staring at them.

"I want everybody to pray real hard." Brady stood on tiptoes, clutching the pew in front of him, looking earnestly at Pastor Hughes behind the pulpit.

Luke stretched his long legs out in front of him and traced the crease in his crisply pressed suit pants. *Brady should be in a children's program this morning,* he thought with a rueful pang, *if only there were one.* In all the time he'd attended this church, he'd never seen a child give a prayer request in the Sunday morning service. Would the parishioners be offended by Brady's antics?

Luke glanced about the sanctuary, looking for the usual two or three children who regularly attended the church. But he saw only one child this morning. His son.

And my son is now throwing a paper airplane across several rows of empty pews!

"Psst, Brady," he whispered. "Sit down." He tried to keep the irritation out of his voice. No telling what might happen next.

"Don't be a doubting Thomas," Brady sang out in perfect pitch, his unruly blond hair a cross between Dennis the Menace's and Opie Taylor's from the old *Andy Griffith Show* reruns, one of Brady's favorite TV programs. "Trust fully in His promise," he sang. "Why worry, worry, worry, worry—when you can pray?"

A tidal wave of deep chuckles and bright laughter swept through the congregation.

Pastor Hughes attempted to restore order, then gave up. He was laughing too hard.

Luke drew a sigh of relief as Brady finally plopped down on the pew. The tyke glanced up at him, looking as pleased as a peacock, his giant smile revealing a missing front tooth. Luke's heart warmed to the boy.

"Brady wants a mommy," Pastor Hughes said good-naturedly from the pulpit. His face took on a serious look. "Folks, never discount a little one's simple faith. In fact, the Lord Himself instructed us to come to Him with childlike trust for our needs. Let's bow our heads and do just that. Let's go to the Lord with childlike faith. Brother Jernigan, will you stand and lead us to the Lord in prayer?"

An elderly man rose slowly to his feet. "Father God, Almighty Lord in heaven, we come to Thee with surrendered hearts. . . ."

Luke closed his eyes and tried to concentrate on Brother Jernigan's prayer. But he couldn't. He was thinking about what Brady had said. *A mommy.*

It was as if Luke weren't sitting on a padded pew in Christ Church in Silver Bay, Florida. Instead it was several years ago, and his wife, Sarah, was telling him about a young woman she'd met at church that morning. . . .

∞

"My heart goes out to this girl," Sarah had said as they drove home from church. "She has a three-year-old son she's giving up for adoption." Her eyes misted with tears.

Luke swallowed hard, feeling her pain. The greatest desire of Sarah's heart was to have a child. But that would never happen. A doctor's recent diagnosis had confirmed it.

"The girl is a good mother apparently, but she got pregnant young—at fifteen—and she's only eighteen now. . .and. . .well, she feels this is the right thing to do, to give up her son. She's looking for a Christian couple who wants to adopt."

Luke realized he was gripping the steering wheel as if he were having a blow-out. He forced himself to relax his hands. But he couldn't relax his inner quakings. He knew what this was leading to, what Sarah might ask.

"Luke. . ."

He kept his eyes on the road, wondering what Sarah would say next. She knew their agreement. They'd made a pact never to bring up the subject of adoption again. They'd reached that conclusion after two adoptions had fallen through and the pain was simply too great to bear. For her. For him. He wanted a child, too.

Sarah reached across the car and touched his arm. "I always wanted *your* child, Luke. One who looked just like you. I wanted him or her to have dark brown hair and dancing eyes like yours. And I wanted him to have a strong sense of what's right, just like you do." Her voice broke. "I. . .we both know. . . that can't happen. At least not in the way we expected it to. But after hearing the girl's story this morning, I'm wondering if God is about to drop a blond-haired, freckle-faced boy into our laps. He's so cute. Just wait till you see him."

Within months he and Sarah had signed the papers and joyfully welcomed Brady into their home as their son. Sarah, especially, had been in heaven.

Two years later she really *was* in heaven. She'd passed away from a fast-growing cancer.

∞

Lord, Luke prayed, *give me the strength and wisdom for the momentous task You've called me to do—to raise a son by myself, at least for the time being.*

Brady pulled on Luke's coat sleeve. "You can open your eyes, Dad," he chirped in his loud, high-pitched voice for all to hear. "Brother Jernigan said 'amen' a long time ago."

Luke felt his neck burning, but he smiled. *Little boys can certainly keep life interesting.*

Pastor Hughes read the scriptures, then began preaching.

Luke pulled a pen and notepad out of his coat pocket and handed them to Brady, hoping they would keep him occupied. As the pastor talked about temples and trumpets, Luke's mind wandered again as he thought about his many conversations with well-meaning friends.

"When are you going to start dating?" they frequently asked. "You need a wife, and Brady needs a mother."

Luke couldn't disagree with them. What they said was true. Trouble was, there was no one in the church to date, at least no one who interested him. He knew he probably wouldn't find a cover-girl, perfect wife like Sarah, but he wanted whomever he married to be attractive and stylish. In his line of work, a financial advisor at Gulf State Bank, he had to attend and host numerous events—parties, banquets, gala affairs, and more—with the elite of society.

Sarah had always loved attending those functions with him, dressed in feminine after-five attire and promenading by his side, making him proud. She'd been the diamond among the rhinestones with her keen sense of style and her unparalleled beauty. She'd even won him a few clients with her charming, amusing ways.

"Why can't you find a wife?" a friend wondered. "You go to plenty of social events. Women are all around you, if only you'd look."

His friends were right. To a degree. For instance, last evening he'd attended a dinner party in a client's home. Among the twenty or so guests, two single women were there. One even flirted with him, pretty brazenly, he thought. But he'd shied away. To his way of thinking, the only women who made good wives were church women—dedicated Christians. Trouble was, all the women he knew at Christ Church were married—or old enough to be his mother or grandmother. So forget that.

"Why don't you change churches?" another friend suggested.

No way. When they'd moved to Silver Bay, the town Sarah grew up in, they'd chosen to join her home church from childhood. Several years ago Luke had been elected to a deacon's position, and he would be loyal to Christ Church no matter what.

"Then why don't you attend some singles' groups in other churches? Surely you can meet someone at one of those. Large churches have lots of singles' events."

Right again. Only he didn't have time to go traipsing all over, scouting out women. Maybe when Brady was older. But not now. Fatherhood was demanding with a capital *D*. And so was his job. How would he find baby-sitters for Brady if he were to go on numerous dates? He could barely find them for his business engagements. Mrs. Nelms, the elderly woman who'd baby-sat twice last week—and many times in the last six months—had recently made it clear that she wasn't finding enough time for her own grandchildren. Last night, for the dinner party he'd gone to, she'd turned him down, and only after several frantic attempts had he found a sitter.

"I repeat, Luke," Pastor Hughes said from the pulpit. "Will you stand and close our service in prayer?"

Luke shot to his feet, smoothed his trousers, fumbled with the buttons of his navy suit coat.

"Dear ones," Pastor Hughes said to the congregation, "shall we bow our heads as Luke leads us to the Lord in prayer?"

Luke led in prayer—shakily—feeling guilty that his mind had wandered during the sermon. When he came to the close of his prayer, he said a respectful "Amen," turned around, and gathered his notepad and pen. "Brady, it's time to go."

"Yippee!"

"Son—" One glance at little Brady, and Luke was squelching a big smile.

"Oh, I forgot." Pastor Hughes leaned into the microphone on the pulpit. "Folks, I really do have a good memory." He touched his graying temples. "It's just short." He burst out into big chuckles. "We have one more thing to do before we go. Everyone, please sit down. I want to introduce you to someone."

The congregation took their seats.

"I'd like for Dr. Jeris Waldron to come to the pulpit. She has a special announcement to make."

Luke heard a slight noise behind him, turned, and saw Jeris Waldron stand up. She was the woman he'd met a few weeks ago after morning worship. Pastor Hughes had introduced them in the church foyer. He'd sat by her during Sunday school a couple of times. Luke hadn't noticed she was sitting in the pew behind him this morning.

Absently he watched as she made her way to the front of the sanctuary. He pushed in the button on his ballpoint pen. In, out, in, out. A few moments ago he'd been thinking there weren't any women of marriageable age in the church. Of course, Jeris Waldron was of marriageable age. But she didn't meet the criteria he had for a wife. He noticed her bland appearance—very little makeup, an ugly black oversized jacket, and a black skirt that was too long. And with no jewelry, it was apparent she didn't know how to accessorize. Last Sunday she'd worn a gray outfit like the one she had on today.

A gray persona. He winced, feeling bad that his honest assessment was so critical. But it seemed to fit her perfectly.

"I believe some of you have met Jeris," Pastor Hughes said. "She recently joined our church. She's a child psychologist and is starting a new practice here in Silver Bay. Jeris is the daughter of a former parishioner in Winter Haven whom my wife and I knew when we pastored there years ago. She was like a daughter to us when she was growing up. When we found out she moved here, we went to see her and asked her to join Christ Church. To our delight she did. Now we've convinced her to accept a new undertaking. She's going to tell you about it." He took a seat to the right of the pulpit.

Jeris crossed the platform, placed a notebook on the pulpit, and adjusted the microphone to her mouth. "Thank you, Pastor Hughes. I'm happy to be a member of Christ Church." For several moments she bragged on Pastor and Mrs. Hughes, how fine they were as pastors, how much they loved their parishioners, and how she had received that love beginning when she was a child.

She cleared her throat and opened her notebook. "I'm pleased to tell everyone I'll soon be starting a children's church program during the morning worship service."

Polite murmurs could be heard from the members of the congregation.

That's wonderful, Luke almost said out loud. He figured Jeris Waldron would be great with kids. She would probably apply her vast knowledge of psychobabble to teaching them, and that would be a good thing.

"Brady, that's your new children's church teacher," Luke whispered.

Brady was drawing circles on four different offering envelopes. He didn't look up but kept drawing.

"I have big plans for the children's church program." Jeris's voice dripped with enthusiasm, and her face lit up. "First of all, I'd like to see it grow. If any of you have grandchildren or know of children who aren't attending church elsewhere, I'd like to find out about them. I intend to make home visits and tell people about our program. Please write down the names and addresses of any children you may know and turn them in to me."

Luke heard whispers. He glanced around and saw pleased expressions on people's faces.

"Second, I'm planning some exciting events for the children. Parties, puppet shows, picnics, and more. This will not only attract new children but it will also minister to the children we now have. If you get a call asking for assistance in chaperoning or for other duties, I hope you'll be willing to help out.

"Third, and most important, I'm doing this for a purpose; and that purpose is to win souls—children's souls—to Christ. Statistics show that most people who are living for the Lord were won to Christ when they were children. It's important for us to provide a climate in this church where young hearts can be influenced for God."

She leaned into the pulpit, probably for emphasis. "It's been said that a man asked the famous minister of yesteryear, D. L. Moody, how many people got saved in his revival meeting on a particular night. Moody told the man two and a half. The man said, 'You mean two adults and one child?' Moody said, 'No, two children and one adult.' The man was surprised, but Moody explained that children were just as important to the Lord as adults. Moody went on to say that when children give their hearts to the Lord, they have their entire lives to work for Christ; but when adults get saved, they have very little time left to devote to Him."

The church members applauded.

Luke clapped, too, but he was fuzzy about what he was applauding for—some minister from yesteryear? Charging through his brain were the myriad things that awaited him at the office tomorrow.

Maybe I should get some work done this afternoon.

He bit his bottom lip, engrossed in his thoughts. When he tuned back in to the pulpit goings-on, Jeris Waldron was filling in the details of her strategy for her children's church program.

Of course he was happy about her plans. Clearly the program would benefit Brady, and that was a pleasant, even welcoming, thought. He'd be taught the Bible on his level during the morning worship service. No more paper airplanes sailing across the sanctuary. And no more prayer requests about a mommy.

But Luke hoped he wouldn't be called on to assist with class parties and picnics. He didn't have a minute to spare.

Even for such a worthy cause.

Chapter 2

Jeris looked across the dining room table at Pastor Hughes and his wife. She was enjoying spending time with them in their parsonage and discussing her plans for the new children's church program. Pastor Hughes was telling a preacher joke, and she and Audra Darling were laughing.

The pastor's wife would always be Audra Darling to Jeris, what she'd told Jeris to call her as a child. It had to do with a Southern thing, Jeris mused. The Hugheses were originally from Alabama. It also had to do with the fact that Audra wanted to be called something special by children, and all children called her this endearing name.

Jeris smiled as she thought about how Audra Darling pronounced her name. It came out as a Southern *Au–dra Dah–lin'*. Jeris smiled again, thinking she was probably the only adult who called her Audra Darling. But that was okay with her. It spoke of the bond between them.

"Thank you for a delicious dinner," Jeris said. "Again." This was the second time they'd invited her for dinner since her move to Silver Bay.

"You're mighty welcome, Jeris." Pastor Hughes drained his iced tea glass and set it on the table. "You have a standing invitation."

Jeris flashed them a big smile. "Do you know what that means to a single woman who's just moved to a new town and doesn't know a soul?"

"It means you can come over anytime you want," Audra Darling said. "Isn't that right, Andrew?"

Pastor Hughes nodded vigorously.

Audra Darling stood, picked up Jeris's plate, and raked the scraps onto her own plate. "In fact, we expect you to." She picked up her husband's plate and did the same. "You're a grown-up version of the fine little girl we used to know when we pastored the church you grew up in, and we're looking forward to some good times with you now that you've moved to Silver Bay."

Jeris felt moisture forming in her eyes as she recalled happy times spent with the Hugheses. They'd never had children of their own, and they'd been almost like a second set of parents to Jeris. She had loved them that much.

Age-wise they were the same as her parents. But physically they were nothing alike. Her dad was short. Pastor Hughes had a commanding presence with his over six-foot height. And her mother was the exact opposite of Audra Darling in the looks department. Where her mother was a jeans-and-T-shirt-type woman, Audra Darling was elegant with her sophisticated clothing and highlighted hairstyles that changed every few months.

Jeris looked over at her now, noticed her bright red manicure that matched her striking red suit, heard the jangle of her silver charm bracelet as she reached for a serving bowl, and pictured the red high heels she was wearing that showcased a red pedicure.

The phone rang.

"Excuse me a moment." Pastor Hughes reached behind him and picked up a phone on the buffet, then stood, gestured toward the family room, and left.

"Isn't it interesting how life turns out?" Jeris handed her salad plate to Audra Darling. "Who knew way back then I'd be working in a town you two happened to be pastoring in?"

"God." Audra Darling's gaze was piercing, as if it could read Jeris's thoughts.

Jeris nodded. Audra Darling could be depended on to assess a person or a situation, and she no doubt was discerning this situation correctly—that God had brought Jeris to Silver Bay. Jeris had prayed for God's guidance before choosing the town to start her practice in, and she believed He had guided her.

"He's got His reasons for bringing you here. And He'll let you know in the by-and-by." Audra Darling chuckled. "And I don't mean in the *sweet* by-and-by either."

Jeris laughed at her reference to the afterlife.

"The Bible says our steps are ordered by the Lord." Audra Darling scraped the salad plates and stacked them.

"I memorized that verse as a child."

"And our stops are, too, as D. L. Moody once said."

"I've never heard that quote. That's pretty good."

Audra Darling wagged her head. "We've had several stops in our ministry, times when the Lord led us to move on to take another pastorate in a different town."

"I'm glad He led you here and that you were willing to come." Jeris envisioned Christ Church. Though the congregation was small and the buildings old, she had confidence the Hugheses would see growth once they'd been here awhile. They'd moved to Silver Bay only months before Jeris did. "I'm glad He led me here, too."

"We love the people. And Silver Bay. I believe we'll be here until we retire. We have big hopes and dreams for the church's future."

"Then I'll be able to sit under your ministry for at least—what? Ten more years? Isn't Pastor Hughes fifty-five now, as my dad is?"

Audra Darling nodded. "And maybe we'll stay a year or two beyond that."

"That's great to hear. Twelve more years with you as my pastors."

"Nothing could please us more." Audra Darling flashed her a brilliant smile. "Maybe when you're married and have children, your kids'll look at Andrew and me as another set of grandparents."

My kids? What a pleasant thought. Jeris had counseled lots of children and had a special connection with them. She looked forward to the day when she had kids of her own. On second thought, perhaps she should say *if.* The years were ticking by fast.

"I'm praying God will send you a fine Christian man, Jeris."

Jeris was at a loss for words. She certainly hoped the same thing. But what could she say? No men were on the horizon, not even within radar range.

Audra Darling picked up the stack of dishes and made her way toward the kitchen. "I'll be back in a jiffy with our dessert."

"May I help?" Jeris stood.

"No." Audra Darling waved her back down. "Sit tight. Won't take me but a minute. You might like looking through the church pictorial directory. It's on the buffet. It'll help you put the names with the faces of our members. It helped me when we moved here."

"That's a good idea." Jeris reached over and picked up the directory, her thoughts on the Hugheses as pastors. She flipped through the booklet, looking at each picture, reading each name. Every church the Hugheses had pastored had grown under their leadership. And, more important, their parishioners had been nurtured and spiritually fed. Everybody loved them.

She remembered when they'd moved away from Winter Haven and how sad the church folks had been to see them go, her family included. She was sixteen at the time, and they'd promised to come back for her high school graduation, which they did.

When Jeris married at twenty, Pastor Hughes performed the ceremony, something she'd planned on since she was a child. He also conducted Jeris's husband's funeral three years later. That was a long time ago—nine years. Now her life had meaning and purpose in her profession as a child psychologist. That was what she focused on these days.

Audra Darling came back into the dining room, carrying a tray with a layer cake on one end and cups and plates on the other. She set it on the table, poured coffee into a cup, and held it out to Jeris. "You take cream? Sugar? Sweetener?"

"Cream." Jeris took the cup and poured cream into it. "Thanks."

Just then Pastor Hughes hurried into the dining room. "I have to get to the hospital."

Audra Darling put her hand over her heart. "Is it Brother Ward?" She turned to Jeris. "He's in the last stages of congestive heart failure and has complications. Diabetes, too. They've given him less than three months to live. He's only in his forties." She shook her head. "Did he—"

"No. As far as I know, he's still okay. This call came from Sister Sloan's daughter. Her mother tripped on a throw rug, and they're rushing her to the ER. She may have broken her hip, and you know what that means. Surgery, usually."

"Poor Sister Sloan." Audra Darling looked at Jeris again, concern etched in her features. "She's a charter member of Christ Church. She's ninety-seven and has dementia." She turned back to her husband. "Do you think she's strong enough to come through it?"

"I don't know. But I *do* know she—and her family—need our prayers."

"Do you want me to go with you?"

"No need to. You stay here and visit with Jeris. I'll call you after I find out the prognosis." He kissed his wife. "But don't look to hear from me for several hours. You know how emergency rooms are. See you." He said good-bye to Jeris and left.

Jeris marveled at what had just transpired. To be cared for by such a fine pastor and his wife was a blessed state, in Jeris's opinion. And she welcomed being cared for. She'd spent the last decade earning several degrees and had taken no time for herself or anyone else. Studying and applying herself to her chosen field had been her way of life. Now she was being pulled into the warmth and loving care of the Hugheses. And the thought was music to her ears.

Audra Darling sat down. "Mind if we pray for Sister Sloan before we eat our dessert?"

"Oh, let's do. Sounds like she's going to need it."

Audra Darling reached for Jeris's hand and led in prayer. When she finished praying, she sliced the cake and handed Jeris a piece.

For more than an hour they chatted about Audra Darling's cake recipe, the church, the ministry, Silver Bay, Audra Darling's interests, and more.

The conversation turned to Jeris, her move to Silver Bay, her interests, and then to her new practice.

"What made you want to become a psychologist, Jeris?"

Jeris smiled, thinking about the twists and turns of life that sometimes propelled one to follow a certain course.

"When you started college, wasn't education your major? Wasn't that what you told us you were going to study when we asked you at your graduation party?"

Jeris nodded, remembering the festive occasion. "I wasn't sure what I wanted to be."

"Like many graduating seniors."

"I thought teaching would be a good thing."

"But you quit college two years later to get married."

"Wesley and I fell in love when I was seventeen. When I turned twenty, he said, 'Why wait?' After all, he was twenty-six and had already graduated from college. He was eager to get married."

Audra Darling placed her hand over Jeris's. "And then you had only three years together as husband and wife. Sometimes life is hard to understand. Who would have thought he'd die so soon?"

Jeris nodded soberly, remembering the exact moment she'd received the news of the small plane accident that took her husband's life.

"My heart went out to Wesley the first time I saw him. He was just a boy—maybe six or seven years old—and he was climbing down from that great big church bus." Audra Darling rubbed the rim of her coffee cup, her gaze fixed on the glass-fronted china cabinet across the room. "His home life. . .it was so. . .tragic. An alcoholic father. . .a mother who didn't have enough backbone to. . .to protect her little ones from his meanness." She swallowed. "We tried to help him. And his family, too. We tried so hard."

"You did a lot for them. Wesley always said that. Through yours and Pastor Hughes's help, he and his family had good things to eat and clothes to wear. And he came to know Christ. That's the most important thing of all."

"When you called and told me you were marrying him, I'll have to admit I couldn't picture you two together." She paused. "Your backgrounds were so diff-erent." Her voice was almost a whisper. "I wish—" She stopped abruptly. Silence hung in the air. "He. . .he was a good Christian boy."

He was a product of his upbringing. Jeris took a sip of her coffee, now cold.

"He died so young." Audra Darling shook her head, her brows drawn together. "Knowing what Wesley went through in childhood, was that what propelled you into the field of psychology? You saw what he experienced, and now you want to help others?"

Knowing Wesley propelled me into the field of psychology. Period.

∞

After a pleasant afternoon with Audra Darling, Jeris felt glowingly good as she drove home, despite the overcast sky. The woman had a way of bringing sun-shine into any situation, it seemed. They'd chatted and laughed like girlfriends who were the same age, not like what they really were—one old enough to be the other one's mother. Audra Darling was fun, but she was spiritually refreshing, too.

A gentle January rain started, and Jeris flicked on her windshield wipers. Recalling a TV weather report, she slowed down. The weatherman said the first few minutes of rain were as prone to cause accidents in Florida as snowstorms up North because of hydroplaning. The water mixed with the oil on the streets and became as slick as glass, causing a car to slide sideways and possibly wreck. Only when the streets were thoroughly wet did the risk of accidents decrease, the weatherman said.

I sure don't want to hydroplane. On this road. Or in my life.

Now that she'd started her own practice, she was excited about what lay ahead. She wanted to set a steady course on what would bring her fulfillment and happiness and not get sidetracked.

In the professional arena, she hoped to become a well-respected child psychologist in Silver Bay with a thriving practice. She ached for children with deep-seated needs and would work hard to help them.

In spiritual matters she wanted to serve the Lord and put Him first. She'd done that since she was a child and would continue. She looked forward to teaching children's church and influencing little lives for God.

She had financial goals, too. She hoped to earn enough money to own a home and take pleasant vacations. She had a good car and a nice apartment, but owning a home would give her a sense of permanency and roots. And vacations would give her rest and relaxation so she could come back refueled and refreshed.

She also desired to make new friends in social settings. She'd always been on the shy side, and friendships had come hard for her. But she planned to reach out more, to show herself friendly, as the Bible put it. And having the dazzling Audra Darling as her mentor, she felt certain of success.

The rain increased, and she turned her wipers on high speed.

Whop-whop, whop-whop, whop-whop, the wipers droned. Combined with the driving rain hitting the car, the noise was enough to drown out her thoughts for a moment.

Good, because the only other area of my life I can think of is romance, and I'm not sure about that.

Romance? She'd had that once. Or at least what she thought was romance. At seventeen, who knew what anything was, especially love? She'd been fooled. Wesley's attentiveness, affection, and tender ways when they dated turned into domination, jealousy, and control as soon as they walked up the aisle.

"The last time I fell in love, I was seventeen years old and as naive as a newborn," she whispered, as if to summon up strength for the determination forming in her heart. "The next time I give my heart away, I won't be as foolish. A good-looking man will *not* sway me."

Movie-star handsome, Wesley had constantly belittled her after marriage. He'd humiliated her for everything, it seemed, particularly her plain-Jane appearance and lack of education. She couldn't seem to find her way career-wise, and he took delight in pressing that upon her at every opportunity. She'd tried several jobs, but nothing worked out. She'd felt worthless. According to Wesley, she wouldn't know how to put fries in the grease at a fast-food restaurant.

With tears and a hurting heart she would try to talk to him about his attacks and tell him he couldn't keep treating her that way. But he would tell her he didn't know what she was talking about, then berate *her* for her audacity to bring up such awful accusations against *him*.

She didn't know then that he was a product of his up-bringing, as she'd thought when listening to Audra Darling today. She didn't have a clue why he treated her the way he did. The only thing she knew was to cry out to God and ask Him to give her a strong, faithful love for Wesley.

And God did. He answered her prayers. She determined she would stay true to Wesley because she'd made a vow before God and man, as her grandmother used to put it. And she determined to love him, no matter what.

To try to please Wesley, she'd enrolled in college again. Perhaps something would click for her and she would find her career path. One of the first courses she took was psychology. During her first semester, she discovered why Wesley was the way he was.

Then he died. She grieved for him as if he'd been Prince Charming. She'd loved him with her heart, soul, mind, and strength; and she'd been more wounded at his death than in living with him, if that could be so. Only a person who'd walked in her shoes could understand that.

It was shortly after his death that she knew what she wanted to do. She would spend her life helping people understand what was happening to them and why they acted the way they did, particularly children. And then she would help them change their behavior.

Nine long years had passed since Wesley died. She was ready for a relationship and had been for some time. Like any woman, she wanted to love and be loved. But she was wiser now; she had more head knowledge and heart knowledge. She would be careful, as cautious as a kid on his first day of swimming lessons. She had decided she would be discerning in her choice, unlike last time.

The last few years, no one had come along for her. Her time clock was ticking. Would she go through the rest of her life single, as her aunt Betsy had?

"I would've married, if only the right man had knocked at my door," Aunt Betsy always said. "But he never did. So I just continued on my merry way. Did I say 'merry'?" she would add with a wry smile.

Jeris saw the windows fogging. She leaned toward the dashboard and turned on the defroster. *Is that how it'll be for me someday? Fifty-four years old like Aunt Betsy and not married?*

Her stomach knotted, and her heart pounded. She didn't want to go through life single and alone, without a man to care for her and her to care for him. She wanted a husband. And she wanted children. Two, maybe three.

Whop-whop, whop-whop, whop-whop.

Was that her heart or the wipers?

∽

Sitting at the kitchen table with her husband, Audra ate a bite of toast. She loved this time of day. They read the Bible and prayed together. After that, they read the newspaper, then began their busy day.

Andrew chuckled. "Listen to this." He described that day's installment of his favorite cartoon, the one about the couple who constantly locked horns in marital battles.

They both laughed.

Audra took a sip of coffee. "Listen to this." She read aloud each frame of the comic that featured the long-time single woman who'd finally found her man. "I wonder if Jeris follows this comic strip? It might give her hope that she'll find Mr. Right."

"Mr. Right?"

"I told her yesterday I'm praying for God to send her a husband. If ever a girl deserves a good man, it's Jeris." She paused as she looked out the bank of windows facing the water. "I can't wait to see her married and happy, with a houseful of children—"

"A houseful?"

"You know what I mean. Two. Several. Whatever she wants. She's going to make a great mother."

"Like you."

She thought of what Andrew had told her many times. He'd said that even though God didn't send them children, He had used her to minister to many women, and by doing that she'd become their spiritual mother.

"I'm glad Jeris moved here. I think one reason God sent her is for you to be a friend to her, Audra."

She nodded. "I look forward to that. She's a neat young woman."

"And I believe the Lord is going to use you to lend your expertise to help her."

"Expertise?"

"Can you take her shopping?"

She knew exactly what he was talking about.

"She wears such old-looking clothes."

"They're expensive."

"I don't doubt that. Jeris has good taste. Unfortunately it doesn't manifest itself in her clothes."

"They're called travel knits."

"But nobody her age wears that stuff. You don't even wear things like that."

She looked down at her outfit. She was wearing a crisp white cotton blouse that had tiny tucks down the front and hung over her tiered brown gauzy skirt. She wore a bronze metallic belt low-slung at her hipline that matched her bronze metallic, high-heeled, open-toed shoes. It was the latest look, and she had several of the new tiered skirts. She could dress them up or down depending on the occasion. Put a fitted t-shirt with a tiered skirt and team them with raffia-beaded wedges, and she could go to a picnic, as she'd done yesterday. Today, for the church office, she'd chosen the dressier look with heels.

"Why don't you take her shopping and get her to buy some outfits like you're wearing? Or something similar?"

She thought about the bland colors Jeris wore and the sameness of the style. A gray knit suit. A black knit suit. A brown knit suit. A taupe knit suit.

"Why don't you two go to the new mall that just opened in Tampa? Take a whole Saturday and show her the ropes. Shop to your heart's content."

"And I could get some new outfits, too, huh?" She grinned at him.

He chuckled.

"I could take her to a cosmetic counter and let the girl give her a makeover.

And maybe I could schedule an appointment at the hair salon so they could update her style."

"And please get her to buy some new shoes."

She laughed, envisioning Jeris's shoes. Like her knit suits, they were all the same. Closed-in loafers with short heels. And she nearly always wore black tights or black hose. "But I wouldn't want to offend her with any of this. I wouldn't want to risk hurting her feelings. She's too sweet a girl."

"She's a psychologist. Explain what you have in mind and the rationale behind it."

"That she should be wearing brighter, younger-looking clothing because she's young and has great skin and facial features and hair, and she should be showing them to their best advantage?"

He winked at her. "You're right on track." He wiped his mouth with his napkin, then stood up. "We need to get going."

"Andrew?" She looked up at him.

He glanced at his watch, then picked up his Bible, put it in his briefcase, and snapped it shut. "Yes?"

"Remember when I said I told Jeris I'm praying that God will send her a husband?"

"Yes, I do."

"I think Luke would be the perfect candidate."

"Don't tell me you're going to do some matchmaking between them." He set his briefcase on the floor and stood there looking at her, his eyebrows drawn together.

Audra playfully jutted her chin in the air. "It worked for Al and Gloria, didn't it?"

"I guess I can't deny that."

"And that's the only time I've ever tried matchmaking, you have to admit." She stood up and pushed her chair under the table.

"Right."

"You know I don't go around poking in other people's business."

"I've seen enough pastors' wives like that, and I'm mighty glad you're not one of them."

"But I definitely felt the leading of the Lord concerning Al and Gloria. All I did was point them in the right direction."

He laughed. "Toward each other. By inviting them both to dinner several times."

"It worked, didn't it?"

He pulled her to him in a big bear hug. "I think they're almost as happy as we are." He drew back and gave her a syrupy look, then grinned.

She smoothed his shirt placket, her mind still on Jeris and Luke. "Jeris needs a husband, and Luke needs a wife."

He nodded. "Luke *does* need a good woman in his life. He needs a special woman, what with having a son and all."

"Jeris could be that woman. In fact, she'd make an ideal wife for him."

"Anything's possible, I suppose."

"The Bible says, 'With God all things are possible.'" She laughed, but she was as serious as she'd ever been.

"True. Jeris is tops in my book. Luke couldn't get a better wife than her. Maybe it'll work out between them."

"I think they'd make a great couple."

"And you said you're praying about it, right?" He rolled his eyes, but he was smiling at her.

She smiled back. Brilliantly. "Sometimes prayers need legs." She pictured a prayer in a cartoon's dialogue cloud. Underneath was a set of legs. They were wearing bronze metallic, high-heeled, open-toed shoes.

Chapter 3

Jeris turned on the portable CD player and smiled as the lively children's praise song filled her classroom. It was early, and she'd have plenty of time to get things ready.

She scanned the room, pleased with the work she'd accomplished this week. A low table in the center would seat eight or ten children—she had high expectations—for coloring and table games. And stations against the walls would provide a variety of activities—a dress-up area with Bible character costumes, a cozy reading circle complete with a rug and bean-bag chairs, a kitchen for the girls, a tool bench for the boys, a track with cars and trucks, and shelves holding building blocks.

She'd collected some things from classrooms that weren't being used. Other items she'd purchased. Besides the stations, the children would have plenty of space to prance around to the beat of the praise music during song time. She couldn't wait to see the classroom filled with activity.

How many children would show up this morning? Besides preparing the classroom in the evenings after work, she'd made calls and visits, trying to drum up some students. She felt sure Brady Moore would be here today. He was a regular. And the other two children who attended Christ Church. But she hoped she'd have at least a few more.

She made her way to the tall metal cabinet and pulled out several new boxes of crayons and two stacks of papers she'd photocopied from the master book. She walked over to the table in the center of the room, placed the crayons on it, and put a coloring sheet at each place.

"Dr. Waldron?"

She turned around when she heard a man call her name, the second stack of papers still in her arms. She spotted Luke Moore and his little son, Brady, standing in the doorway. "Luke, Brady." She rushed over to the door and gave the child an exuberant hug. "Please come in, both of you." She released Brady and thrust out her arm toward the room. "Brady, I have some nice activities planned for you."

Brady stood as if transfixed by the wonderful things he saw.

"Brady," Luke said, "say, 'Thank you, Dr. Waldron.'"

"Jeris," she corrected. "I want the kids to call me Jeris." She tapped the tip of Brady's nose.

"How about *Miss* Jeris?" Luke said. "When I was growing up, I was always taught to address ladies like that."

"That's okay, too. All right, Brady, I'll be Miss Jeris. How about that?"

"Thank you, Miss Jeris." Brady dashed across the room. He stopped at the car track and pushed a tiny truck along the grooves. "Vroom, vroom, vroom."

"See you later, Brady," Luke said.

"Vroom, vroom, vroom."

Luke shrugged his shoulders at Brady's lack of response. "Looks as if he's going to enjoy your class, Ms. Waldron. Or is it *Dr.* Waldron?"

"I'm hoping all the children will enjoy our class. And it's Jeris." She extended her hand and gave his hand a firm shake.

"Well, I'll see you later. . .Jeris. I'll pick up Brady as soon as church is over." He rushed out of the room.

"No need to hurry," Jeris said into the air. She returned to the table and continued putting papers at each place.

She hadn't expected Luke to hang around as some parents might, either clingy parents or parents trying to soothe an unhappy child. She didn't expect Luke to stay ten minutes. Or even five. She didn't think he needed to make a big effort to get to know his son's new teacher. That wasn't important.

But she *did* expect him to stay a few minutes and talk about Brady. She knew Brady's background, of course, how he'd been adopted and Luke's wife had passed away. Audra Darling had told her that much. She expected Luke to ask a question or two about the new children's church program, maybe make some comments and perhaps tell her a few tidbits about Brady, his favorite activities, his spiritual training, and where he went to school.

But Luke Moore had bothered with none of that. He'd rushed out of her classroom—and away from her—like he was a fireman on the way to a fire.

She'd gotten his meaning loud and clear, hadn't she? She was a psychologist. She possessed an inner sense, a knowledge the average person was unaware of. She watched people's mannerisms and body language, their nuances, what they said—and didn't say, which was as important. She could read people like a book, as the saying went. Simple as that.

And she'd just read Luke Moore. In her opinion Luke Moore wasn't interested in Jeris Waldron, with his handsome good looks and his impeccable attire and his fabulous career. To him, she was too plain and too boring. She didn't have enough pizzazz or wit to attract him.

She put the last coloring sheet on the table, then walked over to the countertop and looked in the upper cabinet for the box of cookies she'd put there earlier.

Luke's sentiments were fine with her, because she felt the same way about him, only from a different angle. He was too handsome for her taste. And too full of himself. She was sure she would find that out when she had more interaction with him—no, *if* she did. He probably would remain aloof and no doubt had an ego as wide as the Gulf of Mexico, like most handsome men.

Give her a balding, bookish guy any day. They had no egos. Only tenderness, what her heart craved from a man.

⚭

"Jeris?"

Grasping the box of cookies, Jeris turned and saw Audra Darling at the door. She was pleased she'd stopped by. She motioned her in. "Come and see my classroom."

"I'd love to. You sure I won't hold you up from what you need to do?" She glanced down at her watch.

"It's still early yet. I have plenty of time before class starts."

Audra Darling made her way across the room and gave Jeris a motherly hug. Her gaze swept the area. "It's nice, Jeris, very nice."

"Thanks. I would've painted it, too, with Pastor Hughes's permission, of course. But I didn't have time." Jeris pointed out the various play stations.

"You did a fine job. The children will love it." Audra Darling looked over at Brady who was busy at the car track. "Come here, Brady Moore, and give me a hug." She smiled and held her arms out to the boy. He ran toward her, and she embraced him, their faces lit up by smiles.

Jeris reached down and caressed Brady's chin. "When'd you lose your tooth, Little Man?"

"Last year." He jumped on one foot, then the other, over and over.

Jeris laughed. "You mean last week or last month, don't you?" She knew most children his age had trouble judging time. And from the looks of his gum, the tooth had only recently come out. "Did you get some money under your pillow?"

He nodded vigorously, his eyes glowing like stars. Then he zoomed back to the car track and picked up two more cars.

"Isn't he darling?" Audra Darling stared after him.

Jeris smiled. Audra Darling loved the word *darling*. "That cute little freckled face will steal your heart." She watched him playing with the cars and trucks as he made his "vroom-vroom" sounds. Little Man would be her nickname for him. She liked it.

"You're looking for an assistant, aren't you?" Audra Darling's eyes twinkled.

"Yes. I have a teenage helper this morning. But I'd like an adult on a permanent basis, and then, as the class grows, I plan to have a couple of teenage helpers every Sunday."

"Would you consider a woman the age of a grandma as your assistant?"

"You?" Jeris was surprised. Audra Darling had never mentioned the possibility.

"Well, you know how much I adore kids."

"Yes."

"And I'm experienced. I've taught all age levels in church work."

"Yes."

"And I have a deep desire to do it."

"Yes."

"And. . .I'd really like to work with you. At least for a while. Would that b okay with you?"

"Yes. Yes. Yes." Jeris laughed.

"I've led women's ministry ever since we've been here. But I just handed i over to a woman I believe will do a good job with it. So I'm free at the momen from ministry duties, and I'm ready to take on something else."

"When can you start?" Jeris laughed again. She was ready to sign her up. I would be a pleasure working closely with her. And she needed the help.

"How about right now?"

"That sounds great."

Audra Darling reached into a black canvas bag on her arm and pulled ou a pink stuffed French poodle. The dog matched her tailored pink linen suit an her pink manicure. She barked like a dog and waggled the stuffed animal in th air. "I came prepared."

Brady came running. "Can I hold your doggie?" He jumped up and dow in front of her.

"Only if you sit down. Fifi likes gentle petting. And she likes to sing. Wan to hear her sing a song?"

Three more children dashed into the room, and Jeris found herself occupie with the parents as she answered questions about the children's church program All the while she noticed Audra Darling interacting with the children in the fre play area and how they seemed to take to her and her to them.

Audra Darling played a significant part in my past, she thought. *Maybe she' do that in my future.*

❦

Jeris spotted Luke as he walked into the classroom to pick up Brady. Sh made her way to him, as she planned to do to every parent, today and every Sunday She wanted to greet each one and be available for any questions, maybe give then a recap of the Bible story she'd taught their children.

"How did Little Man do today?" Luke scanned the classroom. "There he is."

Jeris spotted Brady hammering an oversized plastic nail into a workbench So Luke called him Little Man, too? She thought she'd found a private nick name for him.

"Did he miss me?"

She smiled. "To be truthful, no."

"Thanks a lot."

"What I mean is, we kept them pretty busy."

"I'm just kidding." He glanced around again. "From what I can see, it look like you've created a place kids will be eager to come to every week."

"That's my goal. I did the same thing at my office, too." She thought abou her waiting room—low tables with blocks, toys in a large chest, and a playhouse in the corner with working windows and doors. Her philosophy was to make a child feel comfortable and happy, and perhaps he would talk about what was bothering him.

"Brady," Luke called. "It's time to go."

"Let me get his coloring sheets." She walked to the nearby desk and found Brady's papers, then returned to Luke. "Here."

"Thanks." He folded the papers in half and stuck them in his Bible. "Brady, let's go."

Brady trudged over. "Aw, do we have to, Dad?"

Jeris leaned down to Brady's eye level and touched his cheek. "I have a treat for you, Brady. I have a treat for all the children since this is our first day of class."

Brady jumped up and down. "What is it? What is it?" His eyes were starry, like before, and his grin-with-the-missing-tooth was nearly as wide as his face.

"Normally the treasure box is reserved for—"

"The treasure box?" He jumped higher.

"Hold your horses, son," Luke said. "Let your teacher finish her sentence."

Brady kept jumping.

Jeris started again. "From now on, the treasure box will be for when you kids memorize your Bible verse or bring visitors. But today, since it's our first Sunday, I'm going to let everybody get a prize. Go look in it, Brady, and select anything you'd like."

"Yippee!" He raced away.

"Children, let me have your attention." Jeris turned toward the kids and gave instructions about the treats.

Bedlam broke out. The children saw Brady digging in the treasure box, and they all made a mad dash for it, toys flying in the various play stations and costumes left in heaps. Parents arrived, and by the time she'd delivered the correct coloring sheets—as well as the children—to the correct parents, she noticed Luke and Brady had slipped out.

I never had a chance to tell Luke about our Bible lesson on how to pray.

Into her mind popped the prayer request Brady had belted out last Sunday during the service.

"*I want everybody to pray that God will give me a mommy.*"

☙

"Luke!"

Luke turned around in the narrow hall of the church and saw the pastor's wife hurrying toward him. "Hi, Audra."

"Wait up," she called. "I need to ask you something."

"Sure." He leaned against the wall and watched Brady playing with his ball-on-a-paddle he'd gotten from Jeris's treasure box. "Brady, be careful with that

151

thing. Don't hit anybody if they walk by."

"Yes, sir, Dad." Brady hit it into an open doorway, the ball going crazy on the end of the long elastic cord.

Audra reached Luke. "I saw you come into the children's church room and pick up Brady, but I was putting away the paints and paintbrushes and didn't get a chance to say hello."

"It was pretty busy in there."

"Which we're thrilled about. We had six children in class today. Jeris worked hard all week bringing in new students."

Luke nodded. That was good. Brady would meet some new friends at church. "So you'll be helping with the program?"

"Yes, I volunteered to be Jeris's assistant."

"You certainly love kids. . . ." He looked down at Brady, thinking how much his son liked Audra.

"I'm looking forward to working with them. And with Jeris."

"Pastor said you knew her when she was growing up?"

Audra told him they'd met Jeris when they were pastoring her home church in Winter Haven. "She's always been special to us."

"She seems to feel the same way about you."

Surprise etched Audra's face. "When have you two had time to talk? Have you been out or something?"

"No. I only met her at children's church."

"Of course. I didn't mean to presume."

He shrugged. "I just gathered it from all she said about you and Pastor Hughes from the pulpit last Sunday."

"Oh, that's right. When Andrew called her up to make her announcement?"

Luke nodded. "I figured you were pretty close."

"Can we get hamburgers and milkshakes for lunch today, Dad?" Brady piped up. He stood statue still, his eyes imploring, his palms together in a prayer stance, his ball and paddle stuck in his back pocket.

Luke and Audra laughed.

"Please, Dad? I haven't had a hamburger since—"

"Night before last." Luke smiled, then felt his face growing warm. He didn't want Audra to think he didn't feed his son properly. "We eat out almost every night, but it's not hamburgers all the time. 'Course if Brady had his way we'd be at Jolly Hamburgers five nights a week. But most of the time we eat at Dale's Café. They offer a balanced meal."

"I don't have any hamburgers and milkshakes at my house"—Audra put her hand on Brady's shoulder—"but I have a roast in the oven and rice and gravy and—"

"I hope you're about to invite us to dinner." Luke chuckled, thinking about Audra's dining table laden with food, something he'd enjoyed a couple of times.

"Yes, I am. I'll have Sunday dinner on the table in a jiffy. Can you come?"

"Is the sky blue?" He smiled broadly. "Is grass green?"

Brady looked disappointed.

She caressed Brady behind the ear. "As I said, Brady, I don't have any hamburgers or milkshakes at my house. But Pastor Hughes said the fish were biting yesterday. It's been so warm lately. Maybe you can drop a line in the water and see if you can catch one."

"Yippee!"

"So I can expect you and Brady, Luke?"

"You can count on it. My mouth's already watering."

"Wonderful." She paused, looking contemplative. "I didn't even think to ask. Is it okay for Brady to go out on the dock with his Sunday clothes on? Last time I invited you I called in advance so you'd be prepared."

"It's fine. He'll have a blast. And I'll enjoy it, too. I've been needing to do something like this." He rubbed the back of his neck. "My work's been heavy lately."

"You're a hard worker, Luke."

He shrugged.

"Let's go, Dad." Brady tugged on Luke's suit coat. "I want to go catch some fishes at Audra Darling's house. Maybe if we catch some before she gets there, she'll cook them for us."

Luke laughed. "Well, we'll sure work at it, Little Man. But I think she said a roast is on the menu for today."

Audra shifted the chain of her purse to her other shoulder. "Maybe after we eat, we can all take a boat ride, like we did that other time."

"Yippee!"

"That'll be fun, won't it, Little Man?" Luke envisioned the warm sunshine and the sparkle it put on the surface of the water.

"Yes, sir."

Audra laughed at Brady's grown-up-sounding response. "You've trained him well."

"I work at it." Luke rubbed the top of Brady's head.

"It's evident what a good father you are, Luke." She looked down at her watch, her brows drawn together. "I'll be home in about twenty minutes or so. Unless Sister Sasser snags me in the foyer and tries to show me her scars from her latest surgery. This time it was gall bladder, and they did it by laparoscopy. She has scars here"—she poked at her stomach with a bright-pink fingernail that matched her pink suit—"and here"—she poked another place—"and here"—yet another. "She's apt to give us all the gory details next."

"Audra, you are a mess."

Her eyes twinkled with merriment. "Go on in the house when you get there. You know where I hide the spare key. Same place the last pastor hid it."

"Thanks. See you."

"And go on out to the dock if you like. Andrew left his tackle box and some cane poles on the back porch."

"It sounds so relaxing that I think we'll run by the house and change clothes."

"Then I'll probably beat you. I'll see you when you get there." She patted Brady's shoulder again. "See you, buddy."

"Yes, ma'am."

She smiled. "Your daddy's raising you to be a Southern gentleman through and through. He's a fine daddy." She turned back to Luke. "Oh, I invited Jeris Waldron to come, too. I wanted you to know."

Chapter 4

After Luke and Brady changed clothes, Luke drove to the parsonage while Brady sat in the backseat busily engaged with a video game.

Luke's mouth was watering, as he'd told Audra. The woman was a first-class cook. She ought to write a cookbook—she was that good. He was looking forward to her roast and rice and gravy today. He could almost smell it cooking, that distinct roast beef scent. She'd entertained Brady and him last month and served roast then, too. The other time he'd been there, she'd served baked ham. But he could eat her roast every Sunday and never get tired of it. It beat Dale's Café's roast entrée all to pieces.

He wondered what she would serve for dessert today. Last time it was homemade chocolate cake and ice cream. He hoped she'd have the same—he could never get enough chocolate.

He turned onto Trout River Drive. The parsonage was in an older part of town on a body of water that flowed out to the bay. The church had owned the house for decades. But they'd kept it up, painting it through the years and making other improvements. A few months ago, after the Hugheses accepted the pastorate, the church replaced the kitchen cabinets, refinished the wood floors, and recarpeted the bedrooms, compliments of hard-working retired parishioners who'd put in long hours to get the refurbishing done.

As a board member, Luke had heartily approved the costs. He was glad they'd done it, for Audra's sake. A woman liked a well-kept home. Especially a woman like Audra. He knew it the moment he met her when the board interviewed them. She was a class act, with her up-to-date clothing and hairstyle and her sparkling personality. If he married again he hoped he would find a woman like her, only younger, of course.

And he wanted to marry again.

He contemplated his situation.

"Predicament" was what his friend Ben called it.

"Double bind" was what his business colleague Paul dubbed it.

"Straits" was what his babysitter Mrs. Nelms labeled it.

"Sticky wicket" was how old Brother Jernigan put it.

It seemed he was the brunt of a lot of people's comments. And conversations. And that aggravated him. Why couldn't folks mind their own business? At work and at church he was frequently told that he, as a single man, needed a woman in his life in the worst possible way.

He pulled into the parsonage driveway, letting out a long, steadying breath. Deep down, he admitted to himself, what they said was true. He needed a woman, a wife who would love him and Brady. But he would never let anybody know how he felt. He didn't like talking about it. When the perfect woman came along, he'd make his move. Until then he'd have to wait. And people would, too. That was all there was to it.

As he drove down the long driveway toward the house, he saw Jeris Waldron's car parked close to the garage door. He knew it was hers because he'd seen her leave church in it last Sunday.

Nice. It was an expensive, late-model SUV. *At least you have good taste in cars, Jeris.*

He braked, then threw the gearshift into Park with more force than was necessary. He knew exactly why Audra had invited Jeris today. He could add two and two—after all, he worked at a bank, didn't he? Audra must want to get the two of them together. People did things for a reason. And that was the reason Audra had extended an invitation to Jeris for Sunday dinner—when he and Brady would be there.

How convenient.

"Oh, I invited Jeris Waldron to come, too," Audra had said at the church. *"I wanted you to know."*

He wasn't interested in Jeris. She was an okay woman, but she wasn't in his ballpark. He was sure something would have clicked between them by now if a relationship was meant to be. But he'd felt nothing when he'd seen her, even if it was only a few times.

Why would Audra try to push her on him? Maybe Jeris was in league *with* Audra. Maybe she'd put Audra up to this. Now he felt more than chagrined. He jerked open his car door.

Brady clambered out of the backseat and shut his door. "Hurry, Dad. Let's go fishing."

Luke got out slowly. "Remember? We're eating first. Then we'll go fishing. I'm sure Audra has the food on the table by now. Or almost."

"Aw—"

"Watch your manners, son. And no begging during dinner. When we've finished eating, I'll take you outside. You can't go outside alone because of the water. You understand?"

"Yes, sir."

Brady ran to the front door.

Luke trudged toward the door as if he were going to a root canal. As he passed Jeris's SUV, he thought about what he would face inside the house. A sticky wicket? A good description. It would be awkward and definitely *not* relaxing as he'd first thought when Audra invited him and Brady for the afternoon. Because Jeris would be there.

Well, he would show Audra. And Jeris. He would be polite to her. But that was all.

⁓

"Can we go fishing now, Dad?"

Luke looked down at Brady, pleased at how polite he'd been throughout the leisurely dinner. Audra and Pastor Hughes were superb hosts, and with Audra's cooking, a dinner party at their house was guaranteed to be enjoyable. Today had met his expectations and then some—but only because he'd kept a good distance between himself and Jeris. Just the way he intended for things to remain.

"Da–a–a–d, can we go fishing now?"

Luke took the last bite of his cake—chocolate, as he'd hoped—then wiped his mouth with his napkin. "Five more minutes, Little Man, okay?"

"Yes, sir."

Luke touched his midsection. "Audra, you did it again."

Audra looked across the table at him, smiling. "What?"

He gestured at the bowls on the table. "You scored a ten."

"Thanks, Luke. I love to cook."

"You should give cooking lessons." Jeris put her napkin beside her plate and settled back in her chair. "I, for one, could use some."

"I'll be the first one to sign up," Luke said. "All I know how to do is make toast and coffee. And soup and sandwiches." He paused. "Oh, yes, and cereal." He laughed. "Right, Brady?"

Brady threw him a crooked smile.

Everyone at the table laughed.

A shadow crossed Brady's face, and his bottom lip pooched out. "But sometimes you won't make me the kind of cereal I like."

"You can't have that sugary stuff *every* morning, Brady. Oh, and occasionally I grill hamburgers."

"Hamburgers?" Brady's eyes danced.

Pastor Hughes finished his iced tea, then stood up. "Who's ready to drop a line in the water?"

"Me, me, me!" Brady threw his hand up as if he were in a classroom.

"Then let's go, pardner."

⁓

Jeris rinsed the last pot and placed it on the towel on the counter. "Thanks again for inviting me to dinner, Audra Darling. It was delicious as usual. But I want you to know I don't expect this all the time."

Audra Darling stood at the stovetop, wiping it with a soapy cloth. She waved the air as if dismissing Jeris's remark. "I know that. But let's approach it from this basis. If I invite you, I hope you'll accept and know I'm doing it out of genuinely wanting you to be with us and not from some sense of duty or obligation. Agreed?"

Jeris smiled at her. "Agreed. But I can never reciprocate, at least not by cooking for you. I'm sort of like Luke. I can make toast and coffee. Cereal. Bagels. Canned soup and sandwiches. But unlike him, I've never grilled—"

"You *do* need help, child." Audra Darling glanced out the window at the water as she took off her apron and smoothed the front of her pink linen suit. "Are you ready to go outside? Isn't it a glorious day?"

Jeris nodded. "The last time I was at a theme park, one of the gift shops was selling little bottles labeled *Florida Sunshine*. They looked as if they had only air in them. The clerk said they sell out so fast she can barely keep them stocked." She laughed.

Audra Darling laughed, too, then said, "I wonder if the fish are biting today, like they were yesterday. Wouldn't it be nice if that darling little Brady caught one?"

Jeris gazed out the window. "I think I can safely say he'd be as happy as if he were at Disney World. Most little boys like to catch fish." She watched Brady, Luke, and Pastor Hughes on the large square floating dock. Beyond them the sunshine danced on the pewter-colored water, a silver fish jumped in the distance, and birds flew low over the green lake grasses lining the shore. Around the rim of the water, houses were scattered here and there with docks jutting out. Across the way Jeris spotted several colorful boats—a red one, a blue one, a striped one. One boat was pulling a skier in a wide wake of water. Farther out she could see the salt marshes with their brown reedy plants.

Audra Darling bustled about the kitchen, putting away items.

Gazing at the idyllic scene through the window, Jeris was filled with a sense of peace. She couldn't wait to get out there. It was a perfect day for a water outing, not hot and not cold. It was "just right," as Goldilocks said. "It's beautiful—the water—the foliage—the boats. It's like a landscape painting come to life. It's so serene."

"That's a good way to put it. Well, I'm going to go change"—Audra Darling looked down at her suit—"into some loafing clothes. I sure couldn't take a boat ride in this, could I?" She pinched a wad of pink linen at her hipline.

Jeris smoothed the front of her long black skirt and over-sized matching black jacket. "These could be considered loafing clothes, I guess." She squeezed a handful of her jacket. "These jersey knits are so comfortable, even though they're professional. That's why I love to wear them. I have this suit in four different colors: black, gray, navy, and taupe." She paused. "And it doesn't take me long to get dressed every morning. That's another advantage to wearing them."

Audra Darling looked contemplative for a moment and opened her mouth as if to say something. But she turned and dashed toward the bedroom. "You go on out. I'll be there in a jiffy."

"All right." Jeris pulled open a French door. She walked out onto the porch, then down the grassy slope toward the dock. She grasped the rail and made her way onto the narrow wooden walk over the water, then to the floating dock where Pastor Hughes and Luke sat on lawn chairs.

Brady stood nearby, holding a fishing pole, his line in the water.

"Hi," she said to no one in particular, trying to be friendly. "How's it going?"

"As fine as a frog's hair and not quite as dusty." Pastor Hughes grinned as he stood. "That's what Brother Jernigan says all the time."

The three of them laughed.

Luke stood also.

"No need for you two to get up on my account." Jeris waved them back down, then walked a few steps over to Brady.

"Brother Jernigan's quite a character, isn't he?" Luke settled into his chair.

"That's an understatement." Pastor Hughes chuckled. "I'm only kidding. He's a lovable old fellow. But his antics sure keep church life exciting."

Jeris ruffled Brady's hair. Maybe it was the thickness of it. Or its unruliness—the big cowlick at the crown. It seemed everybody ruffled up his hair. "Catching any, Brady?"

He looked up at her, squinting and smiling in the sunshine, then back at the water. His pole bobbed downward. "I feel something!" he shouted. "Something's pulling my pole!"

Luke crossed the dock to Brady's side. "You've got a bite, son. You're catching a fish."

"I am?" Brady let go of his pole.

"Whoa." Luke caught it just in time and put it back in Brady's hands. "Hold on, son. You're about to bring one in."

"Yippee!"

Pastor Hughes stepped over to them.

Jeris took a step backward to give them more room. She enjoyed seeing Brady so excited.

"Bring him in, pardner." Pastor Hughes stood beside Brady, cheering him on.

Luke helped Brady pull the line out of the water, a wriggling fish on the other end.

In moments the fish was in a bucket, and Brady had already dropped his line back in the water.

"Andrew?" Audra Darling called, her voice carrying over the water as if she'd been talking into a microphone.

Jeris looked toward the house.

Audra Darling came through the French doors, leaving them open behind her. She still had on the skirt to her pink linen suit but was wearing a yellow top.

"What's the matter, Audra?" Pastor Hughes walked briskly up the dock.

Jeris watched them as they talked. It was an emergency, from the looks of things. *Lord, help in this situation, whatever it is.*

Luke came up beside Jeris and gestured toward the house. "I hope everything's okay."

"You never know in pastoring."

He nodded somberly.

Pastor Hughes and Audra Darling walked out on the dock toward them.

"Jeris, Luke," Audra Darling said, "we need to go over to Brother Ward's house. He just died."

"I'm so sorry," Jeris said. "Is that the man you were telling me about last Sunday? The one with congestive heart failure and other complications?"

Pastor Hughes nodded. "His family called. They'd like us to come pray for them. They're pretty distraught."

"I can imagine," Jeris said. "We'll leave so you can go."

"Brady," Luke called. "We have to leave now."

"Aw, Dad." Brady's grip on his cane pole was viselike.

Audra Darling stepped forward and put her hand on Luke's forearm. "Please don't leave. Let Brady fish to his heart's content. And you and Jeris sit out here and enjoy the sunshine. And then, when Brady's finished, take a boat ride. Andrew will give you the keys. The life vests are under the seats. And then have a snack. There's plenty of sweet tea in the refrigerator and more chocolate cake on the cake plate and anything else you can find—"

"No, Audra," Luke said, "we'll go ahead and leave when you do."

"He's right," Jeris chimed in.

Pastor Hughes dug in his pocket and pulled out his key ring. "Luke, Jeris, I insist you stay." He worked at getting a key off the ring. "Just because we have to leave doesn't mean you do. It isn't fair to disappoint Brady because we have church duties to attend to. Especially when you don't have to leave. Make yourselves at home. Take a boat ride." He placed a key in Luke's palm. "Explore some of those salt marshes I showed you the other time I took you out on the boat."

"And then go inside and get something cold to drink," Audra Darling added. "Better yet, take some cold drinks with you in the boat. There are plenty in the refrigerator, all kinds. And have some more cake before you leave."

"And when you're finished," Pastor Hughes said, "just lock up before you leave. You know where to put the spare house key."

"I—I don't know what to say," Luke said.

Jeris didn't know what to say either. The sentiments she'd felt earlier this morning when she thought Luke wanted to avoid her washed over her like a wave. And now he was hesitating to accept the Hugheses' kind offer. Probably because of her. He most likely didn't want to spend time alone with her. Well, that was fine with her. She felt the same way about him. She'd looked forward to coming to the Hugheses' house. But the original plans included Pastor Hughes and Audra Darling. Now they were leaving, and she didn't care about staying.

"We insist." Pastor Hughes and Audra Darling spoke the words at the same time.

"I know you need to go." Jeris glanced at her watch.

"And we're not leaving until you both agree to stay." Audra Darling put her hands on her hips and glared at them, a twinkle in her eyes.

Jeris glanced at Luke.

He stared at the dock and traced a knothole with the toe of his shoe. "All right. If you insist." He looked up at Pastor Hughes. "Speaking for myself, I mean. And Brady."

Jeris hesitated. Luke wouldn't look at her or give her a hint he'd like her to stay and wasn't including her in his answer. Was he just being particular in his answer? Or did he want her to leave?

"Jeris?" Audra Darling's tone was soft. "You'll stay? And you'll act as hostess in my stead? Please? I feel badly, leaving my guests."

One look at Audra Darling's pleading eyes and Jeris knew her answer. "Yes, I'll stay." She glanced over at Brady. "We'll have a good time."

Chapter 5

Luke kept busy with Brady for nearly an hour, not necessarily avoiding Jeris, who was sitting quietly behind them on a lawn chair, but because Brady needed his help. He had caught two fish. And then four times fish had nabbed his bait, which meant the hook had to be baited over and over.

He'd already cleaned Brady's fish, scales flying everywhere. That way the chore would be done when they were ready to go. He didn't intend to stick around long.

He saw several fish scales on his sleeve and flicked them off. Another reason he hadn't talked to Jeris was because she hadn't talked to him. She was a reticent one.

He swiped at his sweaty forehead with his arm. His hands were too nasty with fish smell to use right now. On the weathered dock, with the sun beating down and not a breeze to stir the air, it felt almost as hot as summertime. But the sun felt good. He liked the outdoors and the activities associated with it: trail biking, swimming, jogging, hiking—just about anything under the brilliant blue sky.

One more swipe at his forehead and he wondered how Jeris was standing the heat in her black jacket and long skirt.

He glanced over at the boat. Before they left to go home they needed to take a boat ride, what the Hugheses had insisted they do. "Brady, are you ready for a boat ride?"

"Yippee!" Brady threw his pole on the dock and raced toward the boat.

"Whoa, Little Man. Don't get too close to the edge. Get back now."

Brady stepped back.

"That's good."

"Can we go now? Can we go now?" Brady was doing his usual jumping.

"In a minute." Luke cleaned his hands with disposable wet cloths from Pastor Hughes's tackle box, then helped Brady do the same. He noticed Jeris still hadn't said a word. What was going on with her? Hadn't she heard them talking about the boat ride? "Jeris, are you ready to take a boat ride? We won't stay out very long." Still cleaning his hands, he turned around to face her.

"I guess so." She had taken off her black jacket and wore a brown sleeveless shirt. She fanned her hand in front of her neck, her olive skin looking tanner than usual—no doubt the result of the sunshine today. She stood up and stretched. "But why don't I do what Audra Darling suggested and get some soft drinks for us to have in the boat?"

"I'll vote for that." Luke closed the tackle box. "I'm as thirsty as a straggler in the Sahara."

"Miss Jeris, can you bring me a root beer?" Brady asked.

"I sure will. If Audra Darling has any."

"Anything is fine for me."

"Okay. I'll be right back." She turned and headed up to the house.

Ten minutes later they were seated in the boat, life vests on and drinking their cold beverages, not saying anything, just enjoying the drinks in the warm sunshine.

Jeris reached into a plastic grocery bag she'd brought along and retrieved three baseball caps. She handed two of them to Luke and Brady.

"Where did you get these?" Luke asked.

"Inside. On a rack. I figured Pastor Hughes wouldn't mind our borrowing them. He has at least two dozen, and they'll be a lifesaver out here in the sun."

"Thanks." Luke put on his hat, and Brady did, too.

She set her soft drink down on the bottom of the boat and balanced it between her shoes. She removed an elastic band from her wrist, shook out her hair, gathered it into a ponytail, and secured it with the band. Then she put on the cap and carefully threaded her ponytail through the hole in the back.

Luke couldn't help watching her. She wasn't three feet away from him in the boat. For some reason her movements bothered him. They were almost. . .intimate?

She adjusted the bill of her cap.

He noticed she'd taken off her black tights when she went inside. Good. At least she wouldn't be so hot. But she still had on her ugly black shoes. *Sturdy* was how he'd describe them, not like Audra's, those sandal-like heels many women wore.

"This tastes good, Miss Jeris." Brady held up his root beer and smiled his charming smile at her.

"This does, too, Brady." She held up her drink and smiled back. "I think Audra Darling would say you're a darling boy."

Brady giggled, his shoulders shaking, his nose scrunched up.

"Everybody about finished?" Luke had his hand on the key. "Ready to go?"

"In a minute, Dad." Brady held his drink to his lips and drained the bottle.

"One more sip and I'll be ready, too." Jeris collected their bottles and put them in the grocery bag, then put the bag in a side compartment. "Okay."

"Me, too, Dad. Let's go."

"Hang on," Luke yelled, "as we go sailing into the wide, blue yonder!"

"Only we don't have a sail," she added wryly.

Luke smiled.

She held on to the rail beside the seat and told Brady to do the same. Then she reached for his other hand and kept it in hers.

They took off across the river, the wind in their faces. Luke enjoyed the cooling breeze. For close to half an hour he drove, weaving into small fingers of water that extended into the salt marshes, then out again into broad expanses. Pastor Hughes had recently studied salt marshes, and Luke recalled some terms he had used. *Salinity.* Spartina, *a type of cord-grass abundant in the marsh. Spot-tail bass. Blue crab. Shrimp. Alligators, though rare.*

Luke reduced the speed so he could be heard. He wanted to tell Brady something Pastor Hughes had told him. "Brady, Pastor Hughes says you can sometimes see a manatee out here. So be on the lookout."

"Oh, boy! Like the ones we saw on TV last year?"

Luke smiled. It was last week. "Yes, just like those. Manatees are marine mammals, remember? And remember how the documentary called manatees 'gentle giants'? And it said some people call them 'sea cows.'"

"I want to see a sea cow." Brady grasped the side of the boat and leaned over.

"Be careful, Brady." Jeris had let go of his hand at the lower speed but reached for him now and grabbed a handful of his shirt for safety.

"What do manatees eat, Dad?"

"They're herbivores."

"What's that mean?"

"It means they eat plants." Jeris kept her grasp firm on Brady's shirt.

"Oh."

"They feed on water grasses, hyacinths, mangrove leaves, things like that," Jeris said. "I've seen them all my life. I grew up in Florida."

"Me, too," Brady said.

"The documentary said they consume up to 9 percent of their body weight every day." Luke searched the water close to the boat and farther away near the reedlike grasses. He hoped they'd see a manatee for Brady's sake.

"I want a snack, Dad."

"How about a water lily?" Luke laughed.

"Da–a–a–d."

"I'm only kidding. When we get back we'll have another piece of Audra's chocolate cake. How about that? She said to help ourselves."

"Yippee!"

Luke turned off the motor and let the boat float. "Maybe the quiet will bring a manatee to us."

Jeris nodded.

"So you grew up in Florida?" Luke kept his voice low. "In Winter Haven, right? Isn't that what Pastor Hughes said, the Sunday you told us about the children's church program?"

"Yes. In Winter Haven. Where are you from?"

"I'm a native Floridian, too, but I'm not from around here. I grew up in Ocala."

"Pretty area. Horse farms and rolling hills."

He nodded.

"I have an aunt who lives not far from Ocala. When I was growing up, we used to visit her. But I haven't been up that way in ages. How long have you lived in Silver Bay?"

"A little over four years," he said.

"Dad!" Brady shouted. "I have to go to the bathroom!"

"Brady. There's such a thing as manners." He looked straight ahead, not even glancing at Jeris.

Brady jumped up, sending the boat rocking.

"Sit down, Little Man. You'll turn us over."

Brady sat back down. "But I've got to go bad, Dad."

Jeris was laughing.

Luke felt embarrassed. "Brady, you'll have to wait," he said in a low, controlled voice.

"I can't." Brady's feet were dancing on the bottom of the boat, making *tap*, *tap*, *tap* noises.

Jeris put her arm around Brady and smiled at him. "We can't predict when nature calls, can we, Little Man? I guess your great big root beer took a great big toll." She glanced over at Luke and shrugged. "Can you find a place for him to get out?"

Brady's upper body was now shaking.

"Looks like you'll have to," she added.

Luke nodded, cranked the motor, and headed for the closest shore. When he stopped, Brady jumped into the shallow water and headed for land. "Brady, I was going to get out and pull the boat up so you wouldn't get wet."

"I can't wait, Dad."

Luke jumped into the water, sneakers and jeans and all. He needed to guide Brady, his mind on crabs—and alligators. He shuddered as he caught up to him and grabbed his hand. "Come on, Little Man." They took off through the shallow water. "Jeris, can you throw the anchor over the side? We'll be right back."

"I'll 'sit tight,' as Audra Darling says. And I'll take care of the anchor for you."

"Thanks." Luke looked for a sheltered place some distance from Jeris and headed that way with his son.

"Dad, can we go exploring?" Brady asked when they came out from the shelter of trees.

Luke glanced around and saw a copse of trees. Leading into it were some rough trails that probably hadn't been walked on in a long time. "I don't know...."

"Please, Dad? We can pretend we're Christopher Columbus."

Luke smiled. Brady's first-grade class had studied Columbus last week. "Jeris is with us. She probably wouldn't like to go traipsing about in the woods."

"Miss Jeris!" Brady turned toward her and flailed his arms in the air like a windmill. "Can you come over here?"

Luke looked across the way at the boat.

Jeris leaned forward and cupped her ear as if she were trying to hear what Brady was saying.

"Brady, if she's going with us, we need to be gentlemen and help her out of the boat."

"Okay, Dad."

Luke grabbed Brady's hand, and they dashed toward the edge of the water then stopped.

"What did you say, Brady?"

"I'm going to be Christopher Columbus, Miss Jeris."

Luke smiled. "Brady wants to follow a trail into the woods. I know it's getting late. But we won't be long, that is, if it's all right with you. Do you want to go? If you don't, we won't do it. We wouldn't want to impose."

"Please, Miss Jeris?" Brady folded his hands in his familiar prayer stance, jumping on one foot, then the other.

She laughed. "I—" She glanced down at her clothing.

"You're not dressed for hiking. . . ." Luke's voice trailed off. *That long skirt. . . .* "Can you walk in the woods in that thing?"

"Hey, I'll manage. I'm tough. I accept the invitation."

"Yippee!"

"I love traipsing through the woods," she said.

"Okay. But don't climb out yet, okay?"

"Okay."

"I'll pull the boat up on the bank so you won't get wet." Luke turned to Brady. "Stay put." He sloshed through the water to the back of the boat, threw the anchor inside, and pushed the boat with a hard thrust. Then he came around to the front, pulled it onto dry ground, and held out his hand to her.

Jeris stood up, took his hand, and stepped toward him, rocking the boat. She stopped. "Yikes."

Luke clamped down on the side of the boat and steadied it.

"Thanks."

"Try again."

She took another step, then started to climb over the side.

R–r–i–i–i–p.

"My skirt." She looked down. The side slit was now several inches higher, and the fabric was jagged where it tore.

"Oh, my." Luke looked at Brady. "We didn't mean to tear her clothes, did we, Brady?" He felt bad that her skirt was ruined.

Brady's giggles filled the air.

"No problem. Maybe it can be fixed. If not, I'll buy a new one." Her hand still firmly in his, she jumped over the side and landed solidly on two feet.

Good thing she's wearing those—those—oxfords?

She smiled at Luke, then ran her hand through Brady's hair. "Who's ready for an adventure? I am."

"Yippee!" Brady shouted.

"Let's go, Christopher Columbus."

Luke sat down by Brady in his twin bed that night and pulled the sheet up to his chest. He handed him a book from the bedside table, then picked up another book and thumbed through it.

"We had the goodest time today, didn't we, Dad?"

Luke smiled. Brady said that every time he had a good time. "You need to say *best* not *goodest*."

Brady looked up at him with a puzzled expression on his face.

"Oh, never mind." Luke affectionately tapped Brady's chin. He was too young to grasp grammar. There would be plenty of time for that later. My, how he loved this child. Little Man—what he'd dubbed him the first time he laid eyes on him.

He felt. . .how did he feel? He looked down at the book he was holding and saw the word *fuzzy* in the story. That's how he felt. Pleasant images filled his mind. Brady in his school uniform coming out of the front door of his school. Where had the time gone? How could he be in school already? Brady in swimming trunks, jumping into their pool. They'd had some good times together in the backyard. He was glad he'd decided to put in a pool. Brady dressed up in his Sunday clothes, holding his children's Bible and full of questions about Moses and other Bible characters. Brady with his ear-to-ear smile and little freckled face and unruly blond hair. He added joy to Luke's life.

Brady picked up another book from the bedside table and opened it.

Luke thought about the busy week ahead. He would be out three nights. A dinner, a club meeting, and another function he couldn't remember. That meant he wouldn't be there to put him to bed and read to him those nights as he was about to do now. And Wednesday nights were out, too, for bedtime reading. They were always a scramble—church, a quick bath, a prayer, and a kiss. That left just three nights for their ritual.

If only there were more days in the week. Good thing he wasn't dating.

"Look, Dad." Brady held his book so Luke could see the page. "This little boy's fishing, just like I did today. I caught two fishes. All by myself."

Luke looked at the picture. A little boy was pulling on a fishing pole. On the end of the line was a fish. "You sure did, Brady." He caressed Brady's sun-reddened cheeks. "I was proud of you." He tweaked him on the nose. "You're growing up too fast."

Brady pushed up his pajama sleeve and flexed his muscle. "I'm big, Dad, aren't I?"

"Yes, you are."

"Feel it." He thrust his arm out and flexed his muscle again.

Luke squeezed Brady's arm. "It's as hard as a rock."

Brady had that little-boy proud look. "It took some big muscles to catch

167

those fishes today, didn't it, Dad?"

"It sure did. Which did you like best? Fishing? The boat ride? Or our walk in the woods?"

"The goodest part was when Miss Jeris was climbing out of the boat and her skirt went *r–r–i–i–p*." A fit of giggles hit him, and the bed shook with his laughter. "That was so funny."

Luke distinctly remembered the moment.

"She's fun, isn't she, Dad?"

Luke tickled him along the ribs, and Brady shrieked like a fire truck.

He buried the top of his head in Brady's chest, then gave him a bear hug. "You're funner, Little Man."

Chapter 6

Luke stuck his head in the church library and saw the volunteer librarian—a rotund elderly lady—sitting at a desk, engrossed in a book and munching on a cookie. "Miss Ada?"

She threw her hand over her generous bosom. "Mercy me, you scared the wits out of me." Her chest heaved in and out, and the little veins on her nose turned as red as a candied apple. She fanned herself with her lace-trimmed handkerchief.

He walked to the desk and smiled at her. "I'm sorry, Miss Ada. I didn't mean to startle you."

"I guess I was so enthralled with my book—" She stopped talking, fidgeted, and put her hand over the book she'd been reading.

Luke couldn't help seeing the cover. It depicted a man and a woman in a tasteful embrace. Since the library was in the church, he was sure it was a wholesome Christian novel. He squelched a smile—not at the book but at the way she was trying to hide it. Miss Ada was at least seventy. She was the proverbial old maid of the congregation.

"I didn't even hear the door open. Normally it creaks."

He laughed. Most doors in this church creaked.

"I have a title to recommend to you before you leave." She adjusted her glasses. "But, first, did you need to tell me something? You're a man on a mission, aren't you? I can tell by the look on your face. You're definitely not one of my regular patrons. You do much reading? Do you ever read those new Christian novels they're publishing nowadays? I do. Of course I don't get them from this library."

She rolled her eyes. "We haven't had a new book in Christ Church library for more than fifteen years. I check out Christian novels from the public library." She reeled off a few authors' names. "Have you read any of their new books?"

"I. . .can't say that I have. I'm not into fiction."

"Well, you should be. Promise me you'll try them. I know you'd like them. Okay?"

"Okay, Miss Ada. I will."

"But you didn't come here to check out a book, did you? Or hear about new titles, right?"

"Right." He cleared his throat. "Pastor Hughes assigned me to the church library, and I was stopping by to check—"

"Hmmph!" She turned up her nose. "Why don't you deacons fix the creaking doors around here and quit snooping in places you have no business in?"

He didn't say anything at first. The last deacon overseeing the library minis-try hadn't been able to accomplish anything, with Miss Ada being so snippy and all. That deacon had finally given up. That was three years ago, Pastor Hughes had told him.

He took a step toward her and smiled his most engaging smile. "Miss Ada, I stopped by to tell you I have a five-hundred-dollar donation for you to buy some new books."

She jumped up, bustled around the desk, and pulled him toward her in a big hug. "Well, I'll say." She hugged him again.

Luke caught a whiff of dusting powder, the scent his grandmother used. Something purple-sounding. Lavender? Lilac?

"Happy hoedown and all that stuff." She danced a little reel, her elbows flail-ing chicken-style. "Where did that kind of donation come from?"

"Sorry. I can't tell. It's anonymous. But the donor requested that half of it be spent on children's books."

"Children's?" She stopped in her tracks, her sparse gray eyebrows pulled down over her thick glasses. "I haven't had a child in this library in the twenty-two years I've been working here."

"Maybe because you don't have any children's books."

"Well, I can remedy that now, can't I? I'll be glad to pick out some. That'll be nice, spending other people's money. But stuff and nonsense—I want to assure you it's not my fault we haven't had any children's books in here—except for a few."

"No, I wouldn't blame you at all, Miss Ada."

She thrust her hand out sideways, indicating a shelf with only three or four thin children's books. "I've been a public-school librarian and know what a library needs to make it good. Variety—and that includes children's books. I know that as well as I know my name. But I never had funds to buy them. And whenever I asked for book donations, I only received ones for adults. And you'd be surprised at what some of those were."

She leaned forward, her eyes widening, and lowered her voice. "Racy rom-ances, that's what." She wagged her finger at him. "Anonymous, of course. Just like this donated money you told me about."

She tsk-tsked. "Yessirreebob, one Sunday morning when I arrived, a paste-board box was sitting by the door. When I went through it I found some of those. . .those. . .well, the kind of books I just told you about. There's no place in a church library for books like that."

"Only books like this." Luke whisked the book she'd been reading from her desk and held it up. He couldn't resist. He smiled again.

"Right as rain." She took the book from him and brandished it in the air like a politician making a point. "This"—she thumped the cover—"is a good book. It entertains you, and it draws you to God in the process."

He patted her shoulder. "I'm only teasing you, Miss Ada."

She shrugged away. "Well, I'm *not* teasing. I'm speaking a truth here," she said in an authoritative tone.

"I'm sure you are, though I can't attest to the glowing review of the book you're reading." He glanced at the cover. "As I said, I don't read much fiction. And I've never read in that genre."

"Maybe you should." Merriment danced in her faded blue eyes. She held up the book and tapped on the picture of the couple. "Boy meets girl. Boy resists girl. True love wins out. Boy gets girl. And they live happily ever after."

He laughed. Then he glanced at his watch. "Well, I need to pick up Brady from his class."

"How's that boy doing in school? He's a charmer if ever I saw one."

"He's doing fine, Miss Ada. He loves it. He can't wait to get there every morning."

"Every time he sees me, he gives me a great big hug. Makes a person feel as dear as the apple of one's eye. And he's so polite."

"Thank you. He's my Little Man." The warm fuzziness he often felt when he was with Brady hit him now.

"It was you, wasn't it?" She peered into his eyes. "The donor?"

"No. But I wish I'd thought of it first." He glanced around at the meager selection of books. He'd never been in the church library. "It's an excellent idea."

She put her hand on his arm. "I'm grateful for it. Honest I am. Please express my thanks to Pastor Hughes. And if you know who donated the money, please tell them I said thank you. And"—she paused and drew a lungful of air—"I apologize for being so...so...bristly when you first came in."

He patted her shoulder. "That's okay, Miss Ada."

She walked over to her desk and picked up a pamphletlike book. "I've been doing some work in here, contrary to what you deacons think." She winked at him. "I'm not meaning that in a harsh way, honest." She winked again. "And when I was sorting through the shelves I came across an interesting book I'd like to recommend to you."

He looked down at the faded booklet in her hands and scanned the title. *"How to Choose the Right Wife...for Christian Lads."*

"Luke, I think it would be good for you to read it."

He bit his bottom lip. *Oh no, here it comes.* Advice about his *situation*. But then he smiled, somewhat interested in what this colorful lady had to say.

"You know. Your situation and all."

He felt like playfully rolling his eyes. But he kept his gaze steady instead. "Yes?"

"Frankly, I'm not one to be pushy."

He squelched a grin.

"But when I pulled this book off the shelf it piqued my interest, and I sat down then and there and read it from cover to cover." She held the thin book gingerly, as if it might fall apart from age. "Actually, when I saw it, the first person

I thought of was you."

"Me?"

"Yessirreebob. It was the Sunday your Brady made his prayer request during morning worship."

"Oh." Luke rocked on his heels, remembering his embarrassment with a sharp poignancy.

"Soon as I read it, I asked the Lord to bring you into my library so I could give it to you."

"You did?"

"I did. And He did."

"Right as rain?" He laughed as he used her expression.

She laughed with him.

"Technically, though, wasn't it Pastor Hughes who sent me in here?"

She shook her head, the soft part of her full jowls jiggling. "Nosirreebob. It was God. I know it because I asked Him to, and the Bible says, 'Ask, and it shall be given you.' I prayed, and He answered."

He looked down at the title again.

"Even though it was written in 1954, its truths still apply today."

"In 1954?" He nodded slowly, gazing at the cover. What did a book that old have to say, especially about *that* subject? He envisioned women dressed like those in *Little House on the Prairie*, even though he knew that era was the 1800s. But the images wouldn't leave. He chuckled.

"Don't you go laughing till you see what's in it." She looked at him, a twinkle in her eyes. She opened the booklet, moved closer to him so he could see the pages, and ran her finger down the table of contents. " 'Make Sure God Is Involved,'" she read. "That's the first chapter. Here's the second: 'What Kind of Girl to Look For.' And another: 'How Can You Tell If It's the Real McCoy?'" She closed the booklet and held it out. "It has some good things to say about choosing a wife."

To be polite, Luke took the booklet from her. "Thank you, Miss Ada."

She grasped his hand and squeezed it. "You promise me you'll read it?"

He was as interested in reading it as he was in reading *The Iliad*. "I—" He noted its thinness. It would take him maybe thirty minutes. Or less. "Sure."

"Then come over here and check it out." She sat down at her desk and thumbed through a small wooden box, then glanced up at him. "I know my system's archaic. But we have so few books."

"Soon you'll have some new ones. And maybe more donations will start coming in."

"I hope so." She bent over the small box again. "Let's see." Her eyebrows drew together as she kept thumbing. "Here it is." She pulled out a yellowed index card, wrote his name and the date on it, then handed the booklet to him.

"Thanks."

"You can keep it as long as you want. It hasn't been checked out since 1955."

Chapter 7

Jeris finished her client dictation, then tidied her desk. She couldn't get her mind off ten-year-old Lane Felton. His mother, a single mom, had dropped dead three weeks ago at the age of thirty-seven, apparently from a heart attack. His grandmother was bringing him twice a week so Jeris could help him deal with his shock and grief.

"Lord," she prayed, clasping her hands on top of her desk, "please help Lane. Holy Spirit, bring Your comfort into his little heart. Surround him like a cocoon and gather him into Your tender, loving arms. Assure him that You love him and that he'll make it through this trying time—"

Z-z-z-z-z. It was her cell phone vibrating. Z-z-z-z-z.

She picked it up, saw Audra Darling's number on the display, and clicked it on. "Hi, Audra Darling."

"Hi, Jeris. Are you on your way home?"

"No, I'm still at the office."

"You sound like Luke. Work, work, work. That's all you two know how to do." Audra Darling's laughter rippled through the phone lines.

"I'm on my way out. I had a heavy case load today, and I just finished the last of my notes."

"I'll catch you later then."

"No, that's okay." Jeris stood and slung her purse over her shoulder. "I can talk." She picked up her briefcase. "Now is as good a time as any," she said, walking toward the door.

"You sure?"

Jeris stepped outside the building and locked the glass door. "I'm sure."

"You told me to call you."

"I did?" She reached her car.

Audra Darling laughed. "Sounds like you need a glass of sweet iced tea to wind down."

"Or a fat-free latte." Jeris got into her SUV and started the engine.

"I'm calling about the party we need to plan for children's church."

"Oh." Jeris pulled out of the parking lot and threaded into traffic on the busy road. "I haven't thought about it since—"

"Let me guess. Since last Sunday when we talked. That's when you told me to call you."

"Right. I remember now."

"You said something about taking the kids on a picnic?"

"Don't you think they'd like that? Somewhere away from the church? Something different? And fun?"

"Yes, they'd love it. I was reading an article in the newspaper this morning about a beach not far from here where you can hunt for sharks' teeth."

"Sharks' teeth?"

"Prehistoric sharks' teeth, according to the article."

Jeris's mind went into overdrive. *We can have a picnic on the beach and then hunt for sharks' teeth.* She made a left-hand turn, and the phone fell from its perch on her shoulder. *And then I can teach them a brief lesson about Jonah and the whale.* She put the phone back up to her ear. *Only I'll tell the kids the Bible says it was a great fish, not necessarily a whale, and that some Bible scholars say it could've been a large shark and—*

"Jeris? Did you hear me?"

"I sort of did. My phone fell, and by the time I picked it up, well, what you said was spotty."

"I said we could take them. . ." Audra Darling proceeded to give voice to everything Jeris had been thinking.

Jeris laughed. "Sounds fabulous. When I dropped the phone I was mapping out the party exactly as you did, down to the lesson on Jonah and the whale."

"When the Holy Spirit illuminates minds, you never know what's going to happen." Audra Darling laughed. "If it's all right with you, I'll plan the party for you. The food, the transportation, things like that. In fact I've already done a few things. I figured it would help you out—"

"It'd be a big help."

"I'll get a chaperone. Counting us, that'll be three. Don't you think that's how many we should have? Considering the kids'll be on the beach and we'll need to keep a close eye on them?"

"Sounds like a good plan. Who are you planning to call?" *Not Luke Moore, I hope.* At the Hugheses' parsonage Luke had been polite to her, but that was about all she could say for him. Oh yes. She could add *cold* and *aloof.*

"I thought I'd call Luke."

Not him. "What about Denny Roper's grandmother? She's the one who brings him to church. She always shows an interest in things that concern him. She might go with us."

"She's tied up."

"Why not Cheryl Carson? She brings her neighbor's son, Jeffrey, and she might be willing."

"I tried her, too."

"What about Blake Larsen's mother or father?"

"They're going out of town on a business trip, and his grandmother's keeping him. I asked her, but she has two other grandchildren she's watching that day, and they're babies. I can't think of anyone else."

"Looks as if it'll be Luke then?"

"If he agrees."

"I've got the joy, joy, joy, joy down in my heart," she sang inside. Only the children's song was dirgelike. She didn't want Luke to think she was behind this. She didn't want him thinking she was on his trail. Because she wasn't. He clearly wasn't interested in her. And she clearly wasn't interested in him. And never would be.

Chapter 8

After Luke put Brady to bed, he set his iced tea glass on the lamp table in the family room, stretched out on the sofa, and picked up the remote, working the throw pillow behind his head to get it just right. He aimed the remote, turned on the TV, and flipped channels. He flipped through them again. He punched in numbers. He punched in other numbers. He flipped all the way through the channels for the third time, from the lowest to the highest.

I have an evening designated for downtime and no work, and wouldn't you know? I can't find a thing to watch. He clicked off the TV.

Maybe he would catch a short snooze. It was too early to go to bed. Only 8:45. He glanced at the dark TV. Well, he could always work. He looked across the room into the kitchen and saw his briefcase sitting by the door. He'd brought home extra work in case he found some free time.

All right then, he would get some work done. He stretched both arms, his hand hitting the lamp behind him. He sprang up, swung around, and caught the lamp just in time. He set it upright and adjusted the shade. On the lamp table was his Bible. Sticking out from the middle of the Bible was the little book Miss Ada had given him last Sunday.

How to Choose the Right Wife. . .for Christian Lads.

He'd promised her he'd read it. Now would be a good time. He picked it up. "Let's see, Mr."—he noticed the author's name on the cover—"Granfield, if you can tell this lad how to choose a wife." He smiled as he turned to chapter one: "Make Sure God Is Involved."

"The Creator of the heavens and the earth, the Eternal One who is omniscient, omnipresent, and omnipotent, created you, His masterpiece and highest work of creation. Though He manages the vast universe, He wants to be involved in your life, and most particularly whom you marry."

I'll agree with that. Luke took a sip of iced tea.

"God's Word is your road map on the Seeking Road as you make your way toward Marriage City."

Interesting way to put it.

"As you serve God and put Him first in your life, He will lead you in the path He's chosen for you. Your duty is to ask Him to show you His will and way. Let me assure you this will not be a bitter pill to swallow. Conversely, it will bring you joy, for God is a God of infinite joy. Walking in His will, you will be the happiest.

"The girl God has for you will be tailor-made for you. Even if she doesn't have rose-petal lips, cute dimples, and curly hair, you will think she's the darlingest thing on earth."

Luke laughed so hard that he nearly dropped his glass. This sounded as if Audra had written it.

"Some lads pray about their spiritual lives. That's commendable. Some even pray about such things as their jobs, all the way down to the mundane. That, too, is admirable. But God wants you to pray about choosing a mate, the right person, the wife He has planned for you. His Word says in Jeremiah 29:11 that He has definite plans for you. He wants you to seek Him in earnest prayer about one of the most important plans in your life—The Marriage Plan. Have you done that? If not, I advise you to stop reading right now and commit your way to Him, as the scripture says."

Luke laid the booklet aside and put his glass on the lamp table. He'd prayed about many things: the church, its ministries, Pastor Hughes and Audra. He'd prayed about career moves, the right school for Brady, even whether or not to put a pool in his backyard last summer. But he had never prayed about The Marriage Plan.

I've never asked God to send me a mate. And not just any mate, but His choice for my life.

He snapped his eyes shut. "Lord, I'm sorry I haven't prayed about this before. I took this part of my life for granted. I thought it would just happen in its own time. But now I want to commit my way to You, as this little book teaches. From now on I'm relying on You to bring a woman into my life, the right woman who's tailor-made for me."

He drew a deep breath. "Please prepare my heart. Whatever needs changing in me, please do it. I'm open and willing. In Jesus' name. Amen."

Luke dove into the swimming pool, then surfaced, swam to the side, and called for Brady to get in the deep end with him.

Brady jumped in, went under, and came up, his little arms flailing in the water.

∞

Luke grabbed hold of him, and Brady clung to his neck. "Want to swim across the pool, Little Man?"

Brady nodded and started out.

"Go, Brady! You can do it." Luke dog-paddled nearby as Brady swam across the pool. He was staying close for safety. "Go, go, go. Keep those arms digging into that water. Keep those feet kicking. That's it. Go, boy! Go!"

Brady surfaced at the other side and hung on to the tiled lower edge, swilling in big gulps of air, his chest going up and down, his face all smiles. "I did it, Dad. I did it."

"Yes, you did. Congratulations."

"Am I a good swimmer, Dad?"

"The best."

Brady pulled himself along the side of the pool as he made his way to the shallow end. "I'm going to get my mask and fins."

"Okay, Little Man. But don't let go of the edge. You're still in the deep end."

"I won't, Dad."

Luke leaned back against the side, his elbows resting on the tiled lower edge. He was glad for this time with Brady. He'd left work early today and picked him up at the afternoon care center.

He looked at the sky. They had at least another hour of daylight. Each spring day that edged toward summer gave them longer daylight hours, and he was taking advantage of it every chance he could. Tomorrow night he and Brady were going to a PTA meeting, and Wednesday night was church. Thursday night he would be at a board meeting, and Friday night he had to go to a banquet. His week would be gone in a blink of the eye.

Saturday Brady was attending the children's church picnic out on the beach. That was perfect. Luke was going on a boating outing with some of his clients. A group of people aboard six or seven boats would spend the day together, picnicking, swimming, and skiing. One of the clients had just bought a cabin cruiser, and he'd told Luke he couldn't wait to try it out. Luke couldn't either. "We'll have a high old time," the client had said.

With Brady taken care of, Luke could attend the outing and not feel guilty about leaving him. His son would be having his own high old time.

"Look, Dad. I'm going to stand on my hands under the water."

Luke glanced at the decorative clock on the wall of the lanai. He needed to get the hamburgers on the grill.

"Da–a–a–d, look."

"I'm looking." He pinned his gaze on Brady. It was funny how kids wanted their parents to look at them all the time. But it was also satisfying for parents to do so. To kids it meant their parents were pretty much the center of their little worlds. He liked being the center of Brady's world.

Brady went down headfirst into the water and stuck his legs up, his little fins waving like flags in the air. Then he burst up to the surface. "Did you see me, Dad? Did you see me?"

"I sure did. Good going. You held your breath a long time. And you balanced perfectly."

R–r–r–i–i–ing.

Luke bounded out of the water, walked over to the table near the shallow end, and, still keeping his eyes on Brady, grabbed the phone. He scanned the display and clicked it on. "Hi, Audra."

"Hi, Luke. Busy?"

"I'm about to throw some hamburgers on the grill. Brady and I are outside swimming."

"The life of Riley."

"I wish."

"Just kidding. That's the biggest tale of all, accusing you of being lazy. I'm calling because we need a chaperone for the children's church picnic on Saturday—"

"I'm tied up."

"You are?"

He could hear disappointment in her voice. "I have an outing with some clients."

"Oh."

Several seconds passed.

"Audra? Did we get cut off?"

"No."

"I'm sorry I can't help."

"It's okay. I understand. Work's work."

A high old time.

"Well, I won't keep you from the pool and Brady. I'm sure we'll manage."

He felt bad about disappointing her. But he couldn't help it that he had plans. Surely she could find someone else.

They said good-bye, and he clicked off the phone.

"Who was that, Dad?" Brady was standing on the top step of the shallow end, throwing colorful diving toys into the bottom of the pool.

"Audra Hughes. She was talking about the children's church party."

"I can't wait till Saturday, Dad."

"You mean because of the party?"

"No. I get to see Miss Jeris again."

∞

Luke left Brady's bedroom and settled onto the sofa. It was time for session number two with *How to Choose the Right Wife. . .for Christian Lads.* What would Mr. Granfield tell him tonight?

He opened the booklet to chapter two: "What Kind of Girl to Look For."

"Never look down on yourself because you are searching for a mate. Just as a garden needs rain, so a lad needs a wife. It's the same way for a girl, too. She needs a husband. But the question is, what kind of a mate do you look for?

"God has created lads and girls with certain physical attributes. Lads like girls with feminine charm, much like the old nursery rhyme says, 'Sugar and spice and everything nice.' Girls like lads with masculine traits, such as broad shoulders and strong muscles. God planned these things when He created Adam and Eve. He also planned that there would be basic physical needs in both lads and girls. But they are to be fulfilled only within the bonds of holy matrimony. Marriage will be the culmination of your God-created physical longings.

"While marriage is an honorable institution that should be sought, you are not to go into it unadvisedly. Lad, you are not to be swayed by a girl with curls."

Oh, brother.

"If God thought enough of your brain to wrap a skull around it, He expects you to use it."

That's a profound statement, Luke thought. *I need to memorize that. It'll help me at work. And in teaching Brady when he reaches his teenage years.*

"The field to choose a mate from is narrow for the Christian lad. There are restrictions, but they are for your own good. The girl you choose must be a genuine Christian. The Bible boldly proclaims this when it says you must not be unequally yoked. Do not permit yourself to look outside the ranks of the righteous."

I'm on the right track there.

"Don't rush into a relationship. Take your time. Do not have a whirlwind courtship."

I'm good to go. I'm in full agreement.

"It's very important to get the right girl. You will not only have a physical union with your mate but a spiritual one. Two souls shall be one. You will share laughter and tears, joy and heartache, life and death.

"Think on the girls you know. This is where you must start looking. There is a tender love story in the Old Testament about Ruth and Boaz. When Ruth and Naomi came to Judah, the hand of God guided Ruth into the field of Boaz. He was someone with whom she and Naomi were familiar. Likewise, he knew of Ruth. Her sweetness and industriousness impressed him, and he eventually wooed and won her hand in marriage.

"Again, I tell you, think on the girls you know."

Think on the girls I know? The only single ones he knew at church were Miss Ada and Jeris Waldron.

"Do not necessarily look for sweeping eyelashes and wavy hair. The pretty ones with the pink cheeks and hourglass figures might not have those pink cheeks and hourglass figures after marriage."

Luke laughed out loud.

"A girl with average looks oftentimes supersedes a glamour queen. A glamour queen, while she may catch your eye before marriage, might also catch other lads' eyes—after marriage to you. Just because a girl has blue eyes and raven hair and peaches-and-cream skin means nothing in the lifetime you will share together. Sometimes the beautiful-on-the-outside girl expects you to wait on her hand and foot. She might be conceited and selfish.

"Do not think I am putting down beauty. I am just warning you. A word to the wise is sufficient, the Bible says.

"However, lad, it is important to note here that you are not required to marry a girl as ugly as a weathered barn, no matter how good a Christian she is. You are not required to marry a butterface girl. What is that, you ask? A man got married, and his coworker asked him what his wife looked like. 'She's a butterface girl.' 'A butterface girl?' the coworker asked. 'Yes, she's pretty everywhere but her face.'"

Luke closed the booklet. He was laughing too hard to continue.

Chapter 9

On the Friday night before the children's beach party, Luke dialed Audra's number.

"Hi, Luke. 'Sup? as the kids say."

"What does that mean?"

"What's up?"

Luke chuckled. "Oh."

"Working with children will keep you up on the latest jargon—and keep you young."

"You're saying I'm going to pull a fast one on Father Time tomorrow?"

"You're going to chaperone the children's beach party?"

"If you still need me."

"Do we ever. Luke, that's great. We appreciate it."

"Glad I can help. Do I need to arrive early?"

"Just come at the time I told you to bring Brady. Eight o'clock will be fine." She filled him in on the details: what their plans were and what they needed him to do before, during, and after the outing.

"I'll see you then, Audra."

"Wait, Luke. May I ask you a question?"

"Shoot."

"How come you're available? What happened?"

"My plans fell through." He didn't tell her his client's brand-new cabin cruiser hadn't been ready on time, and the client had to cancel the boating party for tomorrow.

"I'm sorry to hear that. But I'm glad you're coming with us. Brady'll love having his dad along for the outing. I think it'll mean something to him."

"I'm looking forward to being with him, too, at his class party. Wouldn't Jeris's term for that be *bonding*?"

"I think so."

"Whatever it's called, Brady is worth all my time."

"Luke?"

"What?"

"I prayed this would happen."

"That what would happen?"

"That you'd go with us."

"You did?"

"Well, my actual prayer was, 'Lord, I'd really like Luke to go with us on Saturday, but let Your will be done.' It appears it's His will for you to go, wouldn't you say? But time will tell."

He didn't know what to say. "Well," he finally managed, "I'll see you tomorrow morning, Audra."

"Okay, Luke. Thanks again."

He clicked off the phone and hurriedly made his way into the family room. Miss Ada's booklet was beckoning.

Luke picked up the book and made himself comfortable on the sofa. He turned to the next chapter, "Inward Beauty Is the Most Important Kind."

"Lad, search for a beautiful woman, meaning one who displays inward beauty, not necessarily outward beauty. The apostle Peter said, 'Whose adorning let it not be that outward adorning of plaiting the hair, and of wearing of gold, or of putting on of apparel; but let it be the hidden man of the heart, in that which is not corruptible, even the ornament of a meek and quiet spirit, which is in the sight of God of great price. For after this manner in the old time the holy women also, who trusted in God, adorned themselves' (1 Peter 3:3–5)."

He flipped to the passage in a modern version of the Bible. " 'Your beauty should not come from outward adornment,' " he read, " 'such as braided hair and the wearing of gold jewelry and fine clothes. Instead, it should be that of your inner self, the unfading beauty of a gentle and quiet spirit, which is of great worth in God's sight. For this is the way the holy women of the past who put their hope in God used to make themselves beautiful.' "

He stared out the French doors, black with the night. "I want a woman with the unfading beauty of a gentle and quiet spirit."

"Lad, true beauty is unselfishness. Let me say here, pretty is as pretty does. If a girl is truly pretty, she will act pretty. In this old world of harshness and ugliness, it's a delight to find a girl who is interested in others. If she is kind to others, she will naturally be kind to her husband and her darling children, too."

Luke considered this. *Though the language is archaic, what the author is saying is true.*

"While I'm addressing beauty, I need to say a word here about her hair. The Bible says a woman's hair is her crowning glory. Do not go after girls with a manly bob or a shorn-to-the-scalp hairstyle that makes her look like a sheep on shearing day. Go after the girls with long, flowing, wavy hair."

Luke laughed.

"If a girl possesses inward beauty, that means she has the qualities of kindness, cheerfulness, patience, industriousness, and thriftiness. Lad, look into a girl's heart to find one like this. And when you find her, latch on to her and never let her go. Joybells will ring in your soul till death do you part."

I'm looking. I'm looking. He flipped to the next chapter, "Check Out the Little Things about Her."

"What does the inside of her house look like? If and when she invites you inside, take her up on it. However she keeps house now will be how she will keep house with you or some other lucky lad. Is the place neat and clean? Are the curtains starched and ironed? Does she live by the motto, 'A place for everything, and everything in its place'? If you are an organized person and you acquire a bride who is messy and slovenly, woe be unto you. The trials you will endure over this issue alone will be multitudinous. This is fair warning."

That's true.

"There are more little things you should consider. Happy is the lad who finds a bride who is a good companion. Perhaps she can ride a bicycle with you, or perhaps she's a bit fond of fishing, hunting, or outdoor life. Maybe she will read the same books as you and will be able to talk intelligently about them (though not too intelligently)."

Luke laughed so hard, his eyes misted over. When he stopped laughing, he flipped to another page. "Choosing a Wife Is Serious Business." *That's for sure.*

"God instituted marriage between a lad and a girl and expects it to last a lifetime. The marriage union is both physical and spiritual as you become one with your bride. For this reason, you must find a girl who will serve the Lord with you and pray with you, one who is involved in the Lord's work. That is of utmost importance. She must love the Lord her God with all her heart, soul, mind, and strength—just as you do. She must put Him first in her life."

I'm all for that. Luke closed the booklet. *That's always been at the top of my list.*

Chapter 10

Jeris came bounding out the side door of the church fellowship hall early Saturday morning, her arms loaded with picnic items. Audra followed closely behind, her arms full, too.

They made their way to the church van in the parking lot and packed the items in the back compartment.

"Here comes Blake." Audra shut the back doors of the van just as a car drove into the parking lot.

Jeris saw four more cars pull up near them. "And Jeffrey Phillips. And Patrice Edwards. And Denny Roper. Do you have a head count of the children? Didn't you say several of them are bringing friends or relatives?"

"Right. I think we're going to have nine children today."

"Isn't that great? Just think. We started with only three."

"God is using you to help build His kingdom, Jeris."

"I feel like it's a privilege to serve Him." She saw several children pile out of cars. "It's good you finally roped in Mrs. Edwards as a chaperone. I wouldn't want the two of us handling all these children at the beach."

"Didn't I tell you? She's not coming."

"She isn't? Then what are we going to do?"

"It's all taken care of."

"Who's helping us?"

Another car turned into the lot and parked. Luke Moore stepped out of the driver's side, and Brady bounded out of the backseat. Luke was dressed in shorts and sneakers.

"Luke?" Jeris was thunderstruck. "He's helping us chaperone?"

"That's right."

She tried to tamp down the chagrin inside her. She didn't like feeling this way, especially since her ill feelings were directed toward Audra Darling. The mere thought made her hurt inside. But she couldn't help it. "How? I thought you told me he turned you down."

Audra flashed her a mischievous smile. "The Lord works in mysterious ways, His wonders to perform."

While Jeris gave pick-up instructions to the parents for when the party was over, Luke assisted Audra in corralling the children and securing them in seatbelts in the van.

Soon they were on their way, with Jeris driving. The children shouted

184

and laughed and jumped on their seats as much as their seatbelts would allow. She was glad they were having a good time, but she wished they would calm down.

Luke sat in the front seat across the boxy console from her, but he was turned toward the back trying to establish order.

Audra, sitting on the bench seat behind Jeris, looked around and clapped loudly three times. "Children, quiet down."

The children ignored Audra's instruction.

Jeris had never seen them act like this. In her classroom there was occasional loudness, but nothing like this. It was the excitement of the party, she decided.

Even Audra's hot pink Fifi didn't do the trick. The children were simply too wound up.

Suddenly one child yelled as if in agony.

"Quit poking Denny, Jeffrey Phillips!" Audra called, near-exasperation in her voice. "I saw that. Keep your hands to yourselves. NBC. No bodily contact."

Luke, still turned toward the children, raised his arms in the air as if he were about to direct a choir. "Do-re-mi-fa-so-la-ti-do!" he belted out.

Every child grew quiet.

Jeris glanced at the kids through the rearview mirror and noted several had eyes as big as saucers.

"Do-ti-la-so-fa-mi-re-do," he sang backward. "Let's sing, kids." He smiled at them, his arms flailing in the air. He led them in a fast rendition of "Jesus Loves the Little Children" and then "The Wise Man Built His House upon the Rock," complete with hammering and raining motions.

The children followed his lead, apparently enthralled.

He led them in song after song.

Jeris noticed the songs were old, not the new praise songs she used in children's church. But that was okay. They were keeping the children entertained and still.

"These are the only kids' songs I know," he whispered to her between lyrics.

"They're doing the trick," she whispered back. "Keep it up."

Twenty minutes later she drove into the beach parking lot.

Luke hopped out, opened the long sliding door of the van, and put the step stool on the ground. He stood to the side at attention, as if he were an army sergeant, his hand in a salute position.

The first child climbed down the stool.

"Aye, aye." Luke saluted the little boy. "Line up here." He pointed to his left.

"Aye, aye." The boy saluted back and did as he was told.

Luke went through this procedure nine times until a long line of kids had formed.

Jeris and Audra were at the back of the van, loading their arms with picnic supplies. Jeris was glad for Luke's innovative control of the children.

185

Calling out military commands, he had them march to the back of the van. "March in place."

They obeyed, their little feet making *tap-tap-tap* noises on the pavement.

"Here," he said to Jeris, where she stood at the back compartment of the van. "Step aside and let me get the cooler. It's too heavy for you."

"Aye, aye, captain." She saluted him.

He saluted her back, then reached into the compartment and lifted out the cooler.

She had thought he was reserved and conceited but had to admit she was seeing a different side of him today. What did it matter, though, what she thought about him? Her thoughts or feelings about him would never amount to anything because she wouldn't let them. And neither would he.

"How did you dream up the military maneuvering?" she asked.

"It just came to me, I guess." He shrugged. "I was in ROTC in college."

"It's the Holy Spirit's illumination." Audra Darling nodded her head with a confident air.

∞

Out on the beach, Luke set the cooler down in the sand under the shade of a palm tree. Like soldiers, the children marched in place behind him.

"Company, halt," he said as he faced them. "We're going to have a good time today, kids. But only if you obey orders. Is that understood?"

Nine "Yes, sirs" came out in unison.

He proceeded to lay down some rules. "No straying from the group. Obey the adults. Line up when you're told to. Come when you're called."

"We claim you as chaperone for every kids' outing," Audra said from behind him as the children waited quietly to be told what to do next.

He looked at her. "Very funny."

"I don't see anything funny about it, do you, Jeris?" Audra had an innocent look on her face.

Jeris was shaking out a blanket over the sand, the middle of it billowing up, then floating to the ground. "I think it's a Holy Spirit-illuminated idea."

Luke chuckled. He noticed Jeris wasn't wearing her usual bland clothing: the too-long skirts and the too-baggy jackets. Today she had on jeans that tastefully displayed her slenderness and a red shirt tucked in at her waist. She looked more casual and comfortable.

Jeris started the party with a vigorous game of dodge ball in the sand.

As they played, Luke watched Jeris, covertly, of course. He didn't want her to think he had bad manners. She seemed to come alive around the children. She was friendly and outgoing. And though she wasn't drop-dead gorgeous, she was pretty in an athletic and outdoorsy way. He liked that in her, something he'd never thought about in wife material.

Later, after one of the organized games, he watched her chase the children, catch them up in the air, and swing them around, laughing, as carefree as the wind. He recalled a few lines from the booklet he'd been reading, something about a lad being happy if his bride could ride a bicycle with him or was fond of the outdoor life.

He laughed out loud picturing June Cleaver in a fancy dress and pearls riding a bicycle beside Ward.

"What are you laughing at?" Jeris was out of breath from playing with the kids.

"Oh, nothing."

All morning he did what he could to be of help, and it looked as if his help was direly needed, as active as the children were. They waded in the water for a time, then picnicked on the blankets Jeris had spread on the sand.

After lunch she told them the story of Jonah, acting it out in front of them and applying the scriptural truths to their lives. Then she asked Luke to lead the kids in singing.

He was proud of himself when he remembered an old song from childhood, "Now Listen to My Tale of Jonah and the Whale." It was a perfect fit to her story.

After the singing, she announced it was time to hunt for sharks' teeth, and the kids squealed. Once they reached the place farther down the beach, she showed them how to hunt, raking her fingers through the sand. Soon the children were on their hands and knees, absorbed in their treasure hunting.

"Dad, Dad, I found one!" Brady came running up to Luke. He was hopping on both feet and grinning.

"Good going, Little Man." Luke hugged him. He examined the small, dark object in Brady's palm. "This is something you'll never forget, finding a shark's tooth on a Florida beach."

"This is the goodest time I ever had." Brady held the tooth in his tight little fist and waved it, smiling his ear-to-ear smile, his eyes dancing.

"It's been a fun day, hasn't it?"

Brady nodded, his cowlick sticking straight up.

"Which did you like best? Hunting for sharks' teeth? Playing games? Or the picnic with the—"

"The root beer?" Brady giggled.

Luke laughed. "You and your root beer. Let's see. What else did we do today? How about when we picked up seashells? Did you like that the best?"

"I liked the story Miss Jeris told us the very bestest. About Jonah and the whale."

Luke looked at the waves lapping at the shore. This was the ideal spot to teach the kids that particular story. "You liked that story the very bestest, huh?" He chuckled.

"Yes, sir. What's a *notion*, Dad?"

"A notion? Where'd that come from?"

"The song you sang about Jonah. Remember? You said Jonah had a very foolish notion."

"Oh. I guess you could say a notion is a way of thinking. And a foolish notion is a wrong way of thinking. God told Jonah to go to Nineveh, but Jonah didn't want to go, so he didn't obey."

"Kind of like when you come to Miss Jeris's class on Sundays and tell me it's time to go, but I don't want to leave?"

"You could say that, yes."

"Does everybody have foolish notions, Dad?"

Luke thought about it.

"Brady!" Jeris hurried over to them, smiling a Brady smile. Enthusiasm laced her voice. "I hear you found a shark's tooth." She crouched in the sand next to Brady. "May I see it?"

"Yes, Miss Jeris." He opened his hand. "It was so fun."

Luke observed closely as Brady told her about the tooth and listened to her response. She was interested in Brady, as she was all of the children. It was apparent she loved the kids. And she interacted with them in an unusual way. It was a gift, something unique and special, he had to admit. He kept watching her as she talked with Brady. She took the tooth from his palm, held it up so it gleamed in the sunshine, and discussed Jonah and the whale with Brady.

"Brady," she said, "Jonah brought salvation to an entire town when he finally obeyed God."

Brady nodded. "That was the goodest story, Miss Jeris."

She laughed.

It was as if Luke were seeing her for the first time. *Does everybody have foolish notions, Dad?* Brady had asked. *I do, Brady,* he could've answered a few minutes ago. *I had a foolish notion that Jeris wasn't my type.*

Brady wrapped his arms around Jeris's neck. "Thank you for bringing us here today."

She hugged him back. "You're welcome, Little Man. I'm glad you had a good time. But, more than that, I hope some deep spiritual truths sank in here." With her index finger she touched his heart. "Maybe one day God will use you to help a lot of people see the light as Jonah did."

A warm feeling washed over Luke—a good feeling, an exciting feeling. *Brady, you certainly helped one person see the light. Me.*

Chapter 11

I t's a good thing we left the beach when we did." Luke glanced across the console at Jeris, then stared at the deluge of rain hitting the windshield, the noise so loud it was almost deafening. "Who would've thought we'd get rain today?" He had to speak loudly to be heard. "With those cloudless blue skies we had at the beach?"

Jeris nodded as she gripped the steering wheel with both hands. "Typical of Florida, I guess. I'm glad it waited until now."

"Me, too." He looked down at his watch. Three thirty.

"The Lord gave us glorious weather for the party."

He nodded.

She tipped her head toward the rearview mirror. "Looks like the rain lulled them to sleep."

Luke glanced behind him. Most of the kids were sound asleep. Even Audra was leaning back against the seat, her eyes closed. "You two did a great job today."

"Thanks. You did, too. We appreciate your help."

He shrugged, feeling a little guilty he hadn't readily volunteered and in fact hadn't *wanted* to come when Audra first asked. Now he was glad he did. He liked the sense of fulfillment it gave him, to know he'd lent a hand to help in the Lord's work. The Lord's work? That's how the little booklet referred to church work. It said a man should find a wife who would serve the Lord with him, one who was involved in the Lord's work.

He glanced at Jeris again. She was certainly involved in the Lord's work. That was good.

The rest of the trip he didn't say any more, and neither did she. He figured they were both a little tired after the full day. But he was looking forward to talking with her more, especially after the revelation hit him on the beach, the one Brady had brought him.

Soon Jeris pulled into the church parking lot. It was still raining heavily. She stopped the van under the wide carport beside the church. "It'll be easier to get the children out under here with the rain."

"Good idea." He unbuckled his seatbelt.

"Children, wake up," she called. "We're back."

Within ten minutes everyone had left the church except Luke, Brady, and Jeris. He offered to park the church van in its usual spot on the far side of the sanctuary. Then he dashed to his car, pulled up under the carport, and let Brady in.

Jeris thanked him again for his help, then ran through the rain to her vehicle.

As Luke drove through the parking lot on his way to the road, he noticed Jeris's vehicle hadn't moved out of her parking space. He backed up and pulled over beside her car. He tapped on his horn and inched his window down. She inched hers down. "What's the matter?" he asked.

"My windshield wipers won't work. I can't drive like this."

Rain was pouring into his car. "Can you make it to the carport?"

"I think so."

"Then come on." He closed his window and drove under the carport, leaving room for her to pull up beside him. "Stay inside, Brady." He hopped out of his car.

Brady was so sleepy that he didn't let out a peep.

Jeris got out of her car and stood there, the car pinging, with the key still in the ignition. She pulled out the key, and the pinging stopped. "I can't imagine what's wrong with the wipers. My SUV is brand-new."

"Some fluke thing, probably. It's under warranty, I'm sure."

She nodded.

"Leave it parked here, and I'll run you home. Then, when it quits raining, I can pick you up and bring you back to get it. On Monday you can take it to the dealership."

"I wouldn't want to impose—"

"You aren't imposing. Brady and I don't have any plans for the rest of the afternoon. It'd be no trouble at all."

"That's okay."

"But what else can you do? You can't drive in this downpour without windshield wipers."

"I could wait it out."

What was up with her? He was trying to be kind, and she was refusing it. Then he realized he was being forceful. "I'm sorry. I didn't mean to order you. I was only trying to be helpful."

"I—I . . ." Her voice trailed off.

"Let's start over. May I take you home and bring you back later?"

She shrugged. "Okay," she finally said.

Luke opened the car door for Jeris, and she got in.

"Hi, Miss Jeris." Brady came alive. "I had the goodest time today." He rubbed the sleep out of his eyes.

"I did, too, Brady." She turned toward Brady and smiled, then gave Luke instructions on how to find her apartment.

Brady held up his shark's tooth. "I'm going to put this under my pillow tonight." His eyes were glowing, and he was smiling broadly, revealing his missing tooth.

She laughed.

Luke laughed, too. "Brady, that's for *your* teeth."

"Oh." Brady looked crestfallen.

"But maybe we can find a special place to display it."

Brady brightened.

"Maybe we can frame it and hang it in your bedroom."

"Yippee!"

After a few minutes Jeris gestured toward a large gated apartment complex on her side of the highway. "Well, here we are. Take the next right."

Luke pulled into the complex. The buildings were painted in complementary hues that reminded him of a Florida sunset—corals, oranges, and burnished golds. Even through the steady rain he could see an architecturally pleasing club-house on the left and guessed a pool was behind it. Most complexes were built that way. Tennis courts were to the right. The landscaping design was superb. "Nice."

"Thanks. I enjoy living here." She fished in her purse. "Pull up to the gate, and you can swipe my card." She retrieved a thick white card from her purse and handed it to him.

He drove up to the huge black wrought-iron gate, lowered his window, and swiped the card. The gate opened in front of them. "Which way?"

"Follow this road a little ways, and I'll tell you where to turn when you come to my street." Within minutes she led him to her garage.

"These units have garages?" He was surprised. He knew this was a luxury complex, but he didn't realize they had garages. It had been a long time since he'd lived in an apartment.

"Some do." She pulled out a remote and clicked it, and the garage door opened. "Pull on in. A garage comes in handy for weather like this. That's why I chose this unit."

Luke drove in, turning off his wipers so they wouldn't flick water on the sides of the garage. A couple of tennis rackets hung on the wall above a bike.

June Cleaver surfaced.

He smiled inwardly.

Other than the bike and the tennis rackets, the garage was spotless.

Jeris opened her car door, then turned to him. "Thanks for the ride, Luke."

"Glad I was there when your mishap occurred." He put the car in REVERSE but kept his foot anchored on the brake.

"Me, too."

"Dad, I've got to go to the bathroom."

Jeris laughed, her eyes twinkling in delight.

"I keep trying to teach that boy manners." He rolled his eyes in a playful manner.

"Da–a–a–d—"

"We'll find a gas station on our way home, son."

"Bring him inside." She put her purse strap over her shoulder. "There's no need to hunt for a gas station in this deluge."

191

"I can't wait any longer, Dad."

Luke could only accept her kind offer. Secretly he was glad she had made it. He would get to spend a little more time with her. "Thanks, Jeris." He put the car in PARK and turned off the ignition.

"You're welcome. Come on in, guys."

"Do you have any root beer, Miss Jeris?" Brady undid his seatbelt and reached for the door handle.

"Brady." Luke rolled his eyes again.

"It's okay. It's no bother at all." She turned toward the backseat. "Yes, Little Man. I have some root beer."

"Yippee!"

Luke was curious as he walked into her apartment.

Brady darted across the room. He reached the hallway, stopped abruptly, and looked over at Jeris.

She gestured to the right. "Hurry, Brady. It's down the hall. At the end."

"Yes, ma'am." He ran like lightning, and the bathroom door slammed behind him.

Luke glanced around the tastefully decorated room.

What does the inside of her house look like? If and when she invites you inside, take her up on it.

He squelched the chuckle roiling up inside as he remembered Miss Ada's booklet again. He seemed to be doing that a lot today. It must mean it was sinking in. The author had said to check out the cleanliness and the neatness of Miss Possible's home.

Miss Possible? He smiled.

"Have a seat, Luke."

"Thanks." He sat down in an overstuffed leather chair that matched the sofa. *Nice.*

"Make yourself at home."

"I think I will." *I like the way that sounds.* He propped his feet up on the leather ottoman.

She crossed the room, stopped at an end table, and picked up a remote. She aimed it at the fireplace and punched a button, bringing up yellow flames on a bank of logs. She walked over and opened the glass doors. "This lets out heat. If you're as damp as I am, it'll probably feel good."

He settled back in the chair comfortably. The heat felt good, just as she'd said. But that wasn't what was making him feel as if he were walking on air.

She turned on a lamp, lit a candle on the coffee table, then sank into the leather sofa opposite him and rubbed her upper arms, making a *br–r–r* sound. "Oh, I forgot. Brady asked for a root beer." She jumped up. "Send him into the kitchen when he comes out, okay?"

"Sure." Luke watched her as she walked across the room and disappeared from sight. But he could hear her in the kitchen, scurrying about.

He looked around the pleasant room again. *You'd be very pleased, Mr. Granfield.* He smiled as he thought of the author of the booklet.

Luke felt pleased, too. The lamp, candle, and flames in the fireplace cast a luminous glow over the room. He admired the sophisticated brown leather sofa and matching chair, the accents of red in the sofa pillows, the flowing curtains at the windows, and the large painting over the sofa. The medium-colored wood of the end tables matched the TV armoire and the dining table he spotted in the alcove at the far end.

Brady came bounding into the room. "Where's Miss Jeris?"

"Did you wash your hands, Little Man?" Luke asked.

Brady saluted him. "Yes, Dad. Where's Miss Jeris?"

Luke stood up. "She's in the kitchen. Let's go find her." Hand in hand with Brady, he turned the corner and saw that the kitchen and dining area were one big room separated by a large island. Four stools with leather seats the color of her sofa were pulled up to the island. Another large painting with red and brown tones hung above a buffet on a far wall. *Nice,* he thought again.

"Miss Jeris, I like your house." Brady ran to her and gave her a hug where she stood near the stove.

She embraced him exuberantly. "Thanks, Little Man."

Finally he let go of her. He spotted a cage against the wall and raced to it. "What's this, Miss Jeris?"

"It's Sparky, my gerbil. He's my pet."

"You have a pet?" His eyes were round with wonder as he looked back at Luke.

She nodded. "I keep Sparky at my apartment on the weekends. But during the week he stays at my office."

"For the children you counsel?" Luke asked.

She nodded again, compassion in her eyes. "Sparky makes them feel more at ease. They seem to open up when they're holding him. They love him."

"Ooh," Brady said. "I love her, too. Can I hold her?"

"You mean *him*?"

"Yes, ma'am." Brady reached through the thin bars of the cage and touched the gerbil on the nose. "Please, Miss Jeris? Can I hold him?"

"Sure. Just be gentle."

"Maybe I'd better help." Luke stepped to the cage and knelt beside Brady, then opened the door. "Put your hand in here, Brady. Let Sparky smell you first."

"Are you a coffee or tea drinker, Luke?" She reached for two canisters on the counter and pulled them toward her.

"That sounds great." He smiled. "I could use a cup."

"You're not helping matters." She smiled back.

He laughed. "I'm game for either one. Really. Which is easiest?"

The teakettle on the stove whistled.

"Tea. You've already boiled the water."

She pulled the teakettle off the burner with a quick movement. "That doesn't matter. I can make coffee in a few minutes."

"That's all right. I'll take hot tea. Sounds good."

She nodded and pulled down two earthenware mugs, then gathered some more items, opening a cabinet door here or there.

"Can I pick him up now, Dad?" Brady ran his hand down the gerbil's back as far as the cage bars would let him reach.

"Okay. Just be careful, like Miss Jeris said." Luke was fascinated as Brady played with the gerbil. He'd begged for a pet for over a year, and Luke always told him they didn't have time for one. Maybe this was the answer. A gerbil. He'd have to ask Jeris how much care was involved. From the looks of things and by the way she talked about transporting the gerbil back and forth, it appeared this kind of animal might work for Brady.

"Luke? Brady? Are you ready for a snack?"

"Aw, Miss Jeris, do I have to put Sparky down now? I want to play with him some more."

"I have some cookies for you."

Brady kept playing with the gerbil.

Luke quickly washed his hands at the kitchen sink, then walked to the island. He was amazed at the spread she'd laid out. He'd been so absorbed in watching Brady with the gerbil, he hadn't noticed what she was doing. She'd put colorful dishes on coordinating placemats, and there was a box holding different types of tea bags. A plate held a variety of cookies on it, and a cheese board had two kinds of cheeses and crackers. At Brady's place she'd set a bottle of his favorite drink—root beer. Beside his plate were a few carrot sticks and a small wedge of fresh cabbage.

"Brady, come and eat your snack now," she said. "When you're finished, you can give Sparky a treat and play with him to your heart's content. Would you like to feed him?"

"Yippee!"

Luke sat down on the bar stool. "Put Sparky back in his cage, Brady, and go wash your hands."

"Yes, sir." Brady did as he was told this time.

In a few minutes the three of them were seated at the island.

Jeris asked Luke to say the blessing.

He prayed, and when he opened his eyes, he saw on the counter a copy of a book the Sunday school class had recently studied. He gestured toward it. "How'd you like it?"

"It was thought-provoking. It's impacted a lot of lives, from what I've heard."

Luke took a sip of his hot tea, remembering Miss Ada's book.

"Maybe she will read the same books as you and will be able to talk intelligently about them (though not too intelligently)."

He nearly choked on his tea, laughing. He grabbed his napkin and threw it across his mouth, still laughing.

Brady giggled. "What's so funny, Dad?"

Jeris put a small slice of cheese on a cracker. "I was wondering the same thing." Her voice had a drone effect, as if she were as interested as the man in the moon.

"Did Sparky make you laugh, Dad? Was it something he did?"

Luke looked across the room and saw Sparky staring at them from the cage, his mouth moving as if he were talking, his whiskers twitching up and down. "Sparky *is* funny, isn't he, Little Man?" Luke rubbed the top of Brady's head.

"You know, Dad"—Brady smiled brightly—"this is the goodest time I ever had."

∽

The rain finally stopped, and Jeris was grateful for the ride back to her car. After she arrived home she took a shower and dressed in comfy clothes, then sat down on the sofa. She turned on the TV but set it on MUTE. She had to do some mental housekeeping.

She hoped she'd managed to conduct herself in the way she'd intended while Luke was there. Her mind replayed everything she'd said and done. She'd been friendly. That was her nature. But she hadn't been too friendly. She'd been hospitable. That was her nature, too. But she hadn't overdone it. Cookies and cheese and crackers weren't too much, were they? Maybe she should've skipped the placemats and matching napkins. And her exuberance with Brady. But that couldn't be helped. She would never be distant with Brady, no matter how much space she wanted between her and Luke.

On and on the scene played in her head as she wondered about this and that. Had she been too harsh when she'd said parents needed to spend lots of time with their children, even if it meant cutting back their work hours? She'd half meant it as a slam against Luke but half meant it out of concern for Brady.

Other questions surfaced in her mind.

Until she felt troubled.

"This has to stop. No more. At least for tonight."

Chapter 12

Jeris drove to the Hugheses' parsonage. Audra Darling had called her a couple of days ago and invited her to dinner tonight. She told her to come early so she could give her a few tips on making lasagna. The plan was to eat it as soon as they pulled it out of the oven. That sounded good to Jeris. She needed all the help she could get in the kitchen and had managed to leave work early.

She braked for a red light. A couple of weeks had passed since the beach party, and she'd stayed busy at work and church. Luke continued to drop Brady off at her children's church class, and he was friendly each time she saw him, though she wondered why.

Was it because of the beach party? Or his visit in her apartment? She was pretty sure he'd come out of his shell because of the visit. He'd called her a couple of times to get advice about gerbils. It seemed he was going to buy one for Brady. Both times he'd called, he'd lingered in conversation. Why, she didn't know. But she was glad Brady was getting a pet. It made children responsible. And gave them something more to love.

She pulled into the Hugheses' driveway and was surprised to see Luke's car. What was he doing here? He said he couldn't cook, so Audra was probably going to include him in the cooking lessons. But why did it have to happen on the same night she invited Jeris?

She bristled as she climbed out of her SUV, shut the door behind her, and walked to the front of the house.

Audra Darling welcomed her and gave her a hug, then led her into the kitchen.

Jeris felt herself clamming up as soon as she saw Luke.

"Hi, Jeris." He was leaning against a kitchen cabinet, his arms folded across his chest, looking like the handsome, self-assured man he was.

"Hi, Luke." Awkward. That's how she felt and wished she were a million miles away. She stopped at the table, put her hands on the back of a chair, and squeezed the maple wood. "Good to see you." *Sort of.*

"Same here. Looks like we're both getting cooking lessons tonight."

"It appears so." She let go of the chair, removed her purse from her shoulder, and set it on the table.

"I readily admit I need them," he said.

I do, too, but with you?

"Neither of you knows how to cook, so I decided to give you some tips tonight." Audra Darling tied an apron around her, nonchalance in her tone. "At the same time."

Jeris was on to Audra Darling's matchmaking. The children's beach party was her first hint. Before that, when she had invited them for Sunday dinner, Jeris hadn't given it a thought. But when Audra Darling had managed to get Luke to chaperone the party, she'd put two and two together. Now tonight—the lessons and dinner. With Luke. She knew Audra Darling was cooking up something.

And it's more than lasagna.

"Here, Luke." Audra Darling pulled out an apron from a lower kitchen drawer and placed it on the counter. "Put this on. It'll protect your shirt."

"Thanks." He put the apron over his head and smoothed out the folds in front.

Audra Darling took out another one. "And here's one for you, Jeris."

"Thanks." Jeris put on her apron, then reached behind herself and tied it.

Luke tried to tie his apron in back. "I need help. You have to be a contortionist to do this."

Audra Darling laughed. "Jeris, can you help him?" Holding a large platter, she tipped her head toward Luke.

If I didn't love you to pieces, Audra Darling, I wouldn't like you right now. Jeris walked over to Luke as if she were a child going to the principal's office.

Luke turned his back to her, and while she tied his apron strings, he and Audra Darling chatted across the kitchen.

Jeris finished her task and moved away quickly.

Luke turned around. "Thanks, Jeris."

"You're welcome." She thought about Brady. "Where's Little Man?"

He pointed to the wide bank of windows over the kitchen table.

Brady stood on the low floating dock with Pastor Hughes, both of them holding fishing poles.

"Looks like they're having a good time." Jeris absently retied her apron.

"And so are we." Audra bustled about the large kitchen, taking things out of the refrigerator and the pantry and setting them on the counters.

Jeris strolled over to the windows, pretending to be interested in Brady and his fishing venture. But she wasn't. She was assailed with doubts about Luke. And about herself as she thought about what lay behind a good-looking man's face—the big ego thing. Wasn't that how it was? Weren't movie-star-handsome men macho and into themselves? Was it true or not?

Chapter 13

Jeris looked at her watch for the umpteenth time as she stood under the church carport. Eleven forty-five. "We've waited nearly thirty minutes. You think we ought to go ahead and leave? I don't think any more children are coming, do you? It looks as if we're only going to have three today."

Audra Darling shrugged her shoulders. "I thought an outing like this would've enticed a few more kids. Maybe it's too soon from our last outing. But that was a whole month ago."

Jeris nodded. Today they planned to take the children to the mall. First they would take them to Jolly Hamburgers for burgers and shakes and then to the kids' playground. After that, they would let them ride the new double-tiered merry-go-round in the center of the mall. Luke had volunteered to chaperone, and Jeris glanced at him sitting in his car with two little boys in the backseat beside Brady. She could see all three picking at each other and giggling.

"I have two church functions today." Audra Darling fished in her oversized shoulder bag. "One is a barbecue at the Winstons' home that starts at noon, and the other was this outing."

"*Was*? What's that supposed to mean?"

"I'm hoping you and Luke will agree to take the kids. Without me." She was still searching through her purse. "That way I can go on over to the Winstons'. I know it'll please them that I was able to come."

"Audra Dar—"

"They're celebrating Ned's sixtieth birthday. It's not just an ordinary come-have-lunch-with-us invitation." She pulled out a key ring full of keys. "They've invited tons of out-of-town family and friends, and they wanted to introduce Andrew and me to them as their pastors."

Jeris gave a resigned sigh. Audra Darling had a good reason to duck out of the kids' outing. But it would make things awkward. Luke was the last man she wanted to be stuck with. In the last few days—since Audra's cooking lesson—she'd spent some time sorting through her feelings, trying to make sense of her qualms, trying to weigh them and determine if there was any validity to them. She'd come to the conclusion that matters of the heart were almost too difficult to understand, even with her training in the field of psychology. Naturally Luke would be a good choice. He was a Christian and successful, but he wasn't her idea of—

"I take it by your silence you're in full agreement?" Audra Darling gave her a dazzling smile.

"I. . ." She nodded. What else could she do? What choice did she have? Audra Darling wasn't needed at the outing with only three children, but she *was* needed at Ned Winston's sixtieth birthday party. And Jeris would help her out. "Sure. Go ahead." She smiled. "But you'd better get a move on if you want to be on time."

"I knew you'd understand. You know how pastoring is. Everybody wants you." She was looking in her purse again. "I'll call Andrew and let him know I'm coming." She pulled out her cell phone and flipped it open. "And I'll go tell Luke my change in plans, okay?" She was already crossing the carport. She stopped and turned toward Jeris, her cell phone at her ear. "Jeris, you're a sweetheart."

"Who's a sweetheart?" Luke approached the carport. He wiggled his eyebrows.

Audra Darling threw her hand over her chest, whirled, and faced Luke. "Your deep voice startled me. I didn't know you were anywhere around. I thought you were still in your car."

"Sorry. I didn't mean to startle you. I came to see what the holdup is."

Audra Darling quickly explained the new plan to him.

"That's fine with me," he said. But he wasn't looking at Audra Darling. He was looking at Jeris. Intently.

Jeris dropped her gaze to the concrete. She had too much to think about concerning him. "Do you want to take your car or mine, Luke?"

∞

Luke marveled at Jeris from where he sat on the parklike bench on the first tier of the merry-go-round. He'd thought she was. . .gray. That was what he'd called it after he first met her. But she wasn't gray at all. She was pink and lavender—carefree and uninhibited. She'd shrieked like a child when they first walked up to the new merry-go-round, which made the boys shriek, too. Instead of the usual horses and tigers and zebras, this merry-go-round had sea animals. Dolphins. Seals. Seahorses. Manatees. Whales.

She'd jumped onto a dolphin and started humming the theme song to the old TV show *Flipper*, making the boys laugh.

She was all smiles and laughter, not her usual quiet self. She'd seemed inhibited every time he'd been around her, except for the children's beach party when she'd been playful and friendly like today. The children definitely brought it out in her, and he liked it.

Could *he* bring out those same qualities in her? If he could, maybe he would get to know her better.

∞

That evening Luke and Brady ate a soup-and-sandwich supper, then swam in the pool until dark. Afterward Luke fixed Brady a snack while Brady took his bath. Later he read him a book, prayed with him, and tucked him in bed.

"Good night, Little Man." Luke kissed him on the forehead. "I love you."

"I love you, too, Dad. And I love Audra Darling. And I love Pastor Hughes." He named six or seven other people he loved. "And I love Gerbil."

"Are you still calling him Gerbil?" Luke had laughed when Brady insisted on naming him Gerbil after he bought him at the pet store. But he'd let Brady do what he wanted. It was his pet.

"That's his name, Dad."

"Okay. If you say so."

"You know who I love almost as much as I love you, Dad?"

"Who's that?"

"Miss Jeris."

Luke wasn't surprised. He knew Brady enjoyed spending time with Jeris. He was always asking about her. "Well, sleep tight, Little Man." He kissed him on the forehead again.

"Yes, sir."

Luke closed the door behind him and walked into the family room. He saw Miss Ada's booklet on the end table. He hadn't read it in a while. He supposed it was time to pick it up again.

He plopped down on the sofa, comparing it to Jeris's leather one, thinking maybe he'd enjoy a sofa like hers. Hers was much more attractive than his. She definitely had good taste in furnishings.

He reached for the booklet and flipped to a new chapter: "Why You Need Marriage."

∞

"Marriage is a companionship, a blending of two souls before God. It is right and fitting and good that a lad should have a wife and that a girl should have a husband.

"God brought the first couple together, Adam and Eve. In Genesis chapter one, we see that as God created the heavens and the earth, He saw each thing that He created was good. Six times the Bible says God saw that it was good.

"But it is significant to note that when God created man in the recording of chapter two, He said (not saw), 'It is not good that the man should be alone; I will make him an help meet for him.'

"God knew it wasn't good for Adam to remain alone. He needed a wife. So God set about creating Eve for him. Then he presented her to Adam, and the Bible says, 'Therefore shall a man leave his father and his mother, and shall cleave unto his wife: and they shall be one flesh' (Genesis 2:24).

"Lad, you need a wife.

"You need a wife to cleave to.

"You need a wife to be one flesh with."

Amen to that. Luke wiggled his eyebrows, smiling from ear to ear.

"And as I've stated before, you need God's choice of a wife. She must be the right one. Rest assured, she's out there, lad, reserved just for you. Your job is to seek the Lord about her, and the Lord's job is to speak to her heart about you."

Luke paused from his reading and bowed his head. "Lord, I'm trying to seek You about this matter. I know it'll take a special woman to agree to a marriage with a child thrown into the deal. But You know just who I need. And You know just who Brady needs. I choose to believe she's out there. And, Lord, if it's Jeris, please soften her heart toward me. In Jesus' name. Amen."

Chapter 14

Jeris looked across the table at Carrie Denton, the office manager she'd hired when she opened her practice. Carrie was doing a great job, and she couldn't be more pleased with her work. She was thankful for this new friend, what she'd asked God for when she moved to Silver Bay. Though they didn't attend the same church, Carrie was a believer, and Jeris had enjoyed their friendship. She also enjoyed the short time they shared each morning before the workday began, when they prayed for God's blessings and for the troubled children Jeris counseled.

"What time do you have to be at the airport in the morning, Jeris?"

"My plane leaves at eight, so I'd like to get there around six thirty."

"Then I need to pick you up at six, right? Will that give us enough time?"

"Plenty. Saturday morning traffic is nothing compared to weekdays."

Carrie nodded. "That's for sure."

"Thanks for offering to take me."

"You're welcome. And I'm to pick you up late Sunday night, right? After you get back from the conference? At 10:30?"

"If you don't mind. I really appreciate your help."

"You're welcome again."

Jeris smiled. "I hate missing my children's church class on Sunday, but Audra Darling said she'd cover for me. Remember I told you about her? My pastor's wife?"

Carrie nodded. "I'd like to meet her sometime. Anybody with a name like that—well, I'd just like to meet her."

"She's a neat person. A charming, Southern lady." Jeris took a sip of her sweet iced tea. "Where's Martin this time?"

"Miami again."

"When will he be back?"

"Saturday night. I can't wait for him to get home. I've missed him like crazy this week."

"Typical sentiments of newlyweds."

"I'm having a hard time dealing with Martin traveling so much. Thanks for meeting me for dinner tonight. I hate eating alone, don't you?" A stricken look crossed her face. "I'm sorry. I should think before I speak. I didn't mean to be insensitive. I wasn't even thinking about. . .about your eating alone all the time. Oh, my. I'm bungling this."

"It's all right. Don't worry about it." Jeris smiled to make Carrie feel better.

"I've been eating alone so long that I never think twice about it." She laughed. But her laugh felt hollow.

Carrie stared down at her plate. "Jeris?" She looked up. "I've been praying about something. . .something for you."

Jeris could feel it coming. Was she going to say she'd been praying God would send Jeris a husband? It didn't offend her if that was the case. On the contrary she wanted all the prayers she could get.

"I've been asking the Lord to send a special man into your life."

"Then that makes two of you praying for that."

"Two?"

"Audra Darling told me she's praying the same way."

"Then why don't you make it *the three of us*?"

"Three?"

Carrie wagged her finger at her. "You need to be joining in this prayer."

Jeris shrugged. "God knows my heart. I suppose if it's meant to be, it'll happen."

"But He wants us to pray in specific ways."

"I guess so."

"And you know what else He wants?"

"What's that?"

"He wants us to be open to *His* plans. Sometimes His ways are not our ways."

"Meaning?"

"Well, for instance, what if God has a beta male in mind for you?"

"Beta? I've never heard the term. I know sanguine and choleric and melancholy and phlegmatic—you know, the personality types. And then there're the Briggs-Meyer classifications. But *beta*?"

Carrie held up a bookstore bag, then laid it on the table. "I stopped by the bookstore on my way here and bought a book. It's about heroes and heroines in romance novels and—"

"How's your writing coming along?" Jeris took a bite of her chicken alfredo.

"I just finished chapter four of my novel. If I write a page a day, I figure I can finish it in about four or five months. That class I told you about—the one I'm taking at the community college every Tuesday night? I'm learning a lot about fiction writing. The instructor is a published author of twelve novels."

"Wow."

"She's been teaching from this book the past couple of weeks." Carrie touched the bag. "I'm going to highlight the things she's teaching so I can learn it."

"Just remember me when you're rich and famous."

Carrie laughed and rolled her eyes, her long dark eyelashes fluttering. "Right, right."

"I'm serious."

"Right, right." She pulled the book out of the bag. "This author says there are two types of heroes. The alpha and the beta."

"And the beta is—?"

"He's the one we don't want to read about in novels, according to the author and according to my instructor. The beta hero is the soft-spoken, supersensitive, easily led gentleman."

Jeris thought about her balding, bookish man. "That's the kind of man I'm looking for. That type of guy is tender, at least from what I've observed. And that's the number one thing I want in a man. Tenderness."

"But what if God wants to give you an alpha male?"

"And what are alpha males?"

"That's basically what this book is all about. The alpha male is described as a strong, powerful man."

"Sounds pretty good to me, too." Jeris giggled.

"They can be tough and hard and arrogant and macho."

She frowned. "No, thanks."

Carrie opened the book, ran her finger down a page, and flipped to the middle of the book. "This says, 'Romances are stories of strong women taming dominant men.'"

"I'll pass on the domination thing."

"It says, 'The heroine needs a hero who's a formidable challenge to her.'"

"Not my cup of tea."

"Have you ever read *Jane Eyre*?"

"It was one of my favorite books when I was a teenager."

"Okay, there's an alpha male."

Jeris ran a slice of Italian bread through the oil-and-herbs mixture on her bread plate, then took a bite. She savored the flavors, recalling the story she'd always loved, the tale of the plain though noble heroine Jane and the dashing though distant Mr. Rochester. She thought about Mr. Rochester, scenes of him and Jane playing in her head as if they were on a movie screen.

"This says, 'The alpha hero can be unlovable *at first.*'"

Jeris sipped her tea, thinking about Jane Eyre's alpha hero. "Mr. Rochester was like that."

"Right. He didn't reveal his vulnerability—"

"Or his true character—"

"Until the end." Carrie nodded her head vigorously. "Here's a second story like that one—*Beauty and the Beast.*"

Jeris nodded. "Another unlovable hero—"

"*At first.* Those are important words. This book says, 'The alpha hero has the capacity to finally temper his toughness and, in so doing, to love the heroine passionately and faithfully.'"

Jeris let out a sigh. It would be wonderful to find a strong, intelligent, successful man like Carrie was talking about and fall deeply in love with him and him with her. He could be brash at first like Mr. Rochester or the Beast, but his loving nature would finally win out, and all would be utopia.

" 'The alpha hero is a powerful man who finds out his life isn't complete unless he wins the hand of the heroine,' " Carrie read.

Suddenly Jeris's practical side surfaced like a diver out of oxygen. Carrie wasn't talking about reality. She was talking about fantasy. Pure and simple.

"This says, 'During the course of the novel, as the heroine comes to trust the hero, the hero comes to trust her, true love wins out, and they live happily ever after.' "

"You forget one thing." Jeris tried to keep a hard edge out of her voice.

"What's that?"

"I'm no heroine in a novel."

Carrie shut the book. "Of course not. I know that. What I'm trying to get you to see is, don't box God in."

"How do you know I'm doing that?"

"I don't know that you are. I just care about you and want to see you as happily married as I am. And that's achieved by not boxing God in. . .by letting Him work as *He* wants to work so He can send you the man *He* wants for you. Sometimes single women are single for a reason. They get too picky and too hard to please. They put all the emphasis on what they want and not on what God wants. It's as if they're putting parameters on God's will—"

"How could you know that?"

"Because that's how I was before I met Martin. I've been down this road. I speak from experience. I was looking for the complete opposite of Martin. I knew what I wanted and thought it was all about that. Now he's the love of my life. But when I first met him I wouldn't give a chewing-gum wrapper for him. Then we sort of grew on each other, and Cupid's arrow pierced our hearts."

Carrie touched her heart and fluttered her long dark eyelashes. Then her brows drew together contemplatively. "No, the heart of the matter is, God had it all planned out that we would fall in love and marry. I just had to be open to Him."

Jeris had a lot to think about. Her balding, bookish man might not be God's plan for her, and a little flutter of fear gripped her heart. That image had been a comfort to her for a long time.

"You can trust in the Lord, Jeris."

"I've been a Christian nearly all my life. I fully understand that."

"Do you really?" Carrie gave her an unwavering stare.

Jeris looked down, studying her nails. In psychological terms, she knew she had "trust issues."

"He wants the best for you. You don't have to be afraid."

"Who said anything about being afraid?"

"I did." Carrie gave her that unwavering stare again. "The first step to conquering a problem is admitting there is one."

"Hey, who's the psychologist here?" Jeris smiled wryly. "You should get your license."

"I'm sorry." Carrie's face flushed. "I just want to help."

"Thanks," Jeris said in a deadpan voice.

Chapter 15

Jeris walked briskly down the hall after children's church was over, thinking about the kids. She'd enjoyed being with them this morning. She'd missed them last Sunday when she was away at the conference. She made her way through the side door of the sanctuary. Audra Darling would be along momentarily—she'd stayed in their classroom to see the last child picked up.

Now that morning service was over, they were going to pack away the puppets in the sanctuary and take down the portable puppet stage they'd set up yesterday. Pastor Hughes had asked their class to do a short puppet show at the beginning of the service this morning, and it had been a rousing success. The congregation thoroughly enjoyed the program as the children worked the puppets to a backdrop of lively kids' praise music. And it had produced some visitors. Several people who normally didn't attend church—parents and grandparents of the new children—had come to see their kids perform.

She walked up the steps to the platform and over to the puppet stage. She stepped behind the heavy purple curtains hanging from white plumbing pipes and picked up Mrs. Mizelle Mouse, then placed her in the packing box. She put Mr. Billy Bear beside her, gathered more of the puppets, and packed them away, fitting them deftly into the box.

Audra Darling joined her behind the curtains. "I'm glad you had a good trip last weekend, Jeris. I'll tell you what, those kids missed you like crazy." She picked up Miss Erma Elephant and placed her in the packing box.

"I missed them, too. I hated to be away. But it couldn't be helped. I'm just glad I had you to take care of my class."

"Luke served as my assistant."

"Really?" Jeris heard Brady in the sanctuary. His chirpy little voice echoing in the vaulted ceiling announced his presence.

"Can I lend a hand?" came Luke's voice.

Audra Darling pulled the curtains apart and stuck her head through the opening. "Sure. Come on up."

"Come on, Brady. Let's go up onstage."

"Yippee!"

Jeris tugged on the curtains and pulled them back farther so she could see out. In a little while they would unscrew the white plumbing pipes from the joints and work the curtains completely off and fold them.

Luke and Brady walked down the aisle and up onto the platform.

"Can I go behind the curtains, Dad?"

"No, son. We don't need you to get in the way. We have to take the stage down. We'll be finished soon. Just sit on that chair over there." He pointed to a high-backed, red upholstered oak chair that stood near the pulpit.

"Aw, Dad." Brady climbed up on the big chair, his little legs dangling.

Luke approached the puppet stage and started unscrewing the joints.

Jeris smiled at Brady and motioned for him to come to her.

Brady hopped off the chair, ran to the puppet stage, and joined her.

She turned to Luke. "I'm sorry." She realized her mistake too late. "I should've asked you first. Is it okay if Brady helps me pack the puppets?"

"You sure he won't get in the way?"

"Please, Dad." Brady held his hands under his chin in his familiar prayer stance.

"Of course he won't. I'll put him to work." She nuzzled Miss Ollie Ostrich under Brady's chin, and he squealed like a banshee.

"Okay, Little Man, you can help Miss Jeris."

For nearly twenty minutes they all worked, packing the puppets, taking down the plumbing pipes, folding the heavy curtains, and putting them and the pipes into the boxes.

"Done." Jeris ran her fingers in a zigzag trail down Brady's back. "Good job."

"Thanks, Miss Jeris."

"Brady, why don't you quote last Sunday's memory verse for Miss Jeris?" Audra Darling winked at Jeris. "It'll prove I taught you tykes something while she was gone."

"Yes, ma'am." Brady walked over to the edge of the platform. He put his little heels together and stood statue still, staring out at the sea of empty pews as if they were filled with parishioners. " 'Man looks at the outward appearance,' " —he said it in a singsong, little-boy style—" 'but the Lord looks at the heart.' First Samuel 16:7."

"Good job again, Brady." Jeris made her way to him, feeling proud of him. All children needed to learn the scriptures, and Brady had memorized quite a few. "You're a smart boy."

"Good going, Little Man," Luke said.

Brady thrust his hands straight out to his sides, hummed the theme to *Batman*, and made a flying leap off the platform.

"Oh, my." Jeris took a deep gulp. The platform was high.

Brady landed on the carpeted area in the space behind the altars.

"Brady!" Luke ran down the steps, worry in his voice.

Jeris hurried down the steps, too.

Luke reached him first. "Son, don't ever do that again. You could've been hurt." He looked him over closely, checking his arms and legs. He touched the top of his head. "Does anything hurt?"

"No, sir."

Concerned, Jeris bent down, touched Brady's upper arm, and gave it a feathery stroke as she looked up at Luke. "Are you sure he's okay?"

Luke nodded. "I'm sure." He chuckled. "I checked out his outward appearance, though only God can see the inside."

∞

As he drove to Dale's Café for lunch, Luke thought about the verse Brady quoted. His son was doing it again. He was helping Luke see the light. With a hurtful pang he recalled the prejudice he'd had toward Jeris when he first met her.

But his hurt eased when he remembered the prayer he'd prayed and how God had answered it. *Please prepare my heart. Whatever needs changing in me, please do it. I'm open and willing.*

He smiled as he drove along, thankful the prejudice had long been plucked from his heart. *Thank You, Lord, for answering my prayer.*

Tenderly he thought of Jeris and her endearing ways. Not only was she beautiful outwardly but she also had a beautiful heart, what Miss Ada's booklet talked about.

"And it's a heart I want to win."

∞

Jeris pulled down the covers of her bed and crawled in. The children she'd been counseling lately in her office popped into her mind. Tough situations that needed the wisdom of Solomon. Three children acting out hostilities following divorces. A rebellious teenager driving her parents crazy. A child slowly going bald and her family not knowing why. But Jeris thought she knew. Friday the little girl had finally told her about the bully at school who'd been threatening her the entire year.

Jeris pushed back the covers and slipped to her knees, remembering Jesus' words in the Bible, His instructions for situations that seemed impossible. *These kinds of problems can be resolved only with prayer.* For several minutes she beseeched the Lord to help the children she counseled and to give her godly wisdom in dealing with them.

"Lord, give me Your words to say as I counsel them, not my words and not some textbook jargon. Help me to give them the living words, the words of life, the words of You, Lord."

She finished praying and climbed back in bed, then reached for her Bible and devotional on her nightstand. It was her pattern every night to read the devotional and the scripture it talked about, then ponder them. She reached for a novel, too. Since she wasn't sleepy she would read for a while when she finished her devotions. Reading always made her drowsy.

As she repositioned her pillows she thought of the novel *Jane Eyre*, the story she and Carrie had talked about. She remembered Carrie's questions about the alpha and beta heroes. Alpha? Beta? Wasn't Pastor Hughes a beta man? He was kind and gentle and compassionate and caring. That's what she wanted in a man. But wait a minute. Wasn't he a take-charge person, too? A strong man with a backbone of steel? She wanted those attributes, too, in a husband. She wanted a man who could sum up a situation quickly and do something about it—a "change agent" the newspaper had called it in a story she'd read about people who made a difference in the lives of others. *But*—the word loomed big in her mind—her future husband had to be tender.

She was confused. Alpha or beta? Beta or alpha? Which did she want?

She flipped open the devotional book and turned to today's date.

"I can't believe this." The devotional featured the scripture Brady had quoted in the sanctuary today, right before he took that flying leap off the platform. She smiled, remembering his Batman antics.

"'Man looks at the outward appearance, but the Lord looks at the heart,'" she read, awed by the coincidence. Hadn't someone said a coincidence was when God didn't get the credit?

But God *would* get the credit for this. She repeated the verse and let it sink in, then slipped out of bed and dropped to her knees again. "Lord, thank You for putting this scripture before my eyes twice today. You must want me to take it to heart. Your Word is living and true, and it speaks to us just when we need it."

She recalled Carrie's encouraging her to pray about God sending the right man into her life. "Lord, I recognize through this verse You're saying You know what's best concerning a husband for me. You can look into his heart, and I can't. All I can see is the outside. Help me to be open to You and Your plan. Forgive me for wanting my own way. Help me to trust You wholly and completely, with no fear or doubt or worry but with a full confidence that You know best and have my life planned out."

She continued pouring out her heart to the Lord. "I submit myself to you." She took a deep breath, the very act seeming to fill her soul with confidence. God's confidence. "I don't care if the man I marry is bald or ugly or handsome or tall or short. Or whatever. I put my trust in You to lead and guide me to the right one. In Jesus' name. Amen."

She climbed back in bed. But this time she didn't reach for a book. Instead she turned off the light and fell asleep as peacefully as Job must have after his restoration.

Chapter 16

I have something to tell you, Audra Darling." Bent over a little girl at the activity table, Jeris glanced up at Audra Darling, then looked back down and picked up a blue crayon. She colored part of the sky on the little girl's color sheet. The child needed encouragement. One of the boys had made fun of her coloring last week, and today she'd refused to participate in the activity. "See what I'm doing, Charity? It's so much fun to color." She put the crayon in Charity's hand. "You try it now."

Charity colored part of the sky, not going out of the lines once.

Jeris smiled at her, then tweaked her button nose. "Good job, Charity. Keep it up, and soon your whole sheet will be colored. Isn't it fun to color?"

"Yes, ma'am."

Jeris stood up and pushed the arms of her jacket up to her elbows. Though she liked the professional look this type of suit gave her, she liked being free from long sleeves when she did activities with the children. Maybe she could find a short-sleeved version of this jacket. She would look in her favorite clothing catalog when she went home.

"I have something to tell you, too, Jeris." Audra Darling whisked over to the metal cabinet, opened the door, and pulled out another box of crayons. She made her way back to the activity table and plunked the crayons down in the middle. "Something important."

"What?"

Audra Darling gestured at the children. "When they leave."

Jeris nodded her agreement. They would talk later when they could concentrate. She looked forward to telling Audra Darling about her trust issues and how the Lord had helped her with them.

All morning they worked with the children, coloring, telling Bible stories, singing praise songs along with CDs, supervising free playtime. Jeris wondered what Audra Darling wanted to tell her. She knew what *she* wanted to say to Audra Darling.

When the last child left, Jeris and Audra Darling cleaned up the room.

"Do you have lunch plans?" Audra Darling pushed the last chair under the table, then picked up her purse and Bible.

"You're not inviting me to your house again. You do that too much, and I don't want to take advantage."

"I've told you over and over. When I invite you, it's because we really want

211

you to come. But don't worry about that right now. I didn't cook today. Andrew's out of town."

"That's right." Jeris remembered. He'd gone on a free trip to Israel for pastors only, and the assistant pastor had preached in the service today. "When's he coming back?"

"End of the week. I wish I could've gone. I've always wanted to see Israel. But he's planning to put together a trip for our church people the first of next year, and I'll get to go on that one."

"That'll be great." Jeris followed Audra Darling to the door of their classroom. They stepped into the hall, and Jeris closed the door behind them.

"Maybe we could grab a sandwich somewhere? And talk?"

"Sounds good." Jeris walked beside Audra Darling down the long hall. "Where?"

Audra Darling named a restaurant.

"See you there."

ఴ

"Okay. So what did you want to tell me?" Jeris took a bite of her pita sandwich, noting how good the blend of chopped apples and chicken tasted.

"You tell me first." Audra Darling put down her sandwich—the same kind Jeris was eating—and took a sip of her fruit drink. "Did you taste the apples in this chicken salad? I'm going to have to try adding them the next time I make it."

"Yes, I did. Delicious. You tell me first what you wanted to say."

"All right." Audra Darling took another sip of her drink, looking as serious as she'd ever looked. "I'm not sure how to say this. . . ."

"You? Miss Talkative-at-the-Drop-of-a-Hat? You don't know what to say?"

"I said *how*. Not *what*. Okay. I won't beat around the bush. I think you and Luke Moore are made for each other."

"That's not surprising. You've been matchmaking ever since I moved here."

"Has it been that obvious?"

"For me it has." Jeris smiled, slowly shaking her head and giving Audra Darling a shame-on-you look. Then something hit her. Luke had probably noticed Audra Darling's matchmaking, too. She could feel her face growing warm. Did he think she'd put Audra Darling up to it? She hoped not.

"I think he's the one for you, Jeris." Audra Darling plunged in, telling Jeris about Al and Gloria Stanfield and how she'd arranged some times for them to be together, including dinner at her house. Within a few months the love bug hit, she said, and they got married and now lived in wedded bliss.

"Wedded bliss?" Jeris smiled. It was an old-fashioned term, but it intrigued her. In fact it sounded enticing. And comforting.

"Somehow I knew they were meant for each other. I feel like the Lord used me to get them together. But, Jeris, that was the first time I ever did anything like it. It's not my usual way. But a strong feeling seemed to come over me with both Al and Gloria, and now with you and Luke. Of course, we have to wait and see how it works out, and maybe I'm wrong about you two, but somehow I knew about Al and Gloria."

"Holy Spirit illumination?" Jeris smiled her brightest.

"You could say that."

Neither said anything for a long moment, as if what had been uttered needed time to germinate in the soil of a heart—Jeris's.

Finally Jeris broke the silence. "What do you think I should do about what you've just told me? I mean, if it's the Lord's plan, this is like a secret knowledge I'll have about us. How am I supposed to deal with it?"

Audra Darling smiled. "That's a typical question from a psychologist."

"*This* psychologist needs some answers."

"It's simple. Be open to God."

That sounded familiar. "That's what I wanted to talk to you about."

"Oh?"

Jeris plunged in this time, detailing everything that had happened to her recently, from her conversation with Carrie to Brady's scripture verse to her prayer. She told Audra Darling how she'd poured out her heart to the Lord. She described how she'd relinquished her cares to Him. "I even told the Lord I don't care *what* the man I marry looks like." She laughed, feeling as light as a seagull's feather.

"That's part of God's plan, Jeris, in all of this. Your relinquishment."

Jeris nodded. She felt her eyes misting over. "He can be tall or short or bald or good-looking or ugly. . .or whatever. It doesn't matter anymore. What matters is if he's the one. . .the Lord has for me." A tear escaped down her cheek. "It's a big thing for me to be able to say that."

Audra Darling reached across the table and patted Jeris's hand in a motherly gesture. "I know."

Jeris smiled. "More Holy Spirit illumination?"

Audra Darling nodded. "Everything's going to work out. In God's timing." She paused, her eyebrows drawn together. "When—and not if—Luke asks you out, be prepared."

The thought was thrilling to Jeris. Even if he was as handsome as a superstar.

As Jeris got in her car and buckled her seatbelt, she was enjoying the feelings of anticipation washing over her.

" 'Anticipation,' " she sang, an old song her mother liked to hum. Audra Darling said Luke *would* ask her out. She'd advised her to be prepared when it happened. Well, she would be.

A knock sounded at the car window.

She was so deep in thought that she nearly jumped. She looked up, saw Audra Darling, and punched her window button.

"Sorry—I didn't mean to startle you," Audra Darling said through the open window. "Are you free this coming Saturday?"

"Why?"

"I have something in mind. Can you check your schedule?"

Jeris took out her pocket calendar, studied it, then looked up. "I'm free. What are you thinking?"

"There's a new mall in Tampa, and I was wondering if you could go shopping with me. We could do an all-day girl thing, you know, shop, eat lunch in a nifty place, shop some more, take our time, enjoy ourselves—"

"It sounds like fun. I'll shop with you, but I don't need to buy anything. I'm about to order a few business pieces from *Officebound* catalog."

"You never know." Twinkles danced in Audra Darling's eyes. "Hold off on your ordering."

Chapter 17

Luke sat on a wicker chair on his lanai late Thursday afternoon, watching Brady at the shallow end of the pool. He also kept an eye on the hamburgers on the grill.

Hamburgers.

The last time he'd chaperoned Brady's children's church outing, he and Jeris had taken the kids to Jolly Hamburgers for burgers and shakes.

He'd been thinking about her a lot lately. Every time he'd been with her, she'd maintained a stiff persona. At least with him. With Brady and the kids in her class, she brightened like the Florida sunshine. But with him she'd maintained a reserved front at all of their encounters.

He picked up Miss Ada's booklet and turned to another chapter: "What Dating Can Do for You."

"Dates can be useful, in that dates provide the venues for relationships to be explored. It goes without saying that the lad should be a gentleman on dates. He should act honorably, and likewise, the girl should act in the same manner. NBC. From the outset, No Bodily Contact should be your rule."

Luke hooted. That was the term Audra Darling had used when the kids picked at and punched each other in the van. He thought it was funny then, and it was funny now.

"Dating should not be looked on as the only method of finding a wife. But it can be of help. Though you won't see every side of the girl's behavior while on dates, if you keep your wits about you, you will be able to determine a great deal. You will observe her in many situations, and thus you can decide whether she has the attributes that are needed to make a good wife."

Luke didn't know what to think. This sounded so. . .so what? All he could think of was a hawk watching its prey. He wasn't a hawk, and a date wasn't a prey. But in a way the author was right. After all, marriage was serious business. It was forever. And it needed careful consideration.

"On a first date, you can decide if you are interested in her enough to pursue further dates. If you are, then ask her out again."

That makes sense.

"Watch me, Dad." Brady's shrill voice echoed across the aqua blue pool water. "I'm going to stand on my hands, and this time I'm going to hold my breath for sixty minutes."

"You mean sixty seconds?"

"Look, Dad."

"Okay, Brady." Luke put the booklet down on the table. "Stand on your hands. I'm looking. I won't take my eyes off of you, Little Man."

Brady went down headfirst into the water and stood on his hands, his little feet barely above the water level. In seconds—but longer than he'd ever stayed down before—he surfaced. "I did it, Dad, didn't I?"

"You stayed down a long time. Good going, son. Keep practicing. It's good for your lungs."

Brady went down headfirst again, then resurfaced.

Luke picked up the booklet.

"When you decide to date a certain girl, make a mental checklist of everything she does. First of all, does she accept the date with coquettishness?"

Coquettishness? What an old-fashioned word. "Sit on the first step, Brady. I need to go inside for a sec."

"Aw, Dad."

"Now, Brady."

"Yes, sir." Brady did as he was told.

Luke dashed inside—the booklet still in his hand—found his dictionary, and hurried back out. "Okay, Brady. You can get in the water now."

Brady jumped in the pool and splashed about.

Luke sat down, paged through the dictionary and came to *coquette*. "That's close enough. 'A woman who endeavors without sincere affection to gain the attention of men.'"

He picked up the booklet again and decided to reread the portion he'd just read before continuing on.

"When you decide to date a certain girl, make a mental checklist of everything she does. First of all, does she accept the date with coquettishness? Or sincerity? Is she agreeable to your plan, or does she insist on hers? Is she punctual or late? (It's okay for her to be a tiny bit late some of the time.)"

Luke chuckled.

"While on the date, is she kind to those around her? Does she treat people with respect? Does she display good manners? Notice these things carefully. Does she order the most expensive thing on the menu, or is her choice conservative? (This will tell you how she'll be as a wife. Need I say here that frugality is your goal?)"

I don't care what a woman orders. If I'm taking her out, I want her to order whatever she likes. I'm no Scrooge.

"Do you feel good in her presence? Does she talk a lot? Too much? Does she have the tendency to talk the hind legs off a donkey?"

Luke laughed hard. This author had a way with words.

"A girl needs to be a good conversationalist on many topics (but not too many topics)."

Oh, brother. Here we go again.

"Does she conclude the date with a sincere thank-you? Does she dally while saying good-bye? If she dallies, does she toy with your affections? Does she try to hold your hand on the first date (horrors!)? If so, run from this girl, and never date her again!"

"Dad, I smell something burning."

Luke jumped up and dashed to the grill, the booklet forgotten. The hamburgers looked like charcoal briquettes. They were burnt to a crisp. He scooped them up with a spatula, put them into a pan, and turned off the gas. "Brady, go shower and get dressed. We're going out to eat."

"Aw, Dad. I want to swim some more."

"Maybe I can get off work early tomorrow afternoon, too. You can swim then."

"But, Dad—"

"Want a milkshake with your hamburger?"

"Yippee!"

⁂

Jeris took a sip of water, then glanced around at the pink, yellow, and green light-tube signs in Jolly Hamburgers. The signs announced the restaurant's specialties. HAMBURGERS. MILKSHAKES. FRENCH FRIES. "Where's Martin this time, Carrie?"

Carrie's mouth was a grim line across her otherwise pretty face. "Miami again. Fifth time in a row."

Jeris's heart went out to Carrie. She was having a hard time coping with Martin's traveling. "At least his trips are only once a month."

"I know. I should be thankful. One of the women in my Sunday school class is alone three weeks out of four. Her husband travels internationally. But somehow that doesn't help my feelings. Martin's been going to Miami so often lately that I asked him about our moving down there so we wouldn't be apart as much."

"You'd leave me? What would our office do without you?"

"It's not going to happen. His company wants him here."

"Whew. That's a relief." Jeris paused, feeling guilty. "For me, at least." She swallowed hard. "Maybe something'll happen so he won't have to travel anymore."

Carrie nodded.

The waitress came and took their orders, Jeris's first.

Jeris settled back comfortably in the red leather booth as the waitress took Carrie's order. She listened to the lively, upbeat music that appealed to adults and children alike. She liked coming to Jolly Hamburgers. Every now and then she craved a hamburger, and Jolly's had the best in town—*after* homemade ones. Her father used to grill a lot when she was growing up, and he always said the best food in the world was a homemade, home-grilled hamburger with a slice of sweet onion on top. She couldn't agree more.

"Have you thought any more about alpha and beta men, Jeris?"

One.

"Remember that book I was telling you about? About heroes?"

Oh, I remember.

"Miss Jeris!" Brady came rushing up the aisle.

Jeris leaned sideways and gave him a big hug when he reached her. "Hi, Brady. What are you doing here?" She glanced down the long row of booths. Luke was probably still in the lobby, waiting on the hostess to get their menus.

"Miss Jeris, Dad burned our hamburgers. So we had to come and buy one. And he said I could have a milkshake with mine."

"I'll bet that suits you just fine, Little Man." She tapped him on the chin, then glanced down the long row of booths again. She could feel her face growing warm. Luke would be approaching any moment. She remembered what Audra Darling had told her. She felt as vulnerable and shy as a kid on the first day of kindergarten.

Luke walked up from out of nowhere, it seemed. "Hi, Jeris."

A bolt of courage hit her. Audra Darling would call it Holy Spirit illumination. She smiled. "Hi, Luke. Well, fancy meeting you here." She jumped up and gestured at Carrie. "I'd like you to meet my friend Carrie."

Carrie extended her hand and gave Luke a shake and Brady a high-five. "Nice meeting you, Luke, Brady."

"Nice to meet you, Carrie," Luke said.

"Carrie's my office manager. She keeps everything flowing smoothly. She helps with the office work, and sometimes she entertains the kids in the waiting room, and sometimes she—"

"Analyzes people and dispenses advice." Carrie gave Jeris a knowing look.

"She's becoming a pro at that." Jeris smiled at her for a long moment, then turned her attention back to Brady. "So you're getting a hamburger and milkshake tonight, Little Man?"

"Yes, ma'am."

"Are you going to ride the merry-go-round after you eat?"

Brady looked up at Luke, his hands folded under his chin as he jumped from one foot to the other.

They all laughed at his cute antics.

Luke rubbed the top of Brady's head. "I suppose so. How can we resist the call of the carousel?"

Jeris turned to Carrie. "Luke and I rode the merry-go-round on a children's outing a few weeks ago."

"Let me guess. Luke rode the wild stallion seahorse, and you rode the gentle sea cow, the manatee."

"There you go again, analyzing people." She batted her eyelashes, Carrie-style, enthusiasm welling up within her. She liked that feeling. It felt good. "No. I rode a dolphin, and Luke"—she gestured at him with a flourish and a smile—

"sat safely on one of those benches on the first tier. Are you going to ride a sea creature this time, Luke? Or sit on the bench again?"

He looked intently into her eyes. "Maybe I won't get on the merry-go-round at all. Maybe I'll stand at the gate and talk with you while Brady rides."

A little tingle surged up her spine. "That sounds...like..."

"Sounds like fun to me, Miss Jeris," Brady piped up.

She smiled down at Brady as she and Luke made plans, the tingles lingering along her spine. They agreed to meet at the merry-go-round after they finished eating. Her heart was singing.

The hostess came and asked Luke and Brady to follow her. Within moments they'd said good-bye and disappeared from view.

"How's your writing coming along, Carrie?" Jeris asked. "How many more chapters have you written?"

"Only two. Lately I've been studying the craft almost as much as I've been writing."

The waitress set chocolate milkshakes on the table, then left.

"Yum, yum." Carrie took a long sip through her straw, sat back against the booth, and let out a lengthy sigh. "This is almost as good as reading a Christian romance novel."

Jeris sipped her chocolate shake, savoring the flavor.

"They may be pure escapism, but they're fun to read. And they always have a scriptural theme, at least the ones I've read. And they're so satisfying. Throughout the story the hero won't admit he loves the heroine, or she him. He's noble and brave and dashing though she may not realize it at first, but he has a toughness about him that puts her off."

"Let's see." Jeris winked as she wrote on a pretend notebook with a pretend pen. "The patient has an obsession for Christian romance novels—"

"I really don't."

"I know. It's entertainment."

"Exactly. Some people sew or watch TV or go to movies or do crafts or whatever. I read good Christian books."

"I read them, too. They're more uplifting than what's on TV. Some of that stuff is getting raunchy."

"You're telling me. I'll take an inspiring novel any day over TV or movies." Carrie sighed the same long sigh she had earlier. "By the end of the book the hero's so hopelessly in love with the heroine and so captivated by her charms that he asks, 'What do I have to do to make you mine?' The heroine is so in love with him by this point that she says, 'I'm yours, mister.'" She laughed, then grew quiet and let out a low groan. "Oh, boy, do I miss Martin."

Jeris sensed Carrie's pain at their forced separation. "Your real obsession is Martin Denton."

"You couldn't be any more insightful, Dr. Waldron." Carrie gave her a sappy look as she whipped out a picture of Martin and kissed it. "I'm yours, mister."

They burst into laughter as Carrie had done before.

"I'm feeling sort of giddy tonight," Jeris said.

"I'd call it euphoric."

"How so?"

"It's because you just talked to the love of your life."

"The love of my life?" Jeris was enjoying their banter.

Carrie nodded, her head bobbing up and down like the trinket on a pickup's dashboard. "From everything you've told me about Luke, I think he's a sensational man. He's the *rara avis*. That's Latin for 'rare bird'—or, in my words, 'one in a thousand.'"

Jeris considered this. A warm glow flushed through her.

"I'll tell you something else I think."

"What's that?"

"I've studied this alpha and beta thing so much that I think I can confidently predict that Luke is an alpha male. But my woman's intuition tells me he's got enough beta in him to make an excellent husband."

"A what?" Jeris unrolled her silverware from the napkin. The fork slipped and landed with a *clink* on the floor.

"You heard me. A husband." Carrie paused. "Jeris?"

"Yes?"

"Amor vincit omnia."

"Latin for—?"

"'Love conquers all.'"

∽

Luke draped his arm on the wrought iron fence that separated the onlookers from the riders of the merry-go-round. He glanced at Jeris standing beside him. She was waving at Brady every time he came around. She looked so pretty tonight.

Her outfit showed off her slenderness, and her hair was just the way he liked it. She was wearing her smooth updo, not her ponytail, though that appealed to him, too. Both styles spoke of casualness, and knowing her love for the outdoors, they were perfect for a woman with those interests.

But the prettiest thing about her was her inward beauty. He remembered the verse in Timothy. Or was it Peter?

"Dad, watch me!"

Luke looked over at Brady as he whizzed by on a seal, hunched forward and jiggling the reins as if he were on a live bucking bronco. "Hang on, Brady." He glanced at Jeris and smiled. "I wouldn't want that seal to buck him."

She laughed, her eyes shining as she looked at him.

He stood there enjoying the pleasant sensation passing between them and the lilting sounds of her laughter as if they were floating across a cloud. Her laughter was musical and sounded better than the enchanting tunes coming from the merry-go-round, and it mesmerized him.

For a long moment he let his gaze feast on her—on her striking olive-toned skin, her pleasing features, her captivating smile, the slimness of her form, her animated movements as she waved at Brady.

"What are you thinking about, Luke?"

It's too soon to put my feelings into words.

She waved again as Brady came by. "I enjoy having Brady in my class. He loves to hear the Bible stories when it's story time."

"He says you either act them out or get the kids to do it. He likes that, dressing up in Bible costumes."

She nodded. "We live in a media-saturated world, and that's what we're competing with in the church. I try to make things as lively as I can. I want the Bible to come alive for the kids."

"I, for one, want to thank you for all you're doing for the children at Christ Church."

"Thanks, Luke."

"I intend to help more."

"You do?"

"I've cut back on my long hours."

"Good." She smiled up at him, playfully batting her eyelashes. "Can you chaperone another outing? We're taking the kids on a picnic and boat ride at the parsonage this coming Sunday, right after church."

∞

Luke and Brady walked Jeris to her vehicle in the mall parking lot. They waved good-bye to her as she drove off, then found their car six or seven aisles away.

As they buckled up, Luke thought about Jeris and her love for Brady.

He blinked hard. *Her love for Brady?*

He could see it every time they were together. Her love for his son shone in her eyes and in her actions.

What did that mean for the future? For *their* future? Was this headed into a future that included the three of them? He hoped so.

He remembered Brady's prayer, when he asked God to send him a mommy.

Was Jeris that person? Would she turn out to be the right wife Mr. Granfield had written about? The wife for Luke Moore?

There was only one way to explore this.

Ask her for a date.

∞

After she got home from the mall, Jeris sat on a barstool in her kitchen, reading Wednesday's and Thursday's mail. That happened sometimes, having to read two days' worth of mail. It had been a busy week.

She read awhile, then grew distracted, thinking about the evening she'd spent with Luke and Brady. She and Luke had talked a lot, and not once had she felt shy or awkward around him. On the contrary, it had been wonderful.

R–r–r–i–i–ing.

She picked up her phone and looked at the readout. *Luke.* Was something wrong? Brady? She clicked it on. "Luke?"

"Hi, Jeris."

"Is everything all right?"

"Why do you ask?"

"I was worried. We just saw each other less than thirty minutes ago."

"We did? I thought it was thirty days ago." He laughed.

The tingles hit her spine. Was he saying time went by slowly when he was away from her? She was finding that was true for her.

"Are you sure we were together tonight?" He laughed again.

She laughed along with him.

"Excuse me for being silly, Jeris."

"No excuses needed." *I like what you're saying, Luke.* She got brave. "I like what you're saying, Luke."

"Hmm." He purred like a cat. Loudly.

The sounds coming over the phone thrilled her. A cat purred when it was happy. Or so the theory went. "Luke. . ."

"Jeris. . ."

"Da–a–a–d!"

Jeris could hear Brady hollering in the background.

"Jeris, can you hang on a sec?" Luke asked. "I'll be right back."

"Sure." She waited a couple of minutes.

"Jeris?" he finally said. "You still here?"

"I'm here. Is Brady all right?"

"He's fine. Thanks for waiting. Brady didn't know I was on the phone, and I had to go check on him. He said he had to tell me he loved me one more time—before he fell asleep." His voice choked up. "That little fellow. . .I'm sorry. I didn't mean to get emotional on you."

"It's okay. I'm a good listener."

"I forgot. You're a psychologist."

"Is anything bothering you? Is there anything you want to talk about? Something I could help you sort through or understand better?"

A long pause ensued.

"I'm sorry, Luke. I didn't mean to sound so professional. Forgive me?"

"For what? You saw a person all choked up, and something kicked in for you—empathy, I'd say. That's probably what makes you a good psychologist."

"Thanks, Luke. Are things going well for you and Brady? I mean, I'm sure they are. Every time I'm around you two, I can't get over how well-adapted he seems to. . .to his. . ." Now she was faltering for words.

"To his circumstances? You mean, a child without a mother?"

She cringed. Had she made him feel uncomfortable? She hadn't meant to.

"That's sort of why I called you." He paused. "At least it's along those lines."

"What do you mean?"

"I called to ask if you'd like to go out with me."

Oh, my. She stood up from the barstool quickly, nearly knocking it over, as surprised as an honoree at a birthday party. Actually she was more thrilled than surprised. If that could be so. *I'd love to go out with you, Luke.*

"Do you have plans for this Saturday night? I know it's awfully soon to spring this on you."

Saturday night? She wouldn't be home in time from Tampa. She and Audra Darling were going shopping at the new mall. Maybe she could cancel her plans. She'd rather be with Luke. Her breath came in short, jerky puffs.

"Jeris? Did we get cut off?"

"I'm here."

"I thought we'd go out to eat at one of those fancy places—a nice steakhouse or a seafood restaurant on the water. We could get lobster if you like. We can go anywhere you want to. . . ."

"Jolly's would be fine with me." *As long as it's with you.*

"It would?"

"Yes."

"Well, I have better places in mind than that. And, after we eat, I thought maybe we could go to the concert at the beach—that is, if you'd like to. People spread blankets on the grassy area, and the orchestra plays from the band shell. The Silver Bay Symphony is performing. Some people eat out there. They bring their own picnics. Or they buy their food at the food stands—"

"I—I can't go." *This is painful, Luke. You don't know how painful.*

"You can't?"

"I already made plans with Audra Darling for Saturday. We won't be back in time."

"O–o–h–h."

She remembered what Audra Darling had said about her and Luke, how she thought they were made for each other. She recalled what else she'd said. *"When—and not if—Luke asks you out, be prepared."* She'd been so. . ."euphoric" this evening—what Carrie called it—that she'd been caught off guard by his call. But she could remedy that.

"Well. . ." His voice trailed off.

"I'm free tomorrow night, Luke."

"You are? You don't mind having only one day's notice for a date?"

"Not at all. I'd *love* to go out with you tomorrow night."

"Yippee!" he shouted.

She laughed.

He laughed, too. "That just slipped out."

Chapter 18

On the way to the restaurant Luke took covert peeks at Jeris. She was beautiful. Her ocean blue eyes sparkled like aquamarines in a necklace. They were noteworthy and so light blue-green they looked almost translucent, as if they glittered. Why hadn't he noticed their beauty before?

He glanced at her again. Her hair was in that style he liked so well, and a few pieces floated softly about her temples and in front of her ears. Her hair wasn't blond, and it wasn't brown. It was in between but not streaky with that dyed stuff some women used. It was natural, he was sure, and it was beautiful. Why hadn't he noticed the striking color before?

He smiled, thinking about Miss Ada's booklet. It had some good advice, though it was archaic. But the basic tenets still held true. *The right wife?* In the book, Mr. Granfield said a man needed to look for a woman who was a Christian before he considered anything else. Jeris met that requirement. Then he talked about finding a woman who served the Lord and put Him first in her life. Jeris met that one, too. Then he discussed inward beauty, which Mr. Granfield interpreted as being kind and good and unselfish. Jeris possessed not only inward beauty but also outward beauty—

"We're both quiet this evening," she said.

He nodded. "I was thinking. . . ."

"Me, too."

"You were?" He cast another sideways look at her, and their gazes held for a moment. He forced himself to look back at the road. Was she thinking what he was? About the *M* word? But he chided himself. It was too soon. Though he'd known her a full three months, he reminded himself he needed to go slowly. "What were you thinking about?"

"I—I was thinking how odd it seems not having Brady with us."

"I know. But I'm sure he's enjoying being with Mrs. Nelms. She reads dozens of books to him when she baby-sits." He paused. "I apologize again for this last-minute date."

"I'm glad you didn't wait."

He took a moment to digest that.

"I'm looking forward to this evening." She brushed a strand of hair away from her temple.

Glancing her way, he took note of her hands as she fiddled with her hair and her simple blue top that accentuated her eyes as if it had been a piece of jewelry.

"Where are we going?"

"I was going to ask you for your preference. Steak? Lobster? Whatever. What are your taste buds craving?"

"I have this idea. . . ." Her voice grew quieter with each word she spoke. "I don't know if you'd like to do it—"

"Try me."

"What if we pick up some sandwiches and chips at the deli and go to the band shell?"

"But the concert is tomorrow night."

"I know."

∞

With Luke behind her, Jeris made her way to a tall palm tree, its fronds swaying gently in the ocean breeze. A pastel-colored light shone up its trunk. She saw other palm trees nearby. All had pastel-colored lights shining up them. The setting was extraordinary. Her heart beat a little trill inside her chest. "What about here?"

"That looks like a good place." Luke caught up to her and spread a beach towel on the soft grass that fronted the gigantic but empty band shell. "Good thing I started keeping a towel in my trunk. I've taken Brady to the beach a few times on the spur of the moment, and it's come in handy."

"It came in handy this evening, too." She sat down on one end. She could hear the lulling sound of the waves behind the sand dunes that separated the grass they were sitting on from the beach—a symphony in its own right.

He sat down beside her, the grocery bags still in his hands.

The confines of the towel were tight. Glancing down, she noticed only an inch or two of orange and yellow between them, forcing her to keep her shoulders erect. He would have to do the same thing. If she'd been fair-skinned, she'd be blushing at their closeness.

"Our own private picnic."

She let the waves do the talking, their constant ebb and flow echoing the beating of her heart.

"I'm glad you thought of this," he said.

"I didn't know this place would be so...so..."

"Romantic?" His eyebrows wiggled up and down, and lights danced in his eyes.

She gave a quick nod. "I haven't been to Silver Bay's band shell before. When I suggested it, I was only thinking *picnics* and *outdoors*."

"Would you have suggested it if you'd known what it was like?" He looked into her eyes, and it was as if their gazes were locked.

"Yes." Her heart beat so hard that she was afraid he'd see her shirt vibrating. But she couldn't draw her gaze away from his. She noticed how the wind was ruffling his dark hair, how his hair seemed to prance about in the gentle breeze. She basked in his nearness. She could smell his masculine cologne and could have felt the smoothness of his jaw if she had reached out and touched it. She wondered what it would be like to kiss him, to feel his lips on hers. . . .

"Goldie!" someone shouted from across the way. "Come here to me. Don't bother those people."

Jeris felt a dog's snout at her back, then at her elbow. "Ooh." She giggled. The dog's nose felt cold to her skin. He touched her elbow again. "Ooh!" she exclaimed. It tickled.

Luke laughed when he saw the dog, a golden retriever. He bared his teeth in fun, and the dog let out a ferocious bark.

" 'Hark, hark, the dogs do bark.' " Jeris giggled. "That's a nursery rhyme."

"Goldie Johnson," a lady's voice snapped. "Quit your nosing around, and come here this instant."

The retriever took off across the grass, as excited as a child running into the waves.

"So much for romantic moments." Luke shrugged his shoulders, but he was grinning from ear to ear, as if what had just happened was hilarious.

They both laughed.

Jeris looked down at the grocery bags he was holding. "Want me to unwrap our sandwiches?"

"Sure." He handed her one of the bags and reached into the other one. "I'll get our soft drinks out." He handed her one. "Want me to pray?"

"Yes."

"Lord, thank You for Your goodness in our lives. Thank You for giving us this evening together in this magnificent place—one created by Your hand. Help us to count for Your kingdom and our lives for Your service. Now bless our food and this glorious time. In Jesus' name. Amen."

"That was a beautiful prayer, Luke."

He smiled and nodded as he held up his sandwich. "Chow down."

She picked up her sandwich and took a bite. His prayer had stirred her. She recalled what Carrie had said about him last night at the mall. She thought he was one in a thousand. The warm glow hit her again, rushing through her with gale forces.

They ate in silence, except for the sound of the waves, then talked awhile, then ate, then talked.

It seemed to Jeris their souls communed as they sat under a velvety, star-studded sky. An Emily Brontë verse came to her. *"Whatever our souls are made of, his and mine are the same."* She shivered, and it wasn't from the ocean breeze.

I wonder if we would've kissed if the dog hadn't come up?

∞

Luke smiled as he drove home after taking Jeris to her apartment. Though he hadn't planned to kiss her on their first date, he might've done it. It would've just seemed right. And good. And fitting.

He couldn't think of any more adjectives.

All he *could* think of was her. He wanted to be with her every minute and couldn't wait until the next time they were together.

When would that be?

Oh, yes. Day after tomorrow. Sunday. She'd asked him to be a chaperone for the children's outing at the parsonage.

How would he make it all day tomorrow without seeing her?

∞

Jeris sat down on the edge of her bed and picked up her alarm clock. The red digital numbers glowed against the black background—1:30 a.m. She set it for 7:00. She had to get up early for her shopping outing with Audra Darling.

She crawled in and settled under the covers, but she was too exhilarated to sleep. She was as wide awake as if it had been 1:30 in the afternoon instead of in the morning. She let out a satisfied sigh. Throughout their evening together, the romantic sparks had never let up. Oh, it wasn't a physical sensation necessarily. He hadn't even touched her.

She remembered when he'd almost kissed her and probably would have, if the dog hadn't shattered the magical moment. She didn't believe in kissing on a first date. But somehow, with Luke, it would've been all right. And it would've been a light, feathery kiss. She just knew.

Later, when they walked on the beach, he didn't even hold her hand or put his arm around her shoulders. Yet something indescribable had happened between them. Their souls communed. That's what came to her earlier, and that's what came to her now.

She smiled when she recalled how late it was as they drove home. One a.m. She had thought of the nursery rhyme "Hickory Dickory Dock," the verse about the clock striking one and "the mouse did run." She had quoted it, and they'd laughed together.

Luke apologized profusely for bringing her home so late, telling her he hadn't realized the lateness of the hour, how time had slipped away from him.

She told him time had slipped away from her, too, as the old adage filled her thoughts. *Time flies when you're having fun.*

Only *fun* was too weak a word to describe what had transpired between them tonight.

Chapter 19

Jeris stood in the fitting room, staring at herself in the three-way mirror. She grasped a handful of lightweight, flowing fabric at thigh level. "You really think I ought to wear a print, Audra Darling? I always wear solids."

"As sure as I'm standing here."

"It's not very businesslike."

"It's perfect. You look like a dream come true, dah-ling."

Jeris glanced down at the outfit Audra Darling had picked out for her. "You're wearing a fine-gauge knit, aqua-colored shrug—"

"Did you say a 'shroud'?"

"Jeris, you are a mess."

Jeris laughed.

"You crazy thing, you. It's not a *shroud*. It's a *shrug*. A shrug is a short knit jacket. And this one has a matching camisole. And your aqua-and-black knee-length skirt has a ruffled hem that's made of lined georgette."

"It's beautiful."

Audra Darling leaned over and peered at Jeris's calf. "You've got a little leg going on there, girlfriend. That's a nice feature. Anybody ever tell you you have well-shaped legs, Jeris? Like a ballerina's?"

Jeris playfully swatted her away and looked in the mirror again, pleased with how the outfit looked, with how *she* looked.

"Aqua's a great color with your eyes. And the skirt's ruffled hemline brings some femininity to the ensemble."

"Ever thought about being one of those—what are they called—a caller?" Jeris giggled. "At fashion shows—when the models walk down the runway and someone describes what they're wearing?"

"I used to sew my clothes years ago. That's why I know some of these terms. And I watch those makeover shows on TV sometimes. You know, the ones where they select new clothing and hairstyles and makeup?" She clasped her hands together. "I love to see befores and afters. I love those shows."

"You can tell. You've got the lingo *going on*." Jeris giggled again.

Audra Darling ignored her. "And your shoes—you have a heel thing happening. And some nice toe action."

Jeris looked down at her black high heels with their narrow ankle straps. "Good thing I painted my toenails last night."

"How late was it when Luke brought you home?"

"I'll never tell." She was having that euphoric feeling again. "But I painted them before we went out. I'm glad I did. We took off our shoes and went for a walk on the beach."

"Ooh–la–la."

"In the moonlight."

R–r–r–i–i–ing.

"That's mine. I'll get it." Jeris reached for her new metallic-colored satchel with the double shoulder straps and rhinestone detail. Audra Darling had insisted she buy it earlier in another store. She retrieved her cell phone, saw it was Luke, felt her heart do a trill, and clicked it on. "Hi, Luke."

"Hi, Jeris. I—I wanted to say hello."

"Hello to you, too."

"I was wondering—what are you doing today?"

Is that longing in his voice? He's missing me. And I'm missing him. "I'm shopping with Audra Darling."

"Oh yes. You told me that. I forgot."

"You know what she's like. She's a shopaholic. She never wears out. We went to three stores before lunch, and she tells me we have four more places to go to before we can call it quits for the day."

"Well, I wouldn't want to keep you then."

Keep me! Keep me!

"I guess I'll let you go."

Don't ever let me go!

"All Brady's talked about is the children's outing. He can't wait to see you tomorrow."

The children's picnic and boat ride. . .and being with Luke.

"And, Jeris? Neither can I."

Luke clicked Solitaire off his laptop in his home office and glanced at the phone. He'd like to call Jeris again. He wanted to talk to her, to hear her voice. But he'd called her less than an hour ago, and he didn't want to be a bother.

He whirled around in his roller chair and came to a stop facing the large palladian window overlooking his front lawn. Maybe he should go work in the yard. Though his yard guy mowed the grass and edged the concrete every week, some of his shrubs needed a deep pruning. No, he'd call the guy and hire him to do it.

Maybe he should take a swim in the pool. No, it wasn't any fun without Brady, who was attending a birthday party and wouldn't be home for hours.

Maybe he should do some of the work he'd brought home from the office. No, he couldn't focus—on anything. All he could think about was Jeris.

All day he'd pined for her. What an interesting way to put it. Maybe he'd seen the word in the old-fashioned booklet. Archaic, he knew. But it spoke of what he felt. He was acting like a lovesick teenager having his first brush with love. But it couldn't be helped. She did that to him.

He'd prayed long and hard and sought God for a mate. He now felt Jeris was the one for him. What was his next step? It was too soon to reveal his feelings to her. He might scare her away. And, besides, he respected her too much to do that. They needed time to be together, to find out things about each other and grow to care for each other slowly. But he already cared for her. Still, she needed time for that to happen to her. He was sure it would. He was confident God would work out everything between them. But he could use some practical tips.

What would Mr. Granfield say? In short order he had the booklet in his hands and opened it to the next chapter: "How to Woo Her." He smiled. " 'Woo'? That's an old-fashioned word." Though he knew what it meant, he wanted to see the exact phrasing. He pulled his dictionary off the shelf. " 'Woo: to court a woman.' " He chuckled as he flipped the pages to the old-fashioned word *court*.

" 'Court: to engage in activity leading to mating.' Oops." He searched through the entry for a more appropriate definition. " 'To seek to win a pledge of marriage.' " He threw his arm in the air in a victory signal. "Yes!"

"Spend as much time as you can with your girl. Seek ways to be with her. There are all sorts of social and church functions you can attend together. Converse with her freely. Come to know, trust, and love her, just as she will come to know, trust, and love you. This is a process and will take some time. Don't rush it. Put the Lord first in your relationship. At times pray together.

"Remember that the Lord wants to help you in all ways as you pursue courtship—the most important area of your life after salvation. Just as God guided Abraham's trusted servant to find a bride for his son Isaac, so He will guide you. God inclined the lovely maiden Rebekah to accept the proposal to become Isaac's bride, and the Bible says when they came together Isaac loved her. It also says she comforted him. One definition of *comfort* is 'a satisfying or enjoyable experience.' "

Oh yes!

"Lad, be friendly. Be courteous. Be gentlemanly."

Of course.

"Though morality is at an all-time low in today's world, the Christian lad and girl will not take liberties with their bodies while dating. Even though God created a lad and girl with innate physical desires for each other, they must not indulge in illicit love. Strive with all your hearts to come to each other in marriage clean and pure. When you say 'I do,' you may enjoy each other's caresses in ecstasy all the days of your lives."

Hallelujah!

"Now for some practical matters. Use plenty of soap and water when preparing yourself to be with your girl. Avoid B.O. like the Grim Reaper."

Oh, brother!

230

"Trim your nails. Comb your hair. Shine your shoes. Wear some good-smelling toilet water."

Luke started laughing.

"And always wear jaunty neckties."

Still laughing, he tossed the booklet in the air.

∞

Jeris finished her salad, then drank the last of her sweet iced tea. They'd stopped in a restaurant on their way home after shopping all day. It was now dark, and she was bone tired.

"I guess it's time to call it a day." Audra Darling discreetly applied pink lipstick as she looked into a miniature mirror clipped to a tube. Then she snapped it shut and dropped it into her turquoise crocheted shoulder bag that matched her turquoise crocheted espadrilles.

"I don't think I'll ever look at clothes and shoes and purses in quite the same way after today." Jeris took out her own miniature mirror clipped to her lipstick tube—identical to Audra Darling's and purchased during today's shopping. She glanced at the bottom of the tube. "Transcendent Sunrise." She applied it quickly, then dropped it back into her purse.

After you eat, touch up your lipstick fast, Audra Darling had said. *People will hardly notice what you're doing.*

"I like your new makeup," Audra Darling said. "It looks good on you."

Jeris touched her cheek. Audra Darling had taken her to a makeup counter in a fine department store, and the clerk had given her a makeover. "I kept telling her to go easy, and she did, from what I can tell. What differences do you see between the old me and the new me?"

"That light touch of shadow is nice. It enhances your eye color even more. And the blush brings out your cheekbones. I never noticed how high they are. And the mascara gives the perfect upsweep to your eyelashes. And the lipstick is the cherry on top of the sundae."

"Thanks for today, Audra Darling. How can I ever repay you?"

"Just wear those pretty clothes."

Jeris nodded, thinking about her new outfits and shoes and two purses.

"You're now the proud owner of"—Audra Darling held out her hand, palm side up. She grasped her pinkie finger, her silver charm bracelet jangling—"a black cropped mandarin-collar jacket, rose-and-black lace cami, and rose crinkle skirt with stretch lace trim." She grasped her ring finger. "And a vanilla long-sleeved V-necked blouse, gold jacquard vest, and brown dress gauchos." She took hold of her middle finger. "And a—"

"All right, already. Just condense it to 'Jeris Waldron is now the proud owner of eight colorful new *feminine* outfits.'"

Audra Darling reached over the table and flicked the ends of Jeris's hair where they hit her shoulder. "And she's sporting a new hairstyle, too."

Jeris touched her sleek, feather-cut, blow-dried hairdo. "I love it. But it'll be back in its twist or ponytail soon, I can tell you that."

"That's okay. I just wanted you to see what you looked like with another style. This'll give you more choices. You know which outfit I like best of all the ones you bought today?"

Jeris thought for a moment. "Let me see if I have the gift of description like you do. Is it my black sleeveless square-neck dinner dress with the flounced knee-length hemline?"

"Guess again."

"My, you're putting me to work. Is it my brown cotton-spandex fitted jacket with the coordinating brown-and-aqua print skirt with the"—she stared out the window, thinking—"what kind of pleats?"

"It's called a yoke skirt with inverted pleats."

"A yoke skirt with inverted pleats." She swiped at her forehead dramatically. "I passed, even if I didn't get one hundred." She smiled.

"That outfit's gorgeous. But my favorite of all the clothes you bought is your white sleeveless, fitted, V-necked Battenburg-lace-trimmed dress—"

"With the princess seams."

Audra Darling nodded and smiled. "You're getting good at this."

"I have a good teacher."

"Princess seams emphasize all the right places. You're going to be a knockout in it, what with your olive skin and aqua eyes. I can't wait for Luke to see you in it."

"You don't have to wait too long. I'm wearing it to church tomorrow." The tingles surged up her spine.

Chapter 20

"Finish your cereal, Little Man." Luke pushed his empty bowl aside, then reached for his Bible on the counter behind them. "It'll soon be time to go to church." He found the chapter, looked down, and began reading his portion for the day.

"Is this the day we get to go on the boat ride?"

"That's right," Luke said distractedly, his eyes on the page before him. "Miss Jeris is having a picnic at the Hugheses' for your class."

"I get to see Miss Jeris. Yippee!"

Luke looked up, focusing on the framed print behind Brady's head. But he wasn't seeing the Italian countryside with its earthy tones of rust and brown and tan that he'd looked at a hundred times and more. He was seeing Jeris. Jeris with her class. Jeris with Brady. Jeris with *him*.

"She's so much fun, Dad." If Brady had been standing, he would've been jumping. As it was, he was still jumping—sitting down, his upper body jiggling in movement. "I get to see her today. I get to see her today. I get to see her today."

I get to see her today. I get to see her today. I get to see her today.

Brady bolted out of his chair. "I'm through eating." He swiped at his mouth with a napkin.

"Put your cereal bowl in the sink and go brush your teeth. Then put on your clothes and socks and shoes. I laid them out in your room. If you get finished with that and have time, you can play a video game."

"Yes, Dad."

In seconds Luke was alone in the kitchen, Brady's high-pitched chirps boomeranging down the hall.

He straightened his tie—jaunty? He smiled as he continued reading the Bible. But he couldn't concentrate.

Mr. Granfield again? Why not? He had a little time before they needed to leave for church. And he was in the mood for some—entertainment?

He scooped up *How to Choose the Right Wife. . .for Christian Lads* and opened it.

"How Can You Tell If It's the Real McCoy?" He could skip that chapter. He already knew the answer. Oh, well.

"How do you decide if this is the Real McCoy? Is this true love or puppy love? Will the feelings you are having last throughout eternity or until the next pretty girl comes along? You must think about the following questions. Did you

233

put this matter in God's hands? Did you diligently seek Him for your mate? Is she a Christian? Does she have sweetness of spirit? Does she possess inner beauty? Do the two of you have common interests? Does she have high moral standards? What are your answers thus far?"

A definite yes on each one.

"Let's hope your answers are in the affirmative."

Oh yes.

"Through seeking the Lord, I assure you, you will be able to determine if it's true love. You will be able to decide if you have found your sweetheart. Here are some more indications. Is this girl constantly in your thoughts?"

Yes!

"Do the minutes turn into hours when you're away from her?"

Yes!

"When you think of the future, does it include her?"

Oh yes!

"Can you see her standing in welcome at the door of your future home-with-the-picket-fence, wearing an apron and holding a spoon?"

"Nosirreebob," he belted out, Miss Ada-style, as he tossed the booklet into the air, laughing so hard that tears came to his eyes.

∞

Jeris walked into Audra Darling's kitchen. The children's party would start when everyone arrived. She and Audra Darling had told the parents to have the children there by one o'clock and invited them to stay for the afternoon if they'd like. The parents were bringing the fried chicken, Jeris had bought the potato salad at a deli, Audra Darling had made her special-recipe baked beans, and Luke had volunteered to purchase soft drinks.

Standing at the kitchen counter, Audra Darling was making peanut butter and jelly sandwiches, stacks of them, for the children who wanted them.

"Can I help?" Without waiting for an answer, Jeris washed her hands, picked up a knife, and cut the sandwiches in two, then placed them on a large platter.

"Shouldn't you change clothes? That dress would look awful with grape jelly down the front."

"I plan to." Jeris glanced down at her white sleeveless, V-necked Battenburg-lace-trimmed dress. "I wouldn't mess this up for the world. It was too much fun wearing it. I feel like a princess."

"You look like one, too. But are you sure it's the dress making you feel that way?" Audra Darling elbowed her and winked.

Luke strode into the kitchen, carrying a big cooler.

"Hi, Luke." Audra Darling tipped her head in Luke's direction, then elbowed Jeris for the second time.

Jeris playfully elbowed her back as she thought about the praying she'd done lately. She'd been thanking God for Luke.

"Hi, Audra, Jeris," he said.

"Hi." Jeris felt little tingles hit her spine. Every time Luke came near, she felt that way. She glanced down at her dress again. She hadn't seen him at church this morning. She wondered what he thought about her new clothing and hair-style. What would he say?

"Where do you want me to put this, Audra?" He gestured at the cooler. "It's full of soft drinks. I have another one in the car."

Audra Darling pointed to the window with a peanut butter-laden knife. "Out there. On the lanai. That's where we're going to eat."

"Okay." He turned and left the room.

"I shouldn't have poked you when Luke came in," Audra Darling whispered. "That was silly. I'll try not to do it again. I'll try to act my age." She winked. "It's just that I'm thrilled with what's happening between you two. But I promise to stand back and let the Lord have His way."

"Thanks. Audra Darling?"

"Hmm?"

"I need to thank you for your part in getting us together."

Audra Darling pointed upward.

Jeris nodded, knowing she was giving total credit to the Lord.

In a few minutes Luke came back inside. "I have the coolers situated. What else needs to be done?" He walked over to them and stood there.

Jeris's heart beat its familiar little trill.

"Luke?" Audra Darling put her knife down, wiped the peanut butter off her hands, and leaned against the counter.

"Yes?"

"You asked what you can do. You can give your opinion. What do you think about Jeris's new look? That beautiful dress she's wearing? And the way she's fixing her hair now? And the makeup?"

Jeris stopped arranging the sandwiches on the platter, feeling her face flush. She sent Audra Darling a you-said-you-wouldn't-do-this glance.

Audra Darling let out a little gasp and shot Jeris an I-forgot-I'm-sorry look. She waved in the air. "Forget what I said, Luke. There's so much to do right now, with the kids coming and all."

"I don't mind giving you my opinion." He did a quick sweep of Jeris, from head to foot. His gaze came to rest on her hair. "I like it." He moved his hand as if to reach up and touch her hair but dropped it back to his side.

Oh, Luke.

He focused on her face, and their gazes locked. Again he had the same hand movement, as if he wanted to reach out and touch her cheek.

Time seemed to stand still for her.

He glanced down at her dress, then looked into her eyes again, his gaze speaking volumes. "Feminine. Nice."

Jeris smiled. The look he gave her warmed her all the way to her toes.

He took another quick scan of her. " 'That fawn-skinned-dappled hair of hers, and the blue eye dear and dewy, and that infantine fresh air of hers. . . .' "

Your voice sounds like the rich, low tones of a mourning dove.

"That's a Robert Browning poem." He took a step closer to her. "Your new look is pretty. But nothing compares with your *inner* beauty."

"Da–a–a–d! Audra Darling! Miss Jeris! They're here. Everyone's getting out of their cars."

Jeris heard Brady, but she couldn't focus on what he'd said. The tenderness flowing between her and Luke was all-consuming.

∞

"Will you ride with me in the boat I'm driving, Jeris?" Luke stood on the dock, fastening his bright orange life vest.

"I'd love to." Jeris felt as if she were walking on air instead of weathered boards.

The parents were helping the children put on their life vests, and the adults who'd been chosen to ride in the two boats were vesting up, as well.

Within minutes the boats were filled, and the motors were idling. Though the children were chattering, they were calm and still.

"I guess we pounded safety issues into them so much that they're paying attention to us." She gestured to the kids. "They aren't horsing around like the usual—Mexican jumping beans." She turned around and rubbed the top of Brady's head where he sat on a low seat.

Luke nodded from the driver's seat, his hand on the steering wheel. "They'll remember this day for a long time."

She drew in a breath of salty air mingled with the slight mildewed smell of her life vest that wasn't entirely unpleasant. It stirred memories of boating trips with her parents when she was growing up.

Pastor Hughes, sitting in the driver's seat of the second boat, revved his motor, then brought it back down to idle level. He explained to the children what they would be seeing on the boat ride, his voice carrying across the water as if he were using the pulpit microphone. He named the flora and fauna of the area, then described the marine life. "You might see some roseate spoonbills today and wood storks and painted buntings and sea turtles." He named a few other animals and water creatures. "We may even see some manatees today. Audra Darling and I spotted one last week."

The children let out oohs and ahs.

"Manatees are grayish brown marine mammals in varying lengths up to thirteen feet. They have two small pectoral flippers on their upper bodies which are used for steering and for bringing food to their mouths. They swim by moving their large paddlelike tails in up-and-down motions. Because they're mammals, they have to breathe air—"

236

"Like humans?" one boy piped up.

"Yes, just like us. Manatees have been known to stay underwater for as long as twenty minutes, but the average interval between breaths is two to three minutes. Sometimes you'll see them bodysurfing in groups. They also play follow-the-leader—"

"Just like us," a little girl said.

Pastor Hughes nodded. "Sometimes they synchronize their activities including breathing, diving, and changing directions. Or you might see a mother and her newborn calf."

The children oohed and ahhed again.

"I'd sure like to see a manatee today." Jeris peered down at the pewter-colored water, then across to the far shore. "I haven't seen one in a long time."

"That would be nice," Luke said.

Pastor Hughes gave a few instructions to Luke, then headed out. Luke followed closely behind him in the wake. The two boats rode along at a steady clip. At intervals Pastor Hughes gave hand signals to Luke, and Luke followed his lead, slowing at times for the children to see certain plants and animals near the shore, then speeding across the water at other times.

Jeris enjoyed watching the children and their expressions of wonderment and glee. She was grateful Audra Darling had suggested this outing. It was good for the kids, and it was good for their parents. Perhaps they'd gain some new church members from it. She hoped so.

After they'd been on the water an hour and a half, Pastor Hughes headed toward the house and waved for Luke to do the same. In minutes both boats reached the dock.

Jeris helped the adults get each child safely out of the boats. She and Luke were the last to walk up the dock to the house. "I think the kids really enjoyed the outing," she said.

He nodded. "It was kind of Pastor Hughes and Audra to host it."

She smiled. "They love entertaining guests out here. It's second nature to them. Who do you think enjoyed it the most? Them or the kids?"

"Me." He shot her a quirky grin.

∽

Luke, Brady, Jeris, Audra, and Pastor Hughes sat at the patio tables on the lanai, chatting and enjoying each other's company in the late afternoon sunshine.

"I'm sleepy, Dad," Brady said.

"Why don't you stretch out on a lounge chair?" Jeris asked.

Brady nodded as he stood up and walked over to the chair.

She followed him and made him comfortable by propping a folded beach towel under his head for a pillow. In moments he was fast asleep. She caressed his cheek, then made her way back to her chair and sat down.

Luke couldn't help thinking how motherly Jeris was to Brady. She was attentive and loving to him. It warmed his heart to see it. "Thanks, Jeris."

She smiled at him.

An hour flew by as the four of them chatted in animated conversation about many subjects, including the children's church class, the church, Luke's work, Jeris's practice, Brady, and other interests they shared.

Luke looked across the water and saw the sun slip a notch lower in the pale blue-gray sky. "I'd sure like to watch the sun set on the water. It must be awesome out here. It's not something I see very often since I don't live on a body of water as you do." He glanced at his watch. "But it's time to go."

"Don't leave yet," Audra Darling said. "Stay and watch it with us. Andrew and I watch sunsets every chance we get."

"They're breathtaking out here." Pastor Hughes took a sip of his lemonade. "It's like nothing you've ever seen."

"I'm sure it's great." Luke motioned with his hand. "A sunset over the water."

Audra Darling nodded. "Out here it's as if you're seeing two sunsets instead of one. I mean, I've seen sunsets all my life over water. But I've never seen anything quite like this. This water"—she pointed to the river—"becomes a mirror. You won't believe it until you see it."

"Wow." Jeris looked toward the horizon.

"Okay, you've convinced us, Audra," Luke said. "We'd like to see it, wouldn't we, Jeris? Pastor Hughes and Audra's Double Sunset Over Trout River."

"Oh yes," Jeris said.

"And Little Man?" Luke glanced at Brady who had just sat up on the lounge chair.

Brady rubbed his eyes. "See what, Dad?"

"A double sunset."

"Can I have a root beer first?"

Jeris stood on the high banks of the water, marveling at God's handiwork in front of her. Oak trees with sprawling limbs stood like sentinels on guard to her right and left. Sharp, pointy palmettos dotted the ground that sloped toward the river.

Surely an artist had painted the sky with masterful, giant strokes. In the late afternoon light it had bands of color, a pale blue gray chasing a swath of yellow chasing a neon orange, all streaked horizontally with black ribbons of clouds interlaced throughout. Where the sky met the river stood a bank of trees in varying heights until they tapered off into the water. Below the waterline to her amazement she saw a second sky as Audra Darling had said, two skies if that could be so, right before her eyes.

"It's like a double exposure, isn't it?" Luke said.

Jeris whirled around. "I didn't know you were standing there." She smiled at him. "It's spectacular."

"Yes, it is." He took a step closer to her, so close they could've held hands. His glance scanned her face, from her eyes to her lips, then back to her eyes.

"Spectacular," he said in a throaty whisper.

Her heart beat like a drum. A flood of adjectives hit her. *Kind. Good. Gentlemanly. Tender.*

"Let's go sit in the swings on the bank and watch." Audra Darling stepped off the lanai and into the soft grass. "It's a perfect spot to see our double sunset."

"The perfect spot. . ." She hated to leave the place where she and Luke were standing and didn't want to break the sweetness between them. But she nodded and followed Audra Darling across the grass.

Brady caught up to her and locked hands. "Miss Jeris, is the sun going to drop into the water two times?"

She laughed. "No. Only once. But it'll be reflected in the water below. Sort of like when you look in a mirror." As they walked along, she peered down at the cute little boy with the unruly blond hair and freckles. A love so thick she could almost slice it seemed to flow from her heart to his. *A mother's love?* A picture appeared before her eyes of a giant red heart overshadowing her, then melting into her skin in shades of scarlet and fuchsia and pink until her flesh was its natural olive tone again. So this was what a mother's love felt like, to be immersed in *agape*.

Luke and Pastor Hughes followed behind Jeris, Brady, and Audra Darling as they made their way toward the two covered swings under a mammoth oak.

Audra Darling pointed to the first swing. "Jeris, why don't you and Luke sit there?" She didn't wait for an answer. "Brady, come with Pastor Hughes and me. We'll sit in the other one."

Jeris sat down in the swing, and Luke took his place beside her. Across the way, maybe five yards from them, Audra Darling, Pastor Hughes, and Brady settled in the other swing.

Luke pushed the ground with his foot, and the swing glided into the air in a gentle sway.

Jeris enjoyed the swing's movement. But she enjoyed Luke's nearness more. With a wide expanse of the sky, the tree-dotted horizon and the second sunset reflected in the water; with Luke sitting closely beside her and pleasant thoughts of their future swirling in her head, she thought surely she'd died and gone to heaven. She could sit there forever in this place of beauty, with him close beside her.

"Look." Luke pointed skyward.

The sight Jeris saw took her breath away—what every sunset did to her. The sun dropped faster and faster toward the water in its wide band of orange, the pale blue gray becoming darker with each passing moment. And then it seemed to drop into the water.

No one said anything for some time.

"Look." Pastor Hughes stood. "See that dark circle in the water? I think it's a manatee."

"A manatee?" Brady exclaimed.

Pastor Hughes moved quickly toward the dock. "I'm turning on the hose. If it's a manatee, it'll come to the fresh water."

"Manatees drink from the hose, Dad? Like I do sometimes? When we're out by the pool?"

Audra Darling stood. "Everyone, follow me. I think we're about to see a manatee."

They followed Audra Darling down to the floating dock below.

Jeris walked over to the garden hose on the edge of the dock, a stream of water shooting from its nozzle into the river. To her amazement a dark object swam toward it.

"It's a manatee all right." Pastor Hughes peered into the water.

"A manatee?" Brady said. "Where?"

Jeris took a step toward Brady and put her arm around his shoulders. She pointed downward, toward the dark object in the water. "There. Keep watching."

The manatee surfaced directly under the stream of water flowing from the garden hose. It rolled over on its back, belly up, and opened its mouth, and the water cascaded down its throat.

Jeris was in awe. The manatee wasn't two feet from them. She spotted something beside it. A baby manatee. "Look!" She couldn't help being as excited as Brady always was. "This manatee is a mama. There's her baby."

"Where's a baby, Miss Jeris?" Brady asked.

Jeris pointed to the manatee's side. A smaller version of the manatee hovered close beside her.

"Right there." Luke pointed, too.

"Can you believe it?" Pastor Hughes said. "That calf isn't two weeks old, I'd venture to say."

"Then it's a newborn." Audra Darling came close to the edge. "Oh, how cute." She hummed a few bars of "Rock-a-Bye, Baby." "Brady, that's Mama Manatee and Baby Manatee."

He smiled and looked up at Jeris. "Isn't it cute, Miss Jeris? Her baby? It looks so happy beside its mom."

Jeris's eyes misted over. A manatee and a calf swimming in the water. A woman and a boy standing on the dock. Her heart was so full that she was too overcome to speak.

"Are you okay?" Luke looked into her eyes.

"I'm feeling—spectacular, Luke." She smiled up at him, so happy she could burst.

I'm feeling the same way, his look seemed to say.

The calf submerged, then resurfaced over and over again, but it stayed within a foot of its mother's side.

The adult manatee twirled in the water, then took her same position, lying on her back and drinking the fresh water, gulping it down in huge swallows. After awhile she closed her teeth but kept her lips open so the water rushed over her teeth. Then, of all things, she rubbed her flippers across her teeth.

"Look, Brady!" Audra Darling exclaimed. "Mama Manatee's brushing her teeth."

"She is?"

"Just like you do after you eat," Luke said.

Brady giggled. "Does she have Fred Flintstone toothpaste like me?"

They all laughed.

"What a show." Pastor Hughes shook his head. "Nobody would believe this unless they saw it with their own eyes. A manatee brushing her teeth." He smiled. "I'm glad I have witnesses," he said playfully.

For close to twenty minutes the manatee and her calf stayed at the dock, drinking the fresh water. Finally they swam away.

The five of them stood on the dock watching, even after they couldn't see the manatees any longer, after the sky darkened and the automatic dusk lights came on.

"Thank You, Lord," Pastor Hughes said in the semidarkness, "for allowing us to experience this special time with two of Your remarkable creatures."

Thank You, Lord, Jeris said in her heart, *for allowing me to experience this special time with two of your remarkable creatures, Luke and Brady.*

Luke walked behind Jeris up the dock toward the parsonage, the dusk lights letting off a dim glow in the darkness. Brady had already gone inside with Pastor Hughes and Audra. Nature had called. It did that a lot with his son. He smiled thinking about it.

He stopped and pointed upward. "Look, Jeris." He leaned against the railing. "I think I see the North Star."

Jeris stopped, too, and looked up. "You're right." She drew in a breath of night air perfumed with a nearby gardenia bush. "It's in the right position."

A fish jumped out of the water.

Luke looked over the rail into the water that was now as black as midnight. "You got your wish today."

"What's that?"

"You said you wanted to see a manatee."

"Wasn't that something?"

"I don't think I'll ever forget it." Luke recalled how Jeris had teared up when she saw the manatee and her calf together. It was a touching moment that would be branded in his memory forever. Somehow the manatees made him think of her and Brady.

"I won't ever forget it either." Her words were a whisper.

"I can't get over that manatee making motions like she was brushing her teeth."

Jeris laughed.

He laughed, too, remembering the sight, the manatee on her back with her big belly up, her flippers furiously flapping at her teeth.

"You got your wish today, too, Luke."

"I did?"

"Remember? You said you wanted to see a sunset out here."

"And, as Pastor Hughes said, it was breathtaking."

"*They* were breathtaking." She shook her head. "Two sunsets, one mirrored in the water below it."

He turned in the direction of the sunset. *And I know where I want to propose. When the time comes, I want to ask you to marry me right here, Jeris. When the time comes.*

Chapter 21

Just as Miss Ada's booklet advised, Luke spent as much time as possible with Jeris over the next few months. They found out nearly everything there was to know about each other. He met her family. She met his. His love for her grew and blossomed and flourished.

He often felt like a runner waiting for the signal as he anticipated the day he would propose, but he wisely bided his time.

∞

Jeris fell in love with Luke slowly. That was the one thing she'd asked the Lord for, if Luke turned out to be the one for her, that she would fall in love with him in a gradual way, not fast like her other love experience had been.

God had let that happen, and now she knew with a surety that Luke was God's choice for her.

They had recently told each other they loved one another. It was the same night they kissed for the first time.

Like a movie, the romantic scene played out in her mind. . . .

∞

"You're tailor-made for me, Jeris," Luke had told her as they sat on a park bench under a starlit sky, walkers and joggers occasionally passing by.

"Tailor-made?" she asked, amused.

"I've been reading an archaic booklet Miss Ada loaned me from the library. The author says the girl God has for a Christian lad will be tailor-made for him."

"Lad?" She giggled.

"It's a hoot. The author says it doesn't matter if the woman has rose-petal lips."

She playfully pursed her lips at him. "Do I have rose-petal lips, Luke?"

He ignored her. "Or cute dimples—"

"Do I have cute dimples?" She poked her fingers in her cheeks.

"Or curly hair."

She patted her head. "Mine's as straight as a board."

"The author says if the girl doesn't have all that, she'll still be the *darlingest* thing in the world."

They laughed as he told her more about the booklet that had kept him intrigued at times, in stitches at others.

Then he told her he loved her, and she told him the same thing, and he called her *my darling* for the first time.

Afterward he took her in his arms and kissed her for the first time.

The only way she could describe it was bliss, pure and simple.

∽

Jeris dressed for her date with Luke, her heart singing as it did every time she went out with him. He'd told her to dress casual. And cool. They would be outdoors, he'd said. She chose a white cotton tiered skirt, a red sleeveless top, and low-heeled white sandals. Luke also told her Brady would be with them tonight. For many of their dates in the past months Mrs. Nelms had baby-sat, though Jeris told him to bring Brady along anytime. And she meant it. She loved Brady almost as much as she loved Luke.

She stood before the mirror, basking in loving thoughts of Luke, and pulled her hair back in the style he liked best, the French twist with the tendrils at her temples.

She heard the doorbell ring, walked to the front door, and opened it. "Luke." She beamed at him.

He stepped inside and hugged her. "You look beautiful, my darling, as always."

She loved the endearing term he frequently called her. "Thank you. You look good also." He was wearing light khaki pants and a gold shirt that accentuated his brown eyes.

He drew in a deep breath. "You smell nice, as always."

She leaned in close and took in a whiff of his shower-fresh, cologne-splashed skin, enjoying this brief bit of closeness.

"We need to be going. We don't want to be late."

"No." What she really wanted to do was be cocooned in his arms forever. Instead she walked across the room and picked up her purse. "You said. . .Brady was. . .coming?" Their close encounter had left her breathless. She cleared her throat. "Where is he?"

"You'll see."

They stepped out into the early evening sunshine, and she pulled the door shut behind them. Why was he being so mysterious?

In minutes they were in his car, headed for who knew where.

"Where are we going?" She was curious.

"You'll see soon enough."

She nodded. He was being mysterious again. But, as he said, she would soon see. For some dates they'd gone to dinner. Or to concerts or church events. Or social engagements related to Luke's work and picnics at the beach—lots of those. Or swimming, boating, and bicycling. He'd even rented a motorcycle once, and they drove over to the east coast of Florida for the day.

Tonight he had only told her they would be outdoors. That suited her fine. She loved the outdoors. She'd always been a jeans-and-T-shirt-type woman like her mother until she'd become a psychologist. It was then that she started wearing the knit suits, the ones Audra Darling finally told her she detested. She'd worn them to look professional. Now, though, she wore the beautiful clothes Audra Darling had helped her select. She loved them and felt feminine in them, though Luke often said he liked her in casual clothes, too. He said they represented who she was, her active self, the woman he'd fallen in love with. Her breathlessness was back, and she was taking in short, jerky breaths.

"You must be doing some deep thinking." He glanced over at her as he made a right turn off the highway.

"I. . .uh." She figured out where they were headed. "This looks like we're going to the Hugheses'?"

"We are."

She nodded. This would be an evening spent with dear friends. Though it wouldn't be as romantic as she'd first envisioned, it would be a fun evening. "Then why didn't you tell me? Why were you so mysterious?"

"You'll see soon enough."

She playfully tapped him on the forearm and laughed. But she grew quiet immediately. Just the mere touch to his arm sent electric sparks flying up and down her spine. It was a sensation she enjoyed. He told her he'd experienced the same thing. They'd noticed it the first time they kissed, when he held her in his arms on the park bench. After that, they both said no more kissing or holding each other except for brief hugs, and she knew in her heart that they were reserving those things for marriage. Just thinking about it made her breathe even more jerkily.

He made several turns and ended up on the road where the Hugheses lived. He pulled into their driveway and stopped the car, then came around and helped her out.

She could smell something grilling. Steaks? Instead of going to the front door, Luke led her around the side of the house to the backyard.

"Hi, Jeris." Pastor Hughes stood at the grill with a long fork in his hand. Soft, romantic music wafted from a stereo on the lanai.

"Hi, Pastor Hughes. How are you?"

"Miss Jeris!" Brady came bounding toward her and grabbed her at waist level.

"How's my Little Man?" She leaned down and kissed him on the cheek. "I love you."

"I love you, too." He pulled away from her, ran to a horse-shoe stob a short distance away, and threw a horseshoe toward it. "Watch me."

It was then she saw it on the banks of the water. An elaborately set table for two surrounded by lighted tiki lamps on tall poles.

"Pastor Hughes and Audra and Brady are eating inside. We're eating out here."

"Oh."

"I thought it would be nice to enjoy a special sunset alone."

∞

They ate a leisurely dinner with a backdrop of the soft, romantic music. As the sun started setting, the song "I'll Always Love You" came on the player. Luke stood up, walked around the table to her chair, and held out his hand.

She put her hand in his and stood up, though she wondered where they were heading.

He pulled her into a tight embrace.

"This isn't a brief hug," she murmured. She thought her heart would burst from happiness. She felt so good, so safe, so secure in his arms, so in love, so head over heels, so...she couldn't think of any more so's.

He pulled her chin up and looked intently into her eyes. Then his face came toward hers, and he kissed her.

"Luke?" she asked, but it came out slurred because of the pressure of his lips on hers. She drew back. "Are we supposed to be doing this?" She was half smiling, wondering what he would say.

"I know. Our NBC policy."

She couldn't help laughing, even in this romantic moment.

He tipped his head toward the windows overlooking the Hugheses' kitchen table. "Look."

Jeris gazed at the windows and saw Audra Darling, Pastor Hughes, and Brady staring out. She laughed. "What—?"

"This kiss is approved. They're our chaperones for tonight."

She felt the tingles start at the base of her spine and work their way up. When they hit her neck, they started back down and traveled all the way to her ankles.

"This kiss is approved, too." His lips came toward hers.

She giggled, then returned his kiss. She grew dizzy, but it was a good kind of dizzy.

At last he drew away from her. "We can't do that anymore."

She nodded. "I agree."

"Until our wedding."

She nodded again, relishing his closeness. She stopped. He said *wedding*. "Luke?"

He dropped to his knees in front of her.

She drew in a stiff intake of air, then reached for the edge of the table to steady herself.

The back French doors flew open.

From her peripheral vision she saw Brady bounding outside.

Brady ran up to them and plopped in Luke's chair. But he didn't say a word.

She held on to the table tighter. Unusual, she thought, for Brady to be so quiet.

"My darling Jeris." Still on his knees, Luke clasped his hands in front of his chest. "Will you take...us"—he pointed to Brady and then to himself—"to have and to hold, from this day forward? For better or worse? For richer or poorer? In sickness and in health? Until death do us part?"

Brady hurled himself out of his chair, knocking it over.

She reached over and righted it.

Brady jumped on one foot, then the other. "Miss Jeris, will you marry us? Please?"

Her heart almost melted, like ice on a hot summer's day.

"Jeris? Will you. . .have us?" Luke gave her a pleading look, his hands still clasped together.

"Oh yes." She looked long and hard at him, then over at Brady, sending out messages of love. She stared down at Luke again. "A thousand times, yes."

Luke stood, brushing the dirt off his trousers.

Jeris grabbed him in a bear hug. "Hugs are allowed, remember?"

"And so is one more kiss." He winked at her, then tipped his head toward the windows again. "They told me up to three."

She giggled.

He kissed her. But this time it was light and gentle. "Oh, Jeris. . ."

Her heart was pounding. And so was his. She could feel it in their closeness.

"The sun just dropped into the water!" Brady yelled. "Can we have our chocolate cake now, Dad? No, I mean, Mom?"

Chapter 22

Standing in front of a floor-length cheval-glass mirror in the guest bedroom of the parsonage, Jeris stepped into her wedding dress and held it together at the back. "Mom, can you zip me up?"

"Sure, honey." Her mother slowly zipped up her wedding dress.

Audra Darling stood at her left, holding the circle of flowers for Jeris's hair. "I know it's cliché, but you're the most beautiful bride I've ever seen."

"I second that." Her mother touched a long tendril at Jeris's temple. She looked at Audra Darling. "She's gorgeous, even if I am her mother."

"You're simply glowing, Jeris." Carrie, standing beside Jeris's mother, wore the bridal garter around her wrist like a bracelet, waiting to give it to Jeris. "I'm so happy for you."

"Thank you, dear ladies." Jeris looked into the full-length mirror, glancing first at the three women surrounding her, then giving her wedding dress another admiring gaze. When she and Luke had decided to get married on the banks of the water—at sunset—in the same spot where he'd proposed, she knew she didn't want a heavy, formal wedding gown. It would be too hot. And, besides, the wedding was to be casual and simple.

After several shopping trips with her mother, Audra Darling, and Carrie, she'd finally found the perfect dress. As she looked at herself from head to toe, she thought about it in Audra Darling's terms.

The dramatic white drape-neck gown has split flutter cap sleeves, a slightly fitted waistline, and an asymmetrical ruffled hem.

She hugged herself, running her hands along the sides of the soft crepe fabric. "It's a dream dress," she said, feeling nearly as dizzy as when Luke proposed.

"For a dream couple." Audra Darling placed the flower garland in Jeris's hair.

"For a dream wedding," her mother said.

"It *is* dreamy, isn't it? The wedding?" Jeris worked to get the flower garland just right.

"A wedding on the water," Audra Darling said. "At sunset."

Jeris's mother nodded. "With two old ladies and one young one as attendants."

Carrie handed Jeris the garter.

"And a little boy as the best man." Jeris took the garter, pulled it up her calf, then over her knee, remembering Brady's expression when Luke had told him he would be the best man. He'd belted out his expected "yippee!" And she and Luke had laughed.

"I'm so happy you and Luke got together." Audra Darling fiddled with Jeris's flutter sleeves.

Jeris nodded. "With a little help from you." She talked about Audra Darling's dinners and cooking lessons. And her prayers. "Audra Darling, you're my spiritual mother." She hugged her. "Thanks for everything you did in getting Luke and me together. I'll be eternally grateful."

Audra Darling waved her hand as if dismissing the compliment. "I did what I felt in my heart I needed to do."

Jeris hugged Carrie. "And you helped me also, Carrie. I needed to hear what you had to say about not boxing God in. I needed your prayers, too. Thanks, Carrie, for all you did."

"As the old saying goes, 'A friend in need is a friend indeed.'" Absently she touched her rounded tummy.

"I want to show my appreciation by hosting your baby shower." Jeris was thrilled for Carrie and her little one who would soon make his arrival.

Carrie smiled brilliantly.

"Audra Darling cooked dinners to get you and Luke together," Jeris's mother said, "and Carrie dispensed advice, but, hey, I provided the bride."

They all laughed, and Jeris gave her mother a hug.

"I hear the bridal march." Audra Darling ran to the door and opened it. She bowed low and thrust out her hand with a flourish. "Jeris, your groom is waiting."

"Yippee!"

⌒

Jeris stood on the banks of the water, encircled by Luke's arms, looking intently into his eyes, posing for a shot by the photographer. They'd said their vows and been pronounced man and wife earlier. Now the sun was setting, the guests were milling about eating the luscious hors d'oeuvres Audra Darling had made, and the photographer was giving commands to turn this way and that.

"I'm the happiest man in the world," Luke whispered to her.

"I'm the happiest woman in the world, Luke."

"No talking," the photographer said.

Feeling as if her heart would burst from happiness, she reached up and traced his jawline, her gaze taking in his every nuance.

"Hold that pose, Jeris," the photographer said. "I like it."

"I love you," Luke whispered.

"I love you, too."

"Let's have a kiss," the photographer said.

"Gladly." Luke came toward her, gazing into her eyes, and kissed her deeply.

Her heart beat its familiar trill, and the tingles started up her spine as he continued to kiss her.

"Keep it up," the photographer said.

"I'll keep this up for all eternity," Luke said.

She giggled in his arms.

"The sun is right behind your heads," the photographer said. "It'll be a perfect shot. No talking. Just keep kissing."

"If he only knew how much I'm enjoying this."

She giggled again.

"Hold still," the photographer said. *Click. Click. Click.* "Okay. I have my picture."

He didn't release her.

"I said I have my picture."

"Come up for air, Luke." Audra Darling stood a few feet away, laughing along with the rest of the crowd.

"Yes, Luke," Pastor Hughes chimed in.

Luke finally released Jeris, and the crowd applauded.

"Speech, speech!" someone called out.

He was winded from their kissing. He took a deep breath. "This lad's heart is bursting with joy."

KRISTY DYKES

A former newspaper columnist, Kristy Dykes is an award-winning author of ten Christian fiction titles as well as over 600 articles in many publications, including two *New York Times* subsidaries. Some of her titles have been on the Christian bestsellers list and the christianbook.com Top 20 list. Kristy has won many awards including second place in the 2007 Barclay Gold, third place in FHL's Inspirational Readers Choice, and third place in ACFW's 2006 book of the year, novella. She has taught at many conferences and two colleges and enjoys speaking for women's and writers' events. She and her husband, a pastor, live in Florida. She enjoys hearing from her readers. Visit her on the Web: www.christianlovestories.blogspot.com.

Merely Players

by Kathleen E. Kovach

Dedication

This book is dedicated to my husband, Jim, with whom I can always be myself. My deepest thanks to the wonderful employees at the Gulfarium in Fort Walton Beach, Florida, for their helpful answers to all my annoying questions. I hope this book generates new interest for all your worthwhile projects. Also to Kim Van Meter, Film Commissioner for Mariposa County, California, and to (Tiff) Amber Miller, author and member of American Christian Fiction Writers, who helped me gain an insider's view of filming movies on location.

Chapter 1

"Whoo-oo! We did it, Bethy!"

It hadn't sunk in yet with Bethany that they had actually graduated, and soon Hollywood High would be a distant memory. Yet, there was her Ricky, loping across the stadium, his crimson robe flapping about his body like a victory flag.

Ricky picked her up and swung her around. "We did it. We graduated!"

When he'd set her down, Bethany looked past the thick lenses of his glasses and into the forest green eyes she had come to love. The excitement she saw there went beyond the celebration of their special day.

Ricky kissed her with a solid smack. "I was going to tell you my news at your party tonight, but I can't wait."

She glanced discreetly at the healing scar on his chin. Ricky had accepted Christ in her youth group last year, but ever since the incident that had caused the ugly scar, she'd felt him pulling away. How she wished his news was about forgiveness. But she knew better.

"I heard from them, Bethy!"

"The agency?" She tried to match his excitement. "You've got an agent?" He nodded, and she hugged him. "That's wonderful, Ricky. Before long, you'll be a famous Hollywood actor."

He removed her cap and kissed the top of her head. "Naw, not without my leading lady."

She smiled. The latest school paper's headline sprang to memory. BETHANY AND RICKY, TOGETHER AGAIN. The article reviewed their final play together, *The Music Man*.

In between congratulations from family and friends, Ricky continued to share his news. "They want me to change my image, though. How do you think I'd look with dark hair?"

She wanted to answer with a vehement *No*. Instead, she scrutinized him, tousling the hair that he hated because of its nondescript hue. Was it dark blond or light brown? "I don't know. I'll have to get back with you on that one."

"Oh, Bethy," he said as he swung her around again. "Our future is set."

Bethany swallowed hard. How would she tell him they might not have a future? How would she ever say good-bye?

∞

Ten Years Later

Bethany drove the scenic stretch of highway along the Gulf of Mexico on her way to work, while light jazz music rippled from the car radio. The sights from Highway 98 between her home in Seaside, Florida, and her workplace on Santa Rosa Island in Fort Walton Beach almost always took her breath away. Emerald-tinted crystalline water kissed the sugar-sand beach with balmy waves. Feathery sea oats swayed like kites in the slight breeze while white dunes hugged their roots in an attempt to keep them grounded.

As she began her ascent onto the bridge that connected the resort town of Destin to the island, a brief weather report interrupted the music. "Enjoy the morning and early afternoon, folks. A winter rainstorm is headed our way with temperatures dropping rapidly right around rush hour."

Bethany frowned at the intrusive voice. On this warm February day, a man jogged mere inches from the waves and a sailboat bobbed in languid disinterest only yards from the shore. She shrugged. Nothing was going to spoil this lovely day.

When Bethany arrived at work, Ophelia barked at her for no apparent reason, probably just to hear the sound of her own voice.

"Hungry, girl?" Bethany threw the seal a fish treat and waved to the trainer who was cleaning the area.

She entered the fish house where she began every day at the Gulfarium. "An assistant dolphin trainer's work is never done!" she said to herself as she chose the fish—mostly herring and squid—used to feed her dolphins in the morning. The food had already been thawed slowly in the refrigerator the night before, and she placed it into cool water to clean. Afterward, she iced it down to keep it from decomposing too quickly.

She carried her buckets of cleaned fish out to her counterparts. Four noses, all bottle shaped, poked from the surface of the water. They followed her around to the lower platform where she threw the food into their wide-open mouths. Kahlua, the young male, chattered, whistled, and clicked to encourage her to throw faster. During this ritual, she gave each a rubdown, something they loved almost as much as the treats. The strength under their rubbery, smooth skin reminded her of her human frailty.

As Bethany threw the last fish, she heard a human voice from the other side of the tank call to her in a gentle Barbados accent. "Good morning."

"Definitely a good morning, Sheila." She never grew tired of hearing the therapist's voice, with her *queen meets the islands* lilt. How she wanted to work with Sheila full time! Bethany had been involved with the training aspect nearly all her life, following her father around when he worked at Marineland in California and then later, when it had closed, at Sea World on both coasts. But it gave her a warm feeling to be able to help special-needs kids with the Dolphin Therapy Project.

"You sound chipper," Sheila said as Bethany skirted the pool to catch up to her.

Bethany spread her arms. "The sun is shining, the sky is clear, and all is right with the world."

"What an optimist! There's a storm on the horizon, you know." Sheila waved her clipboard to signal her readiness to organize the day.

"Nah, just a little rain. What's Florida without rain?"

"Are you joining us today?" the therapist asked as they entered her office. She walked over to a file cabinet and pulled out several folders labeled with children's names.

"For a couple of sessions."

"Have you talked to Simon?"

Bethany picked at her thumbnail. "I've asked him about a promotion so I can work with you as a full trainer, but he's still not too keen on the idea."

"Why ever not?" The therapist raised her dark eyebrows.

"I don't know. Something about not being totally dedicated to this as a career. He's fine with me shadowing Dad, but he doesn't think I can hack it full time." Bethany picked up a pencil from the desk and maneuvered it through her knuckles as if it were a baton. "Sure, I ask for time off for church stuff. Also there's the acting thing. He hates it when I need large blocks of time for rehearsals and then performances. But he can't expect me to live, breathe, and drink saltwater twenty-four seven."

"Why not? He expects it from all of us." Sheila flipped through a folder containing information on the first child to arrive for therapy. "Tell you what—I'll inform the trainer assigned today to let you give the commands, kind of back off, and let you run the show. Simon usually pokes his head in during the first session, so if he sees how well you do, maybe he'll reconsider."

The butterflies in Bethany's stomach banged against her abdomen. A chance to prove herself. *Please, God, don't let me blow it.*

Later, in the Dolphin Encounter Building while waiting for the Spencer family to arrive, Sheila opened the child's folder and updated both Bethany and the other trainer, Lauren. "Let's see. . .Kevin Spencer. . .age ten." She perused the page. "Autistic. . .has never spoken. . .therapy program in place, but not seeing much improvement." She smiled at Bethany. "Hopefully Cocoa can encourage him. You've seen the routine. I use positive reinforcement along with the therapy techniques he's already been using. For instance, if I can get him to look me in the eye, Cocoa will do a behavior for him."

"Got it," Bethany said as she picked at a nail.

"You'll be fine." The therapist placed her hand over Bethany's fingers and squeezed.

Soon Kevin arrived with his family. Sheila introduced herself, Lauren, and

Bethany, then knelt until she was face-to-face with the boy. "Hello, Kevin. We're going to swim today. Would you like that?"

Kevin's father, a nervous man, jingled the coins in his right pocket. "Are you sure it's safe? Those fish are pretty big."

Mammals. Bethany's pet peeve. Why must people refer to dolphins as fish when surely they must know better? She began the speech she'd heard Lauren say to new families. "Kevin will be seeing a pantropical spotted dolphin today. She's a smaller species of *mammal* than her bottlenose cousins in the performance arena. Also, Kevin won't really be swimming with her. He will sit on a ledge, and the dolphin will come to him."

At the pool, Sheila positioned Kevin along the side. His parents took seats in the bleachers while Bethany and Lauren slipped into the pool with Cocoa. Sheila briefly explained the reinforcement system, then asked Bethany to introduce Cocoa. Bethany waved her hand, as she had seen the other trainer do, and the small dolphin circled the pool. Kevin locked his gaze on the sleek animal. When she came back around to smile sweetly at him, he cracked a small, one-sided grin.

His mother cried. His father whispered, "Praise God." Apparently any reaction from the boy was cause to celebrate.

Sheila offered him a choice of two colors and asked him to point to the blue one. When he wouldn't respond, she asked him, "Would you like to throw a ring out to Cocoa?" His eyes swiveled toward the pool, and she asked again for him to point to the blue ring. "I know his at-home therapy uses this technique," she told his parents, "but now he has a motive." Finally, after several minutes of gentle coaxing, he lightly tapped the blue ring.

"Good job! Now would you like to throw it to Cocoa, or do you want me to? If you want me to, you'll have to look at me so that I know." Almost imperceptibly, his eyes darted to meet her gaze. "Okay. I'll do it this time, but I'd like you to try it next. Okay?"

She threw the ring to the waiting Cocoa, and Bethany instructed the dolphin to retrieve it and take it back to Sheila. "Look, Kevin," the therapist said as she removed it from the dolphin's nose. "Cocoa loves jewelry. She has a nose ring."

At Kevin's small smile, Bethany had to swallow the lump squeezing her throat.

When he finally allowed himself to throw the ring to Cocoa, in a somewhat unconventional manner—underhanded across his body—he and Sheila joined the two trainers in the pool.

"You're doing great," Lauren whispered to Bethany.

When they were done, Mrs. Spencer dried Kevin off with a towel while his father praised his efforts. Bethany thought Kevin to be a lucky boy to have such a supportive family. They seemed to want to try anything that would help their son.

"We will hope to see a marked improvement in Kevin with each session," Sheila said to Kevin's parents. "We'll book ten sessions. After that time, I'll reevaluate and see if more would benefit him. Continue his therapy at home.

What we do here should make your time with him more productive."

The seeming weight that had dragged in with the Spencers now vanished, and they walked out with a slight spring in their steps.

Bethany pulled herself out of the pool and caught a glimpse of Simon leaving. Her mind flipped through the last hour. Had she done everything correctly? *Yes*, she decided. He should have no complaint.

"Bethany," Sheila said as she threw her a towel. "You did very well. I think you're a natural. Have you ever thought of becoming a therapist?"

"You're a strong advocate for your profession, Sheila." She shook her head at the absurd thought. How much more schooling would that require? She hoped her life had finally settled down. After the move to Orlando right after her high school graduation, she'd lived at home while attending college and gave stage acting a try. When her father was offered the job as senior trainer at the Gulfarium four hundred miles away, she'd shared an apartment with a friend and paid the rent by acting professionally. Her friend married, leaving her with a home she couldn't afford, so she'd followed her father once again.

She walked out of the building that enclosed the encounter pool. The sun's rays bathed her skin with warmth but assaulted her eyes. Once she donned her sunglasses, she noticed a figure waving to her from across the performance tank. Her handsome father. She couldn't leave him again to go to some university. They needed each other. She was his only child, and Daddy was the only parent she had left.

Two more therapy sessions and several dolphin shows later, Bethany searched out her best friend, who managed the gift shop.

"Are we into circus performing now?" She laughed at Cleo's strawberry curls, which hung sideways while she balanced on an upper rung of a ladder.

"Think they could use a new act out there? Cleo Delaney, acrobat and lightbulb changer extraordinaire."

"Come down from there. You're making me nervous."

Cleo made her dismount, astounding the imaginary audience. "What's up, kiddo?"

"Your husband's been gone for a month—"

"Seven weeks and four days."

"And I thought maybe you'd like to come over for a Girl Night. We could do pizza and a movie."

"Sounds great. I'll bring the ice cream." Cleo's previous exertion caused her cheeks to flush, making the freckles on her face more endearing. She continued her closing chores, chattering even while counting change. Cleo could talk during any activity. Cleo talked all the time. "Ed called this morning. I gotta get used to this overseas stuff. He was just going to bed, and I was just getting up. Isn't that wild?" With a snort, she said, "Air Force life!"

She placed the day's proceeds into a canvas bag from the bank and asked,

"How did your day go?"

"It went well." Bethany started spinning the postcard rack, but Cleo shooed her away to straighten them. "I got to play full trainer during one of the therapy sessions. You know, when that little guy smiled at Cocoa, I knew I was in the right place. Simon was watching. I hope he's more open to promoting me now."

"Here, make yourself useful." Cleo handed Bethany a feather duster and pointed to a shelf housing ceramic knickknacks. "It is so cool that you get to play with the dolphins and help children at the same time. I'm jealous."

"Sheila asked me if I'd ever considered becoming a therapist." She fingered the dusty wisps. "What do you think?"

Cleo's mouth drew to the side as she narrowed her blue eyes. "So you plan on being an actress/dolphin trainer/therapist/whatever-strikes-your-fancy-next. Girl, you're going to have to make up your mind." She seized the unused duster and threw it under the counter. "You're almost middle-aged."

Reaching for a furry dolphin puppet on display, Bethany pouted. "I'm only twenty-eight. Some people haven't even left home at that age."

"Beth, you live with your father."

Using the puppet's mouth to counter the accusation, Bethany spoke slowly through closed ventriloquist lips, "It's sintly a natter oth conthenience."

Cleo dislodged the puppet from Bethany's hand. "Don't play with the merchandise. You'll get it all fishy." She put it back on its stand, making sure the head faced outward.

Sheila burst through the gift-shop door. "Oh good, you're still here. Have you heard?"

"Heard what?" Bethany said with a shrug.

"Come down to the Living Seas room. Simon has an announcement."

They, along with the rest of the employees, filtered into the theater-style seating in front of the large tank. A sea turtle stared at them from beyond the aquarium glass.

Those buzzing with gossip seemed to think the announcement had to do with a call from a movie production company.

Cleo began waving her hands in excitement, as if drying her nails. To Bethany, she said, "What if the call was about you?"

"Me? Why?"

"You're the darling of Community Theater. Maybe he saw your last performance."

"You're delirious. They don't work that way."

Cleo made a square box with her fingers and looked at Bethany through an imaginary lens. "Love it! Love it! She swims like Esther Williams, sings like Judy Garland, and acts like Audrey Hepburn. But that hair!"

Bethany self-consciously glanced around at the gathering crowd. Embarrassed, she covered her head with both hands. "What do you mean, 'that hair'?"

"You look like a sun-bleached moppet."

Bethany scrunched her short tresses, feeling it looked better messed up.

Simon had been talking quietly to those gathered around him. When he saw that everyone had assembled, he held up his hands to gain their attention. "I received a phone call from a man who works for Galaxy Productions. He's a location scout interested in making a movie here."

"Location scout?" Cleo's disappointment showed in her translucent blue eyes.

"He'll be visiting next week," Simon continued, "and I want everything spotless. He asked if he could take pictures so the powers that be in Hollywood could make the final decision."

"What movie is it?" Bethany heard from the middle of the crowd.

"*Danger Down Under*."

"Who's the star?"

"Brick Connor."

Squeals from the women masked Bethany's gasp. *Ricky!* She made a hasty retreat to her car, gulping air and muttering, "No-no-no. . ."

Chapter 2

No! No! No!" The woman's scream came from inside a helicopter as it lifted from the roof of the building. Dan ran to it, grabbing the skid just in time. He dangled over the Pacific Ocean as his black tuxedo jacket flapped in the gust of wind caused by the chopper blades. In two fluid motions, he was inside. His nemesis, the pockmark-faced Shark Finlay, grinned at him with sharp, crooked teeth, then leered at the woman tied up in the back of the bubble.

Dan kicked at his enemy in an effort to gain control of the aircraft. Shark snapped at his foot with broad jaws.

"You scuffed my shoe, Sharky. You'll pay for that."

"No worries, mate." With a gleam in his eye, Shark tipped the helicopter, causing the woman to tumble out the open door.

Dan's head swiveled from Shark to where the woman had just disappeared. "You've left me in a quandary, Sharky. Should I stay and bring you to justice, or save a damsel in distress?" He made a quick decision, grabbed the sides of the door, and placed his feet on the skid. "See you in Sydney."

After a graceful swan dive, he swam to the woman. With a single swish of the hidden titanium blade in his watch, he released her before she drowned.

She threw her arms around his neck. "Thank you, Agent Danger, you saved my life."

"You know who I am. Who are you?" They bobbed in the water, a fishing boat already chugging up to them.

"I'm Agent Risk, the rookie."

With a swarthy raise of his brow, he said, "I wish I'd known the *Risk* before I jumped in."

The scene faded with a long shot of Australia, and the words:

SEE AGENT DAN DANGER

IN HIS NEXT ADVENTURE

DANGER DOWN UNDER

Wild applause thundered in the auditorium where the premiere of the third movie in the series, *Danger on the High Seas*, had just played. Brick Connor sulked in his seat and turned to the man who had played the villain, his best friend and mentor, Vince Galloway. He leaned in, speaking for Vince's ears only, "And for this, we get paid the big bucks?"

Vince's grin showed his now-straight teeth, perfectly tucked inside his naturally pockmarked face. "No worries, mate." He cleared his throat and shifted his square body to sit more comfortably in the upscale leather theater seat. "It's going to take me forever to get rid of this Aussie accent."

"Don't get rid of it too soon. We still have"—he wiggled his fingers ominously—"*Danger Down Under* to make."

Brick had become disillusioned after the first *Danger* movie, when the company had lost their great team of writers in a contractual dispute. The second and third scripts became substandard, and the next one showed no promise of improvement. Now it was just another action/adventure film, and he was locked into a contract to finish two more movies.

Vince's wife, Evelyn, who had apparently caught his snide remark, leaned over her husband and spoke so as not to be heard by the departing crowd. "I take it you don't like the next one any better than the last."

Brick ran his hand through his hair. "I don't know; maybe I'm spoiled." He smiled at the tiny woman who nearly disappeared behind her block-shaped husband. "If I could only wedge in some meatier roles."

"You know," Evelyn said as they all stood up, "if you're interested, I've been looking for a financial partner to back the new production company I want to start."

"That's a great idea." Vince nodded his head. "She has the smarts, but we lack the funds to get it going. Could be a way to break out of your typecast."

Brick had reached the center aisle but stopped in his tracks, nearly causing Vince to plow into him. *My own production company.* He'd heard of other actors doing that, and it helped them take control of their careers. Plus, he could produce films that made a difference—that actually said something.

Vince patted his back. "Think about it. We have these location shoots coming up, but after Florida, we'll be home. Come over and we'll show you the research we've already done."

Brick's mind reeled with the possibilities.

As they were filing out, he heard a female voice talking to a friend. "I just love how they tease you at the end of each movie! This one set in the Pacific was terrific, but I can't wait for the Australian one."

A male voice answered her, "I still think the Washington, D.C., movie was the best. The first in the series usually are."

"What was that one called? I forget."

"*Danger* something. . .something *Danger*. I don't remember, aren't they all just called *Danger* movies?"

Danger Behind Closed Doors. Why couldn't people remember the title?

Not feeling like chatting with the reporters, he artfully dodged them and made his way to the limo. Neither was he in a party mood, but he'd promised some people he'd at least make an appearance.

As the car pulled away, he saw Vince and his wife talking to Bebe Stewart

263

of *Entertainment, Now!* He noticed her looking around and knew she was searching the crowd for him. Her viewers would be disappointed if he didn't give an interview.

He shrugged. Bebe would find him at the party.

When he arrived, he perused the crowd. Several people had greeted him before he heard, "Brick-Bud! Come here. I gotta introduce you to someone."

Brick cringed. The voice came from across the sea of people gathered at the glitzy restaurant hosting the premier party for *Danger on the High Seas*. It belonged to Chez, his best buddy from the early days, when partying was a rite of passage for two Hollywood bachelors. They hadn't hung out together in a while, except at social gatherings.

He reluctantly made his way through the crowd and noted with disgust that Chez wore a girl on each hip.

"Brick! This is—what did you say your name was?" The blond on his right whispered in his ear. "Oh yeah. This is Pixie, like the dust." Raucous laughter followed this announcement as if it had been a huge joke. Brick didn't get it. "And this," Chez slurred as he referred to the redhead on his left, "is the waitress. Get me some of those breaded mushroom cap thingies, 'kay, love?"

Brick shook his head as he pulled up a chair. "You started celebrating a little early, didn't you, Chez?"

"And why shouldn't I?" He floated from Pixie as if en route to Peter Pan's Neverland. Apropos, since he all but declared himself king of the Lost Boys who never grew up. He climbed onto a chair and teetered slightly as he stood on the seat.

"For I am Chad Cheswick." Chez geared up for an oration. "The greatest director in the—oops." He prefaced what was sure to be a great speech by falling off the chair and landing at Pixie's feet.

"Chez," Brick said after taking pity on him and setting him in the chair. "You were the assistant director on this film. No one cares who you are."

"But I shot some of the best scenes in that film. It's exactly what they say. Location. Location. Location." He pointed to three obscure spots in the room for emphasis.

Brick ordered a club soda for himself and coffee for his friend. "Yes, Chez. You are the best at location shots."

"Thank you. That's all I'm saying."

Although Chez was only hired for small scenes, those that the director himself didn't need to be at, Brick enjoyed working with him. If only Chez would grow up, he'd be a great director.

The waitress brought the mushroom caps, smiled, and sashayed away. Chez followed her with his bloodshot eyes. "Hey, Brick. A hundred bucks."

"No."

"Aw, come on! You're no fun anymore, now that you're a *big* movie star." He made quote marks in the air.

"I'm not interested in which of us can pick up the waitress. Keep your hundred bucks." Brick had grown past the silly game playing. Chez had not.

"Just as well." Chez sipped his coffee and made a face. "I'd win anyway. We all know who's the better man here."

Brick had a retort ready on his tongue, when a stir began near the door of the restaurant. Bebe had arrived.

Chez rolled his fuzzy gaze toward the commotion. "Your girlfriend's here."

Bebe spotted Brick, and with microphone in hand and a cameraman over her shoulder, she swept down on him as if she were a hawk snatching a mouse.

"Brick Connor, you ditched me!"

"Sorry, Bebe. I had places to go, people to see. You know how it is." He stood and greeted her with a kiss on her coral-tinted cheek.

Yes, they had been an item, back when she interviewed him for the first *Danger* movie. It only lasted a couple of months, and they broke it off amiably.

He respected Bebe's profession as a reporter over the stalking paparazzi. The latter were sleazy photo hounds who didn't care whose privacy they invaded, as long as they could make a quick buck.

Smoothing her royal blue Dior jacket, she looked into the camera. "This is Bebe Stewart with your *Entertainment, Now!*"

As she began asking questions, he tried to answer professionally, but then she went in for the kill. In a few simple steps, she had him admitting that he'd been unhappy with the last few films and was searching for roles with more substance. He kicked himself. That would come back to bite him for sure. Maybe subconsciously he wanted the world to know there was more to Brick Connor than Agent Dan Danger.

∽

Beth?"

Cleo! She'd forgotten all about her. "Up here."

She heard pounding footsteps, as if Cleo had scaled the stairs two at a time.

Cleo swung open the bedroom door. "What are you doing? You scared me to death." She raced to the floor where Bethany sat cross-legged. "You hightailed it out of there so fast, by the time I got into my car to follow, you were out of sight."

Bethany picked feverishly through her high school mementos, the cardboard box in which they'd been stored turned upside down and the contents scattered around her.

Cleo's heart showed through her clear blue eyes. "What's wrong?"

"That m–movie. . ." was all Bethany could squeeze out of her throat.

"What movie? What are you talking about?"

Bethany finally held up a picture she had clutched in her hand.

Cleo looked perplexed. "Beth, this looks like a very young *you* with a handsome kid, so what?"

"Look closer! See who that is?" Bethany swallowed the hysterics that threatened.

"He looks familiar. Is he someone I should know?"

Bethany rolled her eyes in frustration. "It's Brick Connor!" she ground out, shaking the picture for emphasis.

"Let me see that." Cleo pried the picture from Bethany's white-fingered grasp. "Are you sure? Brick Connor has dark hair and an incredible tan. This kid has light brown hair and freckles."

Bethany rose to her hands and knees to search in the pile further. Finally finding a magazine, she held up the picture on the cover to compare with the boy in the photo.

"I don't believe this," Cleo said. "You knew Brick Connor as a kid? How cool! But, what's the fuss?"

Bethany sighed deeply to gain control. "Brick Connor used to be Ricky O'Connell, my boyfriend in high school. He changed his looks and his name when he started acting." She compared the contact lens-wearing Brick to her horribly nearsighted Ricky with glasses. She preferred the latter.

When Cleo leaned against the bed, Bethany's black-and-white cat made an appearance from under the dust ruffle. She rubbed along Cleo's outstretched leg.

"Hello, Wilhelmina. Were you hiding from Hurricane Bethany?"

"You know her name's not Wilhelmina," Bethany snorted, the last shudders of emotion fading away.

Cleo picked up the cat and snuggled the pink nose against her own. "Sorry, Willy. Whoever heard of naming a cat after a fish?"

"Not a fish, you dodo, a killer whale, after the movie *Free Willy*."

"Then why don't you call her Freebie?" Cleo grinned. Bethany snatched the feline and held her close to her heart. Willy purred ecstatically. "Because she wouldn't answer! Now back to my problem—"

"I still don't see a problem. You dated a boy who grew up to be a multimillion-dollar box office star. It might be fun to see him again, talk over old times, exchange autographs—sell his for a profit."

Bethany placed Willy on the bed and began to straighten the mess on the floor. "We more than *just dated*. We were semi-engaged."

"Semi-engaged is like being a little preg—" Bethany placed the palm of her hand in front of Cleo's face, thereby halting the rest of that sentence. Cleo flicked the hand away. "Well, you either are or you aren't! How can you be semi-engaged?"

With trembling hands, Bethany reached for a small heart-shaped box. She carefully lifted the lid to reveal a delicate gold band with a tiny diamond chip setting.

"He gave this to me the day I found out we were moving."

Bethany thought back to that bittersweet day. She'd waited until after the graduation party to spring it on him. Her father had decided to relocate to Orlando, Florida, and work at Sea World there. They would move the next month. Ricky had the promise ring in his pocket, thinking they'd be together forever.

"We were a good team," she said as she methodically shuffled through some old school playbills. "He was Tony; I was Maria. He was Don Quixote; I was Dulcinea. He was Professor Harold Hill; I was Marian, the librarian." Symbolically she threw her past back into the box and sealed it.

"Shortly after graduation, my father moved us across the country. Ricky stayed in California and dedicated himself to his career. His letters dwindled to a trickle. By the time Dad was offered the senior trainer job here, we'd stopped communicating." She shrugged her shoulders and ran her hand through her cropped hair. "When he became Brick Connor, I ceased to exist."

She had been so afraid her leaving would affect his spiritual life. Ricky depended on her family for guidance. Apparently she was right.

Cleo, after a moment of uncharacteristic silence, finally asked, "You mean, he gave you a promise ring, without any commitment?"

"I thought it was a promise ring. I guess it was more of a 'good-bye' ring."

"I can't believe that all this time you knew Brick Connor and you never told me."

Bethany thought of the real reason her father had insisted on leaving California. *That's not all you don't know about me, Cleo.*

∞

Finally home after pouring Chez into a limo, Brick shed his tux for a ragged pair of sweatpants and an LA Lakers T-shirt. He sank onto his over-stuffed couch, reached for the remote, and placed his bowl of ice cream on his stomach. He wasn't hungry—the sweet treat served more as comfort food than anything else. Mmm. . .Choco-Mallow Swirl. At this moment, better than a woman.

Before he could find the movie-classics channel, the phone rang.

"Argh! It's a conspiracy!" He listened to the answering machine. Best invention ever. Screening his calls kept him sane.

A thick Alabama accent rolled out of the speaker and moseyed barefooted to his ear. "Brick? Brick, honey? Pick up, darlin'. It's me."

Maggie.

He picked up the phone. "Hey, Maggie."

"Hey, Brick." It sounded like an episode of *The Andy Griffith Show*. Should they amble over to Floyd's for a haircut and piece of gossip? "I saw your interview with Bebe Stewart. She worked you over, didn't she?"

"Naw, I had her in the palm of my hand." And she bit him on the thumb. "How's the album going?" When he'd first met Maggie, she had been contracted to sing in the second *Danger* movie. At that time, Maggie was a young, ambitious country singer, just coming into her own. Now, as the lead singer of an all-girl country band, she could belt out a tune that could make a coal miner weep. And she played the fiddle—never call it a violin in her presence—as good as any at Carnegie Hall.

"Recordin' simply drains me. Almost as bad as the concerts. Plus, I'm lonely. If you want to get away from the rat race there, you can join me in Nashville. It's beautiful this time of year."

Brick's upper lip began to sweat under his mustache. Maggie seemed to think she could turn him into a Southern gentleman after sporadic dating and a long-distance relationship. He had a brief vision of sitting in a rocking chair on a wide veranda, him in a white suit and her in a frilly hoopskirt.

With a shudder, he said, "Sorry, Mags, I can't get away just yet. I'm about to go on location for this next movie."

He heard an exaggerated sigh. "Well, when we're through wrapping up this album, we'll be going on tour to kick it off. Chances of coordinating our schedules will be slimmer than a snake slidin' through a picket fence, but let's try when you get back."

"Sure thing." He looked longingly at his ice cream, melting by the minute. Time to wrap up this conversation. "Well, you take care of yourself. I look forward to hearing that new album." Not really. Country music set his teeth on edge.

"Okay. I love you."

Brick hesitated. He had never said the *L* word to anyone in his adult life. "Backatcha, babe." He hung up, mentally going through a list of synonyms that would have been far better than *backatcha*.

After about an hour, the adrenaline of the premiere began to wear off, and Brick fell asleep in the middle of an old western. His dream produced a fuzzy image of someone he had said the *L* word to a long time ago. Her father had just made the announcement. They were moving. Where was it? Far away, that's all he remembered. She clutched his ring to her chest, and he promised he would always *L* word her. Even in his dreams, he couldn't say it. The image faded, and the only person left was a teenage boy surrounded by shards of his shattered heart.

Chapter 3

Ken Kirby, the location scout, showed up with his camera and focused in on every inch of the Gulfarium. Bethany watched him enter the performance area with Tim Grangely, seal trainer, hot on his heels. Tim was assigned to be the tour guide, but it sounded more like he'd assigned himself Gulfarium guardian. Thankfully, Mr. Kirby seemed like a patient man.

While he snapped away at the water, the bleachers, and the surrounding area, he informed them that only a few short scenes would be filmed of the actors running through the aquarium and shooting at each other. In the actual movie, they'd be running through a zoo in Australia.

"Since it's more cost-effective to do most of the action shots Stateside, we've chosen several attractions to film in, and we will create our own park later. You know, piecing it like a patchwork quilt." He knelt and took pictures of the mischievous Kahlua, splashing water with his bottle-shaped nose to get attention. "We only plan to be here about a month."

"A month?" Tim whined. "Won't that be disruptive?"

"We'll do all our shooting in the evening, after the tourists have gone." He further promised that all the large equipment would be set back and hidden with a cover.

As they walked away, Bethany heard Tim's objections again, followed by Mr. Kirby's professional tone. "We use computers, so no animals will be hurt making this film."

A month had gone by since Ken Kirby's visit. Bethany hadn't slept well since finding out that his photographs were approved and all systems were go. She took her concerns to the Gulfarium's oldest living resident. He watched her wisely, as only a hundred-year-old loggerhead turtle would.

"How will I ever get through the next four weeks?"

She tried to think of ways to be absent during the filming. Maybe if she broke her leg. She sighed. No, then she would hurt in two places—her leg *and* her heart.

"You're so lucky, Absalom. You've got that big, protective shell. Would you let me borrow it while Ricky is here?"

Absalom opened his mouth as if he were about to give her the answer of the ages but then snapped it shut. Only a yawn.

Bethany looked up to see Cleo approach, wiping her forehead. "I know we're not supposed to have perpetual summer like the rest of Florida," Cleo said, "but our springs are hardly worth mentioning. Here it is March, and I'm already sweating."

"You're just used to your air-conditioned shop. It's beautiful out here." Bethany turned her face toward the sun, allowing its warmth to soothe her frayed nerves.

"Still, I'd rather skip summer and go right into fall."

"No! Don't rush the calendar. 'B-Day' will be here soon enough."

"Huh?" Cleo tilted her head.

"That's what I'm calling the dreaded 'Brick Day.' This is March, and after that—"

"After that—the actors attack!" Cleo came to attention and saluted sharply. "What can we do to prepare, General?"

"Retreat," Bethany said, trying not to grin. But Cleo's antics got the best of her, and she couldn't keep the corners of her mouth from curving upward. "You're so good for me. What did I do to deserve a friend like you?"

"You're blessed." Cleo's eyes twinkled with mischief. "You know, we have about fifteen minutes until choir practice. You might consider tearing yourself away from that old turtle and giving a little bit of yourself to the Lord."

"Did you hear that, Absalom? Little does she know that you're a sage, just waiting for the right question." Absalom turned his 350-pound body away from the girls. "I guess I didn't ask the right question."

∽

"It's really happening. . . ."

"What is that thing?"

"Glenn, if any of my animals suffer—"

"I need a grip over here."

Bethany walked through her beloved aquarium listening to the various snippets of conversation. By seven o'clock in the evening, the production crew invaded as if all of Normandy depended upon them. Cameras, lights of all shapes and sizes, generators, booms. . . She nearly tripped over a man laying tracks upon which rolling platforms would eventually be placed. Her workplace now resembled a working movie set.

How are they ever going to hide this stuff by tomorrow? Bethany moved to her station near the dolphins. Each trainer was assigned a different area near the animals. As unfamiliar sights and sounds surrounded them, they would have familiar faces and soothing voices to calm their nerves. Bethany sat on the lower platform of the performance pool and dangled her feet in the water. She talked quietly to Lani, Kahlua, Coral, and Ginger, who seemed fine but curious. They chattered and swam in circles, then came to Bethany for a reassuring pat.

"Where's that gaffer!" someone bellowed near the seals, which produced a frenzied barking.

"Keep down the noise!" Tim Grangely yelled a decibel higher. He turned to

Glenn, who had joined Bethany, and said with eyes bugging, "You gotta talk to someone! If this din keeps up, no one will be in performance mood tomorrow, including me!"

"Okay," Bethany's father said, "I'll see what I can do. Meanwhile, why don't you visit all the stations and see how everyone is doing?" He winked at Bethany, and she knew he had already done that but wanted to keep Tim busy.

As Tim marched away, nodding with purpose, Bethany giggled. "I think Tim is having a breakdown."

Glenn squatted next to his daughter and threw treats of fish to four eager mouths. "Tim has a tendency to overreact, but his heart's in the right place. Personally, I think it's going rather smoothly. Once the initial setup is done, it shouldn't take long to transition from tourist attraction to movie set." He looked around at the chaos. "Remember the training film I hosted in California? At Marineland before they closed down? Maybe you were too little."

"You mean when it took Mom and me months to shrink your head back down to size?"

He splashed her playfully. "Okay, you do remember. It was a small production, but they made such a fuss. We wanted a training film and hired local college students, who were good, but not as experienced as this crew." They watched another huge light roll past them toward the bleachers.

Bethany contemplated his words. He had reminded her of Marineland. When it closed down, he was forced to take a job at Sea World in San Diego. While he was away, commuting two hours a day and hardly seeing the family, her mother had been killed in that awful car accident.

"Dad." Bethany fiddled with her fingers. "I have to ask you a favor."

"Sure, anything."

"Don't let on we know Ricky when he gets here."

"Why?"

"Remember when Mom died, and all the publicity? It will start all over again if word gets out that we're here. You know the reporters will dredge up the past."

Glenn nodded. "I understand. I guess I never thought of that. You took most of the brunt of the media. I was wrong to leave you with your grandmother in the middle of that mess."

"Oh, I didn't mean to bring it all up again." Bethany laid her hand on his arm. "I should have moved down there with you, but I selfishly wanted to graduate with my friends." She felt her lips tremble as she tried to smile. That year had been the hardest of her life. Her mother tragically ripped from her, her father abandoning her to grieve on his own—or had she abandoned him? Then the move across the country. She forced herself to brighten up. "And, hey, you've more than made up for it by letting me stay with you all these years."

"Sweetheart, you're my daughter. We should be together." He tapped her on the leg. "However, if your Prince Charming arrives, it's time you donned your glass slippers."

"So what are you saying? That I'm an old maid?"

"If the slipper fits."

At that point, Simon appeared at the railing. "How's it going?"

"Pretty good," Glenn said. "The only one who needs a tranquilizer right now is Tim."

Simon chuckled. "Have you seen that guy with the gray ponytail and wearing a T-shirt that says MAKE FILM, NOT WAR? A moment ago, I saw Tim yelling at the poor guy, who was holding the business end of an extension cord and looking at the otters. I think Tim was afraid he'd electrocute them."

After a good laugh, Glenn said, "Maybe I should send him home."

"No," Simon said. "Then he'd be calling me every five minutes to make sure the turtles were still in their shells."

Glenn stood up and surveyed the chaos. "I'll go find him—maybe give him something else to do."

As he passed by Bethany, he mussed her hair. She knew it was his way of saying, *I'm sorry I hurt you, and I love you more than words can say.*

Simon joined Bethany on the platform. "Got a moment?"

"Sure," she said as she hugged her knees.

"I appreciate your helping out this evening. I know how busy you are with all your other activities."

Here it comes; he hates my other activities.

"I've seen you helping Sheila," he continued, "and I know you'd like to do that on a regular basis. You're good with the children, not to mention your dedication." He motioned to the four gray bodies milling about in the pool.

A compliment? From Simon?

"I'm promoting you to full trainer. You've earned it."

Bethany resisted the urge to throw her arms around Simon's neck. "Thank you, Simon. I won't let you down."

"See to it that you don't."

Bethany was left alone with her thoughts. She'd be elated with her good news if her thoughts weren't on a more pressing matter. Filming would begin tomorrow. Twenty-four hours and she would see Ricky again. She played that first meeting over and over in her mind.

Coolly she looked at him. Icicles hung in the air at her frosty glance. Would he recognize her? She didn't care.

"Hello, B—Bethany," he stuttered. Apparently her rare beauty unnerved him. "You've g—grown up. . .a lot!"

"Richard. How good of you to make your little movie here."

She turned on one heel, leaving him gaping after her like a pimple-faced adolescent.

"Bethany, wake up." Cleo, who had already kicked off her shoes, pushed

Bethany's shoulder while she sat down and placed her feet in the water.

"Hmm?"

"You must have been daydreaming. I stood here talking to you for five minutes before I realized you weren't listening." Kahlua gave Cleo a little splash with his nose. The other three noticed the attention and crowded around for a group cuddle.

"Where have you been?" Bethany asked.

"Catching up on some paperwork. I wouldn't miss this for anything. They promised I could stay if I laid low."

"What else could you do, shorty?" she said with a smile.

"Insults? You've got your sense of humor back? At my expense?"

"Sorry." Bethany leaned into her friend and shoved her with her arm.

"Hey, I'm just glad to see you back with the living. Are you okay?"

Bethany squared her shoulders and took a cleansing breath. "Yeah, I'm okay. It's all in the past. Ricky and I are two different people now. He will give his little performance and move on, and so will I. They'll only be here for a month. I can handle a month. Besides, it's over. I feel nothing for him."

"Good." Cleo looked at her as if trying to read between the lines. "I've been praying for you."

"Good."

"It's all over?"

"All over."

Cleo nodded as if trying to convince herself. "Then do you want to hear my news?"

"Of course! Is it exciting?"

"Not *this* kind of exciting." Cleo motioned toward a camera on a boom. The crew was blocking shots for the next day. "But exciting to me. Ed is coming home in a month."

"I thought he was supposed to be gone a year."

"This is just a visit. He left only a few days before Christmas, so we thought May would be a good time for him to get away. He's taking leave then but has to go back in three weeks."

"I'm happy for you." She gave Cleo a squeeze. "Any plans?"

"We're going to go see his folks in Vail. Do you think it's cold there in May?"

"I don't know. Isn't Vail in the mountains? Maybe you'd better be prepared. What will you do without sand in your shorts for two weeks?"

"Oh, Colorado must have something. Mud, pine needles—I'm sure I'll get into some kind of mess."

The director had promised that by ten o'clock the crew would be finished. Bethany looked at her watch. "How about that? Right on time." The equipment was hidden as promised. Tomorrow evening, filming would begin at seven o'clock and run until the wee hours of the morning.

The craft wagon brought catered snacks. The film crew and the Gulfarium employees all stood around in the snack bar area getting to know one another. The extra light that had been brought in to simulate daylight kept the evening chill at bay, creating a pleasant ambience.

The subject of Bethany's acting skills surfaced again.

"Really?" the director asked. "Have you done anything professionally?" He thrust out his hand. "I'm Chad Cheswick. My friends call me Chez."

She shook hands and introduced herself. "Mostly I performed at the Orlando Shakespeare Festival and in repertory theater here and there. Now it's more of a hobby."

"Have you ever considered moving to Hollywood? You could make it big in film."

"Oh no. We lived in Los Angeles years ago. I'm not ready to go back." She felt sweat break out on her upper lip. No way was she moving back. Even though she fought it at first, her father had made a good decision, and they never regretted it.

Chez interrupted her thoughts. "Why would you deny the camera's eye from immortalizing that lovely face? I can tell you're very photogenic."

Cleo broke away from another conversation. "Bethany's talents are invaluable here. Not only is she an accomplished dolphin trainer, she also sings in the choir at *church*."

Bethany rolled her eyes.

Chez folded his hands in front his chest. "You know, we need more good, moral people in our profession."

Cleo's eyes narrowed, and Bethany nudged her before she could make another comment. She found herself warming to Chez. Not bad-looking, either. His dark hair hung in stubborn wisps over his cool blue gaze. Yes, very attractive. A little short, but easy on the eyes, as her grandmother would say.

Bethany noticed that most of the crew had dispersed to finish what they were doing before the break. Chez turned to answer a question from a man with a cable coiled over his shoulder.

Cleo grabbed Bethany's elbow and whispered, "Something about this guy makes me want to wash my hands."

"Don't be silly. He's just being polite."

The angle of Cleo's mouth suggested she felt otherwise.

Chez took Bethany's arm and steered her away from the crowd. "So, what church do you go to?"

Cleo began to follow, but Sheila ran up to her.

"Cleo," she said breathlessly, "my car won't start, and I need to get home. Can you give me a ride?"

"Again? You need to ditch that antique." She gave Bethany a warning look that said *Don't let yourself be alone with this guy*. But what she said was "Call me later."

Simon entered the area and thanked his workers for a job well done. "You may all go home. I'll see you in a few hours." Everyone groaned. Bethany wanted to leave, too, but she and her father had come together that morning.

She turned to Chez and held out her hand. "I'm sure you're busy. It was nice meeting you." He surprised her by latching on and leading her to a table.

"Actually, I'd like to hear more about Bethany, the actress."

She politely sat with him, worried that she was keeping him from something important.

After a moment's thought, she said, "Our community theater will be presenting *As You Like It* in the fall. Since my training is in that genre, I'm excited because it's the first Shakespearean play we've attempted."

"What other things have you done?"

After reciting her résumé, she moved on to her role as dolphin trainer.

"How did you get into that from acting?"

"Just following the family business." She elaborated by telling about her father.

Before she knew it, they'd talked for nearly an hour. He seemed quite pleasant. She'd have to tell Cleo she was wrong.

"It's been a pleasure, Bethany Hamilton, local actress and dolphin trainer." He reached out and wrapped both of his hands around hers, stroking her palm with his thumb. "You know, Florida can't afford to lose you." He leaned in, piercing her with those blue eyes. "I'd love to get to know you better. Think you might find some time while I'm here?"

It might be good to have Chez as a friend. Keep my mind off you-know-who.

While nodding her assent, she made the mistake of looking over his shoulder. A new player entered stage left: tall and suave Brick Connor.

Chapter 4

*R*icky!

Chez had turned to follow her gaze. He looked back at her, a broad smile on his face and a gleam in his eye.

He turned and called out, "Hey, Brick-Bud."

Ricky—Brick—Ricky—*Oh, what should I call him now?*—who had been greeting some of the crew, turned at the sound of Chez's voice. Bethany immediately looked down.

"Don't be shy." Chez tugged gently and pulled her to a standing position. "Brick's a nice guy. He doesn't bite—hard."

He draped his left arm reassuringly over her shoulders and led her forward. The men shook hands.

"How was Australia? Did you meet any sheilas?"

"If you're referring to kangaroos, only in the Taronga Zoo." Ricky's voice had matured and seemed to take on a sarcastic quality. However, it still melted her insides.

Throughout the exchange, Bethany stood with her hand half covering her face. She must look like a starstruck ninny.

She didn't dare take in the full effect of Brick Connor, as if he were Medusa and could turn her to stone. She tried to focus on his boots, no doubt straight from Italy, but with a will of its own, her gaze drifted upward. Jeans covered lean legs that had done their own stunt work. A manicured hand disappeared into the front pocket, pulling the suede jacket to one side revealing a black button-down shirt. Through splayed fingers, she ventured a peek at the strong chin she remembered so well, a faint hint of the scar still there. Lips. *No, skip the lips.* The actor's trademark mustache, dark under the small but slightly bulbed nose, revealing his Irish heritage. . . She would have to look into his beautiful forest green eyes. No, she would rather jump into the dolphin pool with weights on her ankles.

She felt a squeeze on her shoulders, and Chez said, "Brick, I would like you to meet Miss Bethany Hamilton. Bethany, this is Brick Connor."

Bethany slowly lowered her hand from her face. She looked up, and disappointment washed over her when brown—not forest green—contact-shrouded eyes blinked in surprise. Before he could say anything, she thrust her hand toward him.

"Mr. Connor, we're honored to have you here."

Bethy?

If he'd known she was here, he would have polished his boots and probably wouldn't have pulled his jeans from the bottom of the hamper. *And this jacket!* How long had he owned it? Good thing she couldn't see the hole in the lining. Speaking of holes... There was a gaping chasm in the pocket of his pants. With all the suaveness he could muster, he felt inside for his change. At least the shirt was new.

Apparently she wanted to keep their knowledge of one another private. Shaking her hand, he nodded. "It's nice to meet you, Miss Hamilton."

He noted the territorial arm draped over her delicate shoulders but resisted the urge to punch good ol' Chez right in the nose and wipe away that Cheshire cat grin.

The grin continued talking. To the untrained ear, one would have thought the conversation cordial enough. But Chez's voice dripped with oily sarcasm that only Brick could hear.

"Bethany," *who I saw first,* "is a dolphin trainer here," *where I spotted her.* "Plus, I hear she's quite the little actress." *I've gotten to know her, and I want to know her better.* His smirk communicated: *One hundred dollars if you can take her away from me.*

Clearly, Chez wanted to make Bethany a part of the game.

As Chez droned on, Bethany's eyes locked with Ricky's. Memories volleyed back and forth. If they had been observable, they would have played like a teen flick. She clutched her hair, knowing he'd noticed she'd cut it. He rubbed the scar on his chin with his knuckle—neither would forget that night. When Ricky sent her a smoldering silent message, she knew he was thinking of their intimate moments. She felt the blush rise up her throat and dropped her gaze, breaking the silent communication.

"Hey, Chez, we need you over here," a voice called out.

She almost thought Chez was going to drag her over to the cameraman, but Ricky reached for her hand. "So, you're an actress," he said. When she took a step toward him, Chez seemed to go weak, his arm feeling like a dead fish over her shoulder. He let her go and started barking orders at the crew.

Ricky drew her hand through his arm and led her away from the activity. When they were out of Chez's view, she slid her hand away, aware of the muscles under his jacket that had developed in the last decade.

They wandered to the south edge of the park, in daylight a panoramic spectacle looking toward the Gulf of Mexico. Bethany peered into the darkness. The moon, though a sliver, reflected off the whitecaps that rolled toward the beach. A void stretched beyond as far as the eye could see.

Ricky stopped and gently turned her to face him. "Hi, Bethy." His velvet voice stroked her ear with the familiar nickname.

She dared to look up. The spicy scent of his expensive cologne swirled around her. With determination, she gained the strength to break away.

"Please don't call me that."

He jammed his hands into his pants pockets.

"Ten years, Ricky."

"I know. Why did you stop writing?"

"Why did *I* stop writing?" She reached for her hair and scrunched it, trying to be mature. She would not bring up his queue of girlfriends that, according to the tabloids, began lining up even before her second year of college. She remembered wondering if Ricky had forgotten his promise to God.

She took a deep breath. "It doesn't matter. Water under the bridge. You have your life. I have mine. We've moved on."

"You're clipping your sentences. Apparently you're upset."

How clueless could a man be? "Do you remember who wrote the last letter?" She pointed to her chest. "Me. And that was after a long period of silence from you."

He rubbed his neck. "Look. I had no idea you were here. I don't know what to say, but obviously you do. Give me time to gather my wits." His tentative smile almost reached her heart. "You've kind of thrown me for a loop."

She could see her Ricky reaching out from the other side of the perfectly maintained actor's face. "What do you suggest?" she half whispered with resignation.

"A chance to talk—to catch up on old times and discuss the last ten years without blame."

She considered his words while glancing at the lit-up dial on her watch. "It's too late tonight."

"How about tomorrow?" He looked around. "And preferably away from prying eyes." As if on cue, a flash came from somewhere below on the beach. "Well, that'll be in tomorrow's rag. BRICK CONNOR TO WED UNKNOWN DOLPHIN TRAINER."

With the flash came an unbidden memory. Bethany found herself thrown back to the day her mother died. So many photographers. So many questions. She couldn't take it again. "Impossible. I won't be sneaking around with you while all of America watches. Just do your little movie and get out of my life." She turned and stormed back to find her father.

Brick watched Bethany's exit in stunned silence. He hardly felt he deserved that. So, she hadn't outgrown her tantrums. It was best to let her cool off. He'd be around for a while.

Ten years. Why had they stopped writing? She'd been important to him in his youth, but had maturity dimmed his love for her? By the thumping of his heart, he'd have to guess *no*.

He looked back toward the Gulf. The wind had picked up a little, drawing the salt air up the coast. His eyes stung, feeling the effects—or had Bethany's final remark sunk in?

The next morning, as Bethany prepared the daily herring for her dolphins,

Cleo poked her head in briefly. "You didn't call me last night."

"I'm sorry; I forgot."

Her friend disappeared, then reappeared. "Well, what happened?"

"What happened about what?"

Again, Cleo disappeared. Bethany left her work and walked toward the door. They nearly collided as Cleo thrust her red head back in.

"What are you doing?" Bethany asked while clutching her heart to keep it from beating out of her chest.

"I can't stand the smell of dead fish. I'm getting a big breath of air outside and letting it out inside while I talk to you."

Bethany shook her head in wonder. "How can you work here, then? Stay out here, and I'll wash up." They walked out toward the performance pool. "What's on your mind?"

"What do you think is on my mind?" Cleo flailed her arms. "I left you with a handsome director—who is clearly interested in you, by the way. Tell me what happened."

"He seemed very nice. We talked awhile, mostly about me. Then he held my hand."

"I knew he couldn't be trusted. Then what happened?"

The actress in Bethany stopped for a pregnant pause.

"Well?" Cleo practically danced circles around her.

"Then Brick Connor walked in."

Silence. Bethany's chatty friend had a gaping hole for a mouth, and her eyes were as big as Golden Globes. She finally emitted a shrill shriek that rivaled anything from the dolphin pool. Digging in for the juice of the century, Cleo pulled Bethany to a railing near the penguin port. "Tell me!"

"We talked." Bethany looked out over the water. It was in this same spot she had told Ricky to get out of her life. She related the entire scenario.

"That's it? Didn't you ask if he'd changed at all?"

"Why should I have?"

Cleo sighed. "Remember what we talked about?"

Bethany searched her brain. Oh yes, the conversation about leaving her pity party to pray about what God wanted her to say to Ricky when they met again.

She studied her deck shoes and mumbled, "I guess I got caught up in the moment."

"What an opportunity to share your faith with the man!" Cleo never backed away from a point she was trying to make.

"Ricky accepted the Lord years ago."

Cleo folded her arms and pinched her lips. "And yet, you don't believe he's maintained his beliefs, do you?" Sometimes Cleo could be downright spooky. Bethany's father once said she had the gift of spiritual insight.

"No," Bethany admitted. "But, now that he's the mighty Brick Connor, why would he listen to his ex-girlfriend? He's made his choice, and it didn't include God—or me."

Cleo placed her hand on Bethany's arm. "The man's soul may be at stake, the one thing his money can't buy. Isn't that more important than your hurt feelings?"

That stung. "You're right." Bethany nodded and turned to look out over the water. Her back muscles tightened. "But last night wasn't the right time. I had to tell him how I felt."

"Sounds to me like you told him off. Did you tell him you still love him?"

"What?"

"I'm sorry." Cleo backed away. "I've gone too far. All I'm saying is, don't write the man off because of what he's become." She raised her eyebrows, reminding Bethany of her mother. With hands on her hips, she added, "You know?"

Cleo left her with a lot of thinking to do. Had she been too rough on him? Should she have shown some kind of Christian charity? Turned the other cheek? *No way.* She wouldn't offer him another soggy, tear-stained cheek. He blew his chance to have a life with her. But, she conceded, if the opportunity should present itself, she would talk to him again about God.

That'll be hard, since I intend to avoid the man.

Chapter 5

"H eads up!"

Bethany sidestepped to avoid a rolling floodlight. As she walked to the tank, she appreciated the phenomenal organization it took to turn the Gulf Coast attraction into a working movie set. The production crew had promised to take only a month, and it seemed they would make good on that promise.

This time, a handful of people stayed to take care of the Gulfarium residents. All others, employees and local curiosity seekers, were asked to stay in the bleachers overlooking the performance pool. They were thrilled because, by doing so, they volunteered to be extras and simulate the audience at the fictitious Australian zoo.

Cleo joined Bethany on the lower platform of the performance tank out of camera shot. The four dolphins milled about the pool and, just as the night before, came to Bethany for reassuring pats and words of encouragement.

"This is a great spot," Cleo said.

"The action is going to start over there." Bethany pointed to the right of the pool. "Agent Dan Danger and the villain are going to run to there." She pointed to the left side. "They filled us in so we wouldn't be in their shot."

When Brick Connor made his appearance, Cleo drew in a girlish gasp of delight.

"Now *that's* a man," Cleo said.

Bethany scowled at her—but had to admit that the star's black leather pants and matching leather jacket set off his dark hair and mustache, making him appear dangerous indeed. And gorgeous.

"Look how sure he is of himself," Cleo gushed. "And he hasn't even started the scene yet." Another actor entered the area. "Ooh, I know him. That's Vince Galloway. He always plays a villain because he's stocky and rough-looking, but I've heard he's a Christian."

Bethany watched the two men interact. They laughed together and at one point even hugged. She smiled as her heart did a little happy dance. Had Vince been sent to Ricky in answer to her prayers those many years ago?

Both men talked to the director. They nodded as they received their instructions for the scene they were about to shoot. Each man was handed an AK-47.

Bethany leaned toward Cleo. "Those are going to be used to destroy the aquarium." She shuddered. Thankfully the guns were only props.

Cleo grinned. "Cool."

Chez called for quiet and instructed the cameras to roll. A woman stepped in front of the camera and called out some numbers; then she snapped the top of a slate.

"Don't they use digital slates now?" Cleo asked.

"On such a small shoot, they sometimes use the manual ones." *Just don't ask me how I know.* She needn't have worried. Cleo was so caught up in the action that it apparently never occurred to her how Bethany knew these technical things.

Upon the director's command, Brick Connor ran in from the side with his weapon, looking like a man fiercely determined to stay alive. He sprinted past the dolphin pool, and the director shouted, "Cut!" He motioned to the actor, and they talked a moment more. Then they did the scene over again—and over, and over.

When Bethany had just about decided she was bored out of her mind, Vince came in and did the same thing. Over and over. She looked at her watch. These two scenes had taken two hours to shoot.

Finally Chez called for a break, and everyone dispersed to the craft wagon for snacks.

"You want something?" Cleo asked as she stood up.

Bethany stood and stretched. That was a long time to sit cross-legged. "A bottle of water would be fine. I'll stay here, though."

Cleo cocked an eyebrow. "You trying to avoid somebody?"

Bethany gave her a look that she hoped conveyed *Mind your own business.* Cleo turned and scrambled up the ladder.

It didn't do any good to stay put, however. Someone had brought food to the two actors, and they lounged on tall chairs near the bleachers in her full view.

Look at her.

Brick could barely concentrate on what Vince was saying. It didn't matter. It was just small talk, a winding down from the shoot.

She used to be a cute kid, but the gangly teen had finally grown into her legs. *Bethy, you're a beautiful woman now.*

His heart flipped through hoops in his chest.

He turned to answer Vince. When he looked back, his jaw clenched. Chez had joined Bethany. Brick's eyes narrowed. *Back off, Chez. She's way out of your league.* A thought occurred to him from nowhere. She was way out of *his* league, as well. He shook it off. His first order of business was to protect Bethany from the wolf in director's clothing.

While Chez spoke amiably, Bethany continued to glance Ricky's way. She wished she hadn't put him in his place so quickly. If only it were Ricky instead of Chez murmuring these senseless things to her.

His voice last night—I nearly lost it when he called me Bethy. How many times have I heard him talk to me like that in my dreams? The moment he had come onto the set that evening, she had felt the invisible cord that bound them together—a cord tied with memories, sweet and bitter. She wondered if he felt it, too, or was he anxious to make his movie and leave?

He looked as if he'd just stepped out of a magazine. Not the same eighteen-year-old kid she had dated, that's for sure! Even the camera didn't do him justice. Although Ricky had changed his appearance to equal star quality, she felt herself longing to see the teenager once again.

"Well," Chez said. "Break's over, so I have to get back to work."

Bethany smiled politely. She hadn't heard a word he'd said.

After another hour around the dolphin pool, the action moved to the alligator exhibit.

Cleo hopped up. "Let's go."

"No, I think I'll go to Dad's office and wait."

"Oh no, you won't. Filming by the alligators has got to be more exciting than this was. Come on. It's not every day we get to see stuff like this."

She allowed Cleo to haul her off the platform.

They reconvened at Fort Gator and found only about ten people had stayed to observe. Bethany looked at her watch. Nearly eleven o'clock. "How are we ever going to make it to work tomorrow morning? It'll be after midnight by the time we get home."

"What do you mean, *we*? I'm the commanding officer of my little unit. I've already made arrangements with my assistant manager to open so I can come in late." She gave a smug smile.

Again, the two actors chased each other past the man-made swamp.

Cleo tapped her on the shoulder and said, "I know that Brick Connor and Vince Galloway have just run out of sight, but who are those guys?"

Bethany glanced to where Cleo pointed. The hero and villain were sitting in chairs and drinking bottles of designer water.

"They're the stunt doubles."

Cleo slapped her forehead. "Duh! I should've known that."

Bethany realized that the man standing in for Vince didn't look much like him in the face, but Brick's double was just that: his double. Maybe he looked like him because of the angle or the lighting. But no. When he stood up, he could have been the man's twin. *Weird.*

Brick II moved to the area of filming. While a cameraman worked over Vince's shoulder, the villain took a swing at the original Brick. Chez yelled, "Cut!" and replaced the real Brick with the stuntman. They shot it again at a different angle, and Brick II went flying, ending in a double roll and sprawling over the fenced area dangerously close to the pit. An alligator snapped its jaws as if on cue. Chez yelled, "Cut! Print!" and everyone broke into applause. "That's a wrap, folks. Let's get this stuff put away and meet back here tomorrow evening."

"Well," Cleo said, "that's that. Guess I'll go home and get some sleep."

"I've got to wait for Dad. We came together today because he didn't want me driving home so late." She glanced at her watch. "Or rather, early in the morning."

Bethany almost took Cleo up on her offer to stay at her place, only a couple of miles away, but knew her chatty friend would keep her up until dawn talking about all she had seen that night. So Cleo left, and Bethany headed for her father's office. She knew he wouldn't leave until the crew had put everything away. Simon had placed him in charge while the production company was on the premises.

She entered the office and curled up on the short leather couch. She fell asleep quickly and dreamed that someone had placed a sweet kiss on her temple. When she awoke an hour later, a thick beach towel had been placed over her body, and she smelled the lingering scent of spicy cologne.

Chapter 6

Brick splashed on an extra dose of cologne. He stood in front of the full-length mirror in his hotel room, grumbling. "I've been here two weeks. Why hasn't she warmed up to me by now? What's it going to take?" Since her day ended as his began, they hadn't had a chance to connect. She'd reply to his greetings but then rush out. "You can't get away from me today, Bethy, because I intend to follow you everywhere."

He wore a Disney World T-shirt, blue surfer shorts that reached his knees, brown leather sandals, and he topped off the outfit with a straw hat rimmed with a red Hawaiian print. Once he placed the dark sunglasses on his face, he knew no one would recognize him.

He made it safely to his rented BMW and sped off to spend the day as a tourist.

After paying the admission fee, he headed for the dolphin show. Finding a place on the bleachers, he proceeded to scan the area.

Bethany entered from the side, following her father. They both waved to the crowd, and everyone cheered. He drew in a breath. His heart beat so hard that he was sure the people around him could hear.

There was his Bethy, in a wet suit, her fair hair acting as a halo around her angelic face. Her smile seemed to brighten the already-cloudless day, and he longed for her to look at him that way again.

She put the dolphins through their paces while her father explained their antics. Quite honestly, he wasn't even watching the show. Except for the part where Bethany, while on a high platform, put a fish in her mouth and the one called Ginger leaped up and took it away from her. *Yuck. And I want to kiss that mouth?* He thought a moment. *Yes, I do. Very much.*

Too soon, it was over, and she disappeared. He'd paid to observe a Dolphin Encounter and hoped she was the one doing it. Brick almost felt guilty. Maybe someday he would play a stalker and could have this experience to draw from.

He followed the crowd out of the bleachers and headed for the encounter tank. Grateful there were others waiting to watch, he slid in behind them, hoping to blend in. He hadn't counted on it being inside, however. His sunglasses would probably act as a neon sign to Bethany. He took them off, but left on his hat.

She soon entered the area with a family of three. The boy, who said his name was Steve Eberly, got in the tank, while Mom snapped digital pictures and Dad ran the video camera.

"Because our tanks are small," Bethany explained to the crowd, "Florida law prohibits the untrained to actually swim with the dolphin. Sorry, Steve. But he will touch her and learn how to give her commands."

Brick sat mesmerized. She really was good at her job. She brought Cocoa up to Steve's lap and gave some information on how the dolphin came to be a member of the Gulfarium family. "Cocoa came to us after stranding herself on a nearby beach. She had been separated from her mother and was found with a severe lung infection." She petted the little mammal and began to point out the differences between the pantropical spotted dolphin and the bottlenose dolphins in the performance arena. "As you can see, Cocoa, who is fully grown, is much smaller. She was born without spots, and was probably about thirty-one inches in length at birth. As she matured, the spots started showing up, and now she has grown to a healthy seventy-four inches or. . ." She turned to the boy. "How tall are you, Steve?"

"Five foot six—and growing." This caused a ripple of laughter.

"She is about eight inches taller than you." After a few more facts about Cocoa, she showed the boy some basic moves. Before long, he had Cocoa jumping, dancing, and chattering.

At the end of the exhibition, Brick left with the crowd, resisting the urge to stay behind and watch Bethany talk to the little family. He heard her laughter and wished she'd been laughing at one of his jokes. He did venture near her, as some of the audience clustered around her asking questions. How he longed to reach his hand around her slim waist and draw her to him. *Patience, Brick ol' boy. Patience.*

Bethany spoke a few minutes more with the family. "Well, Steve, now you know about as much as I do about Cocoa. Are you going to be a dolphin trainer when you grow up?"

Steve's eyes sparkled with excitement. "Naw, I'm going to be an astronaut."

Mr. Eberly ruffled his son's hair. "We took a tour of the Space Center on this vacation. I'm afraid the lure of the cosmos is stronger than the mysteries of the deep."

Bethany laughed. "That's okay. With Steve in space, I know my job is safe."

As the familiar scent drifted by, it tapped her senses to get her attention. She knew he'd been there, been near enough for her to catch a whiff of his cologne. It wrapped around her like a warm blanket, and she suddenly felt very content. When she glanced around the area, he was nowhere to be seen.

"Excuse me, folks," she said to the family and to the dispersing crowd. "I hope you all enjoyed the Steve Eberly show." Warm applause from the few who were left pleased her. But she had to go in search of that aroma.

She felt like a bloodhound. An old bloodhound past its prime. She'd lost the scent. But she knew it had been him. Her voice of reason tried to sway her thinking. *It could've been anyone, silly.* No—it was Ricky. She knew it.

Brick peeked over his shoulder for a split second and saw Bethany looking around. She seemed to be searching for someone. Maybe her father. He pushed his hands into the pockets of his shorts and sauntered away from her.

Later, he was pleased to see her again in the Multispecies Show, a performance that included a seal and the dolphins. This time Swisher the seal waddled up to the high platform, dangled a fish from her mouth, and fed the dolphin the way Bethany had earlier. He wondered if Swisher had a boyfriend somewhere thinking, *Yuck!*

At the end of the show, Bethany, her father, and the seal trainer all answered questions from the dwindling crowd, allowing them to get close enough to pet the dolphins. He noticed her looking around again, scanning the crowd. *Who is she looking for? Does she have someone special she thought would be here today?* That thought made his stomach queasy.

With one last round of performances, beginning with the dolphin show, he sat in the middle of the crowd and again watched his girl. This time, he tried to pay more attention.

"Allow me to introduce our dolphin family," Glenn said. While he talked, Bethany gave hand signals to each dolphin. He introduced Ginger first, the oldest and most experienced. Then Coral, the next oldest. Finally, he introduced Lani and her son, Kahlua. With each introduction, Bethany raised her right arm and the dolphins would circle the pool and leap in the air. Except Kahlua, described as the class clown. He circled the pool and then pirouetted on his tail fluke. Brick noticed that Bethany had changed her signal to a rotation of the fingers. When Glenn admonished the young dolphin for not following the examples of his elders, Bethany wagged her fingers and Kahlua clicked as if arguing. He then spit water, but he eventually did what his elders had shown him, with a little twist that Glenn said was uniquely his own.

Since it would be a little over an hour before he could see her in the last show of the day, Brick decided to scope out the rest of the attractions. Even though he'd spent every night there filming, he hadn't had a chance to appreciate it from a tourist's point of view.

He went underground to the Living Seas Show, where he watched a scuba diver swim with moray eels, stingrays, and sharks. In an educational presentation about life under the sea, the diver pointed out sea turtles, snapper, grouper, and tarpon. While wandering the grounds, Brick found the penguins, and just on the other side of the Shark Moat, he laughed at the antics of the otters.

At the touch pool, he picked up a seashell but dropped it when he saw it occupied by a hermit crab. How mortifying when a child said, "They won't hurt you, mister." The little girl allowed the crab to wander all over her hands. "Do you want to try?"

She held it out to him, but he recoiled. *Never did like those things.* "N–no, thanks. I'll take your word for it." He quickly left the area, chastising himself for being such a wimp. *Agent Dan Danger wouldn't be afraid of a little hermit crab.*

He eventually found himself at Fort Gator, where they had filmed the first day.

Bethany waved her arms and whistled commands during the last show of the day. She'd already asked her father if he'd seen Ricky anywhere.

"You think he's crazy?" Glenn had said. "He wouldn't come here in the middle of the day. He'd be mobbed."

"I guess you're right." Still, she'd had a feeling he'd been watching her all day.

She was so preoccupied with thoughts of Ricky that she gave a different command from the one her father had explained. Instead of raising her arm to signal them to flip in the air, she raised both arms and pushed her hands upward telling all four dolphins to dance on the water with their tail flukes. The crowd roared with laughter, thinking it to be part of the show.

Glenn shot her a look, and she knew she was in trouble. Even worse, Simon had been watching from the side. She could sweet-talk her daddy, but Simon was a different matter altogether.

She forced herself to stay for the question-and-answer period, hoping they had a lot of questions, not anxious to be alone with her dad and Simon.

There! She smelled it again. Definitely the same spicy scent she remembered Ricky wearing earlier. Questions were coming at her from all directions, and she answered them as best she could. Finally a deep, masculine voice called out, "Are you free for dinner?"

The crowd parted, and there he stood. Despite the cool breeze blowing in from the Gulf, she felt a heated blush make its way from the top of her wet suit to the roots of her hair. An elderly woman stood nearby, holding a stuffed seal from the gift shop, probably bought for a grandchild. "Ignore him. He might be a masher." Grandma jutted her chin out at Ricky, daring him to be so bold as to speak again.

"It's okay, ma'am. I know this guy."

The old woman looked from one to the other, a slow dentured grin pulling on the wrinkles in her face. "Then what are you waiting for? Answer the man."

Bethany scrunched her hair. "S–sure. I guess so."

Everyone applauded the couple as he stepped forward.

Brick led her away from the group, leaving the rest of the questions to Glenn and the seal trainer.

"How did you get away with this?" she hissed as they walked toward the offices.

"I've been getting away with it all day."

"I knew it! I tried to find you in the crowd."

Brick relaxed. So she hadn't been looking for another guy. "How did you know?"

She breathed in deeply. "Your cologne. I smelled it earlier, and I've been looking for you ever since."

"I tend to go heavy with this cologne. It gave me my start in show business."

"*Gentleman's Agreement?*"

"Were you following my career, Bethy?"

She cleared her throat and looked away. "I don't live in a cave, Ricky. I know you made commercials before you became famous."

"I'm sorry. I didn't mean that to sound so egotistical." He could feel her slipping away again. Why couldn't he keep his mouth shut? "So, when can you get away?"

"Away?"

"For dinner."

"I don't think we ought to go anywhere together. No use in starting something that neither of us intends to finish."

Ouch, that smarts. "All I want to do is talk over old times. Nothing wrong with two old friends getting together for dinner, is there?"

"I don't have time."

"But you have time for Chez?"

She stopped in her tracks, turned, and took him head-on. "That's uncalled for. Whom I choose to make time for is none of your business." She began to walk away, her pert nose stuck in the air.

"You need to keep away from Chez. He's a womanizer. The only reason he wants—"

She swung around and poked a slender finger in his chest. "Chez is kind and understanding. I like being with him. He understands me."

"He's using you. He thinks we made a bet—"

"You gambled on me?" Her nostrils flared.

Brick backpedaled. "No. See, we used to play this game, but I—"

He heard a voice call out to her from behind. "Bethany. My office. Now."

She put her hands to her mouth and blanched. He grabbed her shoulders. "Are you okay?"

"Please, just go away; you've caused me enough trouble." She pulled away from him and turned slowly. Taking a deep breath, she disappeared into Simon's office.

When the door clicked shut, he asked himself, *What did I do?*

Chapter 7

Did you do it?" Cleo asked as she followed Bethany to the parking lot after work. Their first stop would be a fast-food restaurant and then on to choir practice at Safe Harbor Community Church located along the sound.

"Do what?"

"Talk to Ricky about God."

Bethany placed her athletic bag on the hood of her car and dug for her keys. "I. . .um. . .haven't seen him."

"You're not supposed to avoid him. You're supposed to help him get on the right track."

Bethany waved her friend off as if she were a pesky mosquito. "Hey, there's no time for that. He starts his day as I'm leaving."

Besides, a week ago Simon had warned her about not paying attention. He said he'd give her two more chances. By avoiding Ricky, she felt she was saving her job.

"They'll be done filming next week," Cleo said. "Then he'll be out of your life for good. Don't miss your chance, Beth."

A voice called out Bethany's name from the parking lot. She smiled. "Now, Chez is someone I've enjoyed getting to know. He's fun and doesn't seem to want anything but friendship."

Cleo sniffed. "I don't trust him."

"Don't be silly." She waved at Chez who was sprinting around parked cars to catch up to them.

"I'll wait for you in the car, Beth." Cleo took Bethany's keys and disappeared into the passenger side of the silver sedan.

Bethany leaned against her car and greeted Chez. "What's up?"

"I know we haven't had a chance to get away, and the company is leaving next week. What say we go out tomorrow? I've given the crew the night off. We're ahead of schedule, and they all deserve a rest."

"A date?" She picked at her thumbnail.

"Well, more like two friends hanging out together. What do you say?"

She glanced toward Cleo's silhouette. "Sure, why not? What do you suggest?"

"Well, the buzz is that you have a penchant for minigolf. So, how about that with dinner first?" He shoved his hands into his back pockets and rocked back and forth on his heels, waiting for her answer.

"Sure, that sounds like fun." She heard a sound coming from the interior of her car. Was Cleo coughing the word *gullible*? She frowned at the rolled-up driver's side window. "I know just the place." She heard more coughing with the words "Don't do it" between spasms.

"Is she okay in there?" Chez leaned down to look in the window.

"She's fine. Just having problems with her nose lately." *She can't keep it out of my business.*

"Oh. So, tomorrow, after you're done at work?"

"Perfect. Why don't I meet you next door at the boardwalk?" She pointed toward the large wooden structure that served as picnic area, beach deck, and tourist trap. "It has some cute little shops and a great restaurant." *And lots of people.* She thought maybe that would ease Cleo's mind.

Chez shrugged. "Sure."

∞

"Five...ten...fifteen...twenty. Twenty dollars for a job well done." Brick laid the bills in the cameraman's hand and patted his back. "Thanks, Fred. You're sure he fell for it?"

"Oh yeah. I started spreading the rumor around that Bethany likes minigolf. Even got the name of her favorite place from her dad. Chez swallowed the bait like a big ol' marlin."

Brick felt very pleased with himself. "Great. Now, on to Phase Two..."

∞

After choir practice, Cleo followed Bethany home. They had arranged another Girl Night, with popcorn and a movie.

Cleo reached for the popcorn in the cupboard and pulled out the popper. "I appreciate you babysitting me like this. It gets awfully lonely at home without Ed."

"You're always welcome to stay in our guesthouse while he's gone." Bethany loved how her friend took over in her kitchen. With things in Cleo's capable hands, she hopped onto the counter and sat with her feet dangling.

"Thanks, but I love my little home. I just need some company once in a while."

As Cleo poured the kernels into the machine, she frowned slightly. Her mouth opened to speak, but then she seemed to change her mind.

"What?" Bethany knew full well what was bothering her friend.

"I don't want to start a fight." She placed the lid on the popper and turned it on.

"Go ahead. I know what's bugging you, so we might as well get it out in the open."

Cleo leaned against the island in the middle of the kitchen and folded her arms. "I've voiced my concern about Chez."

"Adamantly." The corn started to pop, one kernel at a time. "I don't see what you see. He's been very gracious to me, and he's fun to talk to. It's not like I'm rushing out to marry this guy."

"No, but you are going out on a date with him."

"One date, just as friends, as innocent as if it were you and me. Then he'll be going back to California where he belongs."

"I don't know." Cleo shook her head. "I can't put my finger on it, but something about Chez Cheswick just doesn't ring true."

More corn started popping, and they had to raise their voices. "I'm sorry you feel that way, but frankly, you have no say in the matter."

Cleo looked her straight in the eye. "You wouldn't by chance be using Chez to get back at Ricky, would you?"

The heated corn popped furiously and nearly pushed the lid off the popper. "I can't believe you're still harping on that. Can't I have a normal relationship?" However, she'd had almost that same idea when she first met Chez. But then it didn't sound so sleazy. She hopped off the counter and started melting butter in a small pan. "It's not like I date a lot. Can't you let me have this one moment?"

They were both silent as the popcorn reached its zenith, then slowly finished popping the same way it had begun, one kernel at a time.

When it was done, Cleo poured the hot snack into a large bowl. The aroma wafted around the room. "Just be careful, okay?"

"I'm a big girl. Trust me." She poured the butter over the popcorn. "Ow!"

"What happened?" Cleo hurried to her side.

"I touched the pan."

"Big girl, yeah." Cleo turned on the cold faucet and pulled Bethany's hand under it.

∽

Brick and Vince had just finished a scene when Chez called for a break. They all surrounded the craft wagon, where everyone but Brick loaded up on sugary, carby snacks. He grabbed some cheese squares and a handful of seasoned chicken wings and headed toward the Gulf.

While on the bench looking out toward the water, he glanced at his watch. Shooting would resume at midnight, and they would go until three. He drew in a big breath of salt air. Only a week to go, and he hadn't gotten any further with Bethany. He thought of the trick he'd played on Chez. *This plan had better work.*

Chez plopped down next to him.

"Hey, Brick-Bud."

"What do you want, Chez?" Brick asked without turning to look at the intruder.

"You looked lonely over here by yourself. Thought I'd cheer you up." He jammed the last bite of a cookie into his mouth. "You seem a little down lately."

"I'm fine, just tired of being away from home."

Chez draped his arms over the back of the bench. "Yeah, I know what you mean. It's sure a good thing I met Bethany. She's brightened up this shoot considerably." Brick squished a piece of cheese between his thumb and forefinger and pretended it was Chez's head. "Yep, got her to go out with me tomorrow night."

"I heard." Suddenly losing his appetite, he tossed his plate in the trash.

"Guess that means she likes me more than you."

"Guess so."

"You owe me a hundred bucks."

Brick stood and started walking back to the set. "I refused to bet with you, remember?"

Chez followed at his heels. "Oh no, you don't. I get the girl—I get the money. You can't renege."

Brick thought about *The Plan* and was sorry he'd intervened. What if the whole thing backfired? What if he'd put Bethany in jeopardy? Good thing Chez was incredibly predictable.

Chez's incessant bragging sounded like a dripping faucet. "Yeah, we're going to a nice restaurant, but then we're going to this minigolf and go-cart track place she likes. I think it's a little juvenile, but anything to keep her happy. She may be a child when we get there, but she'll be a woman before she gets home."

Brick snapped. He turned and grabbed Chez by the front of his shirt with one fist. "If you so much as lay a hand on her. . ."

They stood like that together, Brick's glare piercing the smaller man's ice blue eyes. At first he saw fear, but then, maddeningly enough, Chez turned into the Cheshire cat.

The director nodded like a bobble-head doll. "Oh yeah. You've got a thing for the little blond mermaid. But she won't talk to you, will she?" Chez raised his hands in victory. "Yes! The mighty Brick Connor has fallen. She's mine—"

Chez yelped as Brick pushed him against a wall with the ease of pinning a varmint with a boulder. "If you hurt her. . ."

"What? You'll rough me up real good? The reporters would love that. Too bad there's no one around to capture *this* Kodak moment."

With regret, Brick loosened his grip. "If anything happens to her, trust me, you *will* regret it."

Sweat broke out on Chez's lip, giving Brick a small amount of satisfaction.

⚭

After the uncomfortable exchange of words, Cleo and Bethany took their popcorn to the living room. As true best friends, they had aired their disagreement and were now ready to settle down for a relaxing evening. Bethany snuggled onto the soft cushions of the couch, crisscrossing her legs and tucking the large popcorn bowl in her lap.

"So what movie did you rent?"

Cleo shuffled through her big bag, the one in which she kept a change of clothes and a toothbrush, just in case she ever decided to spend the night. "Well, it's not an old black-and-white classic, but it's one I love and wondered if you'd ever seen." She continued to search. "Where did I put it? Did I leave it in the car?" She glanced around, as if it might materialize in a place she hadn't even been. "How's the hand?"

"It's fine. Doesn't even hurt anymore. I never would have thought to let cold water run on it. I was about to grab a stick of butter."

"Wrong move." Cleo was on her hands and knees now, searching under the armchair.

"Why?"

"Because, my medically inept friend," she said, sitting back onto her heels, "butter would hold in the heat, causing it to burn even more. Not to mention the salt in butter."

"Hmm, never thought of that. What about ice?"

"The sudden cold could cause more trauma to the wound."

Bethany threw a piece of popcorn in the air and tried to catch it in her mouth. When she missed, she picked it off her shirt and flipped it between her teeth. "How did you get so smart?"

"Just common sense."

Bethany watched Cleo lift pillows and rummage through her bag again. *Common sense.* Should she have used more common sense before pursuing a friendship with Chez? Was she using him, as Cleo suggested, to hurt Ricky? Had she prayed about what her role should be now in Ricky's life? *Well, no.* Upon reflection, she acknowledged being flattered by the attention Chez showered on her and angry with Ricky. She decided her prayer that night would be for God's direction and for Him to impart on her some of Cleo's insight—like asking for the wisdom of Solomon. She smiled. Cleo had to be the smartest person she knew.

"Okay, it's got to be in the car." Cleo jingled her keys and headed for the door.

"So what is this special movie that we have to watch?"

"It's a romantic suspense, about a small town, something about a mystery. . . there's a guy and a girl. . . Oh, what is the name of the thing?"

"Your favorite, huh?" Bethany threw a small handful of popcorn at the person she'd just decided was so wise.

"I know the actress in it. She was very popular at one time. But she died in a car accident while some photo hound was chasing her. Dee Bellamy." Cleo disappeared out the door to find the video.

Bethany sat in stunned silence, tears threatening to spill down her cheeks. She would force herself to pull together before Cleo returned. She had to.

Chapter 8

You have to try this calamari," Chez said as he shoved another piece in his mouth.

Bethany laughed. "Go easy on that. You don't want to lose it when I beat you in my go-cart. Squid doesn't taste as good coming up as it does going down."

"No way can you beat the 'King of Speed' himself. I live in California, you know."

Using her fork for emphasis, she stabbed the air. "I learned how to drive on the West Coast, so you've got nothing on me, buster!" She used the same fork as a bayonet, savagely spearing a piece of her grilled steak. Then she squeezed the seasoned meat between her teeth.

"So," Chez said, "tell me more about the play in the fall. I'm fascinated with Shakespeare."

Funny, he didn't seem like the bard type. "*As You Like It* is one of his most brilliant comedies, in my opinion. It's about subterfuge and people pretending to be what they aren't."

He colored slightly and cleared his throat. "Doesn't sound very funny to me."

She watched him fan himself slightly with his napkin and wondered if the humidity was getting to him. "It's the twist that's comical. The heroine pretends to be a man to protect herself from evil in the forest. Then, suddenly the one she has feelings for shows up, but she continues to pretend so she can find out what his true feelings are. It's a game."

"And you'll be playing the pretender."

"If I get the part. I've done this play in high school and professionally."

"I applaud your humility. What I hear, you're a shoo-in no matter what play they choose to do."

She felt herself blush. "You must have been talking to Cleo, my best friend. She would host my fan club if I had one. So far, she's it."

"Actually, if you're talking about the short redheaded chick, she doesn't seem to like me very much."

She reached over and placed her hand on his. "I'm sorry. She's very protective of me, as I would be of her. I'll talk to her if she makes you uncomfortable."

His smile showed perfect white teeth. "Naw. As long as she doesn't turn you against me, I'll be okay." He flipped his hand over offering her his palm, and she pulled away quickly.

Those eyes. How can they be ice blue and yet smolder at the same time? She pulled at the neck of her blouse. "It's stuffy in here. Are you about through?"

Brick watched Bethany and the lizard as they entered The Track, her favorite amusement park. Phase Two had worked better than he'd hoped. He watched with satisfaction as they both recognized the Gulfarium employees and members of the filming crew milling about. Vet techs, snack bar employees, and aquarists careened crazily around an oval track, bumping into grips, gaffers, and lighting engineers. Chez's mouth had gone slack, and his eyes bugged like a carp. Bethany smiled broadly, obviously enjoying the surprise.

A cameraman flew past them but then stopped short. Turning, he grabbed Chez's hand and shook it. "Thanks, boss! This was a great idea. We needed to unwind after the grueling schedule you've had us on. You're the greatest!"

Chez stammered. "I—uh—I. . ."

Brick walked up to them and slapped him on the back. "Don't be modest, Chez-*Bud*." He turned to Bethany. "This guy booked the whole park just for us." With a light, *affectionate* slap to Chez's cheek, he said, "You'd better do something about the media, though. They're starting to gather. It'll be a circus soon if you don't gain control now." He motioned with his eyes to the newspaper and television news vans entering the parking lot. Two more slaps and he finished with "Good luck, *buddy*." He took Bethany's elbow and said, "It'll take him awhile to get things in order. Why don't we ride the go-carts until he can join us?"

Before Brick could pull Bethany away, she reached over and squeezed Chez's hand. "Thank you for the wonderful surprise." Brick's guts wrenched inside of him, but he knew he had to play it cool. It was all going as planned, and he couldn't let his jealousy ruin it for him.

As they walked away, he heard Chez call after them, perhaps a bit weakly, "Yeah, well. . .I'll catch up with you guys in a moment."

Brick hoped it would be a long moment. With the park open on all sides, Chez was faced with a security nightmare. *Heh-heh.*

They approached the go-carts, and Brick whispered, "Hey, Bethy, remember driver's ed?"

Her tinkling giggle nearly took his breath away. "You had poor Mr. Ludlow clinging to the dashboard. I think he left fingernail marks."

"What about you? You had the man vowing never to teach a woman driver again."

"Didn't he retire that year?" She had reached a red car and slung herself inside.

"Yeah, I wonder what he's doing now."

"I heard he became a shark trainer." Before he realized she was kidding, she hit the gas and took off. He hopped into a blue mini and followed in hot pursuit.

After the go-carts, Bethany decided a snow cone would hit the spot. While

Ricky stood in line, Cleo arrived. She looked around. "Where's Chez? Aren't you supposed to be with him?"

Bethany shrugged. She realized she hadn't even missed him. "Didn't you see the media frenzy in the parking lot? Chez is in the middle of it, trying to keep his actors safe. He'll join us as soon as he can get away." She looked over at Ricky by the snow cone cart, and a niggling thought crept into her brain. Did she truly hope that Chez would be tied up all night? A feeling of guilt started chinking away at her conscience.

Ricky presented her snow cone and greeted Cleo.

"Cleo," Bethany said, "I'd like you to meet Rick—er—Brick Connor."

Ricky reached out his hand. "It's Brick legally, but I'm Ricky to my family and close friends." He winked at Bethany, and she squeezed her snow cone, almost popping off the rounded top.

Cleo held out her hand. "I'm Cleo, the annoying best friend, a mere subplot character."

Ricky's hearty laugh thundered, and Bethany almost felt jealous that it had been Cleo who'd elicited such a response and not herself. *Chink, chink.* More guilt.

"You're never a mere subplot character," Ricky said. "See that fella over there?" He pointed to Vince Galloway, who was cheering on a child as she somersaulted on the trampoline. "He started out as a subplot character in the first *Danger* movie. We had such a great response that he's now Agent Danger's main nemesis. Everyone loves to hate Shark Finlay." He leaned over to whisper in confidence. "And in real life, he's *my* annoying best friend." He held up his paper cone, which was already beginning to drip. "Would you like something? My treat."

"No thanks, I'm good."

He crunched off a big bite from the top of the ice cone, slurping with satisfaction. "Bethany and I were headed for the bumper boats. You game?"

Cleo looked at Bethany. *Do you want me to come?* she silently communicated. Bethany couldn't think of anything more pleasant than an evening with the love of her past and her best friend, annoying though she may be. Funny, Chez didn't figure into the equation. *Chink.*

The threesome became four when Brick invited Vince along for minigolf. Chez was still busy with the reporters, probably giving an interview to some pretty young thing, no doubt lining up his conquests. Brick shuddered. He remembered when he had been that slimy. Thankfully, he grew out of it. If only Chez would. He'd get a lot further in his career if he'd lay off the drinking and carousing.

Cleo and Vince chose their colored golf balls and moved to the side of the little building to pick up their clubs. As Bethany stepped up to the rack of balls with all the different options, Brick couldn't resist playing an old childhood game. "Wait. Let me guess. Which one would Bethy pick today?" He looked at what she was wearing. A pink T-shirt with blue shorts. On the left leg was a pink embroidered flower. "Pink for the lady."

Bethany colored prettily, her blush complementing her shirt. "Did I always choose according to how I dressed?"

"Always." He couldn't tear his eyes from her. The years scattered and blew away like dead leaves, and they were Ricky and Bethy again. It was all he could do not to lean down and kiss those perfect pink lips.

"Hey, you two joining us, or what?"

"Yeah, we can't be a foursome without you."

The two annoying best friends. Yes, he was in high school again, and Bethy was his girl.

"Blue." Bethy tapped his arm.

"What?"

"Blue for you." He came out of his dream, reluctantly.

"How do you know? I never chose according to what I wore."

"Because, you always picked blue. It's your favorite color." She sashayed away from him, obviously satisfied to have matched him in the game.

"Oh, yeah." His voice cracked. *No way, Chez. No way are you going to have any more to do with this woman.*

☙

They had made it to the sixteenth hole. Bethany felt like a kid again. And why not, when she was practically reliving her childhood. She'd been to The Track dozens of times. Sometimes with a group from church. Sometimes with Cleo. But never with Ricky O'Connell. She knew she would cherish this new memory and never think of this place again without seeing him by her side. Teasing her as she flubbed the ball, or accidentally hitting it over the barrier. . . She would always see the intensity of his concentration as he strove to make a hole in one. How she wished this night could continue. But, of course, that would be impossible.

Suddenly it was over. Chez jogged up to them, putter in hand.

"Man, it's a jungle out there. But I think I got everything under control." He took Bethany's hand and said, "I'm sorry it took me so long. Ended up doing an impromptu interview."

"It's fine. I'm sorry you've missed half the evening."

"You kidding? Now the real fun begins, love."

A sudden movement caught her eye, and Bethany realized Vince had grabbed Ricky's right arm. Something was going on between those two.

"I told the reporters that both of you would give an interview," Chez said. "They were excited that you were such good friends in real life. It'll give them a thrill to see enemies on the screen buddying up. They're waiting for you." When neither man budged, he prompted, "If you don't go now, they'll come looking for you. At least they're corralled in the parking lot."

Ricky looked into Bethany's eyes, and she read regret. It thrilled her to think he'd rather stay with her.

When he spoke, his words belied what she'd just sensed from him. "Oh well, the life of an actor. We're on twenty-four seven. It's been fun, girls."

"So." Chez draped his arm over Bethany's shoulders and looked from her to Cleo. "Let's finish this course and move on to the other one. I hear it's harder."

Chapter 9

C LEO BABY!"

Bethany's best friend whipped her head around to find the voice calling her.

"Ed?"

The large man sprinted over outdoor carpet and around fake jungle creatures. Cleo dropped her club and ran to him, jumping into his outstretched arms. "What are you doing back so soon? I wasn't expecting you for two days."

"I never question the Air Force. If they want to send me home, I'm not going to ask why. Apparently there was a space available, and they offered it to me." The munitions expert dwarfed his pixie wife, yet they were a matched set. He looked over his wife's head and said, "Hi, Bethany."

"Hi, Ed. Welcome home."

Cleo tilted her strawberry curls and asked, "How did you know I was here?"

"Are you kidding? It's all over the news. I got home to an empty house and turned on the TV. When they said the filming crew and the Gulfarium had taken over this place, I knew I'd find you here. You'd never miss excitement like this."

She held up her putter. "We're about to start another game. Do you want to join us?"

Ed's smoldering gaze spoke volumes. Cleo looked at Bethany and said, "Bye!"

"Boy, I know where I rank now." Bethany received a fierce hug from her best friend. "Go, be with your husband."

Cleo needed little encouragement.

When they were gone, Chez spoke with a bad imitation of Humphrey Bogart. "Just you and me, kid. Let's blow this Popsicle stand."

"I suppose things will wind down soon, and I do have work tomorrow." She would rather have stayed, but without Cleo or Ricky, she found her energy waning.

As they walked to the parking lot, Chez said, "Actually, I saw that the boardwalk had a nice nightspot. Maybe we could do some dancing."

"I'm not much of a nightspot type of gal."

"Well," he said, scratching his head, "we have to go back there to get your car anyway. How about coffee at the restaurant?"

He is persistent. Maybe she should cap off the evening with something to eat. What harm could there be in that? "Sure. They have outside tables so we can continue to enjoy this beautiful night."

She found herself looking around for Ricky and Vince. If she caught them in time, she'd invite them along. Unfortunately, the newspeople were packing up their vans, the interview apparently over. She had no idea where the two may have gone.

When they reached his car, Chez held the door open for her. "The boardwalk it is then. I promise I won't keep you out much later. I just haven't been able to spend as much time with you as I would have liked."

Bethany decided this would be a perfect time to get rid of the guilt she'd been feeling about not missing Chez.

∞

Brick headed back to the minigolf course. Bethany and Chez were nowhere to be found. He'd seen Cleo leave with someone, which meant Bethany was alone with the leech. If he hadn't allowed the photo op with Vince in the bumper cars, he may have caught them in time.

He went back toward the parking lot. Chez's car was gone. A man from the camera crew approached him from the direction of the lot. After a brief greeting, Brick asked, "Hey, you didn't happen to see Chez out there, did you?"

"Yeah, I saw him and that blond dolphin cutie getting into the car I parked next to. I heard them say something about the boardwalk. They're going there for coffee. But I'll bet Chez has dessert on his mind." He gave an evil wink, placed his hands in his pockets, and sauntered into the amusement park, whistling.

∞

Chez pulled a chair out for Bethany. When the waitress arrived to take their order, they both decided neither was hungry enough for a snack. Chez ordered coffee, and Bethany ordered hot tea. "Oh." Chez caught the waitress before she walked away. "Make that to go."

"Why?" A rock suddenly dropped into the pit of Bethany's stomach.

"I thought maybe we could take our drinks and walk the beach."

Bethany looked where he indicated. It was well lit, and there were still a few die-hard tourists milling about. "If we don't go far. Like I said, I have to work tomorrow."

"Absolutely." He smiled, but his eyes didn't seem as friendly as the rest of his face.

Once on the beach, Bethany suddenly felt vulnerable. She didn't know if it was the black haze over the Gulf, or the wide expanse of beach beyond the pools of light illuminating the area from floodlights on the building. A breeze had kicked up, and she shivered, wishing she had brought her sweater.

"Are you cold?" Chez slipped his arm around her shoulder and rubbed her skin. "Drink your tea. That should warm you up."

He started walking out of the safety of the lights, where the beach was deserted. She stopped. "Chez, I don't feel comfortable going any farther."

He peered into the darkness. "Just to that bit of wood there. I want to see if it's from a shipwreck." When she hesitated, he said, "Don't worry; I'm here."

She allowed him to pull her along, wanting with all her heart to prove Cleo wrong.

Chez kicked the wood. "Aw, can't tell what it is in this light." He turned to her and cupped her chin. "But you look beautiful. Let's see what's on the other side of that bush."

Bethany pulled away, but he clamped down on her hand. A movement near the bush caught her eye. Bethany's nerves were already about to snap, but seeing a broad figure standing in the shadows caused a scream to form in her chest. *Does he have an accomplice? I can't fight two of them!*

Just then, Vince Galloway walked into the moonlight.

"Vince!" Chez bellowed. "What are you doing lurking in the dark? Studying for a new role?"

"I came here same as you." He indicated the Styrofoam cups in their hands. "Do you mind if I tag along? I miss my family and don't feel like sitting in my empty hotel room."

"Please, join us," Bethany said, grateful to Vince for his intervention. She silently lifted a prayer of thanksgiving. Had Chez lured her out there for a reason? Or was it just her imagination? "That is, if Chez doesn't mind." It wouldn't matter if he did. She was not going to be alone with him.

She received a look from Chez that frightened her. Apparently he did mind. But then, as a chameleon changing its color to suit its environment, Chez smiled and said too politely, "You know, you've been telling me all evening you needed to get home. Maybe we should call it a night."

They walked back to the parking lot, with Vince bringing up the rear, like a watchful guardian.

"Vince, do you mind?" Chez flung over his shoulder. "I'd like to say a proper good night to my date."

"Oh, sorry. My car is over there. See you tomorrow, Bethany."

When they reached her car, she opened her door. Chez caressed her shoulders as he turned her to face him. "I had a good time tonight, despite the fiasco with the reporters."

As he spoke, he drew closer to her. The roof of her car bit into her shoulder blade.

Whoop! Whoop! Scree! Scree! Whoop! Whoop!

Chez jumped back as if electrocuted. Vince's car seemed to be having a conniption fit. The horn blared, and the lights flashed. With a *blip-blip*, it stopped.

"Sorry, it's a rental," Vince called out. "Not used to it, I guess. Hit the alarm button by mistake."

Bethany took the opportunity to slip into her car. She shut the door and rolled down the window only enough to talk. When Chez turned back toward er, she could see his intense disappointment.

"Thank you for the surprise. It was so thoughtful of you to include everyone our night of fun. I'll see you tomorrow."

She backed out of the space and waved at Vince as she drove by. In her arview mirror, she witnessed Chez kicking the pavement in frustration.

Brick watched from his own car, several rows away. After throwing a little issy fit, Chez threw himself into his car and whipped out of the parking lot. rick could imagine him sulking.

As Vince drove toward the exit, Brick saw a thick, stubby thumb raised in iumph from the driver-side window. He responded in kind, very pleased with mself that the plan had gone so well. Not only had he gotten the chance to be ith Bethany, but because of his ex-friend's predictable nature, he hoped he had rchestrated Chez's fall. Surely she must have seen the lizard's true colors.

He followed him back to the hotel.

Chapter 10

Bethany knew about the benefit to help buy resources for the Strande Fund, a charity set up to help animals that had beached themselves. Sh was shocked to find out, by reading a poster in the gift shop, that Galax Productions had agreed to be a part of it.

" 'Brick Connor and Vince Galloway will be available for autographs an pictures'," she read aloud to Cleo. "They've set it for the night after the film crev leaves."

"I know. I taped that up there." Cleo zipped and locked her cash bag, tucke it under her arm, then reached for her purse. "Too bad I'm going to miss it."

"You can't leave and miss the glitz and glamour."

Cleo locked the door for the final time before her vacation as she said, "Sorr but I've had these plane tickets for weeks. I guess I'll have to create my own glit and glamour with the man I love in his parents' mountain lodge. I understan we'll have the guest cabin out back."

"That sounds like more fun than a stuffy benefit. Can I come?"

"Only if you board with the family." Cleo gave a mischievous wink.

Bethany would miss her. But another void in her heart took precedenc Production would wrap up this week, and things would go back to norma *Normal.* That word sounded so—*normal.* Mundane. Boring. Brickless. *Who Where did that come from?* The man whom she told to stay out of her life woul actually be leaving it. How did she feel about that?

Every time she tried to convince herself that she was happy her life woul get back to—*normal,* she would see herself laughing with Ricky, whippin around a track in a little metal car, splashing him with her bumper boat. She had fun last night. Could she let him fade from her life again? What choic did she have? He belonged to the world now. An emptiness engulfed her tha she hadn't felt in ten years.

And what about Chez? She knew the answer to that one. Chez had becom someone else: the person Cleo saw—the person Ricky warned her about. She fe God had opened her eyes last night, probably due to her friend's prayers.

She decided to avoid Chez throughout the week. But when he sought he out the last evening of shooting, she agreed to talk to him. He probably onl wanted to say good-bye. They walked to the bench overlooking the Gulf. A fog over the water filtered the sun as it tried to burn through, causing an eeri yellowish glow.

The crew milled about the Shark Moat, which was nearby, so she wouldn't be alone with Chez. She wrapped her arms around herself and faced away from him.

"I just wanted to tell you," he said as he started to caress her shoulder, "that I enjoyed our brief time together. How about the benefit tomorrow? Would you like to pick me up? I've already turned in my rental."

"Um, Chez." She wiggled away from his touch. "I don't know if I'm going." She didn't know why she hadn't thought that he might ask her to the benefit.

"That's okay. We could ditch the whole thing and pick up where we left off at the beach."

"I don't think so. It's best we say our good-byes."

"I never say good-bye." His hand slipped around hers, and he began to stroke her palm.

She whipped her hand away and turned to face him. *Oh no, you don't, buster. I'm on to you.*

"We'll see each other again," he continued. "Maybe when this movie is done, I'll come back. Then we'll have more time to get to know each other."

When he squeezed her upper arms, she placed her hands on his chest. Apparently he didn't care who witnessed this scene. She tried to push him away, but he had latched onto her shoulders, drawing her closer, obviously for a kiss.

"Stop!" In what seemed like phenomenal strength, she pushed him so hard he flew into the air. However, it had been Ricky who grabbed the smaller man by the shoulders and yanked him away from her.

"What the lady is trying to tell you is that it's over."

Ricky glared down at Chez on the ground. She had never seen him that angry, not even in his movies.

Chez blinked and shook his head as if stunned to find himself on the concrete looking up. "That's the last time, Connor," he snarled through gritted teeth. "You can't bully your way out of this one."

"You going to use your mouth to fight, as usual?"

Chez let out a war cry and took the actor head-on. Bethany held in a scream as the two men wrestled. Alarmed, she watched Ricky get a left handhold on the front of Chez's shirt and prepare to swing with his right. She grabbed his fist. "Stop! He's no match for you. And not worth going to jail over."

A muscle rippled in his jaw. After several seconds, he grabbed the director's clothing with both fists and flung him toward the beach, where he landed in the soft, white sand. While Chez sputtered and spit granules out of his mouth, Ricky thrust a pointed finger at him. "Leave her alone. She tried to be subtle, but you're too thick to see she was trying to get rid of you."

Chez stood up, wiped sand off his face, and hopped back over the railing. "You're going to be sorry you did that, Connor," he said as he retreated back to the set.

Ricky turned toward Bethany, who still stood with her mouth agape. His velvet voice caressed her. "Are you okay?"

Bile rose in her throat like mercury in a hot thermometer, the acid taste a reminder of how vulnerable she had been. How many girls had Chez gotten into the moonlight? How many against their will? She started to shiver, and her chin began to tremble. Ricky wrapped his arms around her. She buried her face into the lining of his leather jacket and dug her fingernails into the pliable softness of the lapel. Her tears came hot and plentiful, but they weren't only because of Chez. The familiar feel of her first love's arms triggered memories. . .his fingers caressing her hair. . .the gentle voice that once spoke tender words of love. . . .

Different hands on her shoulders pulled her away from where she belonged. *No*, she wanted to scream. *I'm not done savoring this moment*. . .the smell of leather mingled with spicy cologne. . .the broad chest and muscled arms created to hold her exclusively. Her father pulled his only child from Ricky's arms and curled her into his own.

"What happened here?"

Only then did she realize they had drawn an audience. Forty concerned faces watched as her father led her away to his office.

As she looked back, a vision of the boy who had adored her blurred into the man she could never have, and she longed to be sixteen again.

∞

Brick punched Bethany's phone number while in his hotel room. He'd left the set early, not willing to be near Chez anymore. What shots were left could be handled by his double. He desperately wanted to talk to her—no—he wanted to hold her again. He could thank Chez for that incredible moment. Bethy nuzzled to his chest, her soft hair tickling his lips. The smell of coconut-scented lotion drifting into his senses, making him long to dip into her slender neck for more.

He counted three rattling rings through the receiver before he heard a male voice. "Hello?"

"Glenn, it's Brick. How's Bethany? May I talk to her?"

"She'll be fine. Just a minute."

The voices were muffled, as if Glenn had covered the mouthpiece. It sounded like they were arguing, but after a long moment, Bethany came on the phone.

"Hello, Ricky."

He swallowed hard. *Get a grip; you're not a teenager anymore.* "Hi, how are you doing?"

An unsteady sigh made his heart break. "How should I be? I feel like a fool. You tried to warn me, but I wouldn't listen. Even Cleo could see what kind of person he was."

"Don't be too hard on yourself. Chez makes a career of deceiving women. I should have stopped him before he had a chance to do it to you."

"Well, fortunately the only thing hurt was my pride. Thank you for intervening tonight."

"My pleasure." He genuinely meant that.

"I guess this is good-bye, then."

His heart constricted. "Won't I see you at the benefit tomorrow?"

"I'm not going. I'm not in the party mood."

"But it's for your animals. How would it look for the Gulfarium's most valued asset to be absent from her own party?"

She chuckled, but there was little mirth in the sound. "I'm hardly an asset, more of a liability, actually. Listen, let's just end it here. It's been great seeing you again. Good luck with your career."

Was she really talking to him as if he were a mere acquaintance from the past? *Oh no, you don't, Bethy dear. I have a plan.* "Uh, yeah, and you with yours. Put your father on, okay? In case things get crazy tomorrow, I'd like to say my good-byes tonight."

When Glenn came back on the phone, Brick said, "Listen, could you do me a favor?"

∽

"That one." Glenn pointed to the second dress Bethany held up. That was her favorite, too, but for some reason, her mind fogged over every time she thought about the benefit. Cleo would normally be helping her make this important decision, but she had already left for Colorado.

"Okay, the pink dress." She tossed the off-the-shoulder number on her bed. "Now, how about shoes?"

"Don't make me sorry I talked you into this, daughter," Glenn groaned.

"Oh, all right. I only have a couple of pairs of shoes that would work anyway."

Her father, who had been sitting at her vanity, stood and walked toward the door. He looked at his watch. "I'm going to eat some lunch, then head over there to help set up. I want to be sure they put the band in the right place."

Bethany was so proud of her dad. He'd been in the swing band for years, and now he not only played lead trumpet but directed, as well. Whenever she'd been at other functions with him, she loved to watch the audience, many of them middle-aged women, swaying to the music and batting their eyelashes at him as if he were Glenn Miller himself.

He continued. "I'll be back to get you in plenty of time. But I'm taking my tux just in case I can't get away."

Bethany picked up the pink dress and looked in her full-length mirror, holding the hanger under her chin and swishing the netted fabric to test the movement. "If that happens, I can drive myself."

"No, I need a date. We can't have the most eligible bachelor in northwest Florida going stag, now can we?" He walked back into the room and kissed her hair. "You just better be ready. None of that *making the date wait* stuff. I'm an old man and don't have time for such foolishness." He winked as he left the room.

Later that evening, while putting the finishing touches to her makeup, she heard the doorbell ring. She looked at her watch, wondering where her father was. Then a thought hit her. "That scamp!" she said to her cat, which was pawing at a round perfume bottle on the vanity. "He's pretending to be my date by picking me up at the door."

She descended the stairs, smoothing her dress and fluffing her hair. With her most gracious smile in place, she grabbed the knob and flung open the door for her date.

"You're right on ti—"

Brick Connor, multimillion-dollar box office star, stood on her doorstep in full tux and holding a corsage.

Chapter 11

Your father regrets his absence and has asked me to take his place. I hope that's suitable for you."

Her mouth lay open with the last word she tried to utter still stuck in her throat. She dumbly nodded her head and allowed him to pin the delicate flowers to her dress. A slight breeze caused his spicy cologne to intermingle with the scent of the tiny pink roses, and the combination muddled her thinking.

Why was she acting so silly? After all, wasn't this Ricky, her childhood friend? She took in the tailored tux, the silk shirt, the imported shoes. His dark hair and mustache, his brown contact-tinted eyes—the whole image was a direct negative of the boy she once loved. Ricky had been a golden child, light hair that only grew lighter in the sun, green eyes that reflected the nature around him. However, she reacted to this man in a perfectly normal way. She became Cinderella, and he was the prince of the silver screen.

She still hadn't said a word when her date lowered himself into the BMW and chuckled. "This kinda reminds me of prom." The compact hummed to life at the driver's touch, and music began to flow from the CD player.

Smooth jazz filled the small compartment, helping to untie Bethany's tongue and her tangled emotions. She wondered about her father but, knowing how much he liked Ricky, sensed he had something to do with this *change of plans*.

She narrowed her eyes and cast a sideward glance at the stranger by her side. "Did you two plan this?" When he feigned confusion, she clarified. "You and my dad."

"I confess. I bribed him." Her skepticism must have been evident because he quickly added, "Okay. I asked him to let me do this. I needed a time to be alone with you, to talk."

"We talked the other night."

"While screaming around a go-cart track? Come on, Bethy. While that was all great fun, we never had a chance to clear the air between us."

"What's to clear? I think I clarified everything that first night. We've both moved on. I'm not the same person, and obviously, neither are you."

He began tapping the steering wheel in time to the music. She had to hide a grin. Maybe he hadn't changed so much. He still fidgeted when he was nervous.

"Look," he said as they turned onto the highway, "I'm not suggesting we get back together." Bethany felt her heart thud. Was that what she had wanted all along?

"Neither am I." Her sullen reflection in the passenger-side window suggested otherwise.

"I would just like to know what happened and renew at least a friendship. Is that too much to ask?"

She turned toward him, taking in his now-mature profile. The baby fat was gone, the freckles had faded away, his neck fit snugly into his collar, and those shoulders...

His mouth was moving. She'd better start to pay attention. ". . .thought someday you'd join me."

"What?"

"We were quite the team in high school. In fact, you were phenomenal. I only stuck with it to be with you. You were a much better actor than me."

"That's not true. How could you have gotten this far if you weren't good?"

"I didn't say I wasn't good. I said you were better. I've gotten this far with an exceptional manager and superb advice. I thought someday we'd be a team, like Taylor and Burton. . . ."

"Divorced, several times."

"Tracy and Hepburn."

"Living in sin."

"Rooney and Garland."

"Just good friends."

He grabbed the gearshift and popped it into fifth. "You're not making this easy."

She felt her ears buzz with adrenaline. "Why should I make it easy? You abandoned me."

He whipped his head to look at her. "You're the one who left. How can you say I abandoned you?"

"You stopped writing." She began to pick at her newly polished nails.

"You did, too."

She drew in a shaky breath. Someone had to be the mature one. It might as well be her. "I guess it's as I said before. We just outgrew each other. It happens."

It happens.

Brick chewed the inside of his cheek. Could she actually be this nonchalant about their relationship? He knew beyond any shadow of a doubt, that if she had stayed in California, they would have married.

"Even if you hadn't moved and we had stayed together, it still wouldn't be the same as it was. People grow up, Bethany. It doesn't have to end simply because we're older."

"It's not because we're older, Ricky. It's because we're different. There was a time we were so in tune we could finish each other's thoughts."

"Because we were together so much. That's the only thing I can be grateful to my father for." The familiar surge of hatred boiled deep under the surface, and he rubbed at the scar on his chin.

Bethany patted his arm. "I know. You spent more time at my house than your own, just to avoid him."

She removed her hand too quickly. He wanted to reach with his left, and hold it against his sleeve, like a captured butterfly. But the elusive fingers fluttered away, leaving the skin under his jacket tingling, longing for another touch.

"If it hadn't been for that," he agreed, "I wouldn't have grown so close to you, or your family."

As they sat in silence, a saxophone drawled a bittersweet tune, somehow musically describing the mood.

Music erupted from Ricky's breast pocket. Bethany frowned as he pulled out a cell phone. "Are you in position?" He glanced around, apparently looking for street signs. "We're almost there." He turned down a dark road with a sign pointing to the beach.

"What's going on?" Surely he wasn't going to try to kidnap her so they could spend time together. That was absurd.

"Your dad told me how you felt about people seeing us together. He's going to meet us and take you the rest of the way. This is going to be a media event tonight, and if you're seen arriving with me, they'll be all over you."

Touched by his thoughtfulness, she realized he had all the power. If he wanted to parade her before the cameras, he certainly could. She remembered back a mere twenty-four hours, when Chez had gone sailing over the rail. Brick Connor was not a man to provoke. And yet his gentleness defined his character.

As a result of this new revelation, she couldn't have kept her next words from spilling out of her mouth if she had jammed something between her teeth. "I hope that doesn't mean we have to avoid each other at the party."

He looked at her and swerved a little but regained control of the car quickly. "Nothing would keep us apart tonight."

They met her father at a parking area near a deserted beach where Bethany traded cars. Ricky gave them a few minutes' head start, and they arrived at the hotel moments before him.

Glenn got out of the car, walked to the passenger side, and offered his hand to Bethany. She sat there, arms folded, staring forward.

"Come on, honey," he pleaded.

The valet stood patiently waiting with a smirk on his face. "Trouble with the little woman, sir?"

Bethany stifled a giggle. She heard her dad say, "The little woman is my daughter," as he bent down, his face scowling at her from the open door, and finished the sentence, "and she's being a brat."

Bethany gracefully turned and stepped out of the car. She was gratified by an appreciative look from the valet. Glenn scowled when he handed him the keys, and the boy quickly said, "Yes, sir."

Bethany refused Glenn's outstretched hand. "I'm not speaking to you."

"Okay, I'm sorry I deceived you. But he's a very persuasive man."

They moved toward the glass doors of the hotel. A gold rope had been placed to form an alley to the ballroom, and on either side were anxious faces looking for their favorite star. Bethany heard whispering, and it was clear they were trying to decide if she and her escort were famous. Then she heard someone over the din. "Oh, those are just the fish people."

That did it. She couldn't keep up her pretend anger any longer. With a chuckle, she turned toward her father. "You shouldn't have conspired with him, you know."

"I know, but he's like a son to me. What could I do?"

"Well, since I'm like a daughter to you, you should have protected me."

She tucked her hands into the crook of his arm and leaned close. "But thank you. It felt good to talk to him without an audience eavesdropping." She placed a perfectly formed *mauvelous*-colored lip print on his cheek and then wiped it off with her thumb.

As they moved into the ballroom and were escorted to the head table, both were struck by the glamour of it all. Bethany turned to her father and whispered, "I don't think we're in Kansas anymore, Toto." She had been in this ballroom for a wedding reception before, but then it never looked like something out of a Hollywood movie. Candles flickered in real crystal vases, causing the glow on the walls and ceiling to dance. Glitter sparkled on tables, on plants, and on the floor. There were two ice sculptures spouting a sparkling beverage. One was a dolphin, in leap mode. The other was a kangaroo, to represent the movie, *Danger Down Under.*

"How delightfully decadent," Bethany said as her father pulled the chair out for her.

Even so, all of that paled when compared to the man entering the room. Brick Connor made his grand appearance with the self-assuredness of Cary Grant, the panache of Fred Astaire, and the mystique of Sean Connery.

Vince Galloway entered with Ricky, but it was obvious whom the crowd was there to see. Cameras clicked wildly as local and Hollywood reporters clamored for a comment. The two men moved to a microphone. After the commotion died down, Ricky said, "I, along with Vince Galloway and Galaxy Productions, would like to thank the fine people of Fort Walton Beach for their cooperation in the making of the film, *Danger Down Under.*" This was met with wild applause and whistles. He went on to thank every organization that offered its support and every official involved.

"And now, I'd like to introduce the man responsible for this event."

Simon Kimball came forward. A large screen had been set up, and he began narrating a computer presentation depicting a dolphin rescue that had happened within the last year. When the presentation was over, he received a standing ovation.

As Bethany sat back down, she wondered briefly who would fill the empty chairs around her table. She assumed Simon would take one. Then she smelled that cologne. The lightest touch of his fingers on her shoulders caused her whole body to react, and she grabbed her napkin to still her trembling hands. The voice behind her betrayed his nearness, and she heard a whispered, "How fortunate that we're seated together."

Glenn, on her right, introduced everyone as the large round table began to fill. This included Vince Galloway, Simon and his wife, the mayor and her husband, as well as Cassie, their teenage daughter, apparently a huge Brick Connor fan. Bethany thought the child would die of pent-up excitement. She had obviously been taught how to behave at functions, but if she sparkled any more, there would be no need for the glitter that adorned the room.

Bethany commented on the empty chair next to Cassie. All eyes turned to the vacant chair, and Ricky answered. "That was supposed to be for Chad Cheswick, the assistant director for this location shoot." He reached for his water and sipped before saying, "He was called away—rather unexpectedly last night." Bethany hid a smile as he whispered behind the goblet, "Or rather *sent* away."

The meal started with a creamy broccoli cheese soup with bits of potato, followed by a crunchy cabbage salad with sesame seeds and almonds. The entrée, a scrumptious apricot-glazed chicken garnished with seedless grapes, was accompanied by a side dish of ginger-fried rice. The entire meal ended with almond praline cheesecake.

While coffee was served, Glenn excused himself. "I'm going to try to work after eating all this food. Forgive me if my trumpet sounds flat. My stomach muscles may not be able to sustain the notes."

The waiter came to Bethany, and she refused coffee but asked for herbal tea. Ricky had been in a conversation with the mayor and hadn't heard her request. So when he also asked for herbal tea, something within her struck a chord. Could there still be hope for the two of them? Perhaps she should pursue what they had in common rather than dwell on their differences.

However, there was one huge difference. Ricky no longer lived for the Lord.

Vince rose, also excusing himself, and motioned for Ricky to follow.

Ricky touched his napkin to the corners of his mouth. "Gentlemen. Ladies." He looked at Bethany, and she felt a blush on her cheeks. "Forgive me, but there is already a line forming at the autograph table."

The swing band began with a crashing beat, and soon the dance floor was filled with jitterbugs.

Chapter 12

Bethany leaned her elbows on the linen tablecloth and cupped her chi
as she looked around the ballroom. Couples everywhere. She longed fo
Cleo's chatty presence. But even if her friend hadn't deserted her to go t
Colorado, Ed would be with her. Just another couple to envy.

Bethany felt like a small fish in a very big sea.

After an hour, the musicians had stopped playing, taking a much-neede
break, so she decided to search out her father. At least if she were standing nex
to a man, she'd feel like a couple, even if she did have genetic ties to him.

When she couldn't find him inside the ballroom, she went out to the pati
that looked over the Gulf. The muggy breeze did little to cool her cheeks as sh
stepped outside.

She scanned the area. Several people had decided to get some fresh air, bu
in the corner, behind the potted ficus tree, was her father. He stood talking t
someone hidden from view. Probably another member of the band. She'd go ove
and say hi.

When she approached, however, she witnessed an arm and a hand wit
French manicured nails wrap around his waist. *Who is this?*

Should she approach them? Would she be intruding? She felt an unexpecte
sharp pain. She'd seen her father with women before but knew he'd never felt seri
ous toward any of them. His body language with this one suggested otherwise.

While she stood in the middle of the patio, pondering her decision, a voic
from behind made her jump. "A lady shouldn't be standing all alone."

She turned to see Ricky's grin, and then she relaxed. "You startled me."

"You were deep in thought. Is everything okay?" He handed her a glass c
sparkling ginger ale.

"Thank you. I need this." She took a sip.

"Let's sit down over here on this bench." She looked around for someon
to spring from the bushes with a camera. He must have sensed her hesitatio
"Relax. I've been mingling with everyone, and you're next in line. Now tell m
what's bothering you."

She glanced over by the tree, but the couple—yes, it looked as though he
father had become a *couple*—was gone.

Bethany set her drink down and began to fiddle with her fingers. Bric
dared to reach over and cup them with his hand. It pleased him when she didn
pull away.

"I guess I'm tired." She shrugged her slender shoulders. "It's been a long evening."

"Yeah. It's exhausting to have to smile and carry on a conversation with people you don't know." He reluctantly released her hands.

She looked at him, her lovely mouth at an angle. "How do you do it? You work long hours, you give interviews. Is there ever a time when you relax between movies?"

"I haven't had a real vacation in years. We've been making the *Danger* movies back-to-back." He sighed heavily. "I'll admit, I'm beginning to burn out."

"Maybe you should take a break after this project. Lounge on a beach somewhere. Go surfing. Do you still do that?"

He shook his head. "I haven't been surfing in years. I still have the board, though."

"You're kidding. As many times as you wiped out?"

He chuckled. "You wiped out a few times yourself, dudette. I remember when we were both on that board. . . ." She squirmed slightly, and he knew he'd overstepped the boundary. "Anyway, a vacation is just what I need. I'll arrange it when I get home."

She glanced around the patio and said, "Looks like everyone's gone inside now that the music has started up again."

His arm acted on its own volition, and he reached around her shoulders. She looked up at him, and in the tiny white lights entwined through a trellis nearby, he could see her emerald green eyes. "You know, your eyes are the color of the coast. You blend in beautifully with your surroundings here."

A light floral fragrance had replaced her tropical-scented suntan lotion. It invited him closer, closer, until their lips nearly touched.

"Ricky." She put her hand on his chest. "I need to go inside."

She stood and walked away from him.

He scratched his head.

Well, that *never happened to Brick Connor before.*

Please don't let me topple off these shoes. She could feel his eyes on her back, and her already-wobbly state threatened to buckle her ankles. *Don't let yourself fall for him again. You'll only get hurt.* But even as she thought those words, she knew it was too late.

∞

Glenn announced they would play "Waltzing Matilda" for their final song in honor of *Danger Down Under.* Like Cinderella, Bethany believed she'd never see her prince again after she left the ball. She mingled while saying good-bye to the crew.

Vince swept her off her feet in a boisterous hug. "It was sure a pleasure meeting you, Bethany." He nodded toward Ricky who was deep in a conversation with Glenn. "I'll take good care of him. He told me he'd accepted the Lord years ago but has fallen away. He has a lot of questions, and I think he may be ready to hear the answers." He winked, and she knew in her spirit, as she had on the first day, that Vince Galloway was indeed an answer to her petitions on Ricky's behalf. "When this young man finds his way back, God and His angels will give you a big thumbs-up for all your prayers."

Bethany threw her arms around her new friend's thick neck. "Thank you, Vince," she rasped. The tears were so close; if she had said any more, she'd have embarrassed herself.

As he walked away, he said, "Remember me when you par the eighteenth hole next time."

"I will." She twirled, her version of the happy dance, and walked toward the table where her father and Ricky were.

Glenn stood, kissed her on the cheek, and offered to meet her in the lobby. He had some final things to do with the band before he could go home.

"Have a seat." Ricky pulled out a chair for her.

"What were you two talking so seriously about?" She fluffed her dress as she sat.

"Guy stuff—you wouldn't be interested."

She never understood the relationship between the two men.

Ricky pulled out a pen and began writing on a napkin.

"Now what are you doing?" Bethany peeked over the left hand that anchored the napkin.

"I'm pretending that you asked for my autograph. We're being watched carefully. I have to make it look like you're just another fan." With a playful grin, he whispered, "Try to look awestruck. You know, totally blown away by my star status."

Bethany pulled off her part to perfection, making her moony eyes drip with admiration.

He chuckled. "I knew you were a better actor than me." He gave her the napkin and shook her hand, making a point to caress her wrist with his thumb before letting go. "Good-bye, Bethy. I'll miss you."

She tucked the napkin inside her purse. "Good-bye, Ricky." With a lump the size of an Oscar statuette lodged in her throat, she turned and ran. She even thought of losing her shoe so he would have to track her down to give it to her.

Bethany waited in the lobby, waving to people as they left. Finally her father walked through the doors. S*he* was with him.

The woman hanging on her father's arm wasn't slender, by any means, certainly not athletic enough to keep up with him. Her short dark hair framed a fiftyish face. He introduced her as Amanda Schnell, a Realtor he'd met the previous December at a Chamber of Commerce Christmas party.

Bethany shook her hand carefully, avoiding the long fingernails. *Schnell, huh? Doesn't that mean* fast *in German?*

"Amanda and I had a couple of dates at the beginning of the year," Glenn interjected. "Then she went out of town, and we lost touch. I told you about her, didn't I?"

Bethany cleared her throat. He expected her to talk? "Yes, you probably did, but you go out with so many women, I can't keep track of them all." *There. That should put Ms. Fast-with-the-Fingernails in her place.* But when she caught the warning look from her father, she immediately felt remorseful.

"When I saw her here, of all places," Glenn continued, "I wanted to make sure she wouldn't slip away from me again." He placed his arm around Amanda's shoulders and gave her a little squeeze.

Amanda patted his hand. With regard to Bethany, she said, "As a long-standing member of the Chamber of Commerce, I received an invitation to this prodigious cause. Knowing your father was involved, I wanted to come and support him."

Bethany watched the two gaze into each other's eyes. She hadn't seen that look on her father's face since her mother was alive. "That's nice." She didn't mean to sound so cold. Or did she? "I'll go have the valet pull the car around." She turned to flee but then remembered her manners. She turned and said, "It was nice meeting you, Amanda."

When she reached the cool night air, the valet grinned at her. "Did you ditch your *dad*? I get off in a half hour."

Before Bethany could think of a snappy retort, she heard her father's voice behind her. "The blue Blazer."

"Yes, sir."

Glenn glared at the valet as he hurried off to find the car. "Smart aleck kid." While they waited, he seemed to search Bethany's face. "You okay?"

Bethany folded her arms around herself and felt the first sting of what she knew would be a bucketful of tears if she chose to release them.

The SUV was brought around. When they were well on their way, Bethany couldn't voice what was in her heart—that she may never see Ricky again—so she voiced what was on her mind. "She's nothing like Mom."

Chapter 13

Bethany awoke the next morning determined to start the day on a positive note. All thoughts of Amanda Schnell had been thrust aside, and Ricky would soon be a distant memory.

She freed her legs out from under Willy, who had mimicked a cat comforter all night long, and padded to the bathroom barefoot.

While getting ready for work, Bethany switched from her beaded purse of the night before to her athletic bag. She retrieved her wallet, comb, and lipstick. Then she noticed the cocktail napkin snuggled against the satin lining. She pulled it out, giggling at the recollection of Cleo's encouraging suggestion to sell his autograph for a profit.

"I wonder how much I could get for it," she pondered, knowing it would go straight into her Brick Connor collection of memorabilia.

She turned the napkin over and caressed the bold signature. "This doesn't even look like his writing," she told her kitty, who was sprawled in unladylike fashion across the bed. Had Ricky changed his identity so much he actually became Brick Connor?

"What's this?" She noticed a slight bleed-through from writing on the inside of the folded napkin. There she found a personalized note that read: *My dearest Bethy, I've enjoyed our brief time together. It will not be another ten years before we see each other again. Yours forever, Ricky.*

She carefully folded the napkin and held it to her heart. Was this just another ring with a diamond chip setting? Something to appease her for another decade? *Please, Lord, no.*

Brick had been back home in the Hollywood Hills about a month when Maggie called him from Alabama. When the cordless phone rang, he was sitting by his pool, reading a script for the next day.

"Hey, Brick." The gentle drawl that had tickled his ear when they first met now set his teeth on edge.

"Hi, Maggie."

"I haven't heard from you in a while."

"Sorry. We're finishing up this movie, working on studio stuff. Guess I've been too busy to keep in touch." What was he going to do? Even before seeing Bethany, he knew things were cooling off with Maggie—on his part anyway. Maggie had told him she would never yield to the Hollywood lifestyle. Short and numerous relationships were not for her. However, that meant she had osen him for serious dating, apparently leading to marriage. He never should ave let it go that far. The time apart, plus seeing Bethany again, cinched the deal. ow, how would he tell her?

Maggie sighed heavily into the phone. "We kick off the tour this weekend my hometown. I'd love it if you'd come." Brick hesitated a second too long. Maggie continued. "I could show you around Florala. Then you could meet my omma and daddy." Yep, he should have said something before she threw down e *meet my folks* card. "You haven't tasted real Southern cookin' until you've eaten y momma's fried chicken and bread puddin'." Had her accent gotten thicker? ow long had she been back home anyway?

"Look, Maggie. . ." He didn't want to break up on the phone. But he had no me to run off to Alabama, either. He tried again. "Maggie, I've got something tell you."

"What?" Her icy response told him she knew what was coming.

"I think we should cool it for a while." Silence. "Maggie?"

"Who is she?"

"Excuse me?"

Are all women so intuitive?

"Is it some sweet young thing you've chosen to *mentor*?"

He shook his head as if she could see through the receiver. "It's just not orking out. A relationship needs two people, ideally in the same area code."

Brick heard a shuddering sigh, intentionally loud enough to gain his mpathy. "I've put a lot of effort into trying to make this work. Apparently it's en one-sided all along."

He pressed two fingers to his closed eyelids. "Not one-sided, Mags. I just ink things moved faster than I had anticipated."

Dead silence.

"Maggie?"

"You can't fool me, Brick." She spoke in an even, controlled tone. What appened to the shuddering sigh? "I know there's another woman, and you'll gret messing with me." He gripped the phone, tempted to throw it into the ool. "Go have your fling. You just blew your chance. Southern gals make terrific ives." A solid click assaulted his ear.

He glared at the now silent phone and slammed it to the table. Suddenly eling the need to cool down, he peeled off his T-shirt and dove into the pool.

∞

hroughout the summer, Bethany found herself drawn into her routine. The m crew soon became a distant memory, and instead of rubbing elbows with ollywood's elite, she found herself elbow deep in dead herring and squid. stead of watching the talented actors work through their scenes, she watched r little finned troupe as she put them through their paces, day in and day out.

By midsummer, she had logged enough hours on her knees in prayer to qualify for mission work. Her future became a serious concern. No longer could she glide through life, particularly under her father's care. Amanda Schnell had begun to claim Glenn's time more each day, and Bethany could see she was losing him. It was only a matter of time before the two would get married, and then Bethany would be like a fifth wheel. She had to make plans now.

One evening, she sat on her bed with her knees pulled up under her chin. She enjoyed the therapy aspect of her job. Maybe she should she go back to school to become a therapist, as Sheila had suggested. But after the Hollywood invasion the call of the curtain seemed to niggle at the back of her mind constantly. Acting was in her blood.

Unbidden, a horrible memory surfaced. She was a teenager and had just opened the door to her home. . . .

Flashbulbs. Questions. "How does it feel to know your mother was in that tragic accident?" She didn't know. That was the first she'd heard.

Her father had whipped his sedan into the driveway and chased the reporter away, then held her long into the night.

The two sequestered themselves as much as possible, but those hounding reporters followed them through every step of the grieving process. Nothing was sacred—from the funeral plans to moving from their home in Beverly Hills. The headlines read FAMILY OF BELOVED ACTRESS, DEE BELLAMY, SELLS HOUSE TO PAY MOUNTING DEBT. There was no mounting debt. Mom simply wasn't there—the fire had died.

Eleven years later, the world had forgotten about Dee Bellamy. Grandma Bellamy was in a nursing home, her memory ravaged by Alzheimer's, and Bethany and her father had built a new life in Florida, blending in with the locals. No one ever suspected that they had been related to Hollywood royalty. Not even Cleo knew, a decision that Bethany had not made lightly. But Cleo was part of her new life.

When she saw Ricky, it all came flooding back. The photo shoots in the house, the publicity events, even visiting her mother on location during summer break. Bethany had been told she could follow in her mother's footsteps easily because she'd inherited her talent.

"We could become a team like Taylor and Burton," Ricky's voice intruded. Was God bringing those thoughts into her head, or was it her own selfish desires? *"I told you that you were a better actor than me."*

"Shut up, Ricky! You're not supposed to be on my mind when I'm praying." Her outburst startled Willy, who, with enormous green eyes and a tail bushed out with fright, perched ready to flee. "I'm sorry, sweetheart," she cooed as she picked up the feline and stroked her long, soft fur. With apparent forgiveness, Willy emitted a pattering purr that pummeled her owner's chest with the feel of a carpeted jackhammer.

Ricky. He'd been gone a month, and she still hadn't heard from him. Fine.

A relationship with him would only throw her back into the lifestyle she had left. She tried to shut out thoughts of him, but instead, the inevitable headlines assailed her imagination.

Hollywood Heartthrob and Bellamy Daughter Reconnect.

New Danger Role for Brick Connor as He Pursues Wedded Bliss.

He Spies, She Shies—Brick Connor Turned Down for Role of Husband.

No, it was best that he was out of her life. No good could come from any kind of relationship with a man who lived in a glass house.

∞

Brick removed his suit and tie, throwing them onto the bed. The silk shirt came next. He hurled it toward the hamper, and it fell to a crumpled heap on the floor. After finding his sweatpants and favorite T-shirt under the bed, he tugged them on. The full-length mirror that doubled as his closet door reflected back a slovenly image. *This is me.*

Agitated from the talk show on which he had just been interviewed, he entered his kitchen in search of anything containing high carbohydrates.

"I'd give last year's salary for a chocolate bar right now," he grumbled as he searched through his refrigerator. What he found was caviar, liver pâté, and deboned meat from a Cornish game hen, all left over from a dinner party a couple of nights ago.

"Ah," he said after rooting through the freezer. "There is a God, and He has excellent taste in ice cream." He grabbed the half gallon of Super Fudgie Nutter, tossed the lid in the garbage, and grabbed a serving spoon from the drawer.

As he sat in front of his big-screen television, he snatched up the remote. Why he wanted to watch *The Ray Silverman Show*, he had no idea. It had been taped delayed and was scheduled to air in a few moments.

The host came out, did his ten-minute monologue, and then sat at his desk to introduce the first guest.

"And now, the man of *Danger*, Brick Connor."

Wild applause and female screams greeted Brick as he walked on from backstage. The band played a spy-sounding riff, and Brick lowered himself into the chair.

"Tell us, Brick; I'm sure everyone here is anxious to know. How many more *Danger* movies do you plan to do?"

"Well, Ray, after *Danger Down Under,* I'm contracted to do one more, but after that, I'm not so sure. Not getting any younger, you know."

Ray and the audience laughed. "You look in peak condition. Surely you can keep on going."

Brick chuckled. "Well, I'll be in my mid-thirties by the time the next one's done. It's a lot of physical work, so I don't know how long I can keep it up."

"We can't imagine anyone else in that role, can we, folks?" Ray tapped a pencil while the audience hooted their encouragement.

"Quite frankly, I'd like to move on to other things, something that will challenge my acting ability more."

"Are you saying you think the *Danger* series is fluff?"

Brick's knee started bouncing. "Let's just say that I haven't grown as an actor like I should have. Agent Danger's entire repertoire of emotions can be counted on two fingers."

"But it's an action role. You can't expect it to be Shakespeare."

"True, and don't get me wrong, this role has elevated my status in Hollywood considerably—"

"But," Ray interrupted, "you're unhappy."

Brick sighed. "Yeah, Ray, I guess you could say that. The quality of these movies has gone downhill, and I'm tired of it."

"I'd like to pursue this further, but I've got to take a commercial break." Ray looked straight at the camera. "We'll be back in a moment with more from Brick Connor."

The commercial showed a family running upstairs to get away from a burglar. The mother's face showed fright but softened to keep her children from panicking. The advertised alarm system shrilled, frightening away the would-be intruder.

"Even those actors have better roles than I do." Brick shoved a heaping spoonful of cold comfort into his mouth.

When the program came back on, Brick skillfully dodged the rest of Ray's questions. Or so he thought.

The phone rang, and the caller ID informed him it was his manager calling. He picked it up and began talking without saying hello.

"I know, Daryl, I have a big mouth."

"You're not making my job easy, Brick."

"Hey, he baited me. I'd have never spilled how unhappy I am on national television."

"But you did."

"Come on, how is it going to affect me? My contract is so solid even I can't get out of it. They can't fire me, can they?"

"That's not what I'm worried about. If you keep talking like this, it's going to get around that you're difficult to work with. Your writer's meetings have already been made public."

"If they didn't stink at their jobs, I wouldn't have to have meetings, would I? Why am I the bad guy here?"

"Because you're the star—and gaining a reputation of a spoiled star. Your agent can't get anything worthy of your talent after the *Danger* contract if you continue this kind of behavior. You avoid the reporters. You're standoffish at gatherings. You've even stopped playing the paparazzi. What's going on?"

Brick thought a moment. What *was* going on with him? Was it really an issue of wanting better roles? Was he tired of the Hollywood game? Or was it how he looked in Bethy's eyes? She'd made it clear she didn't want to be with Brick Connor, the movie star. She had nothing in common with that person. That was why he hadn't called her. He didn't know how to win her over without using the old Brick charm, which was cheap and not worthy of a woman like Bethany.

"Brick?"

"Sorry, Daryl. I don't know what's going on with me. I think I need a vacation."

He heard Daryl's soft but anguished moan and knew his manager must be rubbing his eyebrow to relieve tension. Finally Daryl said, "Okay, you've been working nonstop for several years. We've built a stellar reputation. If you disappear for a month or two, it's not going to hurt us any. Just let me know where you are so I can send more scripts if any of your caliber come through."

The two men hung up, and Brick felt 100 percent better. First, because he liked Daryl, who knew what to say to stroke his ego, and second, because he gave him a great idea. He swirled what was left of the ice cream into a chocolate-nutter pudding and placed a dollop on his tongue. The cool, sweet dessert had changed its purpose. No longer comfort food, it was now something with which to celebrate.

He waved his spoon in the air as if directing an unseen orchestra. "I shall disappear."

∽

Bethany entered the gift shop, seeking out the air conditioning. The last of the tourists had left, and she craved not only a blast of cool air but also Cleo's brand of wacky humor.

However, when she stepped inside, she stopped before making her presence known. Cleo stood at the register counting the dollar bills slowly. The faraway look on her freckled face made her look like the subject of a Norman Rockwell painting.

Bethany stood watching her little friend for a full minute as Cleo counted the change. *Plink. . . Plink. . . Plink. . .* When she finally finished the quarters, Bethany moved toward her.

"Hey, girlfriend, what's up?"

Cleo leisurely looked up from her counting. A slow grin spread across her face. "I'm pregnant."

Chapter 14

I'm so happy," Judy told Bethany after the auditions. "Since you've played the part of Rosalind twice before, I wouldn't trust it with anyone else." The director of *As You Like It* stuck a pencil in her hastily banded ponytail, apparently forgetting the two she already had in there.

It thrilled Bethany to be in the community auditorium again.

⌒

The next morning, Bethany woke refreshed. She opened her window and drew in a big breath. It had rained in the night, and the air smelled crisp, reminding her that autumn would soon paint the leaves yellow on the tree outside her window.

She reached for her robe that lay in her chair. Willy, who had curled up on it, glowered at her with one eye, the other buried somewhere beneath a furry paw. Bethany scooped her up and draped the limp body over her shoulder like a silk scarf. Willy protested weakly as Bethany began to dance around the room, pulling clothes from her closet.

After she had showered and dressed, she found Willy in a much better mood. "Hungry?"

Willy's tail shot up and crooked on the end like a staff. With a flurry, Willy beat Bethany to the stairs and noiselessly maneuvered them. Bethany followed, rapping each wooden step with her sandaled feet.

She'd heard the teakettle whistle while still upstairs and knew her father had already started breakfast.

Willy reached the kitchen first but stopped abruptly, raised her middle, and turned to flee the way she had come. When the cat collided into her legs, Bethany had to fancy-dance to keep from crushing the black-and-white ball beneath her feet.

"What is wrong with you?"

Bethany extracted the cat from her ankles and carried her into the kitchen. She put the cat down and glanced at the figure sitting at the table, his face hidden behind a newspaper.

"Hey, Dad," she said after opening the refrigerator. "Do you have the orange juice behind that paper?"

"No. And you're about out of milk, too."

That was not her father's voice. She whirled, bumping her head, making the salad dressing bottles dance in the door.

"Hello, Bethy."

Slowly, the newspaper lowered to reveal the source of the voice that made her toes curl. She expected the dark, neatly groomed actor named Brick Connor to meet her gaping stare. However, the man leisurely enjoying the Saturday morning paper had a softer look, as if he'd suspended his workout routine. Tousled light brown hair brushed the top of wire-rimmed glasses that enhanced his—she looked closer—yes, forest green eyes.

When she finally managed to dislodge her heart from her throat, she croaked, "Rick—Bri—Ricky! What are you doing in my house?"

"I invited him." Her father sauntered into the kitchen as if a mega-box office star was not sitting at his table, drinking from his favorite mug, and reading his paper. Glenn held out a bakery box. "Muffin?"

Brick had to steel himself from cracking a grin. Bethany looked so cute flustered. She stood there stammering, "But. . . Wha—I don't. . ."

"Ricky is taking a little vacation while researching a role, so I offered to let him stay in our guesthouse," Glenn explained.

He played his part very well. They had begun to plot on the night of the benefit but hadn't finalized the details. When Brick had his epiphany after talking to Daryl, he called Glenn, who then helped set up this scenario. They both knew the strategy of surprise, throwing the enemy off kilter and then moving in to conquer. He looked at Bethany's pale face. *Oh, she's off kilter, all right.*

"Are you both crazy?" She grabbed her hair with both fists. Little blond tufts stuck out through her fingers, making her look like a rare, tropical bird.

The two men looked at one another and shrugged. Her father poured himself a cup of tea. "The man has to take a vacation somewhere. Why not here?"

"Why not *here*? Why not simply invite the cameras in for a day in the life of an actor?" Her eyes suddenly widened, and she ran to the living room.

Brick picked up his mug and followed her. When he saw her peeking out of the drapes, he almost offered to forget the whole thing. He knew of her paparazzi phobia, but he had covered his tracks well.

"Relax." He flopped onto the sofa, already beginning to feel like Ricky—very comfortable in his girlfriend's house. "As far as Hollywood knows, I'm in Fiji, taking a well-deserved rest before I start my next project."

Bethany withered like a day-old dandelion. She sank into the chair across from him and dropped her head into her hands. "Won't they get suspicious when they can't find you there?"

"I sent my double. You remember Phillip? From the location shoot?"

She looked up and nodded. "Cleo and I couldn't believe the resemblance."

"There's a reason for that, beyond the obvious. Just as I can make myself look like Brick Connor, so can a dozen other men. Phillip is naturally dark, but he has my bone structure. We've fooled a few people over the years."

Bethany looked at him as if he'd lost his mind. She tilted her head slightly, her eyes seeking understanding. Maybe he had lost his mind, but he was a desperate man.

She drew in a breath, as if just now being able to expand her lungs after a basketball hit her in the gut. "You mentioned you were also studying for a role. What kind of role? Are you seeing how far you can go before you drive the heroine insane?"

Humor—good. Maybe he could get away with this. "I'm researching what it would be like to be famous and yet live a normal life, out of the spotlight." He offered a smile that he hoped would be irresistible.

Bethany chewed on the corner of her mouth, and he wasn't sure if she believed him or not. In essence, it was true. Everything an actor did went straight into his toolbox.

The cat he'd frightened that morning daintily picked her way to her owner's lap where she began smacking and washing her face. Apparently Glenn had fed her. Brick reached over and plucked the feline from Bethany's lap. The fur ball purred as if she'd known him all her life.

Bethany's lips turned up slightly as she regarded her pet in his arms. "Traitor."

Ricky gazed deep into Willy's eyes. "This isn't Moose, is it?" The whole thing felt surreal to Bethany. Why was she talking to this man about her cat? She should be throwing him out on his ear.

"No, it's her daughter, Willy."

His rich laugh tickled the inside of her stomach. "Okay, I remember Moose was a nickname for Shamu. If you followed tradition and named her for famous killer whales, I'd say this one is. . ." He thought for a moment, continuing to look deep into Willy's eyes, as if the answer could be seen in there. "No, you didn't." Bethany shot what she hoped was a solid glare. "You named your cat after the whale in the movie *Free Willy*?"

Glenn, who walked in from the kitchen, joined the conversation. "My daughter is nothing if not imaginative."

"Remember that gray kitten she had years ago?" Ricky talked as if she weren't in the room.

"She named him Flipper." Her father's eyes twinkled with mischief. "All the other little girls had kittens named Fluffy and Whiskers." Both men let loose with belly laughs.

Bethany sat up straight. "You two think you're cute, don't you? This will never work."

"Sure it will." Ricky put Willy down. "You may have noticed that my appearance has been altered." He lifted his hands and rotated for a full view. "This is what Ricky O'Connell would have looked like if he hadn't become. . ." He struck a pose that looked more like a 007 shtick than his own character. "Brick Connor—Man of Danger." He wriggled his eyebrows in a swarthy manner.

Bethany let a giggle escape. She pointed to the couch. "Sit down, Dangerous, and let's figure this out."

She allowed herself a closer look. He was far from the dark, handsome star who had escorted her to the benefit three months ago. He now wore sweatpants in the purple and gold colors of the Los Angeles Lakers and a faded T-shirt he had apparently slept in. "What did you do to yourself?"

"I quit working out and drank a few milk shakes."

"A few?" She glanced at his midsection.

"Hey, don't get personal." He patted the offended tummy. "It may not be rock hard anymore, but it's far from looking like a bowl full of jelly." Then he stroked his head, flattening a stubborn cowlick. "Also, I had the hairdresser strip the dark color off and then dye it back. Did you know they don't make a dye for dirty blond? This was as close as I could get."

She found it quite attractive. Gold highlights in soft, longish hair, grown out from the snappy, gelled look of the actor. And the wire glasses were much more stylish than those awful, black plastic ones of his youth. The missing mustache made his clean-shaven face look younger. He was more approachable—*more Ricky*. Maybe it could work. He was, after all, researching an upcoming role. Certainly she could help. Still, her initial reservations clung to her like a pit bull.

"I don't know." There would be no peace if he were found out. Up until a few years ago, people still talked about the accident that took Dee Bellamy's life. She had endured it on the anniversary of her death every year. "Aren't you putting us all in jeopardy? You're sure to be recognized."

"You know," Ricky continued to present his case, "people will only see what they want to see."

"I don't understand."

"Have you ever seen someone you knew in a totally different place than you were used to seeing them, and you couldn't quite place them because they didn't belong there?"

Glenn helped out. "Like the time we saw Mrs. Killinger at Disney World on vacation. At church, we would have recognized her instantly."

"Oh yeah." Bethany nodded. "But in the different surroundings, I couldn't place her." She wrinkled her nose. "It was the first time I'd ever seen her in shorts."

Glenn grunted in agreement from his recliner.

"Yes!" Ricky said. "That's exactly what I'm talking about."

"But you're a big celebrity. One who has been here filming recently. Wouldn't it make sense for them to figure you out?"

He stood, took hold of her hands, and shook them for emphasis. "People see only what they want to see."

She pulled away, self-conscious at his touch.

"Why would Brick Connor be acting like a real person with other real people? Believe me, they will buy the fact that I'm an old friend of the family, just visiting. It makes more sense."

"How can you be so sure?"

"How do you think I got from one coast to another without so much as a whimper in the news?"

"You mean you've done this before?"

"Remember when I followed you around at work? Even you didn't recognize me. I'm an actor. I can play different roles. Give me a pair of sunglasses, cutoff jeans, and a three-day-old beard. You can't tell me from any other working stiff."

She drew her shoulder up to her cheek in an effort to shut out what was beginning to sound like common sense.

"Trust me. At the first sign of a camera, or nosy reporter, I'm out of here." He slid to one knee in front of her and again took her hands in his. "Give me a chance, Bethy. Let me prove to you that I'm still Ricky. And even though that Brick character intruded, Bethany Rae Hamilton and Patrick Richard O'Connell deserve a second chance."

Chapter 15

Why was she taking this chance? Distracted didn't even begin to describe Bethany that day, knowing she was harboring a movie star. Since Ricky's arrival that morning, she feared everyone knew. Every tourist seemed suspicious, as if they all wore press badges under their gaudy shirts. She was even afraid to confide in Cleo for fear someone might overhear. What if the gift shop were bugged?

The next morning, she wished she'd made an effort to give Cleo a heads-up. The quick "We need to talk" while they were putting on their robes didn't hack it. When they filed into the choir loft at the front of the church and turned to face the congregation, her friend choked on her first note at the sight of the altered actor sitting next to Glenn.

During announcements, Cleo leaned toward her and whispered, "Is that who I think it is?" Bethany preoccupied herself with the bulletin to avoid having to look up.

Heat rose from the yoke on her choir robe, and she knew she must be turning several shades of crimson. "He said no one would recognize him." She stole a glance in his direction and found him watching her, with a silly smirk on his face and an impish twinkle in his eye. She looked back down at the bulletin and wrung it like a dishrag.

"What's he doing here?"

The other choir members were all within earshot, so Bethany whispered back, "I can't talk here. Can you come over after church? I need an ally." Then, to their extreme horror, the pastor asked for all the visitors to stand and introduce themselves.

"He wouldn't!" Bethany hissed.

He didn't.

But her father did. "Pastor," he stood and made his announcement, sounding much like his trumpet, "I'd like to introduce an old friend of the family. He's here from California for a few weeks of R & R."

Ricky stood, and Bethany was forced to play a part harder than any in her acting career. As two hundred faces seemed to swivel her way, she forced herself to sit straight and smile as if she were happy to have company from back home.

Pastor Wilkes only made the matter worse. "Welcome. What's your name?"

"My friends call me Ricky."

He glanced at Bethany. She jerked her gaze to the mangled, now unrecognizable, bulletin.

"Well, Ricky," the pastor said, "welcome on behalf of Safe Harbor Community Church."

The service continued, and Cleo tugged on the sleeve of Bethany's robe. "Look at the people, Bethany."

"What?" She forced herself to look up from her lap.

"*Look.* No one recognizes him."

Bethany scanned the congregation. Not one person stared or pointed in the star's direction. Not one seemed flustered while searching out a pen for an autograph. They were all acting normal. She felt her heart begin to slow its patter and the blood subside from her cheeks. Could he have been right? A little alteration and no one knows who he is? She prayed with all her heart that God would place them in a time warp so they could get to know one another again.

How long will it last, Lord?

To her surprise, the answer came quickly. *As long as it takes.*

∽

Standing outside the church and greeting her friends felt like a study in human behavior. Erin, a friend from choir, approached with her husband and two children in tow.

"How nice to have company, Bethany. Did you go to school together?"

A million answers zinged inside her head, all betraying Ricky's identity, her feelings for him, or anything that would reveal her past life. She finally decided on three simple words. "Yes. . .we did."

Ricky came to her rescue. "Bethany and I have known each other a long time. When the opportunity presented itself for me to visit, I jumped at it."

Erin's husband joined the conversation while trying to keep his two-year-old daughter from sticking a lollipop in his hair. "How long will you be with us?"

"I've had a break in my work schedule, so it will probably be several weeks."

"What do you do?"

What an innocent question. Bethany held her breath waiting for the answer.

"I do studio work—pictures."

"Oh, a photographer. Do you do baby pictures? We'd love to have a good one of little Marissa." He tickled the baby's tummy, and she giggled.

"Sorry, I don't have the right equipment here." Ricky held out his hand to the baby, and she wrapped her pudgy fingers around his thumb.

Erin touched her husband's arm. "He's on vacation, dear." She gave Ricky an apologetic smile.

Ricky pulled his now-sticky thumb away from the baby while her father said, "I'm sorry, you said that in church, didn't you?" He put the baby down, and she began to fuss. "Well, it's nap time. Nice to have you with us."

On the way home, Bethany fumed in the front seat of the Blazer while Glenn drove. She twisted around to confront Ricky sitting behind her father.

"A photographer?" Sarcasm dripped from every syllable. "I never would have agreed to this if I'd known you were going to lie to my friends."

Ricky shrugged. "Hey, I didn't lie. I told him exactly what I do for a living. He made an assumption."

"But then you said your equipment wasn't here."

"I said I didn't have the right equipment. That's true, too."

"That's a gray area, and you know it." How had he gotten so far away from God's truth? The teenage Ricky would have known absolutes.

"Would you rather I told everyone the exact truth? In my career, I've learned diplomacy—when to back off and when to be straightforward. I've even learned when to fudge the truth. It's called survival."

Bethany raised her eyes heavenward. "God help us all."

∞

Later, Bethany and Cleo put sandwiches and sodas on a tray and took them to the enclosed patio out back.

"How's your husband?" Ricky asked Cleo. "I never did get to meet him."

"He's overseas again. Due back in January, a month before the baby is born."

"And I thought my career was tough."

"You get used to it. Knowing he's keeping us safe is reward enough, and of course, I pray for him constantly." Cleo's smile lost its sparkle. Bethany knew she missed her husband horribly.

Cleo tilted her chin, resembling a little redheaded bird. "You know, you look smaller somehow. Is that an illusion?"

"Cleo!" Bethany couldn't believe her friend's boldness.

Ricky's hearty laugh made her feel better. "The illusion is the character I play. He's larger than life on the big screen. So when I show up as Brick Connor, they see me as this six-foot action figure. But when I become just another ordinary guy, I'm not as imposing."

"That makes sense."

"I've got this changing-roles-back-and-forth thing down to a science." He winked at Bethany and took a bite of his sandwich. "Mmm. You know, I haven't had egg salad in years. You make it just like your mom."

Bethany felt a sting of a tear. Ever since Ricky showed up at work several months ago, he brought with him all the memories she had pushed down deep. She thought she had conquered her grief, but his presence peeled off a bandage to expose the wound that had never quite healed.

"Do you remember when we had that party at your house?" Ricky asked.

"The one the football team crashed?"

"Yeah!"

Glenn looked at Cleo. "We had dozens of parties at our house. It's eerie that they know exactly which one."

"You see," Ricky said to Cleo, "we had the entire cast and crew of *The Music Man* at Bethy's house."

Bethany's cheeks warmed. Did he have to call her that in public? Cleo raised an eyebrow. The endearment had not slipped by her.

"We had completed the last performance," Ricky continued. "Most of us were still in makeup, and I was wearing the striped jacket."

Bethany got into the spirit and continued the tale. "We were deep into our chips and sodas, watching the home video my dad made. We were laughing at ourselves and acting silly, remembering when we flubbed and what was happening backstage, when the doorbell rang. In walked the roughest jocks you've ever seen, expecting to make fun of us and walk out with all of our snacks."

Cleo looked at Glenn. "Where were you?"

"We had discreetly removed ourselves to the back of the house. At their age they didn't need us hovering." He popped a potato chip into his mouth and crunched.

Ricky took up the story. "At that moment, on the tape, we were singing 'Ya Got Trouble,' and as if on cue, we all turned to the jocks—and started singing it to them." He wiped a tear, barely able to contain himself. "Now understand, at school, we would cringe when these guys walked by, but at Bethy's house, we were in our element. We started singing and dancing around them."

At that point, the two began to dance around the patio, lifting their hands to the ceiling. Ricky never missed a consonant as he sang about trouble with a capital *T*.

Cleo giggled while protectively holding her extended tummy. "I think I know how those poor guys felt."

Bethany flopped onto the wicker couch, her energy spent. "You should have seen their faces. We wouldn't let them go. We just dragged them into our world, and before long, they were doing that cadence where the townspeople all chant 'trouble.' They were actually enjoying themselves." She slapped Ricky on the arm. "They stayed for the whole party. One of them even went out for more snacks. It was a riot!"

"The halls at school were much friendlier after that," Ricky said. "They nicknamed me Harold and would chant 'trouble' whenever they saw me."

When they were able to get their breath, Ricky said to Cleo, "You know, I'm glad you're in on our secret. I think having backup will settle Bethy's mind."

"I won't blow your cover." She briefly glanced at Bethany. "In fact, I'll pray for you while you're here incognito. God may have a plan for you in all of this subterfuge."

Bethany said a silent prayer herself. *Please, Lord, bring back the prodigal.*

"Thank you, Cleo," Ricky said. "It's appreciated more than you know."

That evening, long after Cleo had left, Ricky and Bethany continued to reminisce. She had gotten out her box of high school memories, minus the candy box with the ring. They rummaged through them as if the box were a treasure chest full of rare and precious jewels.

"I can't believe you still have that." He held up a small stuffed toy he had won for her in one of those claw machines at the mall. "It cost me five dollars to win that for you."

"And it's only worth a quarter." She smiled at the little blue dolphin, whose left eye hung precariously. She never expected the cheap toy to last more than a few years, but it had found a loving home in her memory box.

The two sat on the floor, where they had room to toss contents as they looked at them. When he noticed the high school annual from their senior year, he moved to the couch and turned on the lamp next to it. Bethany followed him to look over his shoulder.

After adjusting his glasses, he turned the pages tenderly. "I haven't thought of these people in years." Bethany let him get lost in the past. After a while he said, "You know, sometimes I wish we were back there again."

"What do you mean? Would you live those years with your father over again?"

He winced, and she saw him rub the scar on his chin. She wished she hadn't brought up that part of his past. "No, but the time I spent at your house to get away from him is something I'll always cling to in my memories. I have never felt more love than in your home."

Bethany pulled her legs to her chin and hugged them. "My mom had that gift."

He turned to look at her. "It wasn't just your mom." Appearing to weigh his next words, he placed his arm behind her on the couch but never touched her. His spicy scent swirled around Bethany, and her heart started beating a familiar rhythm. After a moment, Ricky said, "I have never felt the kind of love we had."

Ricky searched Bethany's face. Did she understand? Two transparent emerald pools gazed back at him, at first placid but then whirling as her apparent emotions registered what he had just said.

She looked away quickly. "But that was kid stuff. We didn't know anything about love."

He felt a knot in his gut the size of a fist. Surely she wasn't telling him those years together meant nothing. He ventured a touch, just light fingers on her opposite shoulder. He saw her tense but was encouraged when she didn't pull away. She closed her eyes and swallowed; then he felt the tremble. Ah, that was what he wanted. Some indication that she still felt something for him. He pulled his arm back into his own territory and started turning pages again.

Out of the corner of his eye, he saw her squirm and shove her hands under her thighs.

"Ricky. How do you feel about God now?"

Bethany gauged his reaction. How far had he gotten from the Word? Would he be angry? Would he lash out? If they had any future at all, she had to know where his heart was.

He looked at her with pain in his eyes. "I'm so unworthy. How could He love someone like me?"

Was this Brick Connor, who captured a room with his presence? Who commanded every conversation and seemed so self-assured that his very demeanor demanded respect? No, this was Ricky O'Connell, troubled by a turbulent childhood, guilty over the sins of his father. Still doubting, even though he had asked God into his heart years ago, that someone could love him unconditionally.

A trilling Gershwin tune broke the spiritual moment. Ricky grabbed the persistent cell phone from the side table next to the couch. After a quick glance at the caller ID, he said, "I'm sorry; I have to take it. I've been waiting all weekend for this call."

She began to lift herself off the couch to give him some privacy, but he motioned for her to stay. After a moment of listening to the one-sided argument, she deduced it to be business.

He stood and began pacing. "No. . .tell him to keep searching, okay? No. . .I don't want to play another spy. Get me out of this typecast, will you? . . . I don't know, maybe a bad-guy role this time. How about the dredge of society, somebody they'll love to hate? Or maybe a recovering alcoholic, something with meat?" Bethany saw him tense and knew the conversation had taken a turn for the worse. "No, I can't do that. . . . I don't care what you promised. . . . You have my timetable. Work around it." He took a deep breath. "Look, just send me what you've got, and I'll look at them. But I'm not making any promises. . . . Yeah, the address I gave you. . . I'll let you know when I'm back. . . . Thanks, you're a good man. . . . Hug that wife for me. . . . Bye."

He flipped the tiny phone shut and turned to Bethany. "My manager."

"I guessed that."

"He's sending me some scripts from my agent to look through. Don't worry." He must have seen on her face the slight alarm that she felt. "He'll send it to Phillip, who will forward it here. He also wanted me to fly back for a promotional thing. Just a quickie, then I could fly back."

"Does he think you're in Fiji?" She lifted a brow.

He cleared his throat and shuffled his feet. "Well, yeah. He thought I'd be partying with my rowdy friends. . .or with a girl."

"You are with a girl," she teased, knowing exactly what he meant.

He sat back down. "Well, Daryl isn't one for propriety. He'll call anytime, day or night."

"Sundays, as well, I assume." She sat with one leg pulled under and tapped the knee of the leg touching the floor.

"Daryl never rests. Irene calls him the workaholic from. . ." He looked away. "Anyhow, he's good at what he does. He's been working this promotional deal for weeks, but I don't want to do it."

"Why not?" She looked at his altered appearance, wondering if it would be hard to change back.

"I would have to cut my vacation short. Let's just say. . ." He sat up straight, removed his glasses, and allowed Brick to say his next words. "I don't want to leave Fiji just yet."

Chapter 16

B*ethany.*"

"*Mom?*"

"*Bethany honey, time for school. 'This is the day the Lord has made; let us rejoice and be glad in it.'*"

Bethany awoke with a start, searching her room for her mother. It had been years since she'd had these dreams.

After a night of intermittent sleep, she managed to drag herself through another day of work. She was grateful that her last therapy session was with Emily, an eight-year-old child with Down syndrome. She loved Emily, who was no stranger to the routine. After several sessions with Cocoa, she had improved her motor skills and begun to talk more intelligibly.

Emily entered the Encounter building with her mother and ran up to Sheila, wrapping her chubby arms around her waist. "Hi, She-ah." She waved to Bethany, who waited for her by the pool. "Hi, Befany."

"Hi, Emily." Bethany waved her over. "Are you ready to go swimming?"

Emily clapped her hands and began a singsong, "Co-coa... Co-coa... Co-coa."

Emily's mother was a large woman whose belly laugh could be heard over the barking seals. "That means yes."

Bethany recalled the first time they saw this overzealous child, over a month ago. It took effort to keep her on the step and not allow her to plunge in with the dolphin. Over time, Emily realized she wouldn't really be *swimming* with Cocoa. She'd made much progress, and if things went well today, it would probably be her last session, to Bethany's regret.

Sheila spoke to the child as they sat together in the pool. "Say my name, Emily."

When Emily could say Sheila's name correctly, she was allowed to give Cocoa a command. She placed two fingers to her lips, and the dolphin bobbed out of the water to give her a kiss. Then Sheila asked her to say her own name, Emily, since it was the letter *L* that she had such a hard time with. Both therapist and trainer encouraged the little girl with laughter. It seemed more like party time than work.

After several exercises with blended sounds, such as *three, think,* and *bath,* Bethany called out from the middle of the pool. "Say *my* name, Emily." Emily had been taught that if she could say the *th* sound, Cocoa would pull Bethany around the pool. At the end, Cocoa would wave her fluke.

Emily screwed her plump face until it looked like a raisin, put her lips

335

together for the beginning of the name, and let it fly. "Beh-THA-ny!"

"Who-oo!" Bethany signaled Cocoa to slip under her arm, and the two swished around the pool. She gave Emily an extra treat by letting go early and *telling* Cocoa to do a flip.

"Co-coa. . .Beh-thany. . .Co-coa. . .Beh-thany. . ."

When the session ended, Sheila determined this would indeed be Emily's last one. Bethany knelt to be eye level with the wet moppet, who had mummified herself in a large beach towel. "Come visit me, okay?" She looked up at Emily's mother. "Seriously, anytime you're here, have someone find me if you don't see me right away. I don't know what I'd do if I missed a hug from this big girl." Her reward was a fierce squeeze around her neck.

By the time Bethany returned home that evening, she was tired enough to go to bed without supper but found she'd rather put off falling asleep. Would these recurring dreams of her mother prompt the one about the hissing snakes, striking at her with flashes of light outside her door in California?

She found Ricky on the computer in the little office. The sight of him helped jump-start her energy. She wondered fleetingly if she could keep him there indefinitely and turn him into a househusband.

As if he knew her thoughts, he greeted her, "Hi, honey, how was your day? Supper will be ready in a jiffy. We're grilling tonight."

She flopped into the overstuffed armchair by the desk and teased, "You need to get out more. Is this what you do all day? Or do you spend some of your time watching soap operas?"

"Nah, when they turned me down for a role on *The Dead and the Listless*, it soured me on them." He continued to click the keyboard. "Did you know that there are at least ten Web sites dedicated to my career?" He began naming them off on his fingers. "There's the Brick Connor Official Web Site, the Brick Connor—Man of Danger Web Site, the I Love Brick Connor Web Site, the Hey, Brick, Be Dangerous with Me Web Site. . . ."

"Enough! So you're popular. Didn't you know that?"

"Well, yeah, but I never thought I was an obsession. I talked to some of these people today."

Bethany's eyes popped wide open. "How?"

"In a chat room. They didn't know it was me, so they talked normal, not stuttering and flustered like I'm used to."

She shook her head. "I don't believe this."

"It was cool. I used the name Danger Disciple, and I found out all kinds of things."

"I'm afraid to ask."

"For instance, some of them like Agent Danger's hair better in the first movie than the second. One guy told me he thought the gadgets my character used were more realistic than most spy shows, but he liked James Bond's cars better."

"Well, there's no beating the Aston Martin." She smiled at his enthusiasm.

"I agree there. You know, I've been upset over the thin plot in the last two movies. And there's little hope for the rest. Everyone in the chat room agreed with me."

Bethany scooted to the edge of the chair. "Are you trying to cause an uprising? Don't you want people to go see your movies?"

"Of course; that's the point. They'll stop if things don't change." He took off his glasses and rubbed his eyes. Bethany wondered how long he'd been sitting there. "Don't you see? If I complain, I look like a spoiled prima donna. But if the fans rebel or, as you put it, start an uprising, maybe someone will listen." He sat back in the swivel desk chair and chuckled. "I gave them an address to voice their concerns."

He sat there a moment, absently looking at the monitor with his knee bouncing slightly. Something was on his mind.

"Bethy, how long do you intend to be a dolphin trainer? Have you ever considered coming home and starting your own career in show business?"

"How long do I intend to be a dolphin trainer?" She repeated through closed teeth.

Uh-oh. He must have hit a nerve.

"You say that as if it were nothing more than an after-school job. My father has made a very good living at it, you know."

"And your mother was a very good actress. You have her genes, too. Why are you wasting your talents here?"

"Wasting my talents? Just today, a beautiful little girl hugged my neck and said my name, *clearly*, for the first time. That's what I do, Ricky. That's where I make a difference."

"Did you do it, or did the therapist do it? Who made the difference?" He wasn't trying to be argumentative, but with Bethany's unique gift, he couldn't understand why she chose this line of work. There were hundreds in the entertainment field who didn't have half her talent.

"Without me, Sheila couldn't do her job. I'm the reason Emily wants to try harder."

"Come on, any trainer could do what you do. But only Bethany Hamilton can follow in her mother's footsteps. Come back with me and take up where your mom left off."

She pushed herself deeper into the chair. Her eyes had suddenly turned wild, as if a pack of dogs were nipping at her heels. "I. . .can't."

"Or maybe you won't." Now was the time to say what had been on his mind since first arriving in Florida. "Maybe you prefer to continue what you're doing as an excuse to live at home, under your father's wing."

She closed her eyes and balled a tuft of hair in her fist. *That's it, isn't it, Bethy? You're hiding behind your father.*

He spoke to her in what he hoped was a comforting tone. "Bethy, look at me." When she did, he continued. "At the risk of playing an armchair therapist, consider this. Because of your mom's sudden death, you've developed a dependence on the one parent remaining. If you hadn't moved to Florida, I might have been able to take up that slack and help you move on with your life." At least, that's what he'd hoped. They would have married, and he would have protected her for the rest of her life. It wasn't too late for that. He just had to convince her.

Bethany slowly uncurled her body in the chair. She placed her hands on the arms and said, "So, you've made yourself my savior. Where were you those ten years? It was God who kept me sane during that awful time. He was the One who spoke to me when you wouldn't call. He was the One who held me when I heard you were having yet another fling. What happened to you, Ricky? I know you accepted Christ—I was there. Or was that just more playacting? Before telling me what I should do with my life, maybe you should look deep inside yourself. There's a big, black void in there, and only God's love can fill it."

She stood up and walked toward the door. "You said we were grilling. I'll make the salad."

He turned his back to her but nodded. When he knew she had left, he took off his glasses and rubbed his burning eyes.

❦

Bethany ran warm water over the dishrag. Her thoughts turned to the argument before supper. Why was he pushing her? Would he risk demeaning her chosen profession just to get her to move back home? *Home.* She pitched the rag at the kitchen table. That was his word, not hers. California was no longer home. *I belong here, with Dad.* That thought drew her up short. Could Ricky be right? Was she clinging to her father?

She heard the telephone ring once and knew Glenn had picked it up right away. Must have been someone he knew on the caller ID.

Ricky walked into the kitchen as she began to wipe the table. He opened the dishwasher and asked, "Can I help?"

She barely glanced at him. "Our arrangement was when you cook, I clean. Weren't you going to play chess with Daddy?"

He placed a dish in the machine and proceeded to rinse another. "He just got a phone call. I think it's his lady friend. They'll probably talk all night."

Bethany's stomach knotted. *Amanda.*

Ricky continued. "I want to apologize for my earlier remark." He placed the last glass in the dishwasher, poured soap in the special container on the door, and locked it up tight.

When the machine started humming and swishing, Bethany said, "Let's take a walk, get away from this noisy thing."

A balmy breeze blew from the Gulf, and Bethany could smell the salt in the air. Although the sun had gone down some time ago, the temperature was still a comfortable seventy-five degrees. She glanced at Ricky and asked, "You up for ice cream?"

"Sure." He patted his belly. "Don't have to worry about carbs right now."

They headed for the center of town, strategically placed by the developers of Seaside to be within walking distance of the entire community. At the ice cream shop, they ordered a couple of sundaes and then sat outside at a small table. No other patrons were near, so the setting felt intimate.

Ricky swirled the chocolate sauce with his spoon, but before he ate a bite, he said, "I'm sorry. I had no right telling you what to do."

Bethany spooned a small bite into her mouth, the sweet strawberry coolness soothing her ego as much as Ricky's words just now. She had feared her words had been a bit harsh, too, and was grateful for his forgiving nature toward her. "I'd like a second opinion on your diagnosis of my psyche." She offered a tiny grin as a truce offering. "But I do accept your apology, if you'll accept mine."

"Bethy, not everyone is as committed to God as you and your father. I admit, I had a wild side shortly after fame hit, but I've settled down quite a bit."

"Yes, you have. Christianity is a process, and we don't all mature at the same levels. All I ask is that you seek God concerning your career and personal life."

Ricky poked at his sundae. "I have a lot of junk to sort out. I guess I've kept it on the back burner, not wanting to deal with it. Maybe I'm still not ready to deal with it."

"God cares, Ricky. Let Him help you."

When she noticed his jaw clench, she sensed she'd pushed too far and changed the subject. "Since you're playing the role of psychiatrist, how's this? For the last four nights, I've dreamed of my mom. What do you make of that, doctor?"

Apparently he accepted the change of mood, and Bethany marveled at his ability to take on a new role. He pulled his glasses to the tip of his nose and looked over them at her. With a bad Austrian accent, he said, "Vell, vhat ve have here iss a transference of brain waves calling up memories—pictures, if you vill—brought on by an outside influence, causing an automatic response that stimulates said pictures, thereby playing them during REM, vhich is a time vhen the brain is vulnerable to unvanted stimuli." She must have given him a vacant look, because he translated. "I am causing your dreams." He pushed his glasses back up his nose and took another bite of ice cream.

"Huh?"

"It's simple, really. You associate your youth with me, and your mom was part of your youth."

"But why didn't I have these dreams when you were here filming?" She glanced around to be sure they couldn't be heard.

"Because I wasn't Ricky."

That made sense. Brick Connor wouldn't kick off old memories, because he'd never been in her life before. And now, here was Ricky, talking about the old days. She hoped by solving the mystery that it would stop the dreams.

They finished their ice cream and set out for home.

Chapter 17

I hate to leave you home alone tonight. You've only been here a few days, and already I'm deserting you." Bethany grabbed her bag and slung it over her shoulder. She had talked to her guest for too long that morning and found herself running late for work.

Ricky looked up from the toast he was buttering. "Don't worry about it. I know how important choir practice is. Maybe I'll take your advice and get myself out of the house."

She clutched the keys in her hand, wincing at the sharp pain when they dug into her palm. "I was only kidding, you know. There's no use in calling attention to yourself. Maybe I should come straight home. They can do without me for a few practices."

Ricky stood up and escorted her to the door. "I'll be careful. Didn't I prove myself Sunday? Where's your faith?" He kissed her head and shoved her out of the house.

As she stood on the front porch staring at the now closed door, she swallowed hard. Where *was* her faith? Why did she have to second guess everything? Hadn't God already given her peace about allowing Ricky back into her life? She knew He had a plan, but she sure wished He'd let her in on it.

That evening, when she and Cleo walked into the sanctuary, she wondered again about what God might be doing to her when she saw Ricky there—sitting in the choir loft, with a folder of his own!

Gladys, the choir director, was all smiles. "Bethany! You didn't tell me you were hiding this treasure."

Bethany felt the color drain from her face and feared Cleo might have to catch her.

Gladys continued to gush. "Ricky sang a few bars for us just before you came in. He wasn't sure what part he sang." She turned back to Ricky. "You have a beautiful baritone voice. Very polished. Where did you train?"

Ricky's eyes sparkled as he said, "I haven't had any formal training except for high school. Bethany and I were in choir together there."

"Well, you have natural talent then." Gladys pointed to the seat next to Ricky. "Bethany, you can sit next to your friend and show him the ropes. Bass and altos in back, tenors and sopranos in front."

First the surprise appearance in her kitchen, and now this. She leaned toward him and whispered, "You've got to stop. You're going to affect my heart."

He turned, his lips an inch from her ear. "That's what I'm trying to do."

∞

When rehearsals started two days later for *As You Like It*, Ricky knew he was making progress when Bethany invited him along. She stood there, with her hands on her hips, so cute he had to restrain himself from picking her up and swinging her around the living room. "I can't take any more surprises. You've convinced me you can stay incognito. But. . ." She pointed her finger and wagged it in his direction. "You're going to have to promise to be good and just hang out. You are not to be a part of this production. Someone will see through you for sure."

"I promise."

Ricky tried to make good his oath, but when the set director needed an extra pair of hands to build the forest, he couldn't just sit there. Soon he hammered and painted with gusto.

By the second week, the sets were beginning to shape up, and the actors had shed their scripts.

"Where's Jared?" Judy asked the company. They all looked at one another and shrugged. "I wanted to run through Act 3, Scene 2, but I guess we can skip the verses where Orlando places love poems on the trees and begin where Corin and Touchstone enter."

As the two men positioned themselves onstage, a woman ran in from the back of the auditorium. "Bad news, y'all. Jared broke his leg."

Over the gasps, Judy's strangled voice asked, "What about his understudy?"

"Stan was with him. They were on a Jet Ski, and it crashed. Stan broke his collarbone."

Judy clutched the glasses hanging on a chain around her neck and dramatically sank into a theater chair. "What are we going to do? We can't cast someone at such late notice."

Ricky hopped off the stage, where he had been fixing a tottering tree. He walked past Bethany without looking at her and cleared his throat.

Bethany watched Ricky stride past her as if in a dream. By the set of his jaw and the determination in his eyes, she knew what he was about to do.

"Ahem. . ."

No!

"I played Orlando in high school. After watching the rehearsal, most of it has come back to me."

Whispers ranged from inaudible white noise to "But does he have talent?"

"We have no choice." Judy clutched her notebook and started patting her pockets. The assistant director reached over and plucked a pencil from the director's ponytail.

Heaven, help me. Bethany should have tied him to the table at home. She should have hobbled his ankles like they do horses. She should have thrown him out of her house weeks ago, but she never had the strength. Truth be told, she liked having him there.

"Bethany." Judy chewed on the pencil. "What do you think?"

"S–sure. He was good in school. And like you said, what choice do we have?"

"Great! Ricky, are you ready, or would you rather take some time to study while we rehearse another?"

"Oh, I feel comfortable, as long as I can use the script my first few times out."

"Okay, here's the scene, and here are your props. I assume you know what to do with them."

He smiled like a schoolboy given an important assignment. He then launched into Act 3, Scene 2, and became Orlando, mewling his lovesickness for the fair Rosalind and placing poems on the trees he had just set up. "Hang there, my verse, in witness of my love."

∽

"Lord, what are You doing to me?"

As Bethany waited by the indoor interaction pool for her customer, she watched Cocoa move effortlessly through the water. So calm, so serene. Watching the glistening animal suspended in her world, floating without a care, brought Bethany's stress level down considerably.

She prayed that Jared and Stan would heal quickly. However, last night's shock wasn't so much about their accident as more about Ricky.

Lord, please don't let his cover be blown before I've had a chance to talk more about You. She realized her little tirade of the other night was not real witnessing, but rather a dodge to get out from under Ricky's uncomfortable microscope. Yes, he needed to search his heart, but she needed to be more sensitive.

She found herself thanking God for her many blessings, including the second chance He'd given her with Ricky. She closed her eyes and prayed for wisdom. *Lord, please don't let my quick temper and loose tongue destroy what it's taken You ten years to build.*

"Now, that's a beautiful picture."

She nearly fell into the pool when she started at the familiar voice. "You're doing it again! Why are you here?"

He looked at his watch. "I have an appointment."

"*You* booked the encounter? Why didn't you tell me?"

Ricky laughed. "I like seeing you rattled. It fluffs my ego."

"Your ego doesn't need fluffing."

She led him to the wet suits and showed him where to change. When he came out, she stole a glance at his muscled torso. If this was his idea of letting himself go, she wondered what he thought peak condition might be.

Normally there would be a small audience to watch the encounter, family members or others simply curious about the training process. Today, however, they had the building to themselves, and she found herself thankful for her own wet suit. It discreetly covered her in all the right places and made her feel better about any impropriety. They weren't teenagers in the backyard pool anymore.

They sat on the step under the water, and a toothy grin surfaced before them. "Ricky O'Connell, meet Cocoa."

He placed his palm on the surface of the water and Cocoa swam under it for a pat. "Pleased to meet you, Cocoa."

Bethany cocked her head. "Looks like you still remember what I taught you back home."

"Like riding a bicycle. I remember how my friends were so jealous that not only did I have the most beautiful girl in Hollywood High, but we also played with dolphins together."

Were they this close when they first sat down? She didn't think so. Now their legs touched under the water, and Ricky's face was inches from hers. She knew she should move, but her heart anchored her firmly in place.

He reached up with a wet hand to touch her hair, using the same gentleness he had exhibited with Cocoa. "I love your hair like this. You've grown into an extraordinarily beautiful woman."

He cupped her cheek, the heat of his touch contrasted with the cool rivulets of moisture dripping down her throat.

Her heart beat so violently that she felt sure it would start a tidal wave in the tiny pool. She closed her eyes when his lips were less than an inch from hers. Instantly she was transported to another time, a similar situation. She was in that backyard pool with the boy who had become her best friend, the boy who gave her her first kiss.

His lips were as she remembered them, soft, sensitive—his breath warm and sweet.

"Miss Befany?"

With a splash, the couple pushed away from each other. Emily's mother stood near the pool in stunned silence holding the little girl's hand. Bethany felt her face sizzle with the water that had followed her hand.

Emily's mom stammered her apologies. "I–I'm so sorry. I shouldn't have let her burst in on you like that—but we were visiting, and Emily wanted to see you." She pointed weakly toward where they had just come. "They told us you were in here."

"It's okay." Bethany tried to recover. "We were having an interaction—that is—um—this was an encounter—I mean. . ." She took a deep breath and tried again. "How are you, Emily? I've missed you."

Bethany sloshed out of the pool and grabbed a towel. She knelt for a hug from the child.

Over Emily's shoulder, she saw Simon standing at the entrance. Had he escorted the two in? What had he seen? She swallowed hard and tried to force the blush from her cheeks.

"Bethany, when you're through, may I see you in my office?"

Strike two.

Chapter 18

The answer is *no*. Look, I don't want to be difficult, but is there any way we can rework the dates?" Brick squeezed the cell phone as if it were the neck of the person on the other end of the conversation.

Daryl's strained voice sounded tinny with the weak connection. "I'll see what I can do, but this is a great opportunity to improve your image and promote the movie."

Brick caught a glance of himself in the mirror as he paced in front of the bathroom door. This image was not what the public wanted. And what did he want? Was he ready to put on the cloak of superstardom again and resume his career? He answered his own question when his pacing propelled him toward the bay window in the small guesthouse.

Bethy. She had decided to work in the garden after church. There she knelt, creating a portrait, framed by the white, wooden French doors leading to her father's office. Her feather-soft hair blowing ever so slightly, she looked like a dove resting near the azalea bush. He watched as she tenderly worked a yellow mum out of its container. With whimsy, he imagined himself as that mum. Little by little, she had been working him out of his tight container, the restraint of his past. But was he ready to be planted, allow his roots to take hold of something solid—Bethy's faith, for instance?

Daryl's voice drew him back: ". . .getting impatient. I don't know how much longer I can hold them off."

"Hey, if we miss this opportunity, it's no sweat. It's just a commercial."

"Just a commercial? This is *the* commercial. No one else can do this but you. This company gave you your start. A cameo of the now-famous Brick Connor would not only be good for you, but for the men's cologne and the movie. It's promotion all the way around."

Bethany must have noticed his movement in the window. She looked up at him, her genuine smile causing a sensation akin to a warm, healing oil that saturated his heart, a balm to his hurting soul. When he would come home from school to find his father waiting for him, he would remember that smile and couldn't wait to get back to its warmth.

"Daryl, just do what you can, okay? I plan to stay away for at least another month."

∞

After a week of rehearsals, all the players began to feel comfortable with one another. Ricky considered them family. The pastor named Gary looked the part of Jaques to the point of being comical. His basset hound eyes and jowls made him perfect for the morose lord of the banished Duke Senior.

"Gary," Judy called to him. "Have you memorized your speech?"

"Yes, ma'am," he drawled.

Judy called for all those in Act 2, Scene 7 to come forward. The scene progressed to verse 140, where Jaques took center stage. His droopy eyes drew heavenward as he began the famous speech.

" 'All the world's a stage, and all the men and women merely players: They have their exits and their entrances; and one man in his time plays many parts. . . .' "

He went on to describe the seven ages of man: The infant in the nurse's arms. The whining school-boy with his satchel, creeping unwillingly to school. Then the lover, sighing like a furnace. A soldier, full of strange oaths; then the justice, in fair round belly, full of wise saws and modern instances. The sixth age led into the lean and slipper'd pantaloon, an old man, with spectacles on his nose and his big manly voice turning again to childish treble.

Jaques wandered to stage left, scratched his head, and finished the speech. " 'Last Scene of all, that ends this strange eventful history, is second childishness and mere oblivion, sans teeth, sans eyes, sans taste," with a sweep of his hands, palm upward, he finished, " 'sans every thing.' "

Gary slowly sat down on a fake rock, leaving the rest of the company thinking about his words.

Later, after the troupe was dismissed, Brick heard someone say to Gary, "Good night, Pastor. See you in church."

Pastor?

Bethany had stopped to ask Judy a lengthy question. Brick took the opportunity to talk to Gary.

"You know, as many times as I've heard that speech, it still affects me. It makes me wonder, is that all there is? Do we just go through this life and end up *sans every thing?*"

"Well, Ricky." Gary's jowls flapped a little, even in his seriousness. "I often wonder how people handle life without God. I suppose that's the way they see it. But me, I know there is much more; in fact, it's just the beginning. I may end life sans teeth, eyes, and taste, but when my body gives up, my spirit will soar to heaven, and straight into Jesus' arms." Gary closed one droopy eye in a half wink and bore into the younger man with the other. "Do you believe that, son?"

Ricky smiled. Vince would have said the very same thing. He reflected a moment. Did he believe it? He searched his heart as Bethany had suggested. She and her family believed it, and he wanted to because that would mean her mom was in heaven. But if that were the case, where was his father? He felt a chill grip his spine. And if he had prayed the man to his grave, would he suffer the same fate?

Gary waited for an answer. Ricky shoved his hands into his pockets and shrugged. "I'm not sure I'm ready to believe it."

"What's stopping you?"

Dare he go into his past? Sure, he'd prayed a salvation prayer when he was a kid. But should he confess that he continued to have trouble relating to a loving God who would allow a child to be abused? And yet, the Hamiltons took him in and loved him unconditionally. Did God prompt them to do that? Did He care enough to put Bethany in his life?

In answer to Gary's question, Ricky cleared the lump in his throat. "I guess the jury is still out. I have some—issues—to deal with first." He rubbed the scar on his chin.

Gary smiled, which didn't improve his naturally sorrowful look at all. "That's what God is for, son, to deal with those issues for you."

Bethany skipped up to the two men and announced, "I'm ready."

Ricky grabbed the door handle. *But am I?*

Chapter 19

Had he heard correctly? *Surely not.* Ricky went in search of Bethany to ask if it were true. He found her pouring a bag of chocolate sandwich cookies onto a platter in the fellowship hall. The service that Sunday had been moving, but he confessed to himself that singing with Bethy in the choir touched him more than the sermon.

He waited impatiently for her to finish a conversation with a fellow choir member. The woman said, "Bethany, how domestic of you. Did you make those yourself?"

Bethany played right to the gathering crowd. "Why, of course. The trick is to not let the frosting in the middle melt."

When the hoots of laughter died down, Ricky leaned in and said, "I have to clear something up." She looked at him with a curious angle to her brows. He spoke barely above a whisper. "What's a mullet festival?"

Her mouth sprang open in surprise, and an errant giggle escaped her throat. "You're kidding, right?"

"Why would I kid about that? People keep asking if I'm *fixin'* to go, and I don't want everyone to think I'm dumb. Why would they have a festival to celebrate a hairstyle?"

This time, her giggle turned into an outright guffaw. He felt heat rise up his neck as she pulled him to a corner of the large room for more privacy. "It's not mullet as in *short in front, long in back*, silly. It's mullet as in the fish."

"Oh, that makes more sense." He sat on one of the long tables not currently in use. "I kept envisioning a large roomful of bad haircuts."

Bethany leaned her hip against the table he sat on. "They're talking about the annual Boggy Bayou Mullet Festival. It's held in Niceville—"

"Now you're kidding. There's really a place called Niceville?"

"Yes. Niceville, Florida. It's across the bay, a beautiful little town that hosts the festival every year. Mostly craft booths and good eating, but there's also entertainment—local and well-known. Dad's playing there next Sunday with the swing band. Want to go?"

"Sure. Do I have to grow my hair long in back?" He shook his sandy tresses, and she slapped him playfully.

"Okay, you two, am I going to have to break you up?" Cleo closed in on the couple.

Ricky smiled. He knew why Bethany liked Cleo so much now that he'd gotten to know her. He glanced toward her swelling belly and remembered hearing she was five months along. "Hello, Little Mama. How are you feeling?"

Cleo blushed, turning her freckles into tiny pink dots. "Just waiting for the morning sickness everyone insists I should have. It was supposed to hit in the first trimester, so maybe I dodged that bullet. How are rehearsals going?" Then with a conspiratorial whisper, she asked, "No one's seen through the disguise, have they?"

Ricky lowered his voice, as well. "If they had, do you think I'd be sitting here enjoying *homemade* sandwich cookies?"

∞

The week progressed uneventfully, much to Bethany's relief. While she enjoyed Ricky's presence, she still found herself constantly looking over her shoulder. Things were going much too perfectly.

The couple had asked Cleo to attend the festival with them.

"You sure I won't be intruding?" She gave Bethany a look that clearly translated *Give me the sign, and I'll back off.*

Bethany assured her that her presence was more than welcome, and she smiled when Ricky affirmed her stance.

They arrived at the festival, and Cleo asked, "Are we going to see your dad around? When's his group scheduled?"

"They play at five thirty, just before the main act."

"Who's the main act?" Ricky asked.

"I'm not sure. Some country-and-western band. I guess they're pretty popular, but I'm not into country."

Both Ricky and Cleo answered at the same time. "I know." They slapped each other's palms in a high five.

"You two think you know me so well." Bethany's heart felt full and warm as she laughed with her two best friends.

"Jazz and country in the same day." Cleo scratched her head. "Go figure."

"Well, this festival is known to be eclectic." Bethany sniffed the air noisily. "Speaking of..." She sniffed again, this time holding her finger in the air, using it as an odor barometer. "I smell Oriental, and Cajun, and barbecue, and..."

"And mullet." Cleo's freckles paled to an ashen gray. "I'm sorry, you guys, but morning sickness has finally arrived."

Ricky rushed her to a chair under the large food tent, and Bethany went in search of a cold towel.

She returned shortly. "Here. I managed to bum these wet paper towels from the gyro booth." She laid it over Cleo's already moist forehead and fanned her until some of the color returned. "Feeling better? The gyro guy offered ice if we need it."

"No, I'm fine, but only if you promise not to say the word gyro again." She took a small sip of lemon-lime soda that Ricky brought to her. "I think I'll stay here for a little while. Why don't y'all walk around? I'll just sit and listen to the music. When I feel normal again, I'll find you."

Bethany began to protest, but when Cleo insisted, she acquiesced reluctantly. Petting the strawberry curls, she said, "We'll only be gone a few minutes—just long enough to take in the craft booths."

"Go, I'm beginning to feel better already. Oh, look!" She pointed to the crowd. "There's Sheila looking for a place to sit. She can babysit me until you get back."

As they walked into the mob, Ricky said, "I love your loyalty. You're a good friend, Bethany Hamilton." He slipped his hand around hers, thrilling her to her toes.

"Cleo gives much more than she gets. I don't know what I'd do without her. She's my rock. Or rather," she ventured to say, "Jesus is my rock through her." *Oh, Ricky. Let Jesus be your rock through me.* He squeezed her hand slightly, and she took it to mean that he was listening.

They did as they were told and perused the craft booths. They oohèd and aahed over beautiful pottery, paintings, and metal sculptures. They laughed at quirky wind chimes, dolls, and toys. Ricky bought all three of them official Mullet Festival T-shirts, and Bethany bought the baby-to-be a handcrafted quilt.

Eventually they ventured upon a booth of seashell art. Ricky seemed particularly interested in one piece but kept Bethany from seeing it. He shooed her to another booth containing plant slips in hanging glass bulbs.

"I want to surprise you," was all he told her.

"The shirt is enough. You don't have to buy me anything else."

He put his hands on his hips and tilted his head. "Don't you think I can afford it?"

She laughed, as much at the incredulous idea as the picture he created with his body language. "Well, as long as you don't lose your home in Fiji."

He winked. "No problem."

She feigned interest in the hanging philodendrons and ivy until he joined her. He held out a bag, and she eagerly reached for it.

"Oh no, you don't," he said, pulling it back with a teasing sparkle in those beautiful green eyes. "It's all wrapped up."

"That's not fair," she mock-wailed. In truth, she'd rather open it at home, away from the crowd, alone with the man grinning in front of her. Her gaze flitted to the other booths. "I'd like to reciprocate."

"Let's call it a thank-you gift for putting up with me these last few weeks." *No, Ricky. Thank you.*

He gathered the bags she'd been carrying and offered to take the booty back to the car. "I'll meet you at the food tent. Go check on Little Mama."

At the tent, she looked at the table where she'd left her friend and shook her head. "I don't believe this."

Cleo was exactly where they'd left her, but now she was surrounded by empty plates, napkins, and a large plastic cup.

"What? I got hungry."

When Ricky reached the tent, he, too, looked at Cleo in amazement. "How did you put away that much food in such a short amount of time, especially after nearly being sick?"

"It passed." She shrugged as if it were totally normal to be on death's door one minute and ravenous the next.

"Where's Bethy?" He looked around the area.

"She went to get some food." He raised an eyebrow. "Not for me. For you two. She wants you to try some of our local culinary delights."

Bethany showed up at that moment carrying a cardboard tray stuffed with plates from different booths.

"How did you carry all of that? I don't ever recall you working as a waitress." Ricky helped her unload.

"I played Dulcinea, didn't I? The serving wench."

Cleo interrupted. "Okay, Don Quixote, before you break into the chorus of 'The Impossible Dream,' sit down and take a whiff of this stuff."

Ricky looked at the—*what was the word?*—eclectic fare set before him. "What's yours, and what's mine?" He picked at the closest thing with his fork. It appeared to be some sort of meat.

"This is mine." Bethany noted a bowl of something murky. "Mullet chowder."

"Yum," he said with little enthusiasm.

Cleo's eyes danced as she pointed out another dish. "Try this one."

He took a tentative bite and promptly spit it out. "What is this stuff?"

"Smoked mullet," Cleo said.

"I don't think I'm a mullet man." He wiped his mouth and poked at another potentially lethal dish. Deciding against that one, he chose another. "This doesn't look too dangerous." It was a crispy-fried something on a stick. If it came on a stick, it couldn't be too bad, could it? He took a tiny bite, then a bigger one. "Now this is more like it." He ate a whole piece before he said, "This tastes like chicken."

Bethany and Cleo grinned at each other. Together they said, "It's alligator."

"What?" Ricky stood so abruptly that he bumped his thighs on the bottom of the table, nearly spilling the drinks.

Abandoning the feast laid before him, he went in search of a hamburger. Giggly girl laughter danced behind him, making him chuckle to himself.

After their meal, they walked around while listening to light swing music wafting through the festival. When the last note had wailed on Glenn's trumpet, they decided to see who the headliner was that evening. Out came three energetic women in cowboy costume and stringed instruments. Ricky looked frantically for a place to hide.

Chapter 20

O range Blossom Special" erupted from the band, and Bethany started clapping along with the crowd. The redhead playing the violin was especially good, using her whole body to produce the energetic notes.

"Um. . . We're too close here." Ricky tried to pull the girls back into the pressing crowd.

"Are you kidding?" Bethany yelled, trying to make herself heard. She glanced toward the stage and was thrilled that she could practically see the color of the woman's eyes. "This is perfect."

The song ended, and Bethany looked back to say something to Ricky, but he had disappeared. She nearly tripped over a large mass huddled near the ground. "What are you doing?"

"Tying my shoe," Ricky said.

The band began another number. Bethany found herself enjoying the music. It wasn't as country as some she'd heard, and the harmonies of the women, as well as the musicianship, were outstanding. She turned to tell Ricky as much and found herself looking at the top of his head.

"I think I bruised my legs at the table earlier. I can barely stand." He hunched over and rubbed his thighs. "Would you mind if I slipped back and sat awhile?"

"Would you rather leave?"

Cleo heard the conversation and piped in. "You know, I'm getting pretty tired. I probably shouldn't be standing this much." Bethany looked into her friend's clear blue eyes to investigate whether Cleo was actually exhausted or just spoiling the pampered actor.

"Okay," she finally said, interpreting Cleo's heavy lids as the truth. "I can buy one of their CDs later."

As they prepared to leave, she noticed Ricky looking over his shoulder at the fiddle player onstage. That didn't bother her nearly as much as the way the musician looked back at Ricky—not in a flirty way, but with recognition.

After Ricky dropped Cleo off, Bethany turned to him in the little car. "Do you want to tell me what that was all about?"

"What?"

"That exchange back there. At the festival?"

Ricky tried to feign an innocent look, but seeing the determination in Bethany's face, he knew he'd been busted. "Okay. That woman? The one playing the fiddle? She. . .um. . . kinda knows me."

He heard Bethany gasp. They'd just left Destin, where Cleo lived, and there were no more lights for a few miles. He didn't need to see her face. He knew she'd fear his cover was blown and be hurt he'd attempted to keep the truth from her. He didn't want to see that look.

"How does she *kinda* know you? Could she be a threat?"

He turned down one of the many roads that led toward the beach. They parked where they could see the full moon over the Gulf.

As he put the gears into Park, he noted her crossed legs and arms. She'd already begun to shut him out. "Her name is Maggie Carter. I don't think she processed what she saw." At least he hoped not. "We dated recently."

"How recently?"

"Up until July."

"Of this year?"

He gripped the top of the steering wheel and nodded.

"So, you're saying, you and she were a couple while you were making your movie, while we were—getting reacquainted." The pain in her voice broke his heart.

"Bethy." She shot him a look that wordlessly objected to the use of that name. "I actually broke it off with her because of you."

"And this is supposed to make me feel better?" She tapped her foot on the floorboard. "How do they do it in Hollywood? Do I bat my eyelids and feel grateful that you chose me over her? Do I feel triumphant that I won such a grand prize? You tell me."

"Wait a minute." This little temper tantrum needed to be nipped in the bud. "I didn't know I was going to see you again. All I did was renew our friendship. Then," he said, softening his words, "when I got home, I realized Maggie couldn't compare to you."

He reached across the back of the seat and playfully tugged her short hair. She tried to ignore him, but a tiny uplift of her mouth betrayed her. Her arms unwound, and she placed her hands under her thighs.

"Now, I'm sorry." Then she became somber again. "Ricky, you've suspended your life for me, but what happens when it's over?"

"What do you mean? It never has to be over."

She opened the car door and walked toward the beach. Ricky followed, not sure what to expect. She stopped just short of the water. "Look out there, Ricky."

She folded her arms around herself as a crisp breeze suddenly snatched at her thin sweater. He took off his light jacket and wrapped it around her. She never took her eyes from the Gulf. "What am I supposed to look at, Bethy?"

"I'm a fish, and you're a bird. I can't live your lifestyle any more than you can live mine."

He looked out toward a dark cloud blanketing the water in the distance. Lightning lit it sporadically, reminding him of a florescent bulb about to go out.

Turning her shoulders to face him, he said, "Then I'll have to buy a snorkel." He wiped a tear from her cheek and placed his lips over hers. His heart pounded as she returned the kiss. She wrapped her arms around his neck and twirled his hair with her fingers, just as he remembered her doing when they were kids.

When it was over, way too soon in his opinion, she dipped her head and he kissed the top of it, reveling in the herbal scent of the feathery softness.

She looked up at him, and he didn't like what he saw in her eyes. "What about God?" she asked.

That again.

"I've told you: There's a lot of junk to sort out first."

"You've been trying to sort it out for years. It's beyond your capability. Talk to God. Be honest about your feelings. He wants to take your pain away. All you have to do is let Him."

He broke away from her this time, a first in their new relationship. Should he tell her why he couldn't yield this to God? No, he couldn't dig that deep into the wound. She would see him for the ugly person he knew himself to be. He balled his fists and pressed them into his temples. The scar on his chin, though long healed, suddenly throbbed.

"What? Talk to me, Ricky." She touched his sleeve, and he again thought her fingers as gentle as butterfly wings—or was it angel wings? He couldn't handle the pureness of that image and started walking back to the car, but her next words stopped him in his sandy tracks. "Your father is dead. He can't hurt you anymore."

Without turning back, he ground out through his teeth, "But he does. He hurts me every day."

∞

Bethany fell back across her bed. How could she allow herself to fall in love with him again? Had she never fallen out of love?

"Oh, God," she said, feeling her prayers weren't pushing past the ceiling fan. "Why have You brought that man back into my life? He's harboring unforgiveness, and it's hurling him down the wrong path. I can't have a relationship with him when I can see there will always be this hatred hanging over him. That can't be a healthy environment in which to bring children." Swiping at the tears flowing toward her pillow, she added, "What am I supposed to do? Take him by the hand and baby him?"

Willy padded onto Bethany's chest and tickled her hot cheek with stiff whiskers. With the pet's unique chirp, she soothed, using empathetic kitty language. Bethany buried her face in the silky neck and prayed, petitioning for Ricky once again.

∞

The next day, Bethany went through the motions, but her heart wasn't in her work. After the last therapy session, she searched out Cleo. She needed a shoulder to cry on, and Cleo was the only one in on the covert operation. When she entered the gift shop, the assistant manager greeted her. Bethany looked around. "Where's your boss?"

"At home, sick."

Bethany's heart dropped. Had she allowed her to do too much yesterday? Why hadn't Cleo called? "I hope it's not serious. Is it the baby?"

"In a way. Just morning sickness. She called early to tell me she'd have to let it pass, but she'd be in this afternoon. I persuaded her to stay home and rest."

"Good." Bethany wandered out of the shop, feeling utterly alone.

∽

That evening when Bethany arrived home, a candlelit dinner awaited her. A present with her name on it lay on the table, next to a dozen long-stem roses in a crystal vase.

Ricky entered the small dining room carrying a large bowl of creamy chicken Alfredo. The savory bouquet of Parmesan and oregano floated from the steam, and her stomach growled.

"Oh good, you're home." Ricky smiled, prompting her previous image of a househusband. "I hope you're hungry. Sit down, and I'll get the salad." He disappeared into the kitchen.

Bethany followed him, expecting to find takeout containers littering the countertop. Instead, pots and pans, cooking utensils, and various herbs and spices were evidence that someone had made a home-cooked meal.

Ricky pulled a tossed salad out of the refrigerator and turned to look at her. "You seem surprised."

"I didn't know you could cook. Since you've been here, you've either ordered out or grilled."

He took out a smaller bowl, stirred the contents with a wooden spoon, and poured them over the salad. Bethany cocked an eyebrow, and Ricky said, "My own concoction of oil, vinegar, and other stuff I'm not at liberty to divulge." He raised a brow à la Dan Danger. "Top secret, hush-hush stuff." He ushered a still-dumbfounded Bethany back to the dining room. "I've been a bachelor for a long time, Bethy. Did you think I lived on fast food?"

As he pulled the chair out for her, she wondered how he could bounce back so easily. When he'd left her the previous evening to retreat into the guesthouse, his feet dragged as if they were made of lead. She'd upset him, yet here he was, serving her a delicious meal. *Yes, Ricky, you are a very good actor.*

He scooted the present in front of her.

"Go ahead; open it."

In seashell paper tied with a golden ribbon, the box was too pretty to unwrap. "Did you do this yourself?" Thankfully, the gift was too big for jewelry. She opened the lid and found tissue paper wrapped around a square object. A beautiful shadow box lay nestled within the folds.

"I got it at the festival." He looked like a child giving his first girlfriend his favorite frog. "The lady said this is a real sand dollar."

Bethany stroked the round seashell with the tip of her finger. "We don't see too many here along the Gulf because of the sandbar off the coast. They get smashed to bits before they can make it to shore." But this one was broken on purpose. The two pieces were neatly arranged, and little shells in the shape of doves appeared to float out of it.

"She also said that sand dollars really do have these little doves inside them." Ricky pointed out each tiny piece. "A phenomenon, I guess."

A *ding* was heard from the kitchen. "My bread."

When he left, she counted each dove that had been glued to blue velvet. Five. Her eyes drew to two hovering near a piece of coral. The one nearest was Ricky, she mused, beckoning her to follow him, to take a chance. She frowned. Coral, although pretty, was sharp and could hurt you, just like the world into which he wanted to draw her.

"You have it wrong."

This thought was clearly not her own.

"The dove nearest the coral is you."

A peace settled over her. God had answered her rebellious prayer of the night before, giving her a clear directive to take Ricky by the hand and help him through the coral—or was it the world? Unscathed and unscarred.

And the other three doves? There was that voice again. *"They are for your father, your mother, and your grandmother. All symbols of loss. They are free of the sand dollar and in My hands now, as are you."*

Large tears overflowed.

Ricky laid the bread basket on the table and knelt beside her chair, concern filling his eyes. "No, don't cry. Have I done something wrong?"

She embraced him and buried her face in his neck. After several moments, she finally managed to speak. "Ricky, this is the best present you've ever given me. I can't explain right now, but in these last few minutes, my life has changed." She placed her hand on his face. "Because of you." Then she kissed him soundly to assure him as well as herself that not even the storms of life would keep them apart again.

Chapter 21

T ake five, everybody." Judy's stage voice projected from the third row. "Ricky, may I see you down here, please?"

Ricky reached the seats and plopped down next to the director, who had five pencils stuck in the band above her ponytail.

"Ricky," she began, "I've been meaning to discuss this with you. You're very good, and you have your role down pat, but. . ."

He tried to keep his amusement to himself. Upon reflection, he realized he was Ricky, playing Brick, playing Ricky, playing Orlando. The thought tickled him deep down, but he assumed a somber expression. "Have I done something wrong?"

"Oh no, I don't want to discourage you. Didn't you say you had acted onstage before?"

"In high school. Nothing professional, you understand." That was true. He'd never acted professionally onstage.

"I need more stage presence from you. Your actions are too tight. They need to see you in the back row."

"Okay." He nodded. It had never occurred to him before. He'd been trained for the screen. He played to the camera, where simple eye rolls and facial expressions were caught very easily. During close-ups, he'd been taught not to make big gestures, or he could find himself outside of the picture.

"I need more arm waving, more movement." Judy demonstrated with her notebook in one hand and her pen in the other. "Fill the stage with your presence, Ricky."

"Thanks. I'll try that."

He hopped back on the stage and played it big, almost feeling silly as he did so.

During the next break, Judy called them all together. "Remember, dress rehearsal Monday, Tuesday, and Wednesday. Opening night is Thursday. Bethany, I just received a beautiful wig that you'll wear in the beginning scenes until Rosalind becomes Ganymede. Then you will spend the rest of the play with your short-cropped hair, befitting a lady playing a boy."

Ricky leaned toward Bethany and whispered, "I don't think you could ever look like a boy."

"I wonder if I'll get a mustache."

"Hmm. I've never kissed anyone with a mustache before."

She placed her hand on his arm to draw him closer for what he hoped was a flirty remark when Judy's voice intruded.

"And, Ricky, I don't see Orlando with light hair. Think about dying your hair darker. There are products that wash out in just a few days." Judy went on to talk about costumes.

Ricky flinched. The affectionate squeeze Bethany had laid on his arm became a tourniquet-like grip. He knew what she was thinking. If he dyed his hair, his cover would be blown. He'd look too much like that actor Brick Connor. When had Brick become a separate entity? When did Ricky O'Connell insist on his own identity?

He looked at Bethany and saw the answer in her eyes. She wasn't in love with Brick. If anything, she was afraid of the film star. And for good reason. It had been Brick who let her down, who had forgotten about her. But Ricky would always be there for her. Always.

After rehearsal, Ricky managed to convince Judy, with Bethany's help, that Orlando's light hair symbolized his almost-childlike acceptance of Rosalind as Ganymede.

Performances played to a nearly packed house every night, and Ricky soaked in every sight, sound, and musky curtain smell. He could identify with Orlando, who in the opening scene confronted his brother for not providing him the education he felt he deserved after their father's death. Ricky also felt betrayed by the very family who trained him as an actor, then typecast him to a life of action and adventure films.

Then when Orlando met the fair Rosalind, Ricky could empathize. After her exit, his character lamented, "O poor Orlando, thou art overthrown!"

Orlando and Rosalind fled to the forest, him fleeing from his murderous brother, she in search of her father. Ricky and Bethany found themselves in a land not their own—Florida. He, running from his own fame. She, following her father.

When the mask came off at the end of the play, and Ganymede was proven to be Rosalind, she declared her love for Orlando. Had Bethany's masked feelings finally fallen away? Was their relationship back to where they'd left it?

How would it all end? Would Ricky and Bethany close with a kiss to a falling curtain? Was it true that *All's well that ends well*? He hoped so. The final performance was only a few days away, and he planned a very important announcement after the last curtain call.

∞

The weather early Sunday morning began deceitfully. The sun shone as if promising a bright autumn day, but dark storm clouds off the coast confirmed weather reports of yet another tropical storm churning over the Gulf. The Florida Panhandle would feel the effects around lunchtime.

Bethany sighed. She had met her quota of storms for the year. Especially those the weatherman couldn't predict—the torrents that drenched her heart. This one would hit several miles west, but it would drop enough rain to put a damper on their final matinee.

That morning, Bethany fidgeted through the service while struck with the knowledge that in a few short hours, she and Ricky would give their final performance. As the wind picked up outside, invading the century-old building, she swallowed a lump as she realized there would be nothing to keep him near her now. He would have to reenter his real life sooner or later. *Oh God, please make it later.*

After hanging up her robe, she slid into her coat. They'd have to hustle to make it to the theater in time to put on their makeup and don their costumes.

She felt Ricky's hand on her elbow. His voice, that velvet voice, spoke low in her ear, "Is my fair Rosalind wont to take her leave so soon? Nay, may she roost in my heart forever as a gentle dove, and may she lend an ear to I, her feathered lover, who bids her a coo and a woo."

Bethany cocked her eyebrow, trying to look like a modern twenty-first-century woman but feeling very Elizabethan at his touch. "Smooth-talkin' words from someone who's more comfortable with a semiautomatic weapon than Shakespeare. And I don't recall that quote."

"Ah, milady. Thou hast brought out the poetry in this one, thy poor yet humble servant." He bent at the waist and drew her knuckles to his lips.

She withdrew her hand as if he'd placed hot coals on it. Casting a glance around the small music room, thankful they were alone, she cried, "Ricky. We're in public."

"I'll say you are." Cleo walked by the open door, laughing.

Bethany's cheeks warmed. "Uh. . .we'd better get going, Orlando. Curtain's going up in just a couple of hours."

"By your leave, milady."

"Stop that!"

The blustery wind assailed their hair and clothing as they stepped out of the church building. Huge drops of rain bombed the couple and the sea of umbrellas before them as everyone made their way to the parking lot.

"It's here," Bethany said, raising her voice.

They cinched their raincoats, but just as their feet hit the bottom step, cameras began flashing in their eyes. The numerous umbrellas weren't protecting church-goers. They were hiding the dreaded paparazzi, those tenacious bloodhounds who had finally tracked Brick Connor down. They barked their questions at him and viciously tore at his privacy.

"What are you doing here, Mr. Connor?"

"Why have you changed your appearance?"

"Have you left show business?"

Bethany's worst fears were realized, until the umbrellas parted and she came face-to-face with a furious Maggie Carter.

Chapter 22

The paparazzi eagerly made way for this new development. Ricky couldn't believe what or, more specifically, whom he was seeing. "Maggie! What are you doing here?"

"Interesting question, Brick." She spat out his name and ground it under her heel. "I think you should ask yourself that. The whole world has been wondering where you disappeared to. Now we know." Her glare bored into Bethany. "Is *this* what you left me for?"

Ricky pulled the trembling Bethany behind him. What must she be thinking with all these reporters in her face? A nightmare relived, most likely. He frowned at Maggie. "We had nothing, and you know it."

SLAP! Maggie's long musician fingers left a mark on the actor's face.

Bethany came from behind him with her teeth bared. She looked at the reporters. "All of you, leave him alone!" Ricky's mouth went slack. Was this his Bethy confronting the paparazzi?

He barely had time to savor that thought when he found Bethany thrust into his chest, caused by a brisk shove from the fiery redhead. Bethany grabbed at Maggie's arms, which were thrashing about like the winds from the storm that whipped around them. Ricky realized the singer was trying to rip out his ladylove's beautiful blond hair. He thrust his body between the two women, pinning Maggie at the elbows. Glenn, who had just barreled out of the church, held his daughter.

Ricky heard a strangled cry from behind his shoulder. He glanced at Bethany's pale face and followed the path of her startled gaze. A sporty rental car, not noticed in all the commotion, was parked along the street in front of the church. Chad Cheswick had stepped out and now strutted toward them like an arrogant peacock as he opened a black umbrella.

Ricky frowned at Chez. "Why are you here?"

Chez's face showed concern, but Brick knew there was something diabolical beneath that mask. "You're my best bud. I'm here for moral support."

There is nothing moral about you.

"I've been consoling Maggie ever since you dumped her."

Oh brother!

Ricky began to put the puzzle together. No doubt his breakup with the country singer made the news. Chez must have swooped in like a vulture to pick at the leftovers.

"You should have been more careful," Chez said with that insidious tone of concern. "When Maggie saw you here, she and I put two and two together. You wouldn't be the first man ruined by a pretty face." He grinned at Bethany. "Apparently, the news leaked." He spread his arms out to indicate the reporters hanging on his every word. "I'm sure your fans will forgive you for walking out on them. Your fling is over. Come home with us, okay, buddy?"

You slimy. . . "What are you talking about? Are you trying to make it look like I abandoned my career?"

"It's no secret how discontent you've been. I oughta know since we work so closely together." Chez turned toward the paparazzi, making sure they got his good side.

Questions were hurled at the actor from the sea of faces.

"Mr. Connor, is it true you've become jaded with Hollywood and plan to drop out for good?"

"Brick, what will you do now that your career is in the tank?"

Chez grabbed the hilt of the proverbial knife and twisted. He addressed the reporters. "Perhaps Brick has only been on a soul-searching mission." He looked at Ricky. "I see you're coming out of a church. Have you made peace with the father who abused you? Have you *found* religion?"

Tape recorders whirred. Cameras flashed.

Ricky gathered Chez's shirtfront in his fist. In low tones, he said, "I've never told anyone that. How did you find out?"

"We were drinking buds, remember? There was a lot of stuff spilled. Maybe you thought I was too fuzzy to remember. I kept your secret for a long time."

Ricky relaxed his grip. "Why tell it now? Are you that angry that Bethany likes me over you?"

The look in Chez's eyes finally revealed a true emotion. The sadness there caused a lump in Ricky's throat. "This has nothing to do with a girl. When did we stop being friends, Brick?"

His unspoken answer hit him square in the gut. Chez had become a victim to his fame just as Bethany had. When did his career take precedence over his relationships? Was he trying to lose himself in his work, hoping the past would disappear?

A reporter called out, "What did your dad do to you that made you run to God?"

Ricky thumbed the scar on his chin. With his defenses down, the child within, still mad at God, lashed out and answered for him. "No! I haven't found God because there is no God."

He'd suddenly tired of this game. He held his hand out to Bethany. "Come on. We have someplace to be."

When she shrank from him, only then did he realize what he'd said. She bolted down the steps and through the reporters.

"Bethy. . ."

Glenn grabbed his arm. "Let her go, son." He pulled him into the church and shut the door on the bloodthirsty rabble.

Maggie's muffled voice could be heard saying, "Did y'all know that Bethany Hamilton is Dee Bellamy's daughter? Might make a tidy side piece for this story, don'tcha think?"

∞

"Why didn't you tell us?" The pain in Judy's voice broke Bethany's heart. "The play went well with your understudies, but they didn't *wow* the audience like you and Rick—I mean, Brick—Oh, what do you call him?"

You don't want to know what I'm calling him right now. "I'm so sorry, Judy. It started out as an innocent experiment. We didn't mean to hurt anybody."

She hung up feeling as if she were the one who pulled the curtain aside to reveal that the wizard was merely a con man. Last night, the phone calls began shortly after the news broke on *Entertainment, Now!* She didn't watch the program, but she heard all about it through friends from church, people in the play, and coworkers. She also knew that all of America, and worse, her community, knew she was Dee Bellamy's daughter. Her days of living a normal life were over.

With the stress of reporters camped out on her lawn, Bethany sat at the kitchen table having long abandoned the thought of breakfast. Instead, she simply sipped her soothing herbal tea as the memory of the day before pummeled her brain.

The phone rang, and her father yelled from upstairs that he would get it. Let him. She wasn't going to answer another phone as long as she lived.

Bethany's gaze wandered out the window facing the guest-house. Ricky had never come home yesterday. Did that mean he was out of her life forever? He'd promised that at the first sight of a camera he'd be out of there. She took another warm sip and managed to get it past the lump in her throat. She knew he didn't mean what he said at the church, but it still hurt. It hurt that they were back to square one, just when she thought they were making headway. She glanced at the wall where she'd hung the sand dollar gift. How would she lead him through the coral if he couldn't get past his anger?

Her father clomped down the stairs. When he entered the kitchen, his face looked as strained as she felt. "That was Simon. He doesn't want you to come in."

Bethany sighed with relief. "Fine by me. I could use the day off."

Her father sank in a chair beside her. "No, he doesn't want you to come in for a while. He wants you to stay away until things cool off. He thinks you'll be a distraction."

Strike three.

"Have you seen the paper yet?" he asked.

"Have you seen our front lawn?" *Snakes, all of them, coiled and waiting to strike with their cameras.*

Glenn stood and mumbled something while walking to the front door. She heard the click of the dead bolt. A mild hysteria rose in her throat, knowing that lock was the only thing keeping out the world. She heard the noisy questioning, like so many hungry seagulls claiming their meal. Then it stopped, and her father reentered the room.

"You're a brave daddy." She offered a shaky smile.

"I'm angry."

"With me?"

"No. With Simon. This is why he suspended you." He opened the *Northwest Florida Daily News* and flung it on the table. Bethany clutched at her heart to keep it from leaping out of its cage. On the front page was a picture of Maggie's hands reaching for Bethany's hair. But worse, Bethany's hands were reaching for Maggie's throat, or so it looked in the picture. She had actually been defending herself. The headline boasted LOCAL GULFARIUM DOLPHIN TRAINER IN OVER HER HEAD.

She felt her stomach churn. In the background, the sign above the door of Safe Harbor Community Church could be clearly seen: MAY ALL WHO ENTER HERE FIND PEACE.

∞

"Room service."

Brick opened the door slowly. Satisfied the server was authentic, and alone, he granted entrance. After adding extra money to the tip to ensure the man's silence, he pulled the tray into the upscale room of the five-star resort, made possible through Glenn's connections. Bethany's dad had called a friend who'd provided a boat to take him from the church and away from the paparazzi. They sped away from the dock at the back of the church before the intruders knew what was happening.

Now he lifted the cover from the tray and took a long sniff of the ham and sausage omelet. He had already eaten everything in the minibar. That was yesterday. Today he would renew his low-carb diet and get back into shape.

While forking the warm eggs, yesterday's events came unbidden to his mind like they had all night. Before Bethany's tires had squealed out of the parking lot, he made a move to run after her, but Glenn's voice stopped him short.

Together they'd moved back into the church while the rest of the congregation kept the reporters out until the police could arrive. The two men sat in the sanctuary. Glenn's eyes looked weary, but they held compassion.

"You know I've always liked you, Ricky."

"Yes, sir. And you're the father I always wished I had."

"But I love my daughter and don't wish to see her hurt."

"Neither do I."

"I think you two could have a future if you just work at it."

What was he saying? "You mean, you still believe in me?"

"I've always believed in you, Ricky." Brick relaxed, as he always did when having these father/son chats with Glenn. "But you need to shed some old hurts, find some peace, and get on with your life. What you said out there hurt Bethany. Don't you see? She cannot and will not maintain a relationship with you until you've made peace with God. And only you can do that. She can't do it for you—no matter how hard she tries."

Brick's heart hardened. "But you saw what that monster did to me."

"Your father?" Glenn glanced at the scar. "Yes, I saw. Who do you think blew the whistle?"

Brick's eyes had opened for the first time in years. "You were the one who alerted the authorities? That tip is what gave my mom courage to stand up to him."

"I know, and don't think I didn't pray hard about it. I felt God leading me and probably should have called sooner. But see, God cared. He spoke to me, and I acted, albeit late. Sometimes that's how He works in our lives, by using other people. Did you expect lightning to zap your father where he stood?"

"That's what I prayed for."

Brick barely tasted his breakfast as he ruminated on that conversation. He knew God was real, despite his slip on the church steps, and that He had put the Hamiltons in his life.

How could I have gotten through childhood without them?

Apparently he couldn't do without them even now. Glenn had promised to pack his things in the guesthouse and bring them to him.

He looked at his watch. His flight would leave in a couple of hours; then he'd be going home. *Home.* Where was that exactly? Home was Bethy's arms. Home was in her eyes, and her welcome smile the hearth.

A complimentary newspaper had been brought with room service. Brick swigged the last of his tea, but at the sight of the front page, he did a classic spit-take as his unbelieving eyes saw his two girlfriends duking it out on the steps of Safe Harbor Community Church.

"Oh no. Poor Bethy." He knew what this would mean. She had predicted it correctly. Her ordered world would be shattered. He should have stayed away, but he had had to find out if there were still sparks between them.

It was as if they were still going steady at Hollywood High. As if her mother were still alive and he still sought refuge under their roof. . . Was Bethany simply a safe refuge for him? Or was she something more? He reached for the velvet box on the nightstand. The box containing the solitary diamond he had intended to give her after the matinee.

Something more. Definitely.

∞

"Do you want me to come over?" Cleo's voice soothed Bethany's soul through the receiver. Her best friend had called her six times in twenty-four hours.

"No, the press would tear you apart." She sat in the mauve chair by her bedroom window. "The best friend of the home wrecker."

"They weren't married. How can you be a home wrecker?"

Bethany adjusted the phone between her shoulder and ear, then flicked the entertainment page of the paper with both wrists to straighten it out. "I quote, 'Brick Connor has dumped his soon-to-be fiancée, country singer and musician Maggie Carter, for local hometown girl Bethany Hamilton.' It quotes Maggie Carter as saying, 'That *home wrecker* has maintained, in her mind at least, a relationship with Brick for years. Finally her persistence has paid off.' Then it says that I cannot be reached for comment. Can you believe this trash?"

"No, and no one else who knows you will, either."

"Simon must. He's banned me from the Gulfarium indefinitely. He's afraid I'll be a distraction."

"I don't think Simon believes the press. He's just being protective of what is entrusted to him."

"You always see the good in others, don't you?"

"I try, but it's hard sometimes. Have you heard from Ricky?"

"You mean Ricky the deserter?" Bethany stood up with the cordless phone to pace her bedroom. "Ricky, the one who will come away from all this unscathed and more popular than ever? That Ricky?"

"Yes, that Ricky."

"No, and I'm so worried about him." She plopped down in the overstuffed armchair. Willy jumped in her lap and curled into a contented little ball. "I don't know if he meant what he said about God, or if he was just rattled. I'm feeling very guilty about my reaction, but he brought back memories of the old struggle. I don't think I can go through all that again."

"If you love him, you will."

"I don't know what I'd do without you, Cleo. You're so good for me. In return, I promise to spoil that baby rotten. I'll include her in our Girl Nights, and we'll teach her to have an appreciation for MGM musicals."

After a moment of dead silence, Cleo's voice cracked in Bethany's ear. She sounded unnatural when she said, "Is there any way you can sneak past the reporters?"

Bethany sat up, disturbing her kitty, which mewed in protest. "I guess I could go through the guesthouse and hop the fence into the neighbor's yard. She already called to see if she could help. Why?"

"Get some stuff together. I'll pick you up there. You're coming home with me for a few days. I have to tell you something, and I can't do it over the phone."

Chapter 23

Bethany scribbled a hasty note to her father telling him where she'd be. While packing her overnight bag, she listened to the radio. The light jazz helped calm her spirit and gave her something else to think about.

However, the music was interrupted by a tinny voice from the National Hurricane Center. "Hurricane Olga is entering the Gulf of Mexico, where she will most likely strengthen. Those living anywhere along the Gulf Coast should take precautions."

Bethany continued to pack, discounting the forecast. She had other problems to deal with.

After an hour in Cleo's house, Bethany asked, "So, what did you need to say to my face?" She wondered if it had been just a ruse to get her out of the house.

Cleo squeezed Bethany's hands from across the kitchen table, her blue eyes brimming with tears. "Ed is getting out of the Air Force. We're moving to Colorado before the baby is born."

∞

Brick paced his Hollywood Hills home and picked up the phone for the twentieth time that day, and he put it down as he had the last nineteen times. Everything he could think of to say, he had said to the Hamiltons' indifferent answering machine. What more could he tell her?

He'd only been separated from her for a little over twenty-four hours. When no one answered earlier, he'd called the Gulfarium. Her father told him she'd been suspended and was most likely hiding behind the drawn curtains at home. So what else could he think but that she was avoiding him?

What was wrong with him? He knew how she felt about God. Then he went and blurted out such an insensitive thing. He didn't even mean it. Of course there was a God, but he was mad at Him for giving him such a rotten father.

He dialed the cordless phone again and listened to Glenn's recorded message. He tried once more to articulate some sort of apology, but the words wouldn't come out right. With a frustrated growl, he punched the OFF button and threw the phone at the sofa. After a muffled thud, it rang in seeming defiance.

Without checking the caller ID, he stabbed the TALK button and barked, "What?"

Dead silence greeted him. *Bethy?* But then a male voice disappointed him. "Having a bad day?"

"Oh. Hi, Vince. Yeah, you could say that." He sank onto the couch and rubbed the back of his neck.

"I heard about the scandal in Florida. How's our girl taking it?"

"I don't know. She won't talk to me."

"Give her time. Let things cool down. Once all this blows over, she'll come around."

"It goes deeper than that, Vince."

"You want to come over and talk about it? The wife made some awesome lasagna."

Brick briefly thought about his low-carb diet. "That sounds great. I'll be right over." *I hope she made a chocolate cake, too.* He grabbed his car keys. *With frosting!*

∽

"Chess?" Vince asked as they pushed away from the table, their protruding bellies evidence of a fine meal.

"Sure, but you'll probably beat me. My mind hasn't come back from vacation."

Vince brought out the chessboard with his prize collection of Shakespearean pieces. He chuckled. "It's still lying somewhere on the beach, eh?"

"Yeah." *Near a little town called Seaside, with Bethy.*

Throughout the first few moves, they made small talk. Each took turns moving pawns carved to depict Hamlet. Finally Brick worked up the courage to speak. "I can't give her what she wants, Vince."

Vince moved his knight, a small rendition of Nick Bottom from *A Midsummer Night's Dream,* complete with donkey's head. "And what does she want?"

"I guess a normal life." Brick countered with his knight. "I'm worth millions, but the one thing I can't buy her is normality." He nearly swore, but he'd only done that in front of Vince once. He'd never make that mistake again. "She could even have her own dolphin pool in our backyard."

Vince brought out his Friar Laurence bishop. "I could be wrong, but I think she'd take any life you'd give her if you'd only do one thing."

Brick also brought out his bishop, then realized he had been mirroring Vince's moves the entire game. He sat back in the leather wingback chair and pressed his eyes with cool and clammy fingers. "I've gone so long without contact lenses I have to get used to them again."

Great, Brick. . .avoidance. You know what Vince means.

He kept his eyes closed and thought about how far he'd slipped from those days in Bethy's youth group. Her presence made it seem easy. Even this last visit, he felt close to God. But now, so far away from her, he felt far from God, as well.

He heard the other chair creak and knew Vince had shifted his bulky body. When he opened his eyes, he had to smile at the villain of the *Danger* movies, gentle Vince, staring at the board, tapping his temple in contemplation of his next move.

Brick scratched the side of his nose. "You don't have to pretend I'm making this game hard on you."

"Thought I was a better actor than that." Vince's shaggy eyebrows rose with his twinkling eyes.

"I just know you well. You've been a great friend to me."

"I'm here for you, son; you know that."

Brick's throat closed. How he had longed for his father to say those words. A thought struck him so forcibly he flinched. *Have I been looking for a father figure all these years?* First Glenn, then Vince. He'd even warmed to Gary, the pastor who played Jaques in Bethany's play. If he could trust these men so easily, why couldn't he do the same with Bethy's heavenly Father?

"Vince?" Brick leaned forward and placed his elbows on his knees. He clasped his hands and stared at the Persian carpet on the floor. "I want the peace that you and Bethany have, but I think I've been avoiding a relationship with God all these years. She told me to be honest with God, but how do I tell Him..." Brick's voice cracked. "How do I tell Him about the murderous thoughts toward my father?"

"You don't think He knows them already?"

Brick's head snapped up to look in the compassionate brown eyes of his mentor.

"I have a favorite passage of scripture," Vince said. "It's from Psalm 139." Without taking out his Bible, Vince leaned back in his chair and closed his eyes. " 'O Lord, you have searched me and you know me. You know when I sit and when I rise; you perceive my thoughts from afar.' " He opened his eyes and looked pointedly at Brick. " 'Before a word is on my tongue you know it completely, O Lord.' "

Brick pulled out a handkerchief to stop the flow of tears. What was wrong with him? He hadn't cried since that night—that horrible night when he was sixteen. His mother had allowed Bethany to come over to share a pizza and watch a movie since his father was supposed to be out of town. He remembered preparing to pull out of the driveway to take his best girl home.

Suddenly a rough hand pulled him out of the car, away from Bethy.

"What is this, boy?"

Ricky had looked at the back fender. Where had that dent come from?

"I come back early, and this is the first thing I see?"

Searing pain pierced his chin as it hit the back taillight, splintering plastic and spattering blood. That hadn't hurt nearly as bad as hearing Bethany's anguished cry.

His dad had disappeared into the house. Apparently, splitting his son's chin was enough punishment. Ricky drove Bethany home—where he'd stayed, never to return until that monster was out of his house.

That night had been the first time his father drew blood and the first that Bethany had seen the violence. Later, through anguished tears, he'd vowed to her both would be the last.

"You can't change the past, son." Vince's soothing voice nudged him into the present. "But you can change the future. When you invited God into your life years ago, you became a new creation, but you held on to an old hurt. He already sees you as a new creation. If you let this go, you can finally say good-bye to the old person, the one who couldn't forgive."

Could it be true? God knew what had happened to him. God knew what he wanted to do in revenge.

Suddenly it all made sense. Glenn had told him, "I've always believed in you, Ricky. But you need to shed some old hurts, find some peace, and get on with your life."

When he'd told Gary he had issues to deal with, Gary responded, "That's what God is for, son."

And what was it that Bethy had said to him that day in her father's home office? "Look deep inside yourself. There's a big, black void in there, and only God's love can fill it."

And now Vince was confirming what he'd heard from each of these people.

O Lord, You have searched me and You know me. God had been with him through all of it. He knew that now. He put people in his life to ease the hurt. He gave him Bethany. Acknowledging that God hadn't abandoned him through the abusive years allowed the burden of his past to lift enough to where he felt he could breathe. *And, Lord, since You know me so well, You know I'll have a problem forgiving my father. But I want to, and I'll never be able to do it without You.*

Then Brick Connor, the Man of Danger, slid to his knees in Vince Galloway's study and rededicated his life to God.

Chapter 24

I can't believe this rain, and the storm is still miles offshore!" Another feeder band hit, and fierce wind caused Cleo's Volkswagen to swerve. Bethany watched the heaving surf out the passenger window of the little car. "I hope we get home before we're blown into the bay!"

The wind-driven pelt of rain forced them to speak louder.

Had it only been six days ago that the worst thing in her life was the paparazzi? Were her phobias ever as real as this? So what if people took her picture wherever she went? So what if her every move was reported? She'd trade this hurricane for all of that in a Hollywood minute. At least she'd be safe with Ricky.

"I wish we could have stayed put," Cleo said as she shifted gears. "But I don't trust that old house in hurricane-force winds."

"Last I heard it was a Category Four in the Gulf and heading east of Pensacola. We should be safe at Seaside." Bethany remembered her father saying that because it was a newer community the houses had been built to sustain heavy storms. "Better than getting in that long line of evacuees and risk getting tossed by a tornado."

∞

"We should have waited for your dad."

"I agree, but he told us to get home. He said he needed to finish boarding and overfilling the pools. I'm worried. Not only for him but for the animals. Can they do enough to safeguard them from a storm this size?" She prayed for her father's safety and that he'd make it home before the worst hit.

Almost to Seaside, they turned off the highway.

"What *is* that?" Cleo gripped the wheel and pumped the brakes.

Bethany screamed.

∞

Not even a week since his other life as Ricky, Brick threw himself into his work. He reviewed scripts for upcoming projects and researched possibilities for his new production company. He wouldn't allow himself a moment to think of the pain on Bethany's face.

Exhausted, he'd cleared his schedule for the weekend, beginning Friday afternoon. His heart wasn't in the Hollywood game anymore. He no longer needed to be seen at all the fancy bashes, all the premieres, and all the parties. Even before he reconnected with Bethany, he had begun to pull away from the fluff. Now he had a new problem. How would he put in the time to change his image, thus become more involved in his work, *and* convince Bethany that life with him would be normal—even low-key? His head hurt.

He grabbed the television remote, hoping to find something mindless.

"What?" He fumbled for the volume button. The weatherman pointed to a satellite image of the Gulf of Mexico. A swirling mass of clouds completely hid the vast body of water.

"Hurricane Olga has turned and is now expected to make landfall between Destin and Pensacola. Residents all along the Florida Panhandle as far as Seaside are beginning to feel the effects." Olga was heading straight for the Gulfarium—and Bethany.

∞

"It's going to hit us!" Bethany placed her arms over her face and braced herself for whatever was tumbling toward them on a blast of wind. She could feel the car jerk to the left, then right. Tires screeched as the Volkswagen spun out of control, like a spinning cup in the Mad Tea Party ride at Disney World. With a metallic crunch, they jolted to a stop.

Bethany sat in stunned silence, too frightened to move. Soon she felt Cleo's shaky hands stroking her hair.

"You okay?" Cleo asked.

Bethany blinked her eyes, trying to wake up from the nightmare. She placed her palm on Cleo's stomach. "What about you and the baby?"

"We're fine. No pain." Cleo looked back at the road. "What was that?" She got out of the car. The passenger door was pinned shut by a scrub oak, so Bethany had to follow through the driver's side. A lawn umbrella had been the culprit, acting as a giant tumbleweed until it got caught in the brush.

Bethany shook her head. "Who would leave that outside in a storm?"

While watching for Glenn to pass by, they assessed the damage. The front fender had bent into the right tire. With rainwater streaming into her eyes, Bethany tried to pull it away, but with no success.

Tree limbs, plastic flowerpots, and other indistinguishable debris now swirled in the tempest.

"We'd better get back inside," Cleo said.

As they sat there dripping wet, assessing what to do next, the voice on the radio announced that Highway 98 would close within the hour.

"My dad! If he doesn't start for home soon, he won't make it. We'll be stranded." Bethany tried her cell phone. No signal. "The tower must be out."

They looked around. No cars or signs of life anywhere. They deliberated. Should they get out? Try to find someone home who hadn't evacuated? How close was the nearest neighborhood? Too far to walk in a storm... No, they were safer in the car—at least until they were either blown away or drowned in the storm surge.

Bethany felt a silent scream grip her throat. It made her voice sound thin and raspy. "What are we going to do?"

Cleo took her hand and bowed her head in prayer.

∽

"What do you mean there are no flights going that way?" Brick had become irrational. All transportation was heading out of Florida, not entering. Standby was the best they could do.

Local weather reports were sketchy at best. They didn't seem to care that Olga was about to finish what his ex-girlfriend had started—get rid of Bethany.

Brick lowered his head and launched into a prayer, still an unfamiliar act for him. "Dear God? Uh, Ricky here. Please weaken this storm. And watch over my girl, okay? Amen." As an afterthought, he tagged on, "Oh, and, God? If You help me get to Bethy, I'll never leave her again."

∽

Before Cleo could say "Amen," Bethany's father wrenched open the driver-side door.

"Are you girls okay?" Her daddy's face, stressed as it was with worry, never seemed so beautiful to Bethany. When they assured him they were fine, he said, "I just heard that the storm is weakening to a Category Two and beginning to break down, but there's a huge surge in front of her. Probably won't be that high this far east, but we still need to seek shelter."

He helped them out of the little car, and the three of them drove the rest of the five miles toward home. When they pulled into the driveway, Bethany's gaze searched her property. Not a camera in sight.

Nothing like a good, old-fashioned hurricane to blow away the garbage.

Chapter 25

"G o fish."

"Argh! No way, Cleo. I thought you had a five." Now home and safe in a closet under the stairs, Bethany felt like a little girl at a slumber party, a battery-operated camping lantern their only light. Olga ranted outside, but among the heaps of pillows and blankets, she couldn't have felt safer. The radio reported the hurricane had lost its strength before landfall due to a wind shear and had dropped to a low Category Two.

Glenn, who had vacated the narrow space under the stairs long ago, peeked in. "Looks like we fared pretty well. No leaks inside. What I can see outside, there's debris everywhere, but I think the house is okay. I'll know more in the morning." He looked at his watch. "Wait a minute, it is morning. You girls can go upstairs to bed now; the worst is over."

Bethany tilted her head in the way she used to whenever she wanted her own way. "Aw, Dad. Do we have to?"

Glenn poked his finger into her left dimple and said, "That still works, tadpole. Just keep it down to a dull roar, okay?" He looked at Cleo, tugged the pigtail that Bethany had braided, and said, "As for you, little one, we'll look at the damage to your car and check out your house as soon as we can get through."

He disappeared, and Cleo poked her finger into Bethany's dimple just as Glenn had done. "Tadpole?"

Bethany tugged the pigtail. "Little one?" That launched both of them into a fit of giggles.

From upstairs, they heard "Keep it down!" To which they giggled some more.

Cleo finally lay down, her six-month pregnant belly protruding up. "Oh, that feels good on my back. Why are we so giddy?"

"Adrenaline, I guess." Bethany also stretched out. "We were terrified; now we swing the other way into happy oblivion."

"I wish I could call Ed. I'm sure he's worried."

"Hopefully it won't be long before the phone lines are back up working."

Is Ricky worried about me? She wrinkled her nose. He was probably so caught up being Brick Connor again that she doubted if he'd given her a second thought.

The two friends lay there in silence for a moment, coming down from the adrenaline high. Just when Bethany thought Cleo had fallen asleep, she heard "Beth, what are you going to do now?"

372

"What do you mean?"

"What if you don't have a job to go back to?"

"Don't say that."

"Seriously. Even though the storm hit farther west than anticipated, I'm sure the Gulfarium suffered damage. We should prepare ourselves."

Bethany swallowed back a lump. She had prayed for her sweet dolphins and the other animals off and on for the last twelve hours. "I suppose, if Simon will let me, I'll help clean up. I'm sure he won't refuse an extra pair of hands."

"But what if it takes a long time? Will you relocate to continue in another therapy program?"

Bethany sighed. Sometimes her friend could be as persistent as a cricket.

Cleo rolled over on her side and rearranged the numerous pillows surrounding her. "I'm just wondering, after everything you've gone through this week, if you've given any thought to your future."

Bethany reflected on Cleo's questions. It wouldn't be long before her father remarried, a fact she could finally embrace. Bethany would be a fifth wheel, so if she still had her job, she should probably move out. If not, maybe she could move back to Orlando and work at Sea World.

A soft, fluttery sound came from atop Cleo's pillow. Bethany marveled at how fast her friend had fallen asleep. Tears sprang to her eyes. She reached out and gently moved a stray strand of strawberry hair from the freckled face. *What am I going to do without you, Cleo?* This diminutive woman answered the child's cry within her that only a mother could silence. How typical that Cleo would have brought up her future. She must have wanted her *little girl* to grow up.

Bethany turned off the light and quietly left the closet. She tiptoed upstairs to the sanctuary of her room. Two glowing green marbles floated in the dark, and she heard a questioning "Mew?"

"It's okay, sweetheart." Bethany used the cat's eyes as a lighthouse in the sea of darkness to find her bed. She lay down next to the warm feline, nesting her within the curve of her body and stroked her to sleep.

"I don't know what I want to do, Lord." She peered into the darkness, barely able to distinguish her furniture. This was her future—obscure and murky. Her favorite psalm sprang to her mind, as if God had placed it there Himself. She began to recite. " 'O Lord, you have searched me and you know me.' " God knew her better than she knew herself. That thought comforted her.

He taught her one thing this week. The paparazzi weren't nearly as scary as she'd remembered from her childhood. Annoying, yes, but compared to nearly riding out a hurricane in a Volkswagen, those flashing bulbs were nothing more than pesky bugs. And she knew now she had the strength to swat them.

She also learned that she loved Ricky so much; when he was no longer near her, her heart wept. Through her closed eyes, she could see the sand dollar doves hovering near the coral. "You promised that I would help him through the world,

Lord. How can I do that if he remains *of* the world?" A peace washed over her as she felt God's answer. Ricky would be okay.

Another verse from that psalm played in her mind. *"If I say, 'Surely the darkness will hide me and the light become night around me,' even the darkness will not be dark to you."* The tears fell freely. Her future may be murky to her, but her loving heavenly Father could see it. Darkness was not dark to Him.

"Thank You, Father, for taking my hand, just as I'm to take Ricky's, and leading us together through the coral."

∽

The next afternoon, after towing Cleo's Bug back to the house with Glenn's SUV, the phone rang and startled them all. Bethany answered, hoping to hear a velvet voice on the other end. However, it was Simon, so she promptly handed the phone to her father, not ready to talk to the man who had suspended her.

From Glenn's half of the conversation, she gleaned that the coast from Fort Walton Beach west toward Pensacola had sustained most of the damage. But east, Highway 98 between Destin and the Gulfarium had fallen victim to a twenty-foot storm surge that broke it to pieces and washed much of it into the bay. It would be months before they could drive to work.

"I'd like to check out the damage. How about by boat? Mine did pretty well in her slip. . . . Yours didn't? I'm sorry. Why don't I pick you up at your dock? Uh, you do still have your dock, don't you? Good. I'll be there in a few minutes."

Bethany decided to go, too. She had to see for herself how her dolphins fared. She hugged Cleo and apologized for leaving her.

"It's fine," her sweet friend assured her from the sofa, where she and a contented cat curled up together. "Get going and be back before dark."

Bethany kissed the top of Cleo's head. "Yes, Mom."

∽

She hopped into the runabout while her dad started up the motor. The two putted away from shore, Glenn navigating carefully while watching for debris.

They pulled up to the dock where Simon was waiting. Bethany, who chose to sit in the back of the boat, stared in shock at the damage the storm had caused along the shore.

Simon stepped into the bobbing craft. "Sure glad you thought of this, Glenn," he said. "I didn't know how we were going to get over there."

"Sorry about your boat," Glenn said as he maneuvered back into open water.

"I should have tied her better, I guess. Hopefully she'll show up somewhere near here."

"Looks like you got it worse than we did."

Bethany surveyed the coast. Such devastation. Trees, littered about like pickup sticks, lay scattered about a small yacht that had been tossed yards from the water.

She hadn't said a word to her boss since he'd boarded the craft. The callous suspension still stung. Simon turned aft to face her, his greeting stilted. "Hello, Bethany."

She pulled her gaze from the shore. "Simon." She sat tall, lifting her chin. He may have bruised her, but he hadn't broken her. She wanted him to see that.

"I'm glad you're here," he said.

"Are you?" She raised a brow.

He drummed his knee with his fingers. "I can see that you're not going to make this easy."

"What?" she asked with a flash of anger.

"I'm trying to apologize." He let out a frustrated growl. "I'm sorry I suspended you. This storm has changed my priorities. And, well, I think I was unfair to you. We could certainly use your help cleaning up. And your job will be waiting for you when we're up and running again."

Bethany folded her arms. "I accept your apology, but my priorities have changed, too. I've decided to go back to school. I want to help abused children in the same way Sheila helps special-needs kids."

Her father spoke over his shoulder. "You never told me. When did you decide?"

"I had a long talk with God last night. He made me realize that I haven't truly sought His guidance. I know now I can't live at home forever. It's time for me to step out on my own."

She couldn't see her father's reaction, but she saw admiration in Simon's face. "I'll support that decision, Bethany. And if you need anything, please ask."

A weight fell from Bethany's shoulders. She'd never realized until then how much Simon's opinion meant to her. Suddenly she could see herself in his eyes. She realized he had never been antagonistic toward her for the sake of being mean. He simply couldn't trust her because she hadn't fully committed to his life's passion. Now that she had a goal, she imagined he could see her as an equal.

About a half mile from their destination, Bethany spotted a large gray mass on the shore. "Daddy!" She grabbed his shoulder. "Pull over there. I think it's a dolphin!"

∞

After finally getting a flight to Pensacola, the closest he could get to Seaside, Brick drove east along Highway 98. Seventy-two miles lay between him and Bethany. He pressed the accelerator of the rented SUV, his vehicle of choice when big buddy Vince had decided to tag along.

They had no concept of what a hurricane could do. If it had weakened, how bad could it be? They soon found out when they were stopped at a roadblock.

"I've got to get through. It's very important." Brick leaned out his window to talk to the uniformed man directing traffic onto a side street.

"Sorry, sir. Just keep bearing left." He continued to swing his arms.

"You don't understand. I have to see if someone is okay."

"To my knowledge, everyone along this strip evacuated. Now move it along."

Brick flung open his door. Horns blared behind him. Someone yelled, "Get out of the way, you moron."

He ignored Vince's warning to get back in the car. The Man of Danger, who had left home that morning in disguise, took off his hat and glasses and squinted at the officer's now-fuzzy frame. "Do you know who I am?"

The policeman tipped back his cap. "Yes, sir, I do know who you are, but if you were Sean Connery himself, I couldn't let you through. There are boats on the highway."

Brick and Vince looked at each other and mouthed *Boats on the highway?*

Brick meekly got back in the car and turned left onto the side street.

∞

"Is it one of ours?" Bethany leaped from the boat and swam toward the beach. *Oh God, please let it be alive.*

Glenn anchored the boat while Simon grabbed a bucket and several towels from under the bench seat. By the time they joined Bethany, she was on her knees near the mammal, speaking softly to calm it. She looked up at them as they laid the wet towels over the sunburned body. "I don't know this dolphin. She's wild."

The animal's plaintive, high-pitched cry broke Bethany's heart.

They poured buckets of water over the towels they had draped over the large body, being careful to avoid the blowhole. Glenn began digging under the dolphin to help relieve the weight of her body on her lungs. But they needed to figure out a way to get her back in the water. She must have been about four hundred pounds—much too heavy for the three of them.

Before Bethany could finish her prayer for help, she heard an amplified male voice. "You, on shore, do you need help?"

The Marine Patrol!

Glenn stood and cupped his mouth. "We need a large blanket for a sling, and every man on your boat."

∞

Brick glanced toward his friend's sleeping form and felt a stab of guilt. He blamed himself for dragging the big man along, even though Vince insisted he was needed to keep him out of trouble.

They had been rerouted down Interstate 10, taking them thirty miles out of their way. At least they didn't have to go all the way to Seaside. His dogged phone calling finally paid off, but it was Cleo who answered Bethany's phone. She told him that Bethany and her dad had just left for the Gulfarium.

He turned off the interstate, praying that the road had been cleared. Traffic moved smoothly, but he noticed off in the thickly forested area that pine trees had been snapped, as if a large, angry child had grabbed at them in a tantrum.

Vince woke up as the SUV began its ascent onto a bridge spanning a large bay. "Where are we?" He yawned and rubbed his neck.

"We just left a town called Shalimar. This looks familiar. I think if I follow this street it'll get me to the Gulf. Bethany took me the opposite way to the mullet festival."

"Mullet?" Vince asked as he ran his hand over his hair.

"Don't ask."

Another roadblock created yet another detour. Brick slapped the steering wheel. "I can't believe this. I have all this money and clout, and I can't go ten miles to be with the girl I'm going to marry." Vince's shaggy eyebrows shot up on the last word. Brick scowled at him. "What?"

In the distance, they heard *wop-wop-wop*. They each leaned out their windows in time to see a helicopter fly overhead.

Brick grinned as he positioned the steering wheel for a U-turn.

"Follow that chopper!" they said in unison.

Chapter 26

E asy, girl." Bethany continued to talk to the dolphin as she poured water on her scorched skin. She wanted so much to take the lady back to the Gulfarium and treat her sunburn, but from what she could see, the Gulfarium looked like it needed saving itself. The entire beach had blown north and now spilled into the park.

A small boat powered toward them. Bethany squinted. "It's Tim!"

Tim Grangely pulled the motor-powered dinghy close, anchored, and leaped in to help.

"How are the animals?" Simon asked, his voice raspy with uncharacteristic emotion.

"It's a miracle. They're all alive. There's a lot of sand in the pools, but not enough to harm them. But," he said shaking his head, "there's so much destruction. It's going to take us months to get the place up and running again, probably years before we're 100 percent."

Months? Years? Bethany resolved then to stand good on her word. She'd help with the cleanup, but she knew her future was not at the Gulfarium, or with her father. She didn't know how she would do it, but she was going to learn how to help kids like Ricky.

She swallowed hard, suddenly realizing that her dream would have no meaning if he weren't in her life. She wanted him back, and she would make it work.

∞

The helicopter landed in a high school stadium. The two actors ran up to the pilot, who was helping a couple step out of the aircraft. The pilot, a middle-aged man who sported a black ball cap that read POW/MIA—NEVER FORGET, explained that he'd offered his touring service to island residents to see how their homes had fared. But this had been his last run.

Brick presented his case.

The reluctant pilot squinted toward the west at the sun, almost at eye level. "Well, if it don't take too long. Sun'll set within the hour. Soon it'll be too dark to see anything, anyways."

As the two actors climbed into the helicopter, Brick offered the man money, but he refused it. "Nope, I done this for the displaced families free of charge. I can do it for love." He grinned, grabbed the stick, and lifted the bird off the ground.

Brick looked out the open door and down at the devastation. Houses were missing roofs and walls, furniture was scattered about, and boats were dry-docked on asphalt parking lots.

When the sound came into view, the pilot circled an object in the water.

"Hey, boys, you gotta see this."

"Is that what I think it is?" Vince hollered from the back to be heard.

"Yep, it's a house. Yessir, that Olga sure pushed a lot of water in front of her."

Brick could see the thin strip of island that separated the sound from the Gulf. It stretched for miles, barely a bump of sand in the water. Houses built on it were sure to be vulnerable.

"Matthew 7, verses 25 through 27." This was Vince's contribution. At Brick's questioning look, he raised his bushy eyebrows. "Look it up later."

The pilot shrugged and pointed the stick up the coast. Brick pointed to a large shell of a building. "What was that?"

"Five-star resort. Totally demolished."

Brick blinked back tears. It was the hotel where the benefit had been held—the same one where he had sought refuge from the media. How long ago was that? Not even a week? Now it looked like a bomb had blasted every floor in the place.

"We're coming up on your place."

Brick saw what had been the Gulfarium. White sand had infiltrated nearly every crevice. Atlantis must have looked like that, just before its final descent into the sea.

He looked around for Bethany, but the whole place seemed vacant. "Can you put us down over there?" Brick pointed to a flat area on the beach, where the dunes had been.

"No can do. I have strict orders not to land."

"I'll pay you."

"No amount of money is worth losing my FAA license."

They hovered over the area a moment longer. The bench was gone that had looked out over the Gulf, the place Bethany had first told him to stay out of her life, but also where she clung to him after the Chez fiasco. The roof to the Dolphin Encounter Building had been sheared back, and if he used his imagination, he could almost see where they had shared that first kiss—well, the first in this decade.

Where is Bethy? Maybe she'd already been there. Should he ask to be taken to Seaside? The sun was beginning its dip into the Gulf of Mexico.

"Mr. Connor, we've got to be heading back. I've pushed it too far as it is."

Brick nodded. But as they swung around, he noticed a flurry of activity about a half mile to the east. "Can we just see what that's about? They may need our help."

The pilot adjusted his hat, then grasped the stick and pointed the nose eastward.

"Look!" Brick yelled as he pointed. "There are boats and people on the beach."

"That's the Marine Patrol," the pilot shouted. "What are they dragging into the water?"

Brick's heart hammered in his chest. "It's a dolphin. And that fair-haired angel with the bucket is the reason I'm here." That was so true. If it hadn't been for Bethany's love and prayers, no telling where he would be today. "You've got to land."

"With the Marine Patrol there? No way!"

Brick glared at the pilot. "Hover as close as you can. I've got to see her."

"Okay, but I'm not setting it down."

∽

The rescue crew had almost freed the dolphin. Bethany continued to pour water over the towels. With the makeshift sling, the Marine Patrol maneuvered the dolphin to shallow water, taking it slow to keep from injuring her further. Simon had already examined her to the best of his ability without equipment and found nothing to concern him other than the sunburn. If they could get her into open water, she'd heal eventually.

Wop-wop-wop. Everyone looked up to see an approaching helicopter.

"What is that fool doing?" Simon asked. "Those blades are churning the water. Our girl is distressed enough." He patted the dolphin protectively, then started to wave the aircraft away.

Bethany caught his arm. "Wait! It's Ricky!"

Out of the gaping opening, Ricky leaned precariously. Their gazes locked. Her heart flipped when he smiled and waved at her.

She cupped her mouth and yelled, "Meet me at my house."

He cupped his ear and mouthed, "What?"

"He can't hear you," Simon said as he shook her shoulder. "Wave him away. You'll figure it out later."

She caressed the tiny-chip diamond on her left ring finger. *No.* She'd never tell him to leave again.

∽

"They want us to leave, Mr. Connor. We're disturbing the rescue."

"Brick." He felt Vince's hand on his shoulder. "We've got to go."

Brick took off his glasses and handed them to Vince. As he unbuckled his seat belt, he asked the pilot, "How far above the water do you think we are?"

The pilot's face went white. "I don't know. Twenty, maybe thirty feet. Listen, you aren't planning to—"

"Meet you in Sydney," Brick told Vince. Then he turned to the open hatchway and prepared to swan dive.

He felt Vince's meaty hands grab his shirt to pull him back.

"Who does he think he is?" the pilot's voice squeaked.

Vince answered, "Agent Dan Danger."

∽

"Who does he think he is?" Simon frowned, clearly perturbed.

Glenn answered, "Agent Dan Danger."

Bethany wanted to close her eyes but couldn't. She knew what he was about to do, and it frightened yet thrilled her all at the same time. He was doing it for her. *But if he breaks his neck, what's the point?*

She finally took a breath when she saw Vince pull Ricky back into the aircraft. *Lord, please protect my impetuous man!*

To her dismay, the helicopter turned and headed west.

"Finally," Simon said. "Now let's get this lady back into the water."

Bethany continued to keep the dolphin wet but watched the vanishing dot in the sky disappear behind the Gulfarium rubble. Knowing they'd get together eventually did nothing to stop the growing lump in her throat.

The group finally freed the dolphin from her sandy prison, and she floated in the shallow water gaining her strength. All the humans did the same.

"Man," a Marine Patrol member said while catching his breath. "You guys do this every day?"

"Thankfully, no." Simon patted the large mammal. "But we've had our share of rescues."

Rescue. As Bethany listened to their conversation, the idea God had given her the night before finally gelled, and she now knew how she could continue her marine work and rescue abused teens.

"Dad." She turned to Glenn. "Do you know if Marineland has been sold yet?"

He looked at her quizzically. "I don't think so."

Wop-wop-wop.

Like the scene in a movie, the helicopter suddenly appeared over a storm-battered hotel down the shore and sped toward them.

Bethany had to grin at her action hero, looking very Dan Dangeresque while holding firmly to a rope ladder several feet below the helicopter. But she had to remind herself that as an actor he'd done this many times with his own stunt work.

"Doesn't that guy ever give up?" Simon placed his hands on his hips.

"Nope, that's how he's survived all these years."

The aircraft slowed to a hover just in front of them, allowing Ricky to drop the short distance to the white sand still wet from the storm.

The ladder was quickly drawn up, and the helicopter made a circling path around them. Ricky looked up and waved at Vince, who could be seen grinning from the back passenger seat. He waved at Ricky, mouthed what looked like "No worries, mate," and then gave Bethany a thumbs-up. What had he said the night of the benefit? When Ricky finds his way back, God and all His angels would give her a big thumbs-up?

She blew Vince a big kiss.

The dolphin pulled away into deeper water, and Bethany knew her job there was done.

She sloshed her way toward the shore as Ricky closed the gap between them, wading into the water as if he couldn't bear another minute of separation. Feeling the same, she leaped into his arms, sealing their future together. She pictured their kiss on the silver screen and knew no other reunion moment could compare to their real-life romance.

"Bethy," Ricky said when they finally parted, "I have something to tell you. I've made my peace with God. I'm on my way to forgiving my father."

"I know; Vince just told me."

"Huh?"

She squeezed his hand. "I'll tell you about it later." Then she led him to the shore and thanked God that He had seen them both safely through the coral.

Epilogue

This is Bebe Stewart of *Entertainment, Now!*, reporting on Hollywood's golden couple, Brick Connor and wife, Bethany.

"Godinall Production Company, Brick's pet venture, is actively seeking scripts dealing in social issues with messages of hope. No more *Danger* movies for this guy.

"Mrs. Connor's project will be unveiled next month. The Seaside Adolescent and Animal Facility for the Endangered is located in Los Angeles on a newly renovated lot where Marineland used to be. In a recent interview, Bethany had this to say: 'SAAFE is a place for abused teenagers to learn about the care of injured marine mammals and help them return to the wild. In a win-win situation, the mammals love the kids unconditionally. Plans to open a facility in Florida are now underway.'"

Bethany glanced at Ricky, snuggling the baby with his man-sized arm while channel surfing with the other. Just a week old, and Deedee was already beginning to look like her namesake, Grandma Bellamy.

Bethany joined them on the couch and took the television remote away from Ricky.

"Hey," he said, reaching for it playfully. "Never mess with a man and his TV."

"I'll trade it for the baby."

He wrapped both arms around the child and nuzzled her fuzzy head. "No way."

"It's late, and our Hollywood starlet needs her beauty sleep." She kissed his pouty actor lips and contentedly breathed in the scent of his cologne mingled with baby powder.

Before pressing the OFF button, she heard "Mother and baby are doing fine. This is Bebe Stewart, reporting your *Entertainment, Now!*"

KATHLEEN E. KOVACH
Kathleen E. Kovach and her husband, Jim, raised two sons while living the nomadic lifestyle for over twenty years in the Air Force. She's a grandmother, though much too young for that. Now firmly planted in Colorado, she's the area coordinator for American Christian Fiction Writers and leads a local writers group. An award-winning author, Kathleen hopes her readers will giggle through her books while learning the spiritual truths God has placed there. www.KathleenEKovach.com